Emerald City

One month... a lifetime of memories

Emerald City is a gift to my family, mostly my beautiful moon-faced daughter Kinara. I want to inspire her to always dream big and reach for the things she wants in this life. I told her stories of the beautiful costumes I was creating in the story inspired by many out of our tiny island...

Birds of Paradise. Bringing the many lovely species of birds, we have and still are finding in our Caribbean islands to life.
I am remembering and drawing from the bountiful spirits of
Teacher Clifford and Jeweline Roberts...
My darling girl was so happy to come in from school and have a chat about materials and what our evolved and exotic birds should look like. I loved bantering and collaborating with her.
Thank you, my gorgeous girl.

To Montserrat my pillow of dreams. You infuse a strong sense of who I am and who I am still evolving into.
I am one of your beautiful birds like so many.

There are lots of people that I recall and drew on to weave this story. So many that have paved the way and taught me great lessons; by a smile, a kind hand, words of harshness or kindness, even a joke or a photograph, stage presence and showing off their sexuality; and making no excuses about it. You simply just owned it.

I remember seeing you on stage for the first time in Leicester and thought damn I want to be just like you in my next life. The stage presence and that voice, and not to forget the natural beauty that emanated, as well as the electricity when you shook my hand.
You know who you are beautiful lady.

There is another also who is the **Rose** and ultimate gem of our island. I swear if we rise and never hear your sweet melodic voice from our radio airwave, we would surely crumble.
You too know who you are.

Emerald City is my homage to all the women who are still marching strong no matter what life throws at them, and still they rise.

Thank you, Mama Sarah and my mum Patsy, and everyone out there for all the lessons you have taught me. You are all simply the best. Thank you so very much.

Please enjoy and happy reading. Email me at kbuddyroo4@live.co.uk to drop by some kind or positive words please.

Cover Design by **Lesley Mussard**

Previously published: **Time in Head and Heart** by **Authorhouse** in **2009**. It is a mix of poetry and short stories that sorted head and heart when in troubling times.

Chapter One

Nia scrambled down the steps of the ferry with help from a tired looking bushy-faced smelly dark as a sunburnt prune dockworker.

Another then dragged her aboard unceremoniously as though she were simply just another piece of luggage.

"West Indian men; so many have no blasted finesse. It's as if they are always in a constant battle with their nicer selves. As though it is a sign of weakness to be gentle and show more love and respect to their females."

She snatched her hand out of his, and tried to steady her damn self, throwing him an 'if looks could kill stare'.

He shrugged her off and turned his back on her.

He then reached for the next person: a big ship who looked like she could wrestle hippos. Worst yet sink the whole damn boat.

She slapped his hand away. "I could do it me dam-self." She snapped.

"We ain't paying you one red-cent if you fall and buss-up your arse."

"Asshole!" she spat and swatted him away again.

He laughed and challenged. "Rosie gyel, maybe you should stop nham so damn much!"

"Shut de hell up Pike! Is miss you miss all this." She gestured to her person. As she barked and ambled off to find a seat. Two of them proudly. Giving him her middle finger.

"You should cut back. See how you are blowing lek a parpuss."

"You such an asshole. You never did ah complain when you live next to me kitchen. You ole Dutti-dawg. "

"That's why me run lek hell."

"You are always such a jackass!" She called back.

"I still love you though. Good to see you, Rosie. But you had betta heed ma warning." He tossed with a big grin.

One could read between the lines that they had had an encounter.

Nia was certain she had heard way back that the two had a nasty show down aboard this same ferry.

On a better day with her feet planted firmly on the ground she would have laughed. Today though knowing what laid ahead, she pleaded silently with God.

She imagined her auntie Katho sucking her teeth furiously and calling him a "friggin-idiot!"

Nia cursed once again in her mind. She reasoned yet again that she should have followed her intuition. She should have stayed put at the airport and caught the next flight over.

It was just that she had so many treasured packages she did not want to leave behind in Antigua.

1

She had already gone over her budget in Saint Marten and bought more fabrics, laces, toile, buttons, and sequins...
She reminded herself that she wouldn't spend any more money frivolously. She wanted to head to New York for fashion week in the upcoming year. it was one of her ultimate dreams; having her designs displayed on the runway, and competing with the likes of Vera Wang, Donna Karen, and Nicole Miller...

Suddenly the boat lurched. Or was it that she was finally ready to give up the ghost? Her heart took off like a racer hearing the first starter shot. Things started to swirl. She reached out at anything, praying she did not fall on her ass.
"Steady on there." God said. She looked about frantically. She thought she had truly up and left the earth for sure.
"I've got you... I've got you beautiful. You are safe now. Just stay with me."
She obeyed and fell into what felt like a brick wall.
Yes! It was God himself she reasoned. He must have indeed listened and taken pity on her.

Nia closed her eyes. She prayed. She begged her empty stomach lining not to crawl up to her throat and choke the life out of her.
She hated taking the ferry or anything to do with vast amounts of water. It always felt like she was suffocating.
"I am sorry. I just need to sit down. You know I hate this." She ground out as though she was in God's presence indeed. As the blackness threatened to pull her into its deceptive embrace.
"It's okay, I've got you...Just breathe." He kept repeating. "It will pass." Nia felt strong arms guiding her down into a seat. Then she felt a hand massaging her back gently.
"Put your head down and keep breathing...breathe."
"Thank you." She whimpered. "I just hate boats, the ocean, and the vastness of it all." She panted. "Plus, it doesn't help that I keep thinking there's nothing to hold on to down there... Oh God thank you."
He laughed. It was so comforting and melodic. Hypnotic even.

Her eyes rested on her lovely gold sandals and her nicely lacquered pedicured striking orange toenails. As well as the most perfect pair of toes on a male she had ever seen, as they laid clad in mahogany brown espadrilles.
"Any better?" The sonorous voice continued.
"Kinda." Nia mumbled. As she raised a foggy head.
Her eyes took in baggy khaki trousers and loose-fitting white cotton shirt, then up to a long slender milk in coffee creamy neck, clean shaven chin, perfect succulent lips that seem to smile forever showing a perfect set of pearly white teeth, slender nose that looked as though it was surgically enhanced, and two smouldering hazel eyes that seemed to burn right

2

through her all the way to her soul pulling out every secret she held prisoner.
Quickly she tore her eyes away.

He could not resist. He reached out and brought her chin back to centre. "It looks like you are having a tough time." He chuckled softly down at her. Wanting to pull her up towards him. But he resisted. He didn't want to cause her any more distress.
"You don't say." She mumbled, bringing her trembling hands up to her forehead.
"What can I do?"
"Get me off this thing for starters." She offered weakly. Feeling the bile churning around in her stomach and trying to claw its way up and out.
"Just breath...breathe...breathe... It will get better I promise. He coaxed her gently.
"When? Cause I truly hate this."
"I believe you. But I am here now. I will help you through it. Breath... Come on."
Without knowing why, she obeyed yet again. She tuned in to his voice; soft melodic and comforting as he coaxed her being into relaxing.
"How are you doing this?"
"Practise. Plus, I think you already knew what to do. You simply panicked."
"I think so too." She breathed. Forgetting all her training. She did this whenever she was overwhelmed. Even before every performance.
"Thank you." She breathed when she felt some sanity had returned. "You are a lifesaver." She tried to ease out of his grasp. "
"Don't! Stay with me." He offered. He liked her eyes.
"I think I am ok now."
"But I am not." He chortled. Mesmerised it seemed when she looked to him again. It made his heart dance. Just like it had done in Antigua.
"You are funny." She offered lightly, trying to tear her eyes away.
Because his were burning a hole through hers.
She felt as though she was trapped; suspended between a rock and a hard place.
Keep looking and for sure she would tell him everything. Look away, and she would never feel the same again.
"So, are you going to tell me your name now?" He asked lost within her gaze.
Damn!!! He was fine and sexy as hell. His voice had a deep-throated quality that was disarming the hell out of her. She searched her mind to figure out the last time she had thought that of the opposite sex...
Other than wanting to dress them.
"Why?" I mean thanks for the save but I am better now." She pushed out gently. A mistake: because the boat shook, or maybe it was her.
She landed in a heap in his arms.
"Why are you fighting it? Obviously, we are meant to be."
"Look thanks again for keeping me from falling on my behind but

3

I really need to go..."
"Where? We are about a quarter into the journey and surrounded by water. So, in other words we are..."
"I just need some air, and it doesn't help that I find myself shouting over this thing." She gestured. "I am sure everyone is looking because they are thinking we must be having a lover's spat."
He laughed thinking for the umpteenth time how beautiful she was. He couldn't stop his mouth.
"So, since we will be lovers don't you think it's high time you tell me your name?"
"Oh, go away. I need some fresh air." Nia said and shuffled clumsily to her feet and took off towards the back of the boat where she spotted a door.
"Hey we aren't through!" He called after her, remembering that he had legs.

Gingerly she felt her way up to the top of the three dirty steps. He thoughts for the umpteenth time was '**when the hell was their damn government going to find the balls to invest in a ferry of their own**' instead of always kissing the asses of other islands who had somehow seen beyond their own nose.
Antigua was the lead. They seemed to have benefited from any and everything Montserrat since the volcanic crisis occurred. No doubt they were laughing on the way to the bank, each time the ferry docked and left.
Who knows? Maybe she could invest privately into something, especially listening to and witnessing the backlash that happens when travelling in and out of the island for **Festival** celebrations every damn year.

She sank down unto the top step. First though she had to survive number one priority: herself.
"Are you okay? Maybe you should drink this. It's all I have." He extended the unopened bottle of water.
"Thanks, but no thanks." Nia said pushing it away. She remembered her aunties warning to never drink from strangers or leave her food and drink unattended.
"This is when the devil's advocates come out to play. You can even loose your life. Or worst yet go around barking like a dog when you are human. Remember Labordie? That is why he walk and whine/twitch. He loved he liquor, and someone gee he more than he could drink. Get ma drift?"
"I promise you it is perfectly harmless beautiful."
"Said the spider to the fly."
He laughed out loud. "You are funny as hell."
"Why do you keep following me?" She tossed with irritation. Ignoring his comment. She thought she would be a damn fool to accept no matter how godlike he looked and seemed.
"Because I want to make sure you are going to be ok. I am not about to lose you not having just found you."

4

"What? You really are something." She squeezed out, bringing her hand up to cup her head.

"You've noticed?" He teased. Forcing her to hold his gaze.

"No!"

"Liar." He teased.

The boat lurched. This time for sure she felt she was going to hurl. She felt her body being propelled into the air but somehow, she felt cradled like a baby against rock hard muscles.

"You are ok. Just breathe…breathe…breathe."

Nia did as she was commanded until his long hair tickled her face. One of his locks had come undone when he lifted her.

He was indeed God in hiding if he could pick her up as though she weighed nothing. Because her ass alone must weigh a ton. Not to forget her ample bosom; that his eyes kept feasting lustily on in the white cotton tank she wore.

Nia felt heat rise as she tried to conceal them as she pulled her orange cardigan close.

"Not fair." He said, thinking he could just loose himself in her kola nut haven. She took his breathe away each time she looked at him.

There was something elusively familiar, but he couldn't grasp it.

She also reminded him of a warrior princess, she was almost six feet tall and curvaceous in all the right places. Long slender brown legs from that eternal split in her skirt. As well as her neck and her succulent looking lips and white teeth whenever she smiled. Her face reminded him somewhat of the supermodel Tyra Banks, but she was the most beautiful of the pair. Yet they could easily pass for twins. Especially when she smiled.

She'd done it to the ticket agent and looked away. It was in that moment their eyes had met and locked.

Damn! She thought. He sure was one handsome man! Her heart fluttered from an immense lust, and she pictured herself in his arms, acting totally slutty and wanton…

She felt a warmth taking up residence between her legs. Shit! I so need to get laid she thought because he had made her feel naked and oh so damn carnal.

He had thought damn! I need to get laid because he had not had any in months. He pictured them locked away together making hot steamy passionate love for the rest of the month. He even pictured her carrying his babies. He pictured her in a sexy floaty white dress walking towards him as he waited expectantly. SCREEECH!!!!! What the %$&£!!!!

She had broken the connection; she had looked away and continued with what she was doing as though they hadn't formed an attachment in that split second.

He spotted her again when it was nearly time to board. But because he was VIP, they'd swiftly hurried him aboard.

5

Ama had sorted things thus far. He had taken the Lear into **V.C. Bird International** and was ushered quickly through customs and piled into a luxury car to the ferry port.

He had mentioned to Ama that he didn't want bells and whistles from that point on. They had a bit of a tiff. She told him not to call her when he got his ass into trouble. But before she closed the door she spat, "I have a plan Mr. Kiah Corrington."

He loved the woman who always reminded him of Judi Dench and the M character she played in **007**. She had been with him since he took over the floundering real estate development company his grandfather owned majority shares in.

Thank goodness for his auntie. He pictured the face of the woman who has been his guardian angel since he had placed his eyes in hers as a little boy. She lived on the island where he was now heading.

He finally got what Ama meant when he spotted '**them**'. His body was suddenly flooded with mixed emotions. He smiled in the end. She was the best. Time and time she had proven this.

He thought back to the very first day; He was looking for pen and paper and she simply just materialised holding them out to him. He wanted a cup of coffee and there she was.

Down to the day she held a handkerchief out to him just before he sneezed.

"I am that great Mr. Kiah Corrington." She chuffed and blew on the imaginary gun.

She was given a 1% share in the company a couple years later.

She has proven invaluable.

Kiah spotted the beautiful woman again after what seemed like a lifetime. He suddenly felt like he had only begun to breathe.

It was her turn to come aboard. She looked as though she was being forced to stand in front of a firing squad. In another second, he thought she would bolt. Then a rough looking man grabbed a hold of her hand and dragged her down the steps. He never felt so much like smashing another human's face as he did in that moment just by looking at his treatment of her.

You put our entire race to shame he thought. He had to intervene before he followed through on the impeccable urge. Thank God, he had caught her just as another deposited her roughly on the floor.

"Okay maybe if I tell you my name you will tell me yours? Then we can go from there. My name is Hezekiah Carter Corrington, but my friends call me Kiah." He left off the pretentious the third. "I am on my way to visit my aunt in Emerald City and to enjoy Festival 2016. A must she tells me."

He also left off the bit about her nagging; **you should try island-women instead of Yankee ones for a change.**

He waited but she offered nothing, she just kept trying to get far away from him. As though he were contagious.
He could not ever recall having that effect on the opposite sex. They had no qualms it seemed of always throwing themselves at him.
"I am sure woman must always throw themselves at you." Nia tossed.
"What?" It was as if she had read his mind. "You don't know me like that." He offered in shock.

"What the hell!" She cried out as the boat lurched. She fought to regain her balance on two strong legs; that she planted firmly on the floor again.
"You might as well surrender my dear. See the Fates are trying to tell you something."
"That I made a horrible mistake getting aboard this contraption?"
"Then if you hadn't, we wouldn't have met. "He offered and held her close.
"Can you be serious? And why does it seem that I am the only one affected? Look at how everyone is chatting happily and just getting on with it. While I am being tortured."
He laughed. "I am too." He chuckled. "Maybe you should tell me your name, and who knows maybe things will get better."
"Nia...I'm Nia." She wriggled out of his grasp and wobbled over to the railing and held on for dear life."
She thought of the Michael Rosen's children story **Going on a Bear Hunt**. It was one of her favourites now. Pastor Seaton had told her about it. It was her inspiration for dealing with whatever life threw her way. **You must go through it...** That was how she sorted that fool whom she will not name yet.
"Nice name Nia."
"Thank you." She offered. Thankful he had pulled her away from the nameless. He held her captive.
"Does it have any significant meaning?"
"It means aim or purpose in Swahili."
"I like it." He came to stand next to her. Their hands rested inches from each other. He resisted the urge to touch her. "So, is this your first-time visiting Emerald City?"
"No." she spat all too quickly not missing the **TAG** luxury watch on his wrist. She knew it was very expensive. Seba told her President Obama wore one, so he wanted one, but his lover told him they weren't cheap, but he will work on it.
"C'mon cut me some slack here. I am trying Nia."
"Sorry. I just feel as though someone, or something is out to get me." She softened her tone. She wasn't like to this to people unless they gave her cause.
"It will get better." Kiah chuckled devilishly, more so to himself than to her. Thinking 'if only she knew.'
"It had better be soon." She said clutching at the railing for dear life.

7

"Hope so too." Kiah offered fighting the immense urge to pull her in and plant the deepest kiss on her lips. He sucked in his breath slowly as he feasted hungrily.

She looked to him. As his soothing voice seemed to pull her in no matter how hard she tried to resist. Amazing what one could learn by simply just looking at someone.
She forced herself to recall the phrase; **It takes a minute to find something special in a person, an hour to appreciate them, a day to love them, and a lifetime to forget them.**
Come to think of it he was totally distracting her! Plus, the dreadful waves seemed to have calmed sufficiently and was allowing her to finally relax as she continued listening to his hypnotic voice as he locked gaze with her in the blackness that surrounded them.
"So, is this your first time on the island?" She found herself asking.
"No." He beamed over at her. Thanking God, she seemed to be mellowing a bit. "Well, I came here as a boy. Once when I was 6 and another time when I was 10. I had lots of fun, as well as inherited a life changing event...
He shook himself out of the haunting memory. "But my favourite memory was eating ice-cream and watching the masquerades dance in the street. I am long overdue in taking a break. I wanted to go someplace different, not my usual hangouts."
"Where would these hangouts be?" She asked out of politeness. Assuming he would say Europe, Hawaii and on many beaches in California.
I usually travel to the Caribbean, Aruba, the Bahamas, Antigua, Jamaica. Sometimes I go over to Europe."
She smiled. It looked more like a smirk. "So, you are a playboy then." She stated matter of fact.
"Do wipe that smirk of your face dear."
"Just saying if it walks like a duck."
"Shocking! You do not know me, yet you have an opinion? What's that saying? Oh yes! Be careful of throwing stones at glass buildings."
She laughed. "You mean people in glass houses shouldn't throw stones?"
"Exactly." He said loving the way her lips lifted around the edges, the same time causing her eyes to twinkle.
"So, I see I will have to work hard on getting you to change your opinion of me."
"Good luck with that. "She boldly challenged. Beginning to like his company. It kept her from thinking of the murky blackness that surrounded them.
"So, you are an auntie's boy then?"
"I am going to ignore that, Nia. Then again, I am a duck." He did a saga-boy poise. "Auntie B is special to me. Like I was saying before I was so rudely interrupted by that scornful laugh. My Auntie B told me or was it more like challenged me to come and give the island a chance. So here I come."

8

"Well, I think you will have fun, especially since you are coming when we are getting ready for **Festival**. Carnival to you novices. You can witness people at their abandon and wildest. They leave all their troubles and woes behind as Festival approaches."

"What about you? Do you become like others?" He asked. Having a hard time picturing her in abandonment yet relishing the idea of witnessing this first-hand phenomenon.

He could feel his loins heating up, as though someone had started a tiny flame and was blowing it to a roaring fire.

"Wouldn't you like to know?" She asked taking a step away from him.

"Don't do that." He said as he reached out to her and eased her back. His heart settled again in his chest when she inched back. He longed to pull her into his arms. He feasted his eyes on her for the umpteenth time. Thinking he had better not let there be any lapses or else he might lose her for sure.

"So do you live in Emerald City?"

She laughed; it was soft, guttural and oh so sexy.

"Yes, I do. Have done all my life. I do not think I can live anywhere else on earth. Emerald City is my balm, my shelter in the time of storm. I sound really cliché, don't I? But I do not know if I can do a longing in words. Especially when I leave and come back. It's like whatever crap I faced, or hurdle I incurred, setting foot back on E.C soil just heals me, and gives me a new prospective on any trial. Yes, I wish I can change a few things, such as means of travel stopping off in that place we just left and being put through the ringer before we can get home. Not to forget treating us as though we are not worth anything, especially when they have siphoned all our money especially when they know we need to do this just to get home. I wish I had enough money to buy a proper ferry or invest in one or a couple so that our people didn't have to put up with all that bullshit when travelling in and out of the island."

"I know right." He had to play the role. Ama said she herself had a tough time trying to get him into the island. Which was why they had opted for the **Lear** from LAX International. She would have rented a helicopter or chartered an airplane to get him over but again he had declined. Then there was that gut thing again.

"Do you really want to visit your auntie that badly Kiah? It is a two-hour ferry ride; that may or may not run depending on if they have a full charter. Also, there is a tiny airplane that gets you over in half an hour, albeit cramped."

It did not appeal to him. He was tempted to cancel the trip. Tell his aunt he wasn't coming after all, and head out to Maui. But he had a business meeting in the neighbouring island; a prime piece of real estate he had had his eyes on. He had plucked it right out from under a few others and now he couldn't wait to sink his teeth into it: full throttle.

He was going to visit the woman. He could not disappoint her yet again. He would always promise but seize something else over heading to the island.

9

You had better stay the course my friend that feeling said to him. Her voice disturbed his reverie.

"Seriously every time I travel out, I pray it will be different seeing all the time our government says we are working on it. I mean how long does it take to put the proper people and systems in place to enhance and build up tourism? Auntie K says that whoever was is in charge seemed to have eaten their pencil instead of using them to take the proper notes.

He laughed, bringing his hands up to his face. Yes, he would have fired their asses before they could even say wait. He had not made **Forbes** richest page relying on ignorance and lots second chances.

He had a gift; to always go with his gut, it had never failed him.

Even among his family's diatribes. They thought he should have followed them into the rag trade, but his heart was set on real-estate, investing and developing. He could suss out a good thing.

He had borrowed from his auntie years ago and had thrice repaid what he owed, and then some. He had even bailed his parents out a few times. They didn't know. Until when he finally convinced them to sell, and they made a handsome bundle. They are on a world tour; a dream they had for years.

Hopefully they would end up in Emerald City for Christmas.

Guess this was the gut feeling, the Leap of Fate his auntie spoke about.

Just think if he had cancelled, he would never have met her.

From the first look, she had chopped off a huge piece of his heart that he was never ever going to get back if he allowed her to walk away, and out of his life.

Just think if you had flown over. You would have missed this chance. His head reasoned. Thank God he had listened.

"Every day living." Auntie B said. "Just try being a regular guy down in Emerald City; no bells and whistles just let go and let the universe have her way."

His laughter turned into a smile as he continued to look at the woman in front of him.

"So other than being pissed off in Antigua and having the solution to positive traveling to Emerald City. May I ask what it is you do for a living?"

"Are you making fun of me Kiah? I know I must sound irrational, but I just hate stupidity. I don't like people tekkin us mek fool."

Her island dialect slipped out. It usually did when she was upset or boiling about something.

"I could listen to you go on. No judgement here Nia. You have a beautiful accent. Plus, a lot of what you said made sense to me."

"Thank you. We need to sort this if we want to make a dent into our tourism."

"Perhaps we can continue this discussion later. It is very interesting."

"Thanks. "She offered. Thinking perhaps she should be quiet about it. He is vacationing after all. So why should their problem become his?

10

"Let me say in my defence that I am not always such a nasty piece of work. I just don't do well in heat, water, and dealing with shit being shovelled in my lap."

"You go girl!" He tossed doing a drag queen's salute to girl power. It made her laugh. She had lost count now.

Her stomach interrupted with a loud growl. "Oops, I'm sorry. I was so nervous that I didn't eat. Now I am so hungry I could eat a horse. Part of me wished I had taken a flight instead. I could be home and kissing up to some decent food."

"Your heart's desire. Tell me and I will have it delivered to you as soon as we dock. I can give Auntie B a call."

"Bless you. But I am sure my aunties will have your auntie beat."

"Is this a challenge?" He asked. She laughed again. "Seriously tell me what you would like." He loved the sound.

"Just a fact. But I will take a bucket of island spicy wings from Sylvie's with side order of pigeon pea biscuit and gravy, and I will do the rest; a steaming cup of ginger and hibiscus tea." She breathed salaciously.

"Interesting." He muttered over and again as he dug into his pocket and fished out his cellular phone.

"Auntie it is your favourite nephew...We are about an hour and ten minutes out... Me too... Huge favour... Can you please pick up a bucket of someone call **Sylvie's** Island spicy wings and side order of pigeon pea biscuit and gravy please...? I met someone who is craving this as we speak...You will meet her when we get in..."

He held the phone away from his ear... "Yes auntie...I said when we get in... I met her on the ferry coming down actually..."

He held the phone away from his ears again.

"Soon Auntie B... Just please bring me that order... Yes soon... Love you more...Yes Auntie B... I love you too. I will see you soon."

"Are you serious?" She asked, looking at him in total bewilderment. But liking his suave.

"Anything for you my dear. I told you I have no intention of ever letting you out of my sight. Not again."

"You sound like a stalker." She tossed at him. Thinking he was quite pleasing as she looked him over for the millionth time, and that flame that had turned to embers started flickering back to life. He looked like he had just stepped off the pages of a **GQ** magazine.

Stuff like that aren't meant to happen to women like her. Because in her summation guys like him only fell for the girls with names like Buffy, Candy, and Ginger...

They had arms and legs coming out of their neck, with straight hair down their back.

Not black girls with braids, big asses and thick legs and lips. He must be drunk or blind. She busted out laughing.

He reached for her.

She stayed him and pushed him back.

11

"I told you before that I have a black belt in **scream-Kungfu** so if you are going to try and do something …"

"There will be time enough for that Nia." He laughed aloud. "But I promise I wouldn't do anything that you wouldn't ask or beg me to do to you."

"Shit white-boy you got game!"

"Not all of me is white Nia." He confessed. Then smiled at the look of confusion that marred her beautiful face. "My mum is half black."

"Fella stop de lying!" She spat without meaning to. Mouth open and story jump out sort of thing.

"I'm not Nia. I am always delighted to throw that bit in to see what kind of reaction I get."

"You're serious?" She asked. Looking him up and down. "No wonder them locks so fly. But seriously Kiah?"

"I am perfectly serious Nia." It was the absolute truth. He would never lie about that piece of information. It was very important to him and to who he has become.

In a speech to his alma mater **CAL** State LA, he encouraged young people no matter colour, to always, always dream big. Follow dreams; your heart, your beliefs, and equally work just as hard. Never allow anyone to tell you who you are or who you are supposed to be. If you believe you can, therefore just go out and by God's grace just do it. By working as hard as you can and never allow anyone to prevent you turning dreams into reality.

"Hey, are you there?" She snapped her fingers.

"Sorry, but yes, I am half black. Because of my mom. She is referred to as mulatto."

"Wow! You are becoming quite interesting to me Kiah."

"Glad I can spark a smidge of interest Nia." He chuckled yet again.

"Why does it sound like you are trying to get into my panties? Isn't there a Buffy or Lemon stowed away somewhere?" She tossed, voicing her thoughts as she looked around.

"Buffy? Lemon?" He laughed. The first part was indeed true. He salivated at the thought. His face hurt from how many times she had made him laugh since they met.

"Yes, Kiah because guys like you don't bother girls like me. Then again guess you are on holiday. So, what is a little bump and grind gonna hurt, eh? But I am not like your ordinary island girl with a longing to be away from my island. I born yah and I gonna stay right yah." She tried to scramble away.

He pulled her back.

"Nia, I told you I am not ever going to let you get away again, so stop trying to. Now let's see if I can decode that mouthful. You will never leave your island to live anywhere else because you love it too much. Yes?"

"Yes!" She said firmly. But busted out laughing. "You are something else. I must say as well that you are making this trip bearable. Thank you, Kiah."

"You are welcome my Nia." He reached for her hand and held it.

She did not snatch it away. She just stared at their hands until her phone started ringing.

"Seba! Yes, I am on my way. I will be home soon. What are you on about? What pic? **Facebook**? How did that happen? But why? He helped me through a tough time. You know I hate the water.
I understand why you couldn't be with me...Let me check it out...I will talk to you later...No I don't need you to get me I will get a taxi. Yes, I am sure. Love you too. Yes...Yes Seba I will see you soon... Missed you too."
Thankful he didn't insist she stayed on the phone longer.
Kiah flounced away when she said the L word and wandered over to the railing. He turned his back on her. What the FUCK!!! What the hell did you expect? That someone like her would just be free and waiting for you? Get your head out of the cloud man. Snap the fuck out of it. He admonished himself.

Nia swiped the screen to **Facebook**. She took a sharp intake of breath. She hadn't noticed anyone when she came aboard.
The photo was of her staring up at him. Thank God his back was turned.
The caption read **Looks like Carnival Baby found a Man**!!!
Seba tagged her.
She didn't notice Nosey-Ass-Floyd when she'd come aboard the vessel. Which gave the underhanded bastard a chance to catch her with her drawers down at her ankles.
Plus, it was standing room only, so he didn't want to lose his seat. He hated not having a place to park his fat ass. He always had his folding chair at the park.
"Carnival Baby? Is that you?" Kiah asked full of intrigue. Pulling her from her reverie.
"Yes."
"Why?"
"I don't know you that well."
"I thought we were working on that Nia." Silly besotted bastard!!! His head screamed. Thank God his face was unseen. He could just picture Greta his publicist/spin doctor calling him on the phone and demanding to know what was going on.
Then again maybe things would work out seeing his auntie said people in the Caribbean didn't behave like crazy folks in California. They did not follow people about and shoved lenses in their faces to snap pictures. Then sold to the highest bidder.
But he reminded himself that he had to be more careful.
Nia left him and took up residence where he had stood. He walked over to her and handed her the phone back.
"I've messed things up for you huh?"
"It doesn't matter." She stuffed the phone away. "The devil always finds work for idle hands."
"That's social media. You summed it up well Nia." He knew.

13

He had come under fire many times. Over the years he had developed a thicker skin.

He no longer read or entertained idle chit chat. It wreaks havoc. He considered his life boring as shit and did not understand why people would be interested in him at all.

Before it freaked him out. Now he just got on with it. People can be fickle on any given day h surmised. Today for him, tomorrow for someone else. So just take it in stride and don't believe the hype. He kept reminding himself.

"Okay let us change the record. No more talk of social media. Tell me about what's his name? How long have you two been together?"

He couldn't bring himself to say the name. He had to find out more and device a way to get rid of him and for good.

"What are you on about?" She asked. Her eyes catching a glimpse of Emerald City lights in the distance. Her heart took flight.

"We will be home soon." She said nostalgically.

"I am torn." He said coming to stand next to her. As much as he was longing to see his Auntie, he hated having to say goodbye to her.

"I do not want this to end Nia. Nor do I want to watch you go off with this Seba..."

He turned her towards him. He pulled her in. Without another word he brought his lips down on hers. He was ravenous for her more than ever.

He suckled her lips like they were the fount of his existence. When he came up for air, all he could say was, "please don't let this be the last time I see you or get to do this." He kissed her repeatedly.

She did not fight. Her legs became wobbly, her head reeled, as she longed for something solid to bear her up. She loved the way the boat rocked on the water as his tongue expertly eased in and around hers. It was an eternity before they came up for air.

"God, you taste so damn good. I want to bury myself within you." He cupped her face in his hands.

"Kiah, we have to stop this." She finally ground out. "Because if you continue to kiss me the way you, are I fear I may not have the strength to walk away."

He brought his mouth back to hers. He kissed the top lip and then the bottom. He kissed her neck. He kissed the top of her bosom and lingered there...

She cupped his head and held it. "Kiah I am serious." She kissed the top of his head.

He smelt a bit fruity like some kiwi concoction. "You smell heavenly." She said burying her face in his hair. Her head reeled and her body was in chaos.

He lifted his head to look into her eyes. "I am smitten." He said without guilt. "Nia how are we going to do this... walk away I mean?"

"Kiah please. Just let us not think about that, let us just continue to enjoy each other until that time comes." She said feeling bold, and not one bit of ashamedness. For some reason she did not feel afraid either. She loved being in his presence. She loved how he made her feel when he looked at her, touched her, held her...

They continued just holding each other and letting the motion of the ocean rock their troubled soul.

"So, who is Seba Nia? Is he someone that I must go up against? Because I am telling you now that I am not walking away. Not ever."

"Seba is someone I have known for as long as I have known myself. He is my brother, my design partner. He runs the business when I am not there, and when I am designing." She decided too just be honest. She did not want to play games.

"Interesting...So he is not a love interest?"

"No Kiah. I have been far too busy to even entertain that side of things for years now. Plus, I have never been lucky in that arena. So, I have stayed far far far away." She stressed dramatically.

He laughed. "Are you saying there is no one I need to do battle with to win your heart? Not that I am complaining, but someone as beautiful and sexy, and vivacious as you must have a shedload of men waiting on your doorstep."

"No, I do not. Sorry to burst your bubble. But the new craze is stick thin, big boobs and long hair. I could battle in two of those areas but the skinny thing. Nah! I enjoy my food way too much."

"For me having curves is sexy. I like curves. Your curves."

"Seriously dude? Somehow you don't strike me as that kind of person."

"Hence the Buffy and Lemon comment, right? True for a while that was what I was into. But people change. I had to change because most of them bored the hell out of me. Nia, I work too hard, and a lot of females do not have the patience to play second fiddle for too long. Guess timing is everything." He hugged her tightly.

He loved her subtly fruity scent, a mixture of lemon and berries.

"So, if I were to buy into this madness you are feeding me Kiah let me pose the same question to you. Who will I be battling for daring to believe that someone like you could be remotely interested in someone like me?"

"No one Nia? I have not had a committed relationship in a year and then some. Or then again perhaps my job." He too decided he should be honest. He did not want anything popping up to spook her. Just yet.

"So, what is it that you do Kiah?"

"I am a real estate investor and developer." He didn't offer anymore. Thank God she did not pry.

"And you?"

"I am a designer."

"What do you design?"

"Formal and informal gowns and dresses, accessories, clothes and all sorts of stuff."

"Like?" He was intrigued.

15

"I design my own line of furniture and household things; like mirrors, beddings, chandeliers, utensils and draperies, clocks, plates, and forks... Want me to continue? My mind is just always too busy, so I just do what the spirit prompts me to. I even designed my own house/studio."

"Interesting. You will show me soon, yes? How about tomorrow? I can stop by, and you can give me the personal tour."

"I have a few appointments I must keep. I have been away for a week, so I need to honour them. Back to the work first and anything after."

"It is not going to take all day, is it? We could meet in the afternoon. We could have a late lunch. I mean it Nia I need to see you."

"How about if we exchange numbers and you call me around mid-day. I would have a better idea as to a time we can meet. That is the best I can do for now Kiah."

"I will settle for that. Now tell me some more about what you are working on. Because my mind is drifting back to your body, and so help me I need a distraction. Before I toss you up against that rail and have my way with you."

"Do you always say what you're thinking?"

"To beautiful women? Yes, I do Nia." He smiled.

Gosh he is one handsome man! Nia thought, as they continued to talk and stayed wrapped in each other's arms, as the lights beckoned.

As they got more pronounced; welcoming them to Emerald City his heart recoiled.

They did everything to prolong the inevitable. Even deciding to wait for last to disembark.

They kissed one last time before they were rudely disrupted by that same guy who tossed her about earlier.

Again, Kiah felt the urge to teach him a lesson. He made a mental note to not forget him as he forced himself to comply.

He did not want to do anything else to land her or him on social media. She pointed out the guy who had posted the photo.

Kiah smiled when he received the thumbs up. No doubt he was looking for his cell that had sunk to the bottom of the ocean.

True enough he was off in the corner causing a raucous; arguing with officers about it being stolen while he was on that God-awful ferry. She waved to him joyously.

"Karma!" she called out. No doubt he was spying for Ford, her competitive rival for costumes every year.

Kiah forced himself to be strong as they held hands all the way to the immigration desk. He was doing little circles in her palm, that made her tingle all the way down to her toes.

He allowed her to go first.

She could still feel him close; his eyes bore into her. Even when he went across to his immigration officer.

The next time they saw each was out in the luggage section. She was securing all the stuff she needed to declare.

When Nia finally stepped out. The vision of him being embraced by the beautiful Lady Bellot Corrington; one of the island's leading female and society bell; who had her hands in most everything on the island.

They were holding each other as though they were remarkably familiar but had not seen each other for decades.

It gave her heart cause to race sporadically within her chest. She had to force herself to breathe deeply. It made her choke.

Many said she should toss her hat in the ring for the role of Prime Minister. But her excuse was that she was too stubborn and set in her ways to become the leader of any country.

Plus, she loved her role as CEO of the most flourishing department store on the island called **Corrington's**.

Her black dyed hair flowed in a tidy at the nape bob. She was wearing comfortable cream leisure slacks and a dusty pink sweater set and buckled loafers. She always exuded such an air of elegance whenever she stepped out.

Nia was reminded of the parable of the prodigal son when she witnessed the embrace.

Even her auntie Katho was going in for a hug as well and chatting animatedly with him as though it was something they always did.

She wore jeans and blazer over black and white boat neck top. Her long salt and pepper hair was pulled back in a lose ponytail.

At times, the woman stole her breath away because of how much she looked like her mama. They were fraternal twins.

What the...!!! No, it couldn't be she thought quickly as she pieced it all together. She longed to turn tail and run.

Too late. Her auntie spotted her and called her over excitedly.

God help me! Nia thought as she placed one foot in front of the other. The woman had such a way of making her feel like a little girl covered in mud, and who must apologise for having fun.

The two were always a force to be reckoned with. They had been lovers for years. Many had tried to cheapen it or get them to talk.

"We owe no one any explanation except God." Auntie K said.

A couple times reporters tried to get into her face. A mistake they soon discovered. Especially when she told one to kiss her black ass.

The woman was such a disarming ball of contradiction. But Nia loved her to bits. She loved them both. Because they were her force-field and walked hand in hand with her, no matter what life threw at her.

"Hello Auntie Katho." She whimpered. Disappearing into the woman's lavender and rose scent. Her eyes teared up instantaneously.

17

It was her turn to hold her tightly. She anchored herself. She felt guilty at times for not visiting as often as she should. Or checking in just to have a chat other that business. A proper visit was long overdue.

Her watery eyes landed on Kiah. He too looked absolutely stunned.

"Nia dear you didn't tell us you were on the ferry with our Hezekiah!" She released her. "Hezekiah meet my beautiful and **single** niece Miss Nia-Belle."

"Auntie!" Nia squeaked. She could feel the warmth as it crawled about her face, and she prayed even harder for a hole to crawl into.

She tore her eyes away and let them travel from him to his aunt and back to him. Why didn't she put it together? Because the similarities were there if you looked closer. Side by side a perfect match.

She was forced to look back at him.

"Do not auntie me! It's about time you sort your personal life as well as you organise your public. Now tell me Hezekiah what do you think our girl? Isn't she the most beautiful thing you have seen in a long while? Funny I have been telling you about her for so long and you paid no attention. Now look at how the universe worked its magic."

"Pick up your lip boy!" His auntie Bellot teased, bringing him closer. "This is who I had in mind for you to meet all these years I've been telling you to come home." She slapped him upside his head playfully.

"Aaaah..." He spluttered unsure of his next words, never at a loss before. "You mean she is? I mean this is who you wanted me to meet?"

"Yes **Mr- I- am- always- too- busy**. This is who we have always had in mind for you! Now scoop up your lip and say hello to Miss Nia." His auntie said poking him in the ribs.

"But I...we...You mean?"

"Hezekiah just say hello. Sometimes that is all it takes to break the ice. Or bridge a gap." Auntie Katho urged pushing her closer.

"Nia." He stuttered and reached out a hand. His heart was doing all these freaky things in his chest. Shit! He had promised to call her, but he never did. He had lost track of the number. He hadn't put it in his contact like he promised.

They had sent photos of her, he always thought she was cute, but something always distracted him.

She had even answered the telephone a couple times but rushed off to get his auntie after a brief hello...

Shit! Shit! Shit!! He could not believe he...They had fought against it. All these years. He had broken promises after promises of coming back to the island.

He squeezed her hand resisting the urge to pull her to him and cause her further awkwardness.

She looked like she was trying to find a way to hide, as she looked to him with questioning eyes.

"She is beautiful. You are gorgeous. B-darling just think what lovely babies these two can..."

"Auntie K for goodness' sake! Please do not embarrass me any further. I am tired and hungry. I need…"

"Did you stop by **Sylvie's**?" Kiah asked regaining his tongue.

He remembered he had promised her dinner. He hoped his auntie could deliver.

"Speaking of which. You said you had someone you wanted me to meet?" Lady Bellot continued. Hugging him to her again.

"Yes… I…" He saw her shake her head. He stupidly threw her a questioning look. "Maybe later."

"Why? No time like the present." His auntie continued. Looking from him to the jittery looking girl who appeared like she would wet herself any minute.

"Is there something you two are keeping from us?"

"No ma'am! It's just that …Nia and I were talking on the way down and she happened to mention Sylvie's so I promised I would try it. But come to think of it she could have it instead, seeing she won the bet anyway." That was lame. But he had to produce something.

"Bet? What bet?" The woman asked.

"She said we would arrive later than schedule and looks like we did." He was reaching but he had to say something. Seems she was not ready for the ladies to know they had shared more than just hello.

"Mmmh…Well we all know the ferry is hardly ever on time. Come home more often and you will soon discover that. Anyway, yes Silcott did get the meal. It is in the car. But do not think I am not disappointed after you built my hopes up." She released him long enough to walk around to the front of the car and opened the door, lifted out a picnic basket, and handed it over to him.

They remained in that dumbfounded position just staring at each other. Her auntie had even joined in as well.

"Are you okay?" she asked her. "You are quiet. And you… This is the first time I have known you to not have a flippant come back."

She turned to him. "I introduced you to a darling specimen of a woman, more like prime estate, and you appear as though someone stole all your money."

"Sorry Auntie Katholeen. I did not mean to seem disinterested believe me I do not. It's just that I am completely thrown off my game. But it is indeed a pleasure to finally meet your beautiful niece. I look forward to getting to know her a bit more over the next few days. Nia it is my pleasure." He squeezed the hand that he still had in his. Neither realising it seemed.

Her auntie nudged her in the ribs, "play your cards right my dear. He is a keeper." She whispered in her ears.

His auntie passed him the picnic basket that he in turn handed to her. "Please enjoy this, Nia."

"Why don't you invite her over for lunch? We would love to have a catch-up visit. Wouldn't that be great Katho?"

The two women winked over at each other like co-conspirators.

"Hello Miss Nia." Silcott said, coming around to join them. "The bags are all in the car. Shall I put yours in as well? We can make a stop to you first..."
"No! No that would not be necessary." She chimed. "I have too much stuff. Plus, Seba promised he would pick me up."
"Are you certain Miss Nia?" The man asked.
"Yes, thank you. Thank you. I mean thank you as well Kiah. Thank you for dinner. It smells divine." She had popped the lid just to sneak a peek. She could not wait to tuck in. Her dry mouth abruptly sprung a leak.

Suddenly chaos broke out as Seba's black Hummer pulled up with loud blasting music.
"Miss Thang! Your chauffer awaits! Hello ladies! You two look fabulous as usual!"
More cars in the back of him started honking loudly.
"Why don't you blasted people wait your turn? Okay! Okay! You people are trying to give me a major heart attack. I will be back around in a moment baby. Just let me do my thang."
"Why didn't you park the car the right way in the first place Sebastin? Off you go!" Auntie tossed to him.
He blew her a kiss.
"That fella is going to be the death of us all." She clutched her chest hysterically.
"I am so sorry Auntie. I had better go give him a hand. There is lots of baggage to recover."
"Let me give you a hand." He said, wanting to get a little space from the prying eyes. It was his turn to look pleadingly towards her. After a long and hesitant moment, she obliged.

They walked away, crossing the busy road with his hand resting across the small of her back.
"Such the gentleman, and so handsome too." She heard her auntie K say. "I think they are going to make a great couple."
"Even if we have to conspire to get them together." She heard Lady Bellot add.
Nia wanted to look back and say, "I heard you two." But he nudged her along.
"Let them have this." He urged. Loving that they were going to help him win her affections. He couldn't believe his luck yet again. It meant the universe was conspiring in their favour as well. Of all the women in the world and she had come picked straight out of heaven it seemed just for him.
"Nia? Can you believe this?" He asked and pulled her to him. They were standing in a dimly lit area. He had seen it when he was heading out of the building.
"What?" She snapped not meaning to. He put his fingers under her chin and tilted her head up to his.
"That our aunties are trying to get us down the aisle as soon as possible."

Shit! did he just say it out loud? How the hell was he thinking of marriage? He had only met the temperamental women who had somehow managed to blow his mind the first time he saw her. But come to think of it he had already pictured her in a wedding gown, having his child. She was running on the beach with a tiny girl that they were looking upon with so much adoration.

Yes, he had already imagined a lifetime with her. He felt as though she was meant for him because he had never ever in his life felt that pull, that immense connection to anyone like he was feeling towards her.

"Kiah please. I am tired. I am hungry and I don't have any energy left to think about anything. Keep this up and I just might say yes if only to get you to let me go get my stuff and get home and hopefully to my bed."

"I wish I was going with you Nia. I meant what I said to you, I don't want us to lose this connection. I am sure you feel it as much as I do. You feel this invisible pull don't you Nia?"

"If I say yes Kiah, would you just let me go?" She asked. Knowing full well she felt the same thing he was describing. She didn't want to say goodbye either but if she continued to stand there, she knew she would forever be lost to him. She'd even asked God earlier to give her the strength to walk away from him on the ferry. Because it felt as though someone had packed a bag of stones in her chest when she took the first step away. She'd managed to do it, up until it was her turn to cross to the immigration officer.

But when she came out and spotted him again the heaviness descended.

"I don't want you to say anything you don't feel." He urged her, tilting her chin gently, as he stared into her beautiful eyes.

He felt like kissing her again, but he didn't want to cause her another moment of grief.

"Kiah please…Please just let me go…Please… Or I too wouldn't have the strength anymore to say no to you ever again." She pleaded softly.

"So, I am not going freaking nuts here. You do feel it too." He couldn't stop himself. He buried his lips on hers, and her mouth opened to welcome his probing tongue.

He kissed her deeply and hungrily.

The basket dropped from her hands, and she brought her arms up to entwine them around his neck, kissing him back with every ounce of urgency she felt him emitting into her body.

They came away from each other abruptly when a flashlight flooded them with harsh illumination.

"You two okay ova-dey? Maybe a-you need to get a hotel room because this sure ain't de… Lard-have-his-mercy! Miss Nia that you?" Security guard Dyer asked as he brought his hand up to his eyes. "Gosh I sorry."

"That's ok Dyer. I had better be on my way. I need to get my things from customs." She started away. Her heart pounding like a marathoner in her heaving chest.

21

"Nia I am sorry." He said catching up to her. "Please just stop for a second." He pulled her back to him. "Please I am sorry." He said hating she was compromised yet again.

"I have been acting like a wanton female all night. Auntie K always says what's done in the dark will always come out in the light. Not once tonight but on numerous occasions since meeting you Kiah Corrington I have been dancing with the devil. I have even been placed on **Facebook**. Now the biggest man-gossiper there is has found me making-out behind a building like a hot and bothered teenager. What else? What else Kiah? For god's sake just let us find the strength to say goodbye tonight and see if we feel the same in a couple of days towards each other. I mean it that's the best I can do tonight because I am done."

"Nia I am sorry." He buried his face in her braids. "Please forgive me." They stayed that way a while longer.

She was spent. She felt as though she had no strength to fight. She laid against him feeling deflated.

"Let's get your things and get you home and sorted." He offered, feeling her sagging against him. With that he took her hand and urged her on and up the steps to sort her baggage.

Nia felt like everyone was watching her. That they knew something had changed about her. She wished she could say exactly what. But she herself couldn't place her finger on it. So, she kept on walking; one foot in front of the other. Because she was too exhausted to figure it out just yet.

When she got inside to her baggage, they were all stacked like a steep mountain; all 15 pieces. She wondered how in God's name would she get them all to fit in Seba's pristine truck.

"Miss Nia what you got in them bags and cases?" Immigration officers asked. "Any contraband and ting? Seems like every time you leave you bring back another piece to add to the island."

The room erupted in laughter.

"Would there be any work for all a-you if I didn't?" She tossed back. Not one to back down from lip.

"Always giving lip Miss Nia."

"Well don't throw no corn Jaffla."

"By the way, we hear you off de market." He nodded towards Kiah. "Maybe if we spent more time working instead of on social media, things would flow much better coming back into de island?"

"Oh gosh reload no!"

"Well, you started first." Nia huffed.

"So, tell me. He de fella that you tassing us up for?"

"Wouldn't you like that scope, Trevor? Natalie ain't gonna be the next Barbara Walters."

"See she got lip, yes?"

He turned from her to give his attention to Seba. He bestowed upon him the nastiest look.

Seba was dressed in everything from his **HaVana** line; white three-quarter length shorts and tan coloured rolled up to the elbow light linen jacket with the island madras etched about the cuffs (two in one; meaning it could be worn inside and out. Totally lightweight for packing.
He wore it over cloud white tucked in tank. Along with boat shoes in the same madras having worked closely with a shoemaker friend of his to get the style done in sandals as well as dress shoes.
He got the idea from Mr Brown from Tyler Perry's Madear.
Seba claimed, "there is not a damn thing wrong with putting colours and patterns together. Once you wore them with flair. Just like Brown."
The man was gorgeousness personified. He was truly rocking the hell out of the look. She adored the look. Especially his signature look; long thick black permed hair. It was his best feature. That he wore pulled back in a ponytail topped off with a madras fedora.

He came towards her with opened arms. He wrapped her up in his Miyake glory.
"Welcome home darling. I have missed you so damned much." He drawled and squeezed her tightly.
"And I you Seba." She held on with all her might.
"Blasted cock-blocker!" the officers chorused.
"I'll see you... and you, later. Don't forget we have a date." He tossed at the two officers pointing them out. "Now c'mon honey let's get you home."
"I thought you would never say those words. I just want a long warm shower and some tea."
"But aren't you forgetting light and fine over there? He looks lek he gonna haul off and clout me if I don't get me hands off you."
Nia turned. She had forgotten a tad about Kiah. Their eyes met and he started over.
"You had better say something Chicca. Cause I have a hot date later."
"Kiah meet Seba." Nia offered up quickly. His countenance changed. He extended his hand.
"Easy, easy. I love her in the purest of way. Nothing else."
"Got you. Nice to meet you. I look forward to getting to know you."
"Really?" Seba enthused. Dusting himself down.
Nia thought he was fawning and had better put a stop to it.
"If you are done peacocking, can we get a move on?"
"Dang girl!" He bit comically on his fisted fingers. "He so FOINE!"
"Seba please."
"But he is girl. I can feel my teeth sweating and shit!" He whispered up against her ear.
Thank God officer Fatso aka Samson popped up.
"Miss Nia...Madame Butterfly." He tossed scornfully.
A chorus of laughter erupted about the room.
Seba kissed his teeth.
"Where you park? We ready to load up."

"Down by the bluff."

"Down by the bluff? Damn madam. You mean ma guys have to haul all this stuff down there?"

"It is the only spot I could get." Seba waved him off as though he were swatting an annoying fly. "Plus, I am sure you didn't want me parking next to your newly painted gate huh?"

"Just goes to show you don't send a woman to do a man's job." Samson spat, looking like a Samoan-wrestler in his ill-fitted uniform.

"This yah is because we ghat a big tip you know. Otherwise..." He shook his head and clucked his tongue.

"Just get on with it." Seba tossed over at the man. "You sure could lose some..."

"Seba!" Nia snapped. "Let's go."

"Seriously? Cause that overweight slug like to start shit..."

"Please Seba. Not now."

"You better warn him. He way to damn plentiful with he ugly self."

"Samson! Please tell Miss Darcus a brand-new church hat is on the way from **Corrington's.**" Nia interjected before the calamity brewing, escalated.

"Oh, shucks Miss Nia she sure would love that. But on a serious note. Let that one go, and let that one in." Samson gestured toward Kiah who was helping the men to get her bags together.

Samson pranced off no doubt to oversee.

Seba was left to make faces at his receding back.

"You always stopping me giving them bigoted bastard a piece of my mind. What right do they have to look down on me living my authentic life? When we friggin know for sure some of them living on the down low right here in this island?

"Seba, I love you truly, dearly. But my love, tonight is not the platform for sorting that limited way of thinking."

"But they are so conceited."

"Seba, I know. But please I am to damn tired for a fight tonight."

"You had better roar the next time they come for me. Long and loud sistah."

"I promise." She hugged him close. "You know they must go through me to get to you. Now come on. Let's go home."

"Seriously Nia. I get sooo tired of them and their shit."

"We choose our battles brother. This is not where we do it." She kissed him atop his forehead, then released him and pulled him along.

Kiah bounded back up the steps and over to them when they emerged outside.

"The bags are being loaded in your truck." He said to Seba. His eyes zoomed in on Nia's arm about him. He felt a stab in his chest. He tore his eyes awa and reached for the case she had in her other hand.

"Let me help you with that."

"Not necessary. I've got it." She huffed when she felt his fingers on hers. She was certain she saw sparks. It burned.

"Don't you think you have kept the aunties waiting long enough? Why don't we say good night now? Seba will help me with the rest."

A heaviness sat up in her throat having travelled from the pit of her stomach.

"No-no Girl! You dang well know Sebastin don't do grunt work honey. Oh No!" he crooned; a look of consternation plastered all over his face.

Kiah looked at him comically.

She wanted to burst out laughing. He sure was funny. He had missed part of his calling. For she had no doubt that he could be something on the big screen.

He had acted in many theatre pieces in and around the Caribbean. He was truly gifted. He reminded her of Marlon Wayans from the Wayans Brothers at times.

"Oh, stop being such a wimp." Nia tossed at him brushing him away.

"Oh no she didn't" He spluttered cat-walking away.

"Nia why don't you come home with us?"

"Kiah you know I can't. Please don't make this any more difficult."

"I am sorry." He reached for her hand ignoring his feelings. "I hate this. I don't want to say goodbye yet." He squeezed it tighter.

"Please Kiah."

"Your chariot awaits Mo Cherie!" Seba called from across the road. His music blaring loudly once again.

"Bye Kiah. We will talk soon. Thanks for helping me on the ride down." With that she snatched her case and took off running as fast as her legs could carry her.

Thank goodness the traffic had all but disappeared now.

The port was quiet once again, except for Seba's ruckus.

At the junction the two vehicles met up. Seba eased the window down. Silcott did as well.

Her Auntie called. "Night night Nia-Belle. Don't forget to call before bed."

"I will not Auntie." Nia groaned inwardly. She could feel his eyes on her.

Thank God Sebastian had had the good sense to turn the music down, and he hadn't bothered her with any questions, but she could feel his eyes on her questioningly.

"You know the deal Nia-Belle just before you close those beautiful eyes."

"Yes, Auntie. I promise. I love you. Talk soon."

"Good girl. I love you more. Master Sebastin?"

"Yes ma'am." Seba answered like a little boy.

"Just remember who you are driving. Remember if anything happens, I will come down upon you with force of the Almighty. Understand?"

"Yes, mam I know, and yes I understand."

"Love you two. So, you two please be safe. See you soon." She blew them a kiss.

Seba waited for them to make the turn before he started off in the opposite direction.

"I hope you two exchanged digits?"

"Why?"

"Oh, stop pretending! You know that light-boy has your heart doing all kinds of flip flops."

"You can tell?" She nudged him gently.

"Anyone who know you as well as I do can. But seriously you need to wet that garden girl. It has been too long."

"Seba!!!"

"Don't Seba me. Honestly girl life is too short. We need a little sunshine. Plus, he looks like he would do all the groun wok if only you let him. I should know. Tek it from me, he sure is panting and rearing to go."

"Seba! I don't know him to just up and have sex with him."

"Girl just do what your body wants to for a change. Look how safe you played it with that idiot. And what did you get out of it? I say just live your life, and whatever happens is between you and God and them high thread count sheets, and nobody else you hear me?"

"Gosh Seba I am feeling like a schoolgirl. Each time he looks at me I just want to throw abandon to the wind. He makes me feel desire in ways I have never. I just feel like taking my panties off and throwing them at him. I feel so slutty."

"Is about time you treated your personal life like you do your professional. See yourself as desirous." He laughed. "Sista stop wasting that great personality behind all work and no play."

Nia became quiet, she knew he was right, but she had gone through so much with David. He had done a number on her. So much so it made her lazy in the end to try anything with the opposite sex. So, she had simply lost herself in her many areas of work.

"You, okay?" She felt him nudge her.

"Sorry I slipped away for a moment. But yes, I am. Plus I need the basket. I am starving."

"It's in the back there. He told me not to forget to remind you to eat something."

"See what I mean. Seba he was so brilliant with me on the trip coming down, and you know how I hate those journeys."

"I know girl. But you are home now. Just take it one day at a time."

"I hate to sound like a broken record Seba." Pausing between mouthfuls of the succulent chicken. "But why would someone looking like him be interested in me?"

"Shut your mouth! I can ask the same about Gupta. But that man loves me for me, and I love him. No matter what is going on in his household, he chooses me when I need him to. Plus, I told you if I didn't love dick no other fella would have a chance to get near you."

"Seba!"

"Don't Seba me! You know your ass is one fine looking woman. Even a blind man can tell just by listening to your voice. I loved you from the first

26

day I laid eyes on you Nia. Especially for you being the first to truly love me for me. Despite what anyone has to say."

"Seba. You always know what to say to cheer me up. Plus, I love you too. But gosh he a white dude. Well, kinda. He says his mom is part black."

"I don't care Nia. Black, white, purple, pink. Fuck him! Let us pray he knows how to work that half and half dick. Plus, what is the worst that can happen? He is the aunties' nephew... Hold up! So, he is the one they wanted you to chat up and you never did huh?"

"Uh huh. OMG!!! Seba and to think I had his number all these years tucked away!"

"Girl, I think the universe is trying to tell you something. So, you had better wake up and pay attention. Just think this time around you will be better able to arm your heart."

"Dear God, I do hope so." She paused to look at her phone; it had gone off in her lap as she was making light what was in the basket. She wiped her hands, then picked it up.

Are you home yet? I miss you something fierce. Call me. Kiah.

"Shit Seba! It's him!"

"What did he say?"

"He wants me to call him when I get in."

"So will you?"

"I don't know. I mean maybe...I mean I want too."

"Ah-you-ooh! Look at you being cute and shit! You horny bitch! Girl who cares. Just call the love-sick-fella. He's got great taste. I must give him that."

"He really is fine." She pictured him for the hundredth time and the kisses they had shared and could feel a warmth enveloping her being.

She couldn't remember the last time she felt so damned open and raw. He had done this to her.

"Oh, Seba I'm in lust."

"Halleluiah child! Welcome back to the land of the living. You had better open wide and fuck him when the time comes. Don't let him end up with all the fun."

"Seba!"

"Don't forget that damn class we paid an arm and leg for. So, let's put Lady Selah's commandments to good use. I mek Gupta purr each time I am finished with his in-de-closet-ass. He doesn't even want to go home."

"Seba!"

"You yourself told me that her **'mas and toy'** session is what you been living on these past few years. So now you can practice what you paid for."

"Seba!"

"Take ma-name in vain one more time Nia! Call ma-name one more time and so help me I will tek you up that damn hill and strip your ass foo him."

"Seba!"

"I mean girl that is how you should be taking that fellas name. C'mon my friend. Do give him a chance. Tis the season."

27

"Speaking of season. How are plans shaping up for the opening of Festival Village? Did we get all the sponsorship in from the back benchers?"

"You betcha! All plans are a go for Sunday. I manage to procure a hefty sum from Gupta as well. His girls are coming in from London. So, we must give them something they will remember for a long while. Just like I told you to do to that Kiah. I promise at the end of the season I will sit and eat buckets of Sylvie's with you and wash it down with Chico's melted ice cream."

"I am going to hold you to that. But right now, I just need a long hot shower."

"Then you are gonna call him? I mean you look like someone done strung lights up on your insides and put you atop Evergreen tree every time you think of him. I mean who would have thunk that scrawny thing hanging on Lady B's wall would be Mr.**GQ**?"

"Which is why I get troubled Seba."

"Stop fishing for compliments sweetie. I know you know you are FOINE. Tell me you remember Sheik Ravi? He was itching to get you to be a part of his harem when he saw you in your sexy-ass **Spotlight** costume. The old fool almost lost his damn mind."

The truck's interior erupted in a gale of laughter.

"Shit! I forgot about him. He was a blasted chauvinistic pig, and I hated all that friggin bowing. They would have whipped my disobedient ass every second of the day. Plus, I detest all that black."

"Preach it girl!" Seba tossed. "They probably would have lynched my high yellow ass."

"You mean behead right?"

"Uurrgh let us not go down that road. To damn depressing. I say live and let live."

"Amen. Especially when you and I and so many others know that so many are out there living on the down low. Hey what did brother Bas say?"

"He says he will take the gig. Anything for you."

"Bless him. This time we got to drop more gold in his envelope."

"Truth. Seeing he is trying to bring Burning flames, Claudette Peters, Jam band and a few more names on board. Says he is there if it's a worthy cause."

"Bless him. That guy does not get enough praise for the things he does throughout the Caribbean. He is an unsung hero."

"How come it never went anywhere with you two?"

"Because I love him something fierce as I do you. Why ruin a good thing huh?"

"Truth Sista. He is good folk."

"Anything else I need to know Seba? I have a feeling you are keeping something from me."

"What are you talking about girlfriend?" He tossed. His voice sounded too high pitched.

"See right there. You just hit that high note."

28

"You know me to well. But seriously not now. We can catch up tomorrow. Home sweet home."

He pictured that Sadie in his mind. She was seeing her man again on the DL. She had broken curfew a few times.

The man had even showed up at the gates of **Safe Haven** a couple times and they had to call the police.

Kiah settled back against the cool interior of his aunt's Rolls Royce. He had shipped it down to the island for her 60th birthday after he had the boys from **Pimp my Rid**e do a few adjustments to the car.

It was nice to be sitting in it with her. But it didn't stop his mind from wandering.

It took all his strength to not say to Silcott, 'follow the truck.'

He clutched the handle for dear life as the cool salty air blew through the rolled down window.

"So how was your journey down my boy?" His auntie asked and poked him with her stick.

"Sorry?"

"I asked how you enjoyed your journey down on the ferry."

"It was interesting."

"I can see that. But I can't say that I was not disappointed. I was all hyped up to meet this person." She was fishing.

" I know. We got cold feet Auntie." He could feel his breathing getting troubled as he pictured her face, and recalled the taste of her lips, and the melding of her body against his.

The interior seemed like it was closing in. His head reeled.

In another second, he was pleading with Silcott to pull over.

"Not gonna happen Sir."

"Please for God's sake Silcott." He spat, gripping at the man's seat. "Stop the car now."

"Yes Sir."

A couple cars rushed by honking their horns loudly. One even had the nerve to call out "cunt!!!"

But he didn't give a shit. He jumped out just in time to empty the contents of his stomach on the side of the rode.

He could hear waves breaking below. Slowly he lifted his head until he could once again feel his feet beneath him. It didn't help when Silcott shun the beam of the flashlight full force in his face.

He brought his hands up defensively. "C'mon man are you trying to blind me."

"Sorry Sir." The man offered feebly.

"No worries. And please stop calling me sir."

He was thankful when the man lowered the thing.

"Boy what's going on with you?" His Auntie asked looking out the window.

He turned his back to her and just stayed still so the salty tranquil air could do its magic on him in the semi darkness. He thought about her for the umpteenth time and wondered if she had gotten home yet. They had said it would take twenty minutes.

Plus, she hadn't responded to his message.

He wanted to call. However, he thought against it. He didn't think she would answer. He knew he was acting irrational. But he had to be patient and let her come to him.

"Bel, can't you tell he is lovesick sweetie? Couldn't you see how he and our Nia-Belle were eyeing up each other? I think they got on like a house on fire and are now trying to keep us out of the loop. Isn't that true dear boy?"

He offered nothing.

"You know my niece can be as deep as the ocean when it comes to her feelings."

"Pot calling the kettle black." His Auntie tossed at the women. Remember how hard I had to work?"

"Shush Bel."

"Don't shush me. You know it's the truth."

"Bel, just sit down and stay in the car dear. You know how these teenagers can be on these roads at night."

"She is right. Please just stay in the car." Silcott urged the women.

"Give him this." She handed a bottle out.

"Thank you, Silcott." Kiah said and took the bottle. He brought it to his mouth. He spat a couple of mouthfuls before he could swallow any of the liquid. It bought some calm.

"So is Nia-Belle the one you were going to introduce us to Hezekiah Carter Corrington the III?" She scolded. But felt the urge to shout in praise.

"I'm a grown man Auntie B. A damn multi-billionaire a couple times over. I make deals with sheiks and presidents all over the world. But she makes me feel like a damn idiot. Worst yet like some lovesick teenager. I become tongue tied and act a damn fool. I need to pull it together."

"Yes, you do." His auntie tossed laughing loudly.

"What can I offer her? I am only here for a couple of weeks. I leave the island in a few days..."

He couldn't pull the last part back. He had said too much. He tossed his hands to the heaven wondering what the hell was wrong with him.

"Where are you going Hezekiah?" She too was now trying to get out of the car. Silcott tried to stay her.

"Sir I think you had better get back in and let's get you all home."

"Good idea. You better get you skinny behind in here and let's talk about where you think you are going."

"Grown up." He tossed as he scrambled back into the car.

"Please don't tell me you are going to pull the under my roof bit."

"Not a chance. Especially seeing it backfired when dad tried it with me." She gestured over to Katho. "Dear boy love makes idiots out of us all. So let me just say amen amen and amen."

"Bel finally, the playboy has met his match."

"Just think it took all this time for those two to listen to us. I am sure when you two finally laid eyes on each other it must have put the biggest smile on our Creator's face."

"Amen" Auntie B said and pulled him closer.

He buried his face in her ample bosom. He had forgotten how great she always smelt.

"Welcome home my boy. Welcome home. But where the hell are you off to again? You only just got here."

"Not to worry Auntie B. You have me for the next couple of weeks, but I do have a business meeting on Heart Island in a few days."

"I thought Nia-Belle had scared you off." Auntie Katho chuckled. She touched his thigh sympathetically. "She does have the tendency to be a handful. But she is a caring person to the exclusion of herself. She needs to slow down. So, I hope you can be that balm to let her. Let the universe. I do believe like Bellot does that you two could be great for each other. Just think even footing."

"What do you mean? I don't follow." He came up to sitting as he looked from one to the other of the females, who looked him over as though they were cats that swallowed canaries.

"You have your money. She has hers of course." Katho tossed over at him in her thick accent. So, all you need to do is settle down and let your personalities work to complement each other."

"But she..."

"But she nothing. Just don't take our simplicity for being backwards." She pointed over at him.

"No ma'am." He said throwing his hands up in surrender.

She popped up in his head yet again. He wondered if she was already at home. He looked down at his watch. They would just be pulling up. The fella seemed to drive like a maniac. He was such a character.

"Tell me about that guy who picked her up."

"Sebastin! God Lord! I hope you know you have nothing to worry about there. That fella is like a brother to her. Two peas in a pod."

"I would go a step further by saying if you don't learn to get along with him, you will not get close enough to her. Get what I mean Hezekiah?"

"Yes ma'am." He said catching the drift of the conversation.

Simply put. He was the key to getting close to her. Which meant he had some homework to do.

"So, are you going to give her call? Take her out to lunch or something tomorrow? You must strike while the iron is red hot." Auntie Katho said.

"Don't give her a chance to think too long my boy."

"Geez you two! I get it. But I don't want to come off like a lunatic and scare her away."

"Never happen. You baited the hook, she bit, now reel her in." Auntie B finished.

"Are they always like this?" He asked looking to Silcott.

"Worst if it is something they want badly. You had better get used to it sir."

"Dear God help me."
They all laughed. It was grand in the car. He was glad to be home and with his beloved auntie once again. It had been too long.
"Get some sleep Hezekiah. We will talk some more after you have rested. In the meantime, welcome home."

They went through a parted gate and drove up a well-lit long palm driveway.
The white house gleamed welcomingly out to them with its well-manicured lawn and hedges, as well as beautiful rose bushes in an array of healthy-looking blooms.
Gosh it all looked so stately and majestic. It was truly the understatement of the day; to say he wasn't impressed.
The house put his square-footage in California to shame.
"Dang! Auntie B the pictures do not do this place justice. I am way impressed. You can compete for a spot-on **Millionaires Mansions**." Kiah tossed as he came out of the car and stood looking at the expansive layout before him.
"Glad you are impressed. You have supported so much of this. So, I say thank you."
They hugged him close. They stood for a while simply just drinking in the lighted expanse displayed before them.

Getting the bags back and forth from the back of Seba's truck was like competing in a decathlon. She was thankful the only house close enough was **Safe Haven**, but not to close that they could hear how Seba was carrying on.
"You are as annoying as hell." She tossed over laughing at him.
"Bitch you know I ain't cut out for hard labour."
"Just a few more. We are nearly finish."
"I keep telling myself this, and every time another one pop up." He wiped at his brow and used his hat to fan himself with such dramatics.
"I told you I found a steal and I was not planning to leave any of it behind."
"Dang girl! Look at the time! I told the crew I would meet them around 11:30..."
"That's why I told you I would take a taxi, but you farsin-ass didn't listen. You just had to come down to get melee."
"Glad I did too. Cause knowing you... Please girl. You know I had to digest Mr Foine-Ass for myself. Oh Jesus! I am going straight to hell! But just come on let's get this donkey-wuk over and done wid."

Another thirty minutes and she was peeing like a racehorse, and then stripping and standing under a pulsating cool shower.
Glad she had listened to Raheem and updated into the real 21st century with power jets and all kind of gadgets some of which she hadn't even

32

tested out yet. But what she had was like being washed and massaged by heavenly beings.

She longed for her 500 count sheets on her king-sized bed like a dessert for water.

Just then he popped back up in her head. She pictured the way his lips felt on hers. The triggers that kicked in, made her entire body jump to life. Much like it was doing now. Before she realised what she was doing she was touching her soapy body sensually venturing into the deepest of places.

By the time she came up for air she was splayed on the bathroom floor. Minutes later she wondered into her bedroom just as her house phone blared to life startling her. She reached for her bed throw and wrapped herself up pulling a deep sigh and sucking her teeth.

"Yes Auntie. I am fine. I just got out of the shower." She ground out in annoyance.

"Why didn't you call me? I could have joined you, Nia."

"Shit! Fu…" Nia mumbled, looking around frantically expecting him to be standing right there.

She breathed a sigh of relief. He wasn't. It was just her dang gone imagination.

"I can oblige. All you must do is ask."

"Can't you just go to sleep like any tired person?"

"I want to sleep next to you." He said as a picture of her in her naked glory standing before him popped up in his head.

"Kiah please. I am shattered." She said sinking down on her bed and throwing herself against her pillows, looking up at the chandeliered ceiling.

"Me too. But I couldn't sleep. I just kept getting these images…"

"Kiah." She purred. "I am tired."

"I know baby." He took a deep breath. He had to bite the bullet. They couldn't just sit outside her gate for much longer. "What if I say I am outside your gate?"

"Kiah please." She said bolting upright.

"I'm not kidding. I begged Silcott. He brought me down. All you need say is come in and I am there."

He had given the man the wad he had in his money clip.

"Damn man!" Silcott tossed, reaching for his clothes and yanking them on. "You don't have to ask me twice. Le awe go!" He stuffed the bills in his pocket. "She only lives maybe a good 10 minutes away in the other direction. You can even glimpse her in her backyard on the opposite side of the house atop the bluff."

Money always had a way of loosening tongues. He ought to know. He had used that skill numerous times.

"You can't be serious Kiah. I just met you and you want a bootie call?" Who do you think I am?"

"Nia I can just sleep next to you. Nothing will happen. That is if you don't want it to." Kiah added. He knew he would have to fight the urges. Cut his dick off as a last resort.

"Said the spider to the fly." She tossed. Getting pissed that he thought he could score with her and on the first night.

Then again first or tenth what's the difference? She had waited and given herself purely to David and yet that was not enough. So, what the fuck!!! Why was she even thinking of him? She hadn't even seen high nor heck of him in nearly three years now.

"Nia? Are you still there?"

"Yes Kiah."

"Are you going to let me in?" He hated sounding like a cunt. But he had come too far.

"You know what. I am too God-dam tired to think about right from wrong anymore. Tell Silcott to use the code. I will meet you at the door. Give me a couple minutes to get dress."

"You don't have to on my account."

"Kiah nothing is going to happen. Plus, I hope that Silcott told you I house share." She hung up quickly before she could change her mind.

Fuck!!! The man had left that part out. Or maybe he didn't. He was only thinking of her and her face, her lips her body on the way down.

He must have gone through a few scenarios. One of which he wouldn't even be able to see her. She struck him as the sort to make a guy work to get between those long legs of hers.

He was obscene with the images he conjured up of her.

"You! How come you didn't tell me she lived with someone?" He asked the man accusingly as he punched the numbers in, and they waited for the gate to open.

"I did Sir!" Silcott offered not able to contain the laughter that spread across his face. "But you got nothing to worry about. It is her brother Sebastin. You know the fella she went home with."

"Shit Silcott! But hell, we are here already. I don't care now if I am just in the same space as her."

"You sound whipped Sir." Silcott said laughing hysterically.

"Damn! I think so too Silcott." He said laughing along with the man.

He didn't mind. Because he could not remember the last time, he had felt this lovesick. Being able to throw caution to the wind and let the chips fall where they may in his personal life.

He didn't have time to think anymore as they parked in the front of one of her huge wooden doors. He jumped out before they'd even parked.

"Slow down no man! I ain't even want to tell those two that I took you out and you got hurt in the process. I tell you hell would have no hole for me to crawl into. Plus, you had better take care of that lady in there. I warn you."

"Yeah yeah!" Kiah tossed. Closing the car door hurriedly.

"Sir? Sir? You want me to wait, or you want me to come back?"

Kiah ran back and hurriedly gave the man his digits. "If truth be told. I hope you never have to come get me again."
He jogged to the door waving the man off. His dick standing at attention in his pants.

Five minutes later she peeked through the door. "This is crazy! I don't do shit like this Kiah!" She said opening the door a bit wider.
Silcott beeped the horn as he started down the drive.
"Be good to each other you two." He shouted out and prayed they would last because she was a good one. He was too. Because in his opinion anyone who took care of the two women, he loved more than his own life. Was tops in his book.
"Get in before you cause a scene." She scolded and pulled him in.
"Sorry Nia. It's just that I missed you so damn much baby." He devoured her lips in his. She tasted of toothpaste. He was ravenous. He noticed she was also kissing him back in the same manner he was kissing her.
His head begun to reel.

It was almost five minutes before they both came up for air. No doubt she had felt the massive hard on he had in his pants. But once again he threw caution to the wind as she laced her legs about his waist as he went in for her succulent lips once again.
Her arms entwined around his neck gave him all the fuel he needed.
"Nia I am giving you one last chance baby." He ground out, letting go of her tongue. He fought to stay on his feet as he bore her up, and she wrapped herself about him like a python.
"Don't talk Kiah!" The words could not be pulled back. She was lost in her wantonness for the man. Plus, he smelt so damn good. She wanted to inhale all of him. "Just kiss me again."
He did as he was commanded. That was until a picture frame came crashing down from the wall behind them.
It brought them sharply to their senses. Well for a quick second. Then she murmured, "Let's do this now Kiah because I don't have the strength to resist you anymore."
"No need to ask twice sweetheart." He ground out as he stepped over the picture frame. "Where is your...?"
She understood what he asked. She pointed down an infernal corridor, pass a couple closed doors, to one that was open.
He rushed her in. Never was he so thankful for the huge bed that welcomed them.
He deposited her atop it falling into her. They never lost the lock position.
His hand found her legs and snaked hungrily up them.
She purred happily. It excited and spurred him on. He ventured on the inside of her thighs, running his hand up.
Lord have mercy!!! His heart stopped and his head did a reel like he was upside down on a rollercoaster. She had nothing on. His fingers played

around the edges. He dared not let them venture in or he would explode right then and there.

"Nia." He moaned. "Do you feel what you are doing to me?"

He extricated himself from her and slid down her belly like a hungry snake. He did not stop until he was staring at the entrance to heaven's gate.

"God woman! You are so fucking exquisite! May I?"

"Please." She whimpered. Feeling like she had lost all sense of reason as he licked and blew soft breaths.

She screamed his name when he buried what seemed like a lightning bolt straight into her crevice. Her body convulsed sickeningly.

Never in her wildest dream had she ever felt this wanton.

She reached for his head to keep him buried in 'that' spot until she exploded wildly in his mouth.

"Nia, I want to fuck you!" He pleaded insanely as he licked her clean like an animal who had just given birth to its young. Her body slowly but surely started springing back to life, as though someone had ignited a tiny switch.

She hauled him up and fiercely kissed him. Loving the taste of herself on him.

"Please." She murmured and reached out and helped him out of his clothing. "God you are beautiful." She moaned running her hands and tongue all over his body. "I can look at you all night." She said and brought her mouth to him.

Her tongue did all these things imagined that caused more electricity to course through his veins. He had to remind himself to stay the course. He did not want to finish unless he was plunged deep within her.

But before he could do or say anything else she had flipped him down unto the bed and was using her tongue on his Johnson like a hungry feline.

Sounds that he had never made before with anyone else escaped his tortured being, especially when she hot-dogged him between her gorgeous amble bosoms.

It was his turn to plead. He couldn't hold it any longer. But a sound distracted him; more like saved him.

She held up a hand. He spotted a small purple square plastic.

"Are you sure? "He asked her just as she deftly dressed his dick in the smooth material and tossed her leg like a lyrical dancer across his thighs straddling him.

Before another word could escape him, she deftly inserted his dick inside her heated furnace.

He screamed like a frightened boy to the point of whimpering.

She covered his mouth and trapped both his hands in hers as she slowly started moving rhythmically.

"Nia! Nia!" He moaned trying to get some air into his tightened lungs.

It didn't work. He squeaked as she held him with a vice like grip deep within her. Her breast was doing something magical to him as she moved them mesmerizingly across his chest. Her long curly braids had somehow gotten undone. She reminded him once again of a beautiful amazon warrior.

"God you are so fucking beautiful Nia. Where have you been all my life?"

"Shush!" She whispered bending to devour his mouth within hers hungrily.

He was totally and utterly delirious as she rode him to her content.

When he couldn't contain it any longer, and where he felt he would surely die beneath her from pure delight. He e flipped her.

"I am dying Nia." He breathed raggedly. Having the advantage now...

Oh so he thought. Until she spread her legs wide like she was atop a balance beam. Full of lust he began to ride her deliriously.

Suddenly she wrapped them around his neck with such agility.

Fuck! Did I bite off more than I can chew? He became frenzied!!! Thinking she was going to be the death of him as he anchored his hands to the bed and delved deeper.

"Slow down baby!" She moaned as she released his neck and wrapped them about his waist. "Slow down Kiah. Slow down."

He had totally forgotten all of Madame Ito's tutelage. She was the only one who had ever brought tears to his eyes during intimacy.

Now Nia had done it.

Unashamedly he pulled her up to join him. Their eyes locked and held. She brought her hands up to his eyes and wiped the tears.

"Sorry baby. But this is what your body is doing to me." He offered apologetically.

He felt her wrap her arms about him. He held her tightly.

"I want to enjoy you Kiah." She began kissing him delectably as she moved slowly atop him... After a while she pushed him back roughly.

"You bring me joy." She offered as she rode him gently picking up the tempo as she felt him deeper and deeper within her.

This time for sure he was certain of death. So, he allowed it to take his body until he heard her purr.

"Come with me baby." She whimpered in tortured delirium as she writhed, and her body squirmed atop his.

He slapped her firm ass a couple of times before he flipped her on her hands and knees, then plunged like a maniac deep within her.

"Kiah!!!" She screamed in delirium.

"Yes Baby!!"

"Fuck me!!!"

He obliged, grabbing her breast as he pumped with such veracity deep within her. Seconds later their explosion happened like the fourth of July. He gave her everything he had within him.

They laid like marathon runners next to each other in naked abandon huffing and puffing. Never in a million years did she imagine sex to be so delectable. David was okay but he never managed to bring her to such fits of frenzy.

Kiah made her body hissed and hummed in so many ways. She had experienced so many different types of orgasms; that rocked her body to its core. Sex was utterly delirious, and she wanted more.

"Are you ok?" He finally asked. Begging his limbs to follow suit as he turned to her.

She was openly crying. Tears streamed down her face.

"I didn't hurt you, did I? Fuck! I am sorry Nia. It's just… Shit!!!"

He came up on his elbow and cupped her beautiful face.

"I tried my best to let you enjoy, but I fear I might have gotten a bit carried away. God you are so fucking delicious! Both on the inside and outside." He covered her face with kisses.

"What's wrong? Talk to me Nia. You can tell me anything sweetheart."

"You…It…Kiah you were magnificent! I just never knew it could be like that." She said and tried to look away.

"Don't. Please don't do that."

"What?"

"Please don't look away when you speak to me. I love looking into your eyes. You are beautiful."

He buried his mouth on hers. He kissed her hungrily.

When he released her. He urged her to continue.

She said, "I mean I never knew it could be so…" She searched her mind for the words. "So raw, so lustful, so delectable… Kiah my mind is blown."

"What do you mean Nia? A body as delicious as yours has never been worshiped. But you aren't a virgin?"

"Don't remind me of that disaster. I don't even want to think about that."

"I'm sorry baby. It's just that you were so fantastic! You knew exactly what to do."

"I just listened to my body and went with what you were doing."

"That works too." He laughed. "Because it was fantastic!" He said kissing her again. He couldn't seem to get enough.

She smiled.

He thought her so beautiful for the umpteenth time. He said what he was thinking.

"You are so fucking gorgeous! You blew my mind!" He kissed her neck and moved down to her breast.

"Your body drives me totally insane." He slid down to her cinched waist lingering on her stomach. He loved how she moaned and writhed as he flicked his tongue in and out of her navel.

"Oh Gharm! Kiah you can't go again, can you?" She screeched in disbelieve. She thought of David; he would always drop off to sleep snoring annoyingly loudly. He always left her so unsatisfied and yearning.

"Want to see?" He asked coming up on his knees.

Nia couldn't believe the sight that greeted her. He was rearing and ready to go again. She wanted to ask how, but she herself was in that place of acceptance, pushing back the thoughts and images of how wanton and enraptured she had behaved earlier.

"You are gorgeous Kiah." She offered him truthfully as she reached up and joined him on her knees, kissing his lips hungrily. "You make me so raw with want." She kissed his neck, as she felt fingers slip in and out of her.
"Kiah! Oh God!"
"Shush!"
It was his turn to show her again how she made him feel.
He knew he possessed what it took to rise to the occasion. He had learnt from one of the best Asian sex therapists that money could buy.

He pushed her back against the head of the bed, and among the many pillows while he supported her back with his arm, meanwhile using his free hand and fingers to awaken her insides while he bit and licked and blew on her boobs until they were straining at the peaks for him.
She opened her legs in a graceful extension so he could gain further access to explore deeper.
She cried out his name each time in delirium as he tickled her on that spot, he knew would drive her insane.
"Kiah!!!" She purred enthusiastically. Especially when she felt his other hand at the rear entrance of her anus.
"Have you ever had this done to you before?" He asked loving all the sounds that were escaping her.
She shook her head in delirium.
"Do you want me to continue?"
"Yes!!" She cooed lost almost in a trance as she felt a wet finger snaking its way slowly in. She slumped against the weight of his body.
"Stoop a little baby." He encouraged as she relaxed on his hands; front and back.
"Safe word is **mercy** Nia. Say **mercy** if you want me to stop. I will stop once you say this. So, if it gets..."
"Shush Kiah! Just get on with it!"
He laughed. "Yes Ma'am!" He whispered hotly against her ear, as he drove his tongue into it and continued with the onslaught.
He felt her hot and wet and oh so pliant. He inserted another as he took one of her ripened nipples into his mouth. He suckled the succulent tip and bit it daintily. He felt her nearing the brink; her body was nice and pliable now for him to explore at will. He used his thumb and forefinger to gently squeeze her clit as he bit at her straining hard nipple.
She squealed in delirium. She swore and called his name in a crazy torrent.
It incited him as he continued to pleasure her.
"I am dying Kiah!" She sang out repeatedly.
"Not yet! Not without me baby!" He sang in her ear as he brought her over unto his wet cock in a stooping position.
She whimpered, and shook, and sang his name prayerfully, as she gripped the head of the bed.
He kept his fingers inserted in her ass working her magically.
The sounds that came from her made him totally insane. But he couldn't end it there.

"I am going to enter you from the back Nia. Do you remember the word?" He whispered, as he slipped his fingers out slowly and eased from her front and gingerly inserted the tip of his wet cock up her rear end. She groaned. He could tell she wasn't too far from exploding again. She howled sickeningly.

"Let go baby!" He encouraged gently, as he eased her down on his shaft. Slowly...slowly...until he disappeared after a while deep within her. She moaned in delirium.

Her tightness drove him to the brink of madness. But once again he feverishly recalled his tutelage. He reminded himself that it wasn't about him, as he drilled rhythmically like a well-oiled bit.

She quickly learnt the beat and followed the melody meticulously.

He inserted fingers into her opening.

Her breathing was laboured as she swayed like a ship in tempestuous waters.

"I'm dying...I'm dying...I'm dying!!!!! She screeched loudly.

"Go ahead...Go ahead baby." He coaxed softly.

She came like a gushing river all over him.

He dislodged his fingers and kept her screwed to his cock deep within, until he himself followed suit seconds later with the ferocity of an angry gorilla.

Chapter Two

The alarm woke her it seemed like days later. She reached out and found that she was entangled. It startled her. She turned in the huge bed.

For a quick second she was disoriented. She felt someone beside her. She almost panicked.

Then her eyes came to rest on him. He was half covered sleeping against her pillows. His locks splayed about his chiselled face.

Her heart settled back in her chest. She reached out and swiped the alarm, then pulled her braids of her face to look back at him.

He stirred and reached out for her.

Immediately images of what they had done the night before jumped up in her mind, as well as parts of the conversation.

He said he had gotten tested for all sexually transmitted diseases only a month ago. She had done the same.

He showed her his card and she showed him hers. They both agreed that it should have been done before they had even engaged in the act itself. Then someway along the line the sleep fairy had visited; they'd fallen asleep entwined in each other's arms.

She eased up on her elbows and realised she was naked. To make matters worse her body was seriously aching on the inside as well as the outside.

Plus, she desperately needed to pee. How am I going to do this? She reasoned. Realising that one of his legs was draped over her, as well as an arm. She was trapped. But seriously she had to get out. Because if she didn't, she would wet her bed for sure.

She tried wriggling and easing...

"Aww! Aww!" She muttered softly, as though it had crawled from her throat with vengeance.

He stirred. But he didn't wake.

God! I need to wee so badly she thought in a tizzy. She prayed he didn't wake. She couldn't contemplate looking him in the eyes again. Lord God! She sure had been brazened. It seemed she did not have an ounce of control whenever he looked at her or touched her.

I had better bolt! She followed through.

Too late!!!!

"Hi sleepy-head." He muffled, rising and coming nearer. He reached out and held her tight. He kissed the top of her shoulder. He loved the feel of her next to him.

Come to think of it!!!! He never slept with females in his bed!

He would always go to another room for sleep.

But he had slept even though he had awakened a couple of times, simply to confirm that it hadn't all been a dream.

He ran his hand along her smooth creamy body, loving all her curves and edges. Kissing her all over.

"Kiah no!" She moaned and wriggled away from him. Carnal images flashed in her mind for the hundredth time. "I need to go."

"Go? Go where?"

He flipped her over to kiss her lips hungrily. "Feel what you are doing to me." He covered her body with his easily.

"Toilet Kiah!" she squealed continuing to wriggle which gave him the perfect access between her legs, where she felt him hard and strong against her.

Next thing she realised was that he was slithering down the length of her and bringing his lips to rest at the mouth of her being.

He pushed her legs up and buried his tongue deep within her.

"Oh God Kiah! I really must go!" She clenched her legs against the sides of his head tightly.

"God, you smell divine."

"C'mon Kiah please. Or else I will truly wet myself." She pleaded.

"Okay Nia! Hurry right back!"

She didn't wait around. Quickly she scrambled off the bed and bolted in her naked glory straight for the bathroom.

"Naughty Nia. Hurry up and don't keep me waiting. I want to eat you up!" His laughter followed her along with his words

She ignored him, although she could feel her body responding to the rawness.

"God you are one gorgeous woman!" He called out. His voice following her.

Five minutes later he wandered in.

"Sorry. I need to go as well." He tossed. His voice so near caused her to jump clear off the toilet.

He grinned at her as she stood there like a deer trapped in headlights. "Kiah privacy!"

"After what we've been through Nia!" He kissed her lips. "Sorry baby but I really need to." He turned from her and aimed straight into the toilet bowl. "By the way you have a lovely home from what little I can see."

He had no hang-ups about his body or nudity. His parents never did.

"Thank you." She mouthed, as she reached for a towel and draped it about herself.

She walked over to her sink and reached for her toothbrush. She spread some toothpaste and commenced to brush her teeth.

Her eyes drifted to his gorgeous, flawless and chiselled body. She couldn't seem to tear her eyes away. She was hungry for him. It begun to affect her breathing. She spluttered.

She hadn't missed the Yin and Yang sign tattooed on his left ass cheek. The fella was an Adonis.

42

Tings and pings went off again inside her body. She brushed her teeth vigorously.

She jumped out of her skin when she suddenly felt him behind her.

He placed his muscular hard limbs up against her and his hands about her waist.

She felt him spring back and forth to life behind her.

"There is a spare toothbrush in the drawer." She offered pathetically and pointed to it.

"Thank you. Guess I stink huh?" He chuckled. But not before planting a kiss on her neck.

She burned as though someone had sprinkled her with acid. As she watched him pull the drawer open and reached in.

Couple minutes and they were brushing together like a seasoned couple.

Thank God he didn't reach for her toothbrush like David liked to do when he stayed over. Which was why she had so many in the drawer.

He had given her a quizzical look.

She quickly turned her gaze back to the mirror. But she was certain he had not missed the looks she would steal at 'Johnson' as it perked up each time, he glanced at her.

He watched as she went through brushing, rinsing, gurgling and followed suit with each action. Even down to when she reached for the other cup.

But when she turned to leave, he reached out and yanked her back.

"Kiah!" She squealed. Loving his brazenness. She wanted to step into the shower, but she didn't think she had the nerve to do it.

But it seemed like by magic, when he once again read her mind.

"Let's shower." He said, "Nia you have no hang-ups about your beautiful body, do you?"

"Aaarm..." Shit! She thought. She didn't. But standing there adoring his. Made her think of hers.

The man looked like he was built by God himself.

"You are beautiful woman. Let me show you." He whispered, untying her towel. "I want to wash you from head to toe, as I wipe away any disbelief you hold as to just how amazing your body looks and feels to me."

He buried his lips against her neck. "Tell me you want me as much as I want you, Nia." He breathed. As he ran his hands up and down her body.

The towel had fled.

He felt her trembling against him.

"Kiah...it...I hurt." She squeezed out throwing her hands around his neck their bodies melding together. Shock wave now ran through it. She wandered again if he was for real.

"No worries... Let's just have a shower then." He said easily. Thinking he could forgo the massive temptation for now because she mattered more in that moment.

He released her and went over to turn the taps on in the wet stall.

"Kiah..." She chanced, feeling a sense of remorse sneaking up.

"I'm sorry." Her arms came about herself.

43

"Don't worry about it." He offered, turning to her once he got the water to the right temperature.

He reached out to her. "I can wait. Don't forget the mind is a powerful sex-organ as well."

"Do you always say what you think?" She asked in disbelief.

"Yes Nia." He kissed her, turning her face up to his, as he looked deep into her beautiful eyes. "Beautiful woman please do stop over thinking. I am planning on enjoying you if you will have me."

He kissed her deeply again. He knew he would never allow her to slip through his fingers. She was going to be his.

"Kiah... I have not had much luck with whatever this is that is happening between us. So let me tell you now that I am afraid. Perhaps this is a conversation we should have had in the light of day, before any of what we did happened."

"You didn't like it?"

"Kiah please. I am being serious."

"I know. Well let me tell you my serious. You are never ever getting away from me ever again. Yes, Nia! Believe me when I say this. You are mine, and I will never ever let you go. Got that?"

He forced her chin up and held her faltering gaze.

"Kiah..." She squeezed out, wanting to say more. But he held her firm.

"Nia, I made myself that promise on the ferry. Call me crazy, impetuous, whatever we call it these days. But I go with my gut on most every deal I have made. It has never steered me wrong. I have the same feeling about you. That is from the instant I met you."

"But how Kiah?"

"Great alignment of the universe perhaps. I don't care. All I know is that I am not ever leaving your side, ever again."

"Kiah you are crazy!"

"About you woman!" He turned her about. "Feel how you make me feel?"

"Dear God Kiah!" She whispered, as tears slipped down her cheeks. She wrapped her arms about his neck." Please don't ever ever think of playing me." She offered tightly. She wanted to say more, but she held it back. Because she knew she could call people from all around the island. They would have her back. She smiled.

"Trust me, Nia."

"One day at a time." She said, calling on her faith that she had tapped into again the last couple of months.

She reached up on tip toes and kissed him one last time before she eased out of his grasp, and that soul-searching stare, to reach for the hats hanging on the peg.

She slipped her hair up in one. "Bend your head Kiah." She said matter-of-factly. But her heart was banging away loudly in her chest, as she wondered again, what the hell was happening?

He obeyed her. His eyes not leaving hers once, as he sensed her disbelief and mistrust.

He allowed her to put it atop his head. Then he couldn't resist anymore, he kissed her hungrily.

"One day at a time Nia." Was all he offered, as he swept her off her feet and walked with her to the shower.

He placed her on her feet and reached for her shower gel and poured some in his hands and anointed her beautiful wet body in the gentlest way.

Her body of course betrayed her, but he pretended not to notice.

She loved how his hands felt on her body and resisted the urge to claw out at him. She did the only thing she could; hit the button that allowed the jet to emerge from the wall so water would massage their bodies from all angles.

"Nice." He said liking the feel of her and the way the rivulets were hitting his body. He wanted to rip her apart but resisted the urge yet again.

He had to take care of her not just sexually.

He also had to prove to her that he was solid. That he had no agenda except winning her heart and treating her royally. She had intrigued him, and he wanted to learn more, so he could keep that spark alight that he had glimpsed so many times when she had given herself so openly to him.

The water cascaded down and around them as they lathered and caressed each other hungrily in silence.

He reached for her leg and wrapped it around him using his hand to gently wash her.

She exhaled ruggedly. They both knew without saying anything what was happening to their bodies.

His hand wandered between her legs. A finger touched her. It was swollen and it felt glorious. It caused her to yelp and meld her body tighter around him.

She kissed him hungrily.

"Are you ok now?" he asked, bringing the other leg up around him before reaching for her lips again.

She purred.

They kissed hungrily for God knows how long. Just letting the water do its magic.

Couple minutes later when she thought her body wouldn't survive for much longer. He hit the buttons and shut the taps off.

He tried to disengage her, but she refused to let him go.

She bit gently into his neck, tiny bites that gas lighted him everywhere.

"Nia are you sure?" He asked feeling the urgency expelling from her. "I don't want to hurt you." He said gently.

"I want you Kiah!" she nuzzled into him. "So, fucking much!"

45

He backed her up against the stall and kissed her hungrily splaying her arms wide.

"Are you sure?" He asked her again, pausing to look her straight in the eyes.

She nodded wildly, filled with some sort of intoxication.

"Then put your legs down Nia, only if, you are sure." He commanded her. When she did, he used his to open hers wide. "Nia this is your last chance..."

"Fuck me Kiah!" She ground out harshly in an animal like voice that scared even her. She screamed as he plunged deep within her.

The house phone rang loudly. They were towelling themselves down.

"Shit! Shit!" She spat. Then she remembered she hadn't called her Auntie like she had promised.

"Kiah you are a bad influence. I forgot to call Auntie last night." She tossed the towel at him and ran towards the bedroom.

He followed chase and caught her just as she slid across the bed and picked up the phone. She shushed him.

It was indeed her Auntie. She apologised profusely and said she got distracted.

"Bet you did!" Her auntie cackled. "Don't think I don't know that high Yella-boy is with you!"

"Auntie!" she gasped feigning horror. But more so because he had nipped and kissed her bare ass.

"Just take care. Glad you are both together. I will speak to you later. I just wanted to know you are ok."

"Yes, I am Auntie. Love you too. Talk to you later...Ouch!"

He suckled her backside cheek gently. She did devilish things to his body every time he looked at her.

"You have got to be kidding Kiah. Did you take Viagra or something?"

"Just you baby. I told you I have no intentions of letting you out of my sight." He tossed and flipped her over. He laid atop her.

They kissed and touched like horny teenagers. Until they were feverish with want.

He trailed fiery kisses all over her body.

She loved how he adored her boobs. How he seemed to worship them as he licked and suckled knowing just when to continue gas lighting her all over.

She grabbed his head.

"Seriously Kiah. I wouldn't be able to wear any panties today. It hurts."

"I hurt to baby. But I just must have you. I am ravenous."

He kissed her breast taking an already hardened nipple hungrily into his mouth.

"God help me. I want you again." He said, as his hand snaked once again between her legs and disappearing within her heated crevice.

"I want you too Kiah." She moaned. Thinking she didn't even require lubricant like she did with David.

46

"I know you do baby! I can feel just how wet you are." He brought his hand up to his mouth and licked it greedily. He then touched her lips. She tasted herself. It ignited something fierce within her all again. So much so she reached for him with a strength she didn't know she possessed and pulled him up, and pushed him back on the bed, and straddled him. She inserted his ample lengthy dick delicately within her.
The pleasure mixed with the pain was so intense and so damn intoxicating, that she screeched loudly.
He was delirious. As she bathed in the luxuriousness of his delectable strokes, and he took in the different fusions of her face and enjoyed the wicked guttural sounds she made.
He told himself he was a goner for sure. She had him by the balls and was holding tight to his heart. He knew he was certainly going nowhere anytime soon.

It could have been a couple hours later when she unwrapped herself from his arms and went back to shower.
He didn't stir.
She thanked God and slipped to the bathroom. She was truly in so much pain.
Thank God Seba had gone back into town with his friends. He told her he would probably stay there. His truck wasn't parked out when Kiah came over. She prayed he kept his word. Because the fits of screams she had let roar forth he would have thought she was being gutted alive.

She reached for Vaseline and gently placed some all around her privates swearing and awing. Even siting caused her immense pain. She avoided it like the plague. She couldn't recall ever been turned out so much.
David hadn't managed to do a quarter of the things he had done to her. He wasn't selfish either. He made certain she enjoyed herself as much as he was.
The two were so different.
She thought of Kiah as she placed the rose oil all over her body. She scolded herself when she thought of the many ways, he had made her sizzle and crackle.
She smiled like a Cheshire cat at herself in her huge mirror.
It suddenly dawned on her that she should be getting ready to go down to the office. However, she did not see that happening. She oiled her hair with rose oil and piled it high atop her head.
She applied make-up taking special care to highlight her treasured features, her eyes. She then played up her cheek. She thought to continue with the application of her lipstick and gloss after a strong cup of coffee. She gently applied balm to her swollen lips.
She then walked to her huge closet and chose something without too much restriction; a flowing sea-island cotton ankle length dusty rose-pink dress with a plunging neckline. She felt like getting her sexy on.

47

She walked over to her many shoes; most of which she had designed for her line, along with handbags, clutches, backpacks...

They nestled comfortably while she ran her fingers along them and chose a gold strappy toe out with kitten heels and sea-shells motif.

She laid everything out before she headed out to the kitchen for some strong black coffee.

"Hello my sunshine!" He greeted her. She stopped herself from bursting out in laughter as he modelled the white silk robe, she had abandoned the night before.

"Cup of coffee?" He gestured comically to the coffee dispenser.

It was the most heavenly thing. It was the first smell that got to her as soon as she stepped out into the hallway. She had followed it like a junkie.

"Are you God?" She asked him. "I could kiss you... But wait!" She made the sign of the cross. "Shit, I get into too much trouble just by looking at you Kiah."

He laughed out loud, and it echoed around the walls. "So, I take it that's why you slipped away and left me to nurse my woody?"

"What the hell is the matter with you? Do you know how much it hurts just to move?"

"I am sorry baby. You are so tight, and I can't seem to get enough of you!" He planted a kiss on her lips. "You look and smell divine by the way."

"You are so good for my ego!" She kissed him back. She too could not seem to get enough of him. "But first I need coffee."

"Your wish is my command. By the way where do you keep your cups?"

She laughed and pointed out the cupboard. Not missing the plate of fruits, he had put on the island's counter.

She became ravenous instantly. "When did you have time to do that?" She gestured to the platter.

"I got up when you did. I resisted the immense urge to follow you. Especially when I heard you awing. I'm sorry baby." He gestured between her legs.

"Kiah! And to think I must go to work." She tossed covering her face.

"Do you really?" He asked, reaching for her hand and taking it down from her face, placing a cup of coffee in them.

"Yes, I do. I have a meeting with your Auntie B." She said, closing her eyes and inhaling the intoxicating smell wafting up to her.

"I am certain she doesn't expect you to attend. Especially seeing how late you got in. Plus, your auntie must have told her I am down at your place."

"Kiah!" she screeched. Feeling a warmth snaking about her face that had nothing to do with the coffee.

"But seriously I have a crazy work ethos, my word is my bond."

He truly understood what she meant. He did not like breaking promises, especially to others who meant something to him.

"Postpone at least."

"Don't you dare!" Especially seeing as I know what you are thinking." She tossed pointing at him. "I can't even sit! It hurts so much!"

"Who me!" He said, putting his hand up in feigned ignorance. "And to show you a gesture of good fate. I am going to go get myself sorted, while you contemplate what you will do next. By the way here is some food for thought"

He ripped open the robe. Then he reached out to take a piece of mango from the plate using his mouth.

"Tell me that you're not interested, you little minx. He slapped her derriere and disappeared down the corridor.

"By the way your place is gorgeous. That is some view you've got out there."

Nia couldn't help the huge grin that crossed her face or the pride she felt as she reached for the plate and took her cup of coffee out to the veranda.

Her house had been a labour of love. For there were moments when she did not think she could get it to the standard she wanted.

She also remembered the immense pain she felt when she walked in, and her mama was not there to share in the greatness. It was hard.

Those last words were an understatement.

She had grown up in a two-room house that had an outdoor toilet and bathroom. As well as a kitchen attached haphazardly and built up by a couple neighbours of theirs.

She wasn't complaining because she never wanted for anything. Not even a father. Her mama and her Auntie Katho and basically most that her mama knew had in some way along the line stepped up to support her growth.

It was true statement; the village raised a child.

All her mama said when she asked about him was, "What's the use of having someone around who didn't want to be there Nia-Belle? God sent you to me. So, we are the only comp'ny we need. Never ever forget that you are just as great and can do even greater things if you just keep your faith in the one above."

The first prayer she had ever learnt from the woman was the one she repeats every day.

"I Nia-Belle will always do good to myself, to others, and to the universe."

In this house she had four bathrooms in her space. One attached to each bedroom. There were three on the second floor, and three in Seba's apartment.

Each bathroom had a bedroom to accompany it.

Her house at times served as a safe place for abused women and their children who were in conflict; with their spouses, when **Safe Haven**; a village compound she built about five years ago had a crowded capacity.

49

It comes complete with vocational classes where women can improve or upgrade a skill that makes them viable for today's society.

Everything was difficult and at times she didn't understand how she came out on top. Other than it was destined by God.

She touched her hand to her chest and repeated her mama's mantra; **"Do good... Do good... In all you do. Do do good."**

She brought her coffee cup to her lips and looked off at the panoramic view displayed before her.

On a clear day to her left, she could see Montserrat, Antigua, or Redonda. Then Star Island in the middle. To the right the notorious Heart Island. She had heard so many things about the place.

It was known as the playboys' hideaway. At nights the views could be even more spectacular as lights and movements could be spotted.

Her wrap around veranda offered her that glorious blessing.

Especially when she worked outside and witnessed so many colourful scenes as they danced before her eyes. In the flora and fauna, as well as the birds and animals. Not to forget the sunrises and sunsets.

She recalled the stories she researched and heard from the aunties of the early stages of the volcano in Montserrat.

She had glossed over many pictures from West and others, of the majestic displays that unfolded from her majesty Soufriere once she raised her petticoat.

The splendour and colour the mountain showcased to onlookers all over the world was spectacular yet intimidating. As it tossed mushroom plumes of cloud filled with huge boulders, smoke or ash and firestones high cascading down into the sea. Sometimes sending ash-rain to the neighbouring islands.

Her aunties said **Psalm 46** became their prayer at the manse. Because they didn't want to pick through things and pack up and move anywhere else. Emerald City was their home. Where they had met and grown. It was their life. Especially when they investigated the faces of some of the friends and families who stayed with them. Or with other families throughout the island. Where some were taken advantage of, and mistreated, or simply couldn't cope...

Some have since migrated to other islands as well as around the world. So, they could in their opinion do better.

There are many books detailing the arduous journey many undertook. But with faith and perseverance many are now venturing back. Some mentioned that they realised the grass was not greener.

Others have formed a new commitment to infuse life and culture back into their island.

Her **Fire & Ice** line had strategically emerged from the immense love of many in the stories they told for posterity, and the knowledge she gleaned off her aunties, also from the pages of some of those documented spectacular and mesmerising information that no doubt still haunted many. Because it nearly wreaked havoc on her being. She had been consumed by it all.

Thank goodness the grumpy Her Majesty's Madam Soufriere's nasty cough has not gotten any worst. She had stopped spewing.

So, Montserratians as well as all the supportive islands could get on with living. But still according to many it was truly very difficult.

Gingerly Nia inched her aching body down into one of the many rattans. She took a sip of her hot coffee. He had done a fantastic job; not to strong not to weak.

Not many people could make her a good cuppa.

The man was FANTASTIC!!! Graphic pictures of how he had turned her body on its axels, flashed across her mind's eye. She bit down on her lips hungrily.

"Girl, you had better pull your whorish self together!!!" She chastised herself. "Because you frown on one-night stands, yet here you are going against everything you were raised to believe.

"But God it was so good though." She whispered. "I promise I will do penance for it all when I get into town today."

She reached for a piece of kiwi and popped it in her mouth hungrily.

The breeze was succulent. Just as the slices of strawberry, guava, pineapple and mango displayed on her plate.

Before long it all disappeared and so did her coffee; of which she could use another but just the thought of getting up again, or shifting...

She laid back and allowed the lapping of the waves on the beach below to lull her thoughts.

Her mama came for a visit.

The woman was described as a Nomad. She loved the wide expanse of water. She also loved fishing and crayfish hunting.

Nia recalled she headed to the beach first thing each morning for a quick swim before starting her day. Sometimes on balmy evenings it was the last thing she did, as she pulled her along.

She was a beautiful being. Men and even women fell in lust with her all the time.

"You are the only priority Nia-Belle. You and a way to make your life easier than mine has been. You must become something to reckon with on this island my girl."

Nia could never remember her bringing anyone of the opposite sex to the house. If the need arose for any male figure to fetch anything from her, or for their respected others, she would always bring it to them outside.

Her auntie was the only one she could recall that she was ever left with.

Her mama was known for her flamboyant costumes; that you could be sure got mentioned in papers all around the Caribbean and even worldwide.

She also had a knack for creating some of the most beautiful costumes imagined on stage. Some of the other islands even hired her to create ostentatious pieces for many contests.

Her mama had inherited the name **Carnival Mama**. Because she was also an excellent designer and seamstress and would sew fabulous dresses for the festival and carnival contestants, as well as evening and wedding, and social event dresses.

Her dream was to open a little boutique that she would simply call **Belle;** it was her name after all.

Nia recalled asking her why she had given her the same name.

"Simply put sweetie. Because I am you, and you are me. Together we can do great things my girl. Please do not ever forget that. So, I am happy to share."

Nia also remembered that many would say to her mama constantly.

"You need to let the child fall and get bruised. You shelter her too much."

All her mama would do was smile; seems like she was forever smiling.

Even in tough times, they had almost lost the dilapidated house they were renting from Mister Zacharias nickname Mis'ta.

He was one of the richest men on the island. He owned many houses and lots and lots of lands.

He also was the fattest human Nia could recall ever meeting. He reminded her of the caricature of Humpty Dumpty.

He scared her and she could tell he had scared her mama.

Nia couldn't forget the way he had touched her mama's face, and how he whispered against her.

"You had better bring that fine piece of ass... Or we can trade." He tossed cockily.

Her mama sprung to action; she suddenly pushed her behind her. It was the only time she could ever recall seeing stark raving anger mixed with hate on her mother's beautiful face.

"Lay a finger on her. Ever Mis'ta, and I swear to God you filthy bastard that you will join your son in hell." She hissed.

"Well, you had better get creative, or the both of you will be out on the street come night fall."

Only God knows what transpired after they watched him set off in that shiny black trophy car of his. Because he never bothered them again.

Another of her mama's favourite things to say was. "You treasure gifts Nia-Belle. Especially the ones the Creator gives. So, I treasure you. You are my gift, child."

She never ever allowed her to think otherwise.

Nia pictured her face the day she told her she had finally saved enough money. She had also taken her into town and showed her the spot she had sourced out to open her boutique. She had even paid a hefty deposit to get the work sorted. All unknown to her.

So, she owed her everything she had accomplished to this day. She had even taught her from an early age about the **Rag & Wire** trade.

Nia at the age of 9 could already cut cloth from a pattern and use the sewing machine. As well as sketch like a pro.
"That's your God given talent my girl." She would always say. "I only supported what our Creator had already given."
She drew costumes her mama spoke to her about, and even helped to create most when she got stuck.
They would sit together for long periods, and fuss over what would make a sketch or a costume pop.
Many said her mama was never destined to remain in this world for too long. She believed it was the gospel truth. Because the woman was generous to a fault, and surreal and kind.
She would give most of her money to make sure others had what they needed. That was why it had taken her so long to get her store. Because at times she would be sewing curtains, blankets, bed sheets, or uniforms for children just so they could attend school.
All the children throughout the neighbourhood knew they could call upon her mama whenever they needed uniforms or a new dress.
The woman believed all children should be given a chance to grow as children, and not be bothered by negativity.
So, her team always made school uniforms for a different school that showed a need for them each term.

Nia also started a mobile library that went about the island weekly and gave children the opportunity to borrow books; they liked or needed to further support their studies or interest.
Pass it On: is another service they ran two times out of the year; during Easter and Christmas.
They would choose three schools who had pioneers and leaders emerging in a strong sense of community, diversity, and skills in any field of interest.
They or anyone can write a letter stating what has been done by this school or child.
The aunties at **Corrington's** and **Belle** put together funds that they donate.

Her mama loved the idea of always supporting schools. She would easily say, "school was where one went to continue to learn with structure and guidance."
She was a veracious lover of books. She had so many. Especially those on fashion and architecture. Sometimes she would regale her with imaginative houses and layouts; for what her boutique would look like.
Somewhere deep in her mama's mind she must have believed the edict because she was always teaching her the art of making flowers, sewing sequins, painting and sketching…

Little girls at that age loved running about in the sunshine, and chasing butterflies with their friends, or planning parties or their weddings even. Not her. She loved spending time with her mama wilding the moments away, and languishing in her company.

Her mama never seemed to tire of having her around. She loved listening and explaining this or that in the art of fashion and design to her.

She would always say, "Never hide your light under a bushel. You must always shine Nia-Belle."

So, she taught her all she knew. They had loads of sketches in pads all over their house. She still had many in her studios; at home and in town to look at when she felt the need to reminisce.

Then the sadness came. It always does. She recalled the day her mama had finally saved enough money. She had even discovered the location she wanted.

It was July11th 2002. She had taken her into town to show her. It was exactly where **Belle** stands to this day.

They had eaten at Red Pole's fried chicken, and shared an ice-cold Malt, and had an ice cream cone to celebrate. While relaxing on the bayfront wall.

Couple months later J'ouvert morning the last day in December the accident occurred.

Nia had just turned 11years old a couple weeks before. They had celebrated with her auntie; her mama's fraternal twin, Lady B, some of her friends from school and Seba; whose mama died from ovarian cancer a couple years after her mama; who was so happy, especially because they had won another $5000.00 to put towards her shop. She had won best evening wear and costume segment that year.

It was about 7:00 o' clock in the morning, and she was sound asleep in bed with Auntie Katholeen; she had come down from the manse to stay with her.

They were awakened by the most unholy raucous coming from outside the door. When they opened it, they were met by frantic revellers who shouted, "there had been an accident. Her mama was dead."

When auntie Katho managed to calm them enough to understand what they were saying, she deciphered that a stampede had ensued and she had fallen, and the music truck had run over her. As did some of the drunk and crazed revellers.

Some claimed she died instantly, others said on route to the hospital. But whatever scenario it was, all she knew was that in that instant something had shifted for her and her family. Things would never ever be the same.

Nia's eyes stung, and before she could stop them; the tears she had always shed whenever she thought of her mama and the cruel way, she had met her end, came freely.

The anguish caused her to double over. It rocked her to the core.

It happened every time it visited.

He called out to her when he came back into the room. He had stayed longer getting himself sorted just to give her some breathing space.
He needed it too. For none had managed to have this effect on him in a long time. Also, her shower stall was amazing. It reminded him of his at home.
He paused in her hallway to inspect the pictures she had on the wall; he replaced the one that had fallen the night before.
It was a family photo; the aunties, her, and the Sebastin fellow, as well as Silcott.
They looked so happy together. It brought a smile to his face.
There was a black and white eight by ten chicken wire painted photo frame of an African girl. She looked almost ethereal as her long curly hair fell on her shoulder.
Her skin was indigo. Her black corneas against eyeballs that looked as white as freshly fallen snow looked ferial as she stared back. She wasn't smiling. She looked quite wearily towards the photographer, like she had a story to tell behind those sad eyes.
There were lots of other photos; some he didn't yet know but hopefully would. The other side of the wall had sculptors and artefacts from around the world and even the Caribbean.

When he walked out, she did not turn to acknowledge him. Not even when he called out her name.
He started over to her. That was when he saw she was rocking back and forth in what looked like immense agony. He fell to his knees before her.
"God Nia! What is wrong? Are you hurting?" He asked her anxiously.
His first thought was that he had been way to selfish and stupid. He had taken her to many times.
"I am sorry baby. I am so deeply sorry. I did not mean to hurt you." His heart was battling away in his chest.
"I'm sorry." She wrapped her arms around his neck. "It's not you...I was thinking of my mama." She mumbled against him. "It hits me harder some days. But more so around festival time."
"It's okay sweetheart." He held her to him. Thank God. He thought selfishly. She was not hurt because of something he had done. He squeezed her tighter.
He hated seeing her this upset. He had called his aunt and spoken to her and managed to rearrange their meeting. He was on his way to say as much to her.
He lifted her in his arms and sank into the plush wicker and brought her down unto him. That done, he simply just held her. He said nothing.
For what could one say who hadn't had the misfortune to have lost a parent?
His eyes wandered to the lush beauty and the vast expanse of the majestic land on display before him. Then off to Heart Island, that he had just bought, with the thought to redevelop. But he had to assess the island

55

for himself rather than be satisfied with just the aerial view he was given by the previous owners, who wanted a speedy sale.

He had always gone with his gut, which was and still is the way he went about doing business. So far it had not done him wrong.

He had come out gracing the cover of **Forbes** magazine as the youngest multi-billionaire just this year.

He had transformed real estate challenges and walked away holding the money bag all over the world.

His portfolio was vast; he owned shares in transportation and many sporting arenas. Not to forget shopping malls, theatres, parking garages, hotels, a few islands... He never gave money to anything he couldn't buy into.

He had a knack to see beyond the deal itself. Which was why he had jumped on **Heart Island**. He had an elite task force team in incognito checking things out.

He was eager to sink his teeth into the project.

She shifted on his lap and gave another of those "aaawhs."

He squeezed her gently. "I've got you gorgeous." He whispered down to her. Wrapping her up tighter and kissing her face gently.

"Thank you, Kiah." She offered weakly, coming away from him.

She dabbed at her face with cupped hands.

"Want to talk about her. I will listen." He offered taking her face in his hands. "You can talk to me about anything Nia. I am here."

"It is just that I still miss her so terribly. Sometimes it hits me harder than others. I know people say time heals all wounds, but that's a lie. Because I still miss her as though it were yesterday. Sometimes I wish she were here to share in everything she helped me so diligently to accomplish. She never wanted bells and whistles. She just wanted a spot here on earth, so she can continue to sew, sing, and dance. Simply just to bring others joy. I don't battle with God for too many things because believe me he has been tremendously good to me. But I have often asked him why? Because she was never a wilful person who sets out to hurt others. She loved him dearly. She couldn't give a shit what anyone thought of her. Only him. So why did he take her and in such a horrible way?"

"I don't have an answer for that. But all I know is that he never gives us more than we can bear." He kissed her gently.

"That's what most everyone says." She mouthed.

They laughed. He squeezed her tighter.

"Nia sweetheart. None of us has the answer to why we must die. Nor do I dare to presume to know why he does the things he does. His ways are mysterious. But sweetheart let us believe he needed her elsewhere. That she is in a better place."

Those were the words the Dali Lama said to him. Not verbatim. But they were close. He had questioned him about death.

"None of us will ever understand Hezekiah. Ying and Yang is the earth's balance. So, if there is life, there must be death, yes? But let's look at it another way. If we were never made to die, do you think this earth could sustain us, at the rate we are siphoning its supplies?"

The simplistic way had made sense to him. So, he had taken some comfort in that. He was glad that he could recall them now to offer her some solace. He said them to her.

"Kiah do you think I don't get it? But still, I miss her. Don't get me wrong, because everyone from the aunties right down has given me a reason to live. But still, especially around this time is when I wrestle with my God."

"I think he knows, and he understands."

"I know it is utterly selfish to say this, but why didn't he take someone else?" She threw her arms around him.

"Sweetheart all I know for sure is that we live, and we die. I am no philosopher. But from what you just said your mama made sure she poured herself into you. You are the special person you are because of her. Yes? You are the continuation of her to carry on all the things she started... Believe that. Believe it and pull yourself together... You've got this baby." He said wrapping her tightly in his arms.

"Thank you, Kiah. I am glad I was not alone today. Thank you for listening to me."

"You are welcome."

"Now I had better get me behind in gear. I have a meeting with the aunties."

"Uh... About that...I hope you don't take my head off. But I spoke to them earlier... Don't shoot the messenger babe please... They said to get some rest and they would speak to you bright and early on Monday morning."

"Kiah!" She jumped off him. "Ouch! Ouch!" she chorused, pulling her robe about her.

"How do you expect to go out today if you make those sounds with every move you make?" He fought the urge to laugh. "Just take today as reflection time. Fresh perspective so to speak."

"Perhaps you're right." She thought rationally. "I am too damn worn out to argue." She walked over to the edge of the veranda and looked down into the vast backyard.

There was a swimming pool she never used. Her eyes trailed past the fauna and flora down to the beach. She could hear the waves breaking.

"You should be so proud Nia. Do you know how many people would like to have all this?" He came up behind her.

"I know Kiah." She nestled into his embrace. It felt as though she was meant to be there. Like they were hand and glove. She felt as though she could be honest and open with him. That he would listen, support even if she asked. She smiled. She felt in some strange way that her body and mind was at home. She trembled.

"What's causing that?"

"You...Just yesterday if anyone had said that I would be like this with anyone today. I would have laughed in their face."

"I know what you mean. Not that I had given up. Let's just say it feels like I've truly found...Can I say home? Is that a great way to describe how I feel being with you?"

"Oh Gham! Kiah this is so creepy! I just thought that! I like how I feel being with you too. "

"Nia, I pray I never disappoint you." He whispered against her ear. Closing his arms tightly about her.

They remained just that way for a long while, until he broke the silence. "Do you know that island?" He pointed to it.

"All I know about that..." She pointed to the island. "Is that some wealthy Lothario has just bought it. Yet again. Heard there was some sort of human trafficking thing going on over there. Young women and men were being exploited, and there was a raid. I don't know how true that Is. But I am glad it got sorted."

"Lothario?" He asked smiling to himself closing his arms tighter around her. He had indeed heard whisperings of the same thing. But Dominic Lazar had assured him there was no truth to the rumours.

Well, that was until he had his men do further diggings.

They had indeed found a couple people who said they had been exploited, trafficked even. He also heard that some had disappeared because they had dared to speak...

That was how he had sweetened the deal and gotten the man to take his lowest offer.

Thank God he was as boring as heck when it came to being a Lothario. He was not into heavy shit like most. He didn't do drugs. If he got a whiff of drugs, he would be the first to get his ass up and away.

He recalled an instance where a female had kissed him, and the next thing he knew he had signed over 10% of a deal he only just brokered. Funky shit happens all the time. So, he tried his best to keep out of its way.

Another time he had jogged upon a robbery. He'd saved the wife of the guy who is now head of his security team while Deryck was here with him. Kiah thought his lifestyle was as boring as heck. Does knowing American sign language count as uninteresting? Well, that was more a description of him rather than Lothario. It made him smile.

Even his publicist had said as much to him.

In the beginning he did almost everything she wanted. Now he simply picked and chose what piqued his interest.

At one point he threatened to fire her ass if she kept accepting shit that distracted him from what he wanted to achieve.

Well having money afforded getting your ass licked. But he never allowed it to get to his head.

Many have asked how. But all he would say is. "If misfortune knocks, he hoped that someone would have a smidge of pity. So, he kept his feet planted firmly on the ground with how he was in his dealings with others.

He was no push-over, he could kick ass when the need rears its head. That was why he had the team.

So now invitations got tossed especially if he wasn't getting something from the deal.

Give to Get was his motto. Even though he could be like Scrooge. Especially when it comes to a contract and negotiating. Not to forget any money transfer.

So, Lothario? It was so not him. But he listened. His dad always reminded him to pay no attention to noise that stifles. So, until the time was right, he would listen. Who knows what else he would glean?

"Yep." She continued. "There is a saying on the island; when dog ghat money dey run and buy cheese, or is it chocolate? Anyway, some people act de damn fool when they have a bit of money or power. Any-who I don't like water like that." She waved the island away.

"Yet you have that?" He gestured to the inviting body of water below. "C'mon let's go grab a swim."

"Hell no! That's Seba's thing not mine." She wriggled from his embrace. "I would much rather go through my cases. You are welcome to go down if you like."

She walked away and back into the house.

"Do you play?" He followed pointing to her white Steinway baby grand piano. She also had a guitar on a stand, as well as a twin conga drum set.

"Yes." She offered easily. She loved making music.

David had taught her to play. He was a gifted asshole.

"Play something for me." He tested. Just to see if she indeed could.

Like some people would say they can and when prompted they could not do shit!

He looked at her as she went over and ran her hands along the keys. She played the scales artfully and sang them as well.

"Wow! Is there anything you can't do Nia?"

"Not really." She said easily. "That is if I put my mind to it. Plus, I must give credit to my mama and the aunties." Nia paused. She thought of May. She had distanced herself from the family for so many years now.

She prayed that the girl was safe with that family in America.

"So how many instruments do you play?"

"What's here. But I am certain if I had the time, I could master others."

"Cocky."

"Truth. Music is my drug. It is therapy, my path when all seems lost."

"I understand." He thought back to his self-defence moments. It was his north star. He loved working out. His guys kept him in fighting form. He only had to call on them.

"I can see you get my drift Kiah."

"I do. I really do."

His eyes caught the picture above the piano. He saw the resemblance. Nia was the more beautiful version in his book. Although he could see why others could get drawn into her. Because her eyes were mesmerising. Like she could draw anything out of you. You could tell her your deepest secret and not feel ashamed. She almost appeared to be smiling.

It sort-of made his heart skip as he looked up at her.

"Is that your mama?" He asked pointing to the photo. The smile seemed to have deepened. It reminded him of her Auntie Katholeen, who was the darker of the three. So where had she gotten that colouring, he wondered?

Maybe it was from her dad. But he didn't feel like digging into family history anymore. Especially seeing how raw she had been earlier.

The artist had given her mama extended white angel wings. "I like the depiction. Who is the artist? The work is brilliant on the wall."

"I am Kiah." She said easily. He opened his mouth, but nothing came. He pointed out other pieces.

"That too and that too." She offered. "I did them along with most of the furnishings, designs and layout of the house."

"You are one talented individual Nia!" He said in awe. As he remembered coming in on the drive.

One would think there was only one floor to the property. Now standing atop the rise and looking about, he spotted another access across from the dining room.

"If you go through that door Kiah you still have a view of the island when you step out. Also, from all the rooms throughout the house."

She stepped down into the sunken living room; home to a massive single crescent moon wicker sofa filled with colourful fabrics on the pillows and throws. To the right in the corner was a huge driftwood table.

"My television is in that table."

She walked over picked up the remote and pressed buttons. The television slowly rose to greet them.

"There is surround sound for music also." She demonstrated.

Soft music permeated throughout the room.

"You like?" She asked smiling with much pride.

"I love!" He said his eyes following her and drinking in her every move.

She continued with the tour, pointing beyond the arch.

He knew that it led to the huge entryway. He had paused there on his way back in to look. Noticing the different artefacts from all over the Caribbean and the world, as well as a beautiful wide full-length mirror; adorned with dried plaited coconut fauns all around.

"Don't tell me. You?" He asked pointing to the clock. He was beginning to now be able to see her touches around her home.

He was truly impressed.

He had picked up the picture of her mum and her aunt that fell the night before and put it back in its spot. But not before he said, "I know you want me to know you have your eyes on me. So, I want to promise that I will be honourable to her."

The picture shifted. There were other photos as well, and many with the guy Seba. As well as others that he would no doubt get to know later.

He noticed that the aunties played a prominent part.

He hadn't missed the huge chandelier that descended from the ceiling. It was made of the same polished and stained driftwood, with colourful teardrop glass shimmering from it.
She had more siblings' semi attached to her, as well as sprinkled around the house.
Some of the glass resembled origami cranes or flowers and other animals.
"Can you guess what made those?" She asked pointing to the teardrop."
"Tell me." He would have said blown glass.
"They are pieces of glass collected from the shoreline here, and even all around the Caribbean. So is the driftwood. A friend of mine and his team are into Eco-technology on a massive scale. They recycle tons of the waste that floats or get collected from our oceans."
"That's brilliant."
"If you are interested, I will take you down to his place one day. You will be blown away by the things done."
She left the pieces out that she was responsible for their massive success by the things she designed with the pieces they procured.
They had even won the coveted design award to furnish the posh and trendy **Heliconia Hotel**.
Couple brothers from Dubai had bought the run-down place and after renovating wanted to revamp the inside. Just on a fluke Glassford encouraged her to submit some of her designs.
They were gaga over them. Her designs; won the contract along with a hefty sum. She was featured in quite a few magazines around the Caribbean.
Including their famous island glossy **Interpretation** started by Miss Indiria Osbourne the islands' Barbara Walters. As well as her **Mi Casa**, that featured the rich and famous people and their homes around the island and the Caribbean.

The **Heliconia** was the playground for the many rich and famous who wanted privacy when they vacationed on the island.
They had an exclusive boutique in the place. It had done them quite well.
But she had heard a couple of weeks ago that it was up for sale.
It was on one of her pieces of land thanks to her bastard of a grandfather. God rest his black and damned hellish soul. But another day for his shit.

Kiah perked up even more at the Eco-Tech talk. Saving our planet was where huge chunks of his money was found.
He thought of Kancy; she was from Trinidad and had started a vegan restaurant that continues to be a success.
She liked to say to him. "We all blow about the same stuff Kiah when it all boils down. Unfortunately, we do not have lots of investors who are willing to give without getting something back in return. So, at times the price we pay is to damn heart-breaking. But we must not give up. We have an

obligation to make this world sustainable for our next generation. The pressure is real my friend."

He had promised to meet with the Caribbean delegates in Turks and Caicos on his way back from Emerald City.

He spotted a massive sundial emerald mirrored clock. "I love that. That is simply breath-taking Nia."

Closer inspection he saw that it was her mama's face; half in sleep the other awake; a hint of a smile kissed her lips. It was so incredible the honour that went into the depiction.

"Just believe that wherever she is she must be so damn proud of you. I mean it woman. That is mind blowing!"

"It was an immense labour of love Kiah. That picture is the one I have known from forever. That one is from when I wake from sleep, and crawl into her arms. That one is a rarity. She hardly slept it seemed.

She said, "there would be enough time for that when I am dead."

Nia's heart rattled in her chest. "I love you mama." She whispered.

"She seemed remarkable." He kissed her gently. "I have only known you for a day, and woman you've got my mind boggled. I think I am in a dream loop." He kissed her again just to prove to himself.

"I thank God for the people he placed around me to carry out all the things that swim around in my head. Glassford is a Messiah, and so is his team. He manages to bring all my crazy creations to all this. Sometimes we hate each other and need to be separated. But he always gives me what I ask for. All this Kiah. I have my own cup, glass and dinner ware service and utensil line, as well as linens and sofa-coverings and drapes...."

"Amazing!" He said as she pulled him along to continue the tour. She reminded him of Vanna White.

His eyes went to another mural; it was a representation of the Last Super, but with children. They sat around with her mama at the head of the table; that was laden with food. It made him chuckle.

"I get it Nia. It's epic! You say she is gone but she is right here. I can see it...Feel it even."

"That is exactly what I wanted. I wanted her here Kiah... She was one friggin-awesome and amazing woman! Do you know I once saw her drape a piece of cloth without cutting or sewing, into the most incredible dress ever for a tourist visiting here on island?"

"I can imagine. Just look at what you do because of her."

He bent to closer inspect what lay at the bottom of the huge glass top table, that reminded him of a clear translucent blue sky.

It appeared to be a nest where tiny baby birds were protruding some from their shells. Under the same polished driftwood that finished off as a table stand. It drew him in as he realised that two birds held it on their backs.

"That's my depiction of our national bird; the Oriole." Nia said beaming from ear to ear. "It's freaky. But that's how my mind operates at time. I make no excuses for it."

"I love that too." He offered. Thinking he really needed to device a way to get her over to the island with him. He could use her talented eyes. Not that gilded shit he saw running throughout. He wanted the island to be his home away from work.

Something pulled him back to her.

Tall screens were coming together to separate the massive open planned kitchen from the formal dining. He looked quizzically over at her.

"Look I planned to get them done, but never got around to it. But on closer inspection I like them plain."

"Me too." He agreed... "Love the greenery... They aren't real?" He touched them. His voice laced with feigned awe.

"Disappointed Nia." He wagged his finger at her.

"There's not enough time in the day Kiah. I too can say that I am allowed to drop a ball or two."

"So, I am forgiven for talking to Auntie?"

"I'll let it slide." She went to the refrigerator and poured herself a glass of water. "Would you like something? I am sure Rosaria left lots in the fridge."

"I'll make a sandwich. I'll make you one." He offered kindly.

"Nah! I think I'll have leftovers. It's nearly twelve any way."

She grabbed chicken that Rosario had indeed left her. She popped it on a plate; from her **Calabash** line; she had done glasses, dinnerware and dessert, as well as utensils service.

"That's nice...Yours?" He asked. She nodded.

She placed the last two of the biscuits from the night before on it.

"What? You've never seen a woman eat Kiah?"

"I am glad you are feeling better." He smiled over at her. Then proceeded to develop his sandwich, stacking cheese and tomato, lettuce and cucumbers.

"Not a lover of pork then?" She asked him. Noticing he bypassed the ham.

"You didn't ask that question after last night, did you? Have you forgotten already? Perhaps I need to show you again how much?" He teased.

She tossed him a confused look.

He busted out laughing recalling the first time Night Ninja his good buddy from Jamaica had referred to a woman's vagina in such a way. He had spent a couple nights with him in California and had asked where he could get some pork.

Stupidly he'd thought of supermarkets and delis, and rattled off a few names, even pointing out one to him.

Night Ninja had the same look on his face like she did now.

That was until it dawned on her what he was talking about.

"Kiah you're a freak! Plus, it still hurts. So, no more. You are on lock down bad boy." She scolded his dick.

A warmth begun to spread around her body. As a thought came to mind; **white men can indeed jump**. He was very much blessed in that department.

She flicked the screens back into place by touching a switch on the side of the wall. Then joined him at the island. Before long they were eating of each other's plate.
She promised to take him to **Sylvie's** so he could get curried goat and rice; one of his favourites. She also learnt he liked Ital, Rasta pot.
She told him she would get him some as well.
"By the way I noticed your friend hasn't shown his face. I thought he lived here."
"He's already at work, I'm sure. Plus, he went into town after he dropped me last night. But if you must know his place is on the third floor. He likes his solitude, and so do I."
"You really must give me a proper layout of this place Nia. Who's on the second floor?"
"For me to explain that I would have to have you sign a waiver."
She reached into a stationary basket and pulled out paper and pen and scribbled something quickly.
Then she placed it in front of him and said, "Sign."
"Seriously?" He asked in disbelief, reading what she wrote.
I Hezekiah Carter Corrington will agree to pay the sum of $5000.00 to Belle Foundation if I want to acquire the knowledge of what lies on the second floor of this property.
"As a heart attack Kiah." She tossed easily. But already judging by his attire, and the watch he wore, she assumed he could afford most if not all the amount she'd put on the paper.
"Now sign if you want to know about the second floor." She tapped the paper with her forefinger impatiently. "Or you can promise me your first born. By the way do you have kids?"
They never got around to that in all the shenanigans. Which brought warmth to her face of all the ungodly things she had allowed the man to do to her. But not to get it twisted she had enjoyed every little bit of it and would probably go for more if her mee-mee was cooperating.
Thank God they both had done their sexual tests and swapped cards.
"No, I don't." He offered a bit too quickly. But now was not the time to get into any of that shit either.
The girl popped up in his head... and just as quickly he pushed her away.

"Hey? Hey you, you, ok?" He had taken on a faraway look on his handsome face. Taking up the Thinkers pose.
"Sorry. So, are you going to tell me about the second floor? I am way intrigued now." He signed swiftly. Piece of cake in EC currency he thought to himself as he listened to her voice.
"Well, I started this charity called **Belle Foundation** years back when I was a teenager. The aunties supported me on this. **Safe Haven** is one of its

64

babies. It came out of a desperate need to offer women who are being abused a place where they can come to feel safe with their children. It also offers them their own private space to decompress. They are also given opportunities to access learning that allows them to be viable in today's job market. Or even to enhance a skill that they already have. Or didn't even know they had and wanted to improve on. While they are studying their children can attend the onsite crèche. Or the older children have a bus that offers pick up and drop off to school and vice-versa. The only thing they are asked; no contact with the abuser while they are sorting themselves out. We have in-house counsellors for both the adults and the children."

"Completely and utterly floored Nia."

"Abuse is so prevalent here on the island. I just had to do something. Not just for the abuse, but for the abuser as well. Because if we can repair and support families in a positive way, we are all for it. So, we have clinics on the outside that they, meaning the abuser can readily access. That is if they want to integrate their families. So, the second floor is an extension of **Safe Haven**. Families are welcomed to stay here until a space becomes available over there. So, you see why confidentiality is key for the success of the charity?"

"Wow Nia! I know I am sounding more and more like a broken record around you. But wow! I do have one stipulation though."

"What?" She asked smiling, as she climbed down from the stool and cleared their plates.

"That you never hesitate to let me know what help you need in the future... I am serious Nia." He insisted. She had said her okay too quickly. He reached for her hand and stilled her. "I mean it. If even, you have to say it to Auntie B Nia."

He made a mental note; to get the info from his Auntie so he could toss a hefty contribution into the project. He had done it for many others all over the world. So why not here and for her.

He recalled the biggest challenge he had done, and still to this day was the greatest in his opinion. It was when he had gone undercover and work in his company for a month before anyone realised who he was. He worked as the janitor at night, and the mailroom during the day. That was why he'd ended up investing in a couple reality television shows. Some of which are huge hits.

He recalled paying the debts off for the first 500 people, who entered a contest his company set up. Quite a few had gone back to their old ways while some had done extremely well. He checked in regularly.

They had taken the show global. Another 1000 has now tripled their wealth and had gone on to become the heads of their own destinies, with the tools provided by him and his company.

"Who do you think my partners are Kiah? They have been with me every step of the way. I could not do the things I do if they were not supporting me with huge chunks of it."

"But I am serious Nia." He offered vehemently. "I will always only be one phone call away." He meant every word. The woman was truly amazing. He got up and came around to help with the dishes, washing and drying them and placing them in the cupboard. Where he spotted glasses and plates made from the same sea-glass concoction.

"Great work Nia. These are gorgeous pieces as well." He offered. Pointing to the pieces in the cupboard.

The house phone rang. It made them jump guiltily. She reached out and picked it up saying a breathy hello.

It was Seba. "I take it you will not be in the office today." He said matter-of-factly. Seeing he had already received word from Auntie B to say the appointment had been cancelled.

"Are you ok? I know you were tired. I figured you would sleep in."

"I did." She offered coyly. Pictures of the night before popped up in her head as she looked at him drinking a glass of water.

"By the way. Did you call that sexy thing yet?" He pictured the guy in his head. He started to fan himself hotly.

"No." She spat guiltily praying he didn't pick up on anything. For he knew her that well.

"By the way. It ain't like you to stay away from the office and cancel appointments. You didn't even call to let me know. I had everything ready to go girlfriend."

"I'm sorry Seba. I just woke with the nastiest headache, and it got progressively worst, so I thought to just call and cancel with Lady B. I am so very sorry that I didn't check in."

"How are you feeling now? I can stop by Birds' pharmacy and bring you something…"

"No! No don't! I mean I have stuff at home. I am sure it's nothing that a little bit more sleep can't fix. Just stay at the office and look after things for me. Give my apologies to everyone. But seriously don't rush home on my account."

"If you are sure…But seriously pick up the phone and give Mr. Sexy a call… Or I will invite him over to the house myself. I am giving you until 3:00 pm. Then I will call you again, okay?"

"Yes Seba." She offered. She felt him beside her. He kissed the nape of her neck so subtly. It was delicious. His hands snaked around her, slipping into her robe and caressing her nipples. She tried to maintain her cool, but it was slowly slipping with the way his hands and lips were beginning to make her feel.

"Nia? Nia? Girl! Hey, are you ok?"

"Yes Seba!" She whimpered, as she melded into him.

He turned her around and started to kiss the tip of her nipple, then in the crevice.

"Seba." She crooned. "I will call you later, but seriously don't worry. I am going back to bed now!" She didn't wait for him to reply. She quickly placed the receiver down.

"Kiah! You are going to be the death of me!" She purred as she felt him snake his way down her belly, and his tongue flickered languishingly into her belly button.

"Nia! Nia! Bitch!" Seba called out through the receiver. He was rewarded with her pleasure moans.

He dropped the instrument from his trembling hand. It landed with a sharp thud on the table when he realised what it was, he was hearing.

After a couple seconds of listening to her purr like a satiated kitten he reached for the receiver and stealthily placed it on the hook.

Then he proceeded to jump around the office gleefully as he realised the bitch had had the good sense to call Mr. Handsome. Not only that! He was over at the house, and he was fanning her flames

It was long overdue he thought. She deserved a little happiness, and he was doing it for her so why in the hell not. Thank God she had realised that not everything you loose is truly a loss. She had spent enough time yearning for a curse. Well now let the real game begin.

He jumped and cheered in his office. Totally ecstatic for her blessing. He squealed with delight. Thinking he had better make plans to stay elsewhere for the rest of the weekend.

Nia didn't think her kitchen would ever be looked at in the same way by her ever again.

He had placed her atop the island, and the things he had done to her body was enough to make the pope blush.

The pleasure commingled with the pain seemed to heighten the arousal. At one point she whispered naughtily, "Kiah...she can see us!"

He answered, by pulling her down on the floor, and they hid behind the island, and continued on the cold marble tiles.

They ravished each other blaring like jungle animals, as their screams of ecstasy echoed throughout the cavernous house when they bodies constricted and convulsed together.

It seemed like hours when they came up for air again. They had tried watching television and had only ended up making out again.

Somehow, they ended up on the floor wrapped in her colourful throw that she had pulled from a drawer of the sofa. Sleep had thankfully come.

They were wrapped in each other's arms. His mobile went off, and while he scrambled to answer, she once again ran for the toilet.

When she emerged again after a quick shower and changed into shorts and a tank top. He was sitting outside speaking in a different language to someone.

Her eyes also caught sight of a couple suitcases and toiletry bag, along with a computer case at the door.

She recognised the Gucci insignia. A friend had gifted her the same printed luggage.

She ran to the hamper to inspect knowing it was from the aunties. They sold them in store at **Corrington's'**.

The hamper contained cheese scones, potato salad, fried chicken, prawn and pasta bake, coconut turnovers and carrot cake.

"I love you two so much, aunties!!!" She sang joyously.

Then she buried her nose in the cello-wrapped plate. She thought she had died and gone to heaven.

There were chilled bottles of sorrel, ginger, and passion-fruit juice.

She was so ravenous as she sorted through the hamper.

"So, you saw our treats?" He asked as he came into the room. He wore only boxers. "Let me grab a quick shower." He said and reached for his cases and disappeared.

No doubt Silcott had dropped them off. He was one of the few that had the gate's combination. He had worked for the family for almost a decade and was very trustworthy.

She remembered when he would drive them for ice cream at Chico's or anything they fancied on a Friday, and never once said anything to the aunties.

She reminisced; once he had come upon a couple girls being nasty to her and she had sworn him to secrecy. He never said anything to this day to her recollection to the aunties. Because they had never brought it up. Those girls never bothered her again.

She also recalled he had picked her and Seba up from a party where they had gotten drunk. He sorted them out and got them to bed without the aunties knowing.

Many say, "show an islander a wad of cash and they would sell out even their mothers."

However, he was a jewel in the crown. He was the aunties' go-to man and so much more.

He was a father to her, Seba and even their May.

Nia wondered for the millionth time what the girl was up to. Because she hadn't contacted the family in a long time.

While she waited, she felt the urge to sing. So, she went over to the piano and ran her hands along the keys. Before long she was singing.

She sang a couple of her favourite songs from the Broadway adaptation of The Colour Purple **Dear God** and **I'm Here.**

She thought of May and hoped she was doing well.

She was so engrossed in song she hadn't heard him come in until she ended and was rewarded with a lovely applause.

She spun around and he hugged her tightly.

"You smell amazing! But why didn't you let me know you were there?"

"You held me spellbound."

He wore khaki shorts and white polo shirt. His hair was neatly pulled up in a ponytail. He was bare foot.

"You look nice too."

"Thanks, compliments of the aunties. I tried but I got lost in you. In your voice. That song. I have heard it done on so many levels by the best. But fuck! The depth and rawness that you just put in was kick-ass Nia! Why the fuck did it take this long for us to meet?" He squeezed her in his arms.
"Nothing happens before God says so Kiah." She kissed his cheek. "Come on let's get something to eat."
She untangled herself and walked to the kitchen. She took the food from the oven she'd put to heat.
"Grab the potato salad. Let's eat outside. Then again let's eat in here. The sun looks fierce out there already."
"But seriously. Tell me about that in the meantime." He pointed back to the piano.
"It's second nature Kiah. I also sing in the **Emerald City Community Gospel Choir; ECCG** for short. Mama had me enrolled in church choir as well since I took my first step. The aunties' insisted and you know you can never say no to those two."
"True. But you were freaking amazing!"
"Thank you and thank God. Now enough about me. Let's go eat some grub!" She started off towards the dining room. Because the sun was hitting the veranda full on. She knew she could bring the blinds down, but she hardly used her dining room.
Once again, she gave thanks that the aunties had remembered her prawn pasta bake; she took a healthy piece unto her plate.
He looked at her and waited.
"Kiah, I love food!" She said and popped a fork full into her mouth and did a greedy-whistle blow to cool the succulent mouthful.
"This is my favourite dish and auntie makes it for me a lot when this time comes around. Bless the woman."
"For my suitcases as well." He left out the note that was placed on the top; **I've got my eye on you Mr Slick.** He imagined her.
But now he was in, there was no way he was going to let her escape ever again. He knew he sounded bizarre. But so be it. He recognised a great person and there was no way he was going to allow her to slip from his grasp now.

He reached for chicken and potato salad. He would allow her to enjoy her treat. But she teased him to try some; by popping a forkful into his mouth when he tried to protest.
"Shit! Seems like I am doing everything backwards. I forgot to ask if you have any allergies."
"None that I know of."
"What do you think?"
"Just as tasty as you."
"Kiah!"
"Well, it's the truth. You must know I don't say things I do not mean."
"I am beginning to get it." She tore her eyes from his gaze to take a huge gulp of her passion-fruit juice.

"What language was that earlier?" She asked trying to stare the conversation out of dangerous territory. Because she believed if she were to have another round of what he did to her body earlier. She reckoned she would surely die.

She searched her mind to recall if anyone had ever died from too much sex. She drew a blank.

"Mandarin." He offered smiling coyly. He recognised what she had done. "Do you speak any other?"

"Just some French and Spanish." She offered. She chided by saying something in both languages.

He answered her right back and they spoke sexily to each other. She was gagging for more by the time they stopped.

"How many languages do you speak?" She asked curiously.

"Ten or more." He offered as a matter of fact.

"Fuck!" It flew from her mouth without thought. Causing her to splutter and send juice flying all over the table.

He chuckled and demonstrated as she reached for the towel to wipe the mess. He said hello in twelve. She had lost count.

"Talk about impressive Kiah. Are you a **U.N** interpreter or something?"

"No. I told you I am a real estate broker/property investor." He left off all the bells and whistles. They weren't important.

"Where?" She asked making a mental note to do her research when she came up for air.

"California." He offered again. Giving nothing away.

"How long?" She quizzed becoming intrigued now.

"Ten plus years."

"Have you done anything else?"

"I was a chauffeur for a while for one of the world's richest stockbrokers in California. I was a rebel. I didn't want what my parents wanted for me. I was sort of rubbish at school as well, so I quit. Auntie B has always been there. Nia at times it is not what you know, but who. She gave me such a tongue lashing and set me up in a small development company my grandfather had some stake in, with the stipulation that I head back to school. So, I enrolled in night classes and persevered and kept my head in the game and my eyes on the prize. I graduated. Later an opportunity came up in the company, selling shares. I pitched it to auntie, and she thought it was brilliant, so she lent me most of the money. I became the head honcho. The rest is history."

"I think if I am not mistaken, I heard somewhere along the line that your family was in the rag trade?"

"I didn't have the head or the heart for it. Which is why I went in another direction."

"Seems like you have done well." She gestured to his watch.

"I have." He smiled.

Gosh he sure was gorgeous. She thought, how come he wasn't snatched up already? Because he was one fine piece of ass. Plus, he knew how to

wield his big-lengthy-stick. Granted she did not have many to stack him up against. But the things he did to her body...
She shook herself out of that pathway because between her legs was still telling the tales for being so starved.
"You certainly have."
"I really can't complain." He offered. As he looked keenly at her having finished his food. "What else do you want to know Nia?"
"How come you are unattached?"
"Answer the same question."
"It's different for a female Kiah."
"Can be the same for men too."
"C'mon! Someone that looks like you? Desirable, and you can, you know?"
"No, I don't."
"C'mon Kiah you know what I mean."
"No, I don't." He insisted knowing full well what she meant. Seeing she had had gestured to his groin. But he wanted to hear her say it.
"You know how to make a woman's body shout." She said it just above a whisper and tried to look away.
He caught her face in his hand. "Are you trying to say that you love my dick?"
"Aah huh." She whispered and lowered her gaze. His eyes mesmerised her. She felt trapped.
"How much?" He asked his mouth crinkling into a smile, as he teased her mercilessly. "Tell me Nia."
"Very much Kiah...I said very much... Okay a lot!" She spat and signed unknowingly. Because he had pretended, he couldn't hear.
"You just signed Nia! Do you know sign language?"
She shook her head and signed yes.
"Damn woman." He signed back to her. "You have a very dirty mouth."
He bent to kiss her deeply.
"You are amazing. How long have you learnt?"
"Since I was fifteen. You?"
"Since I was twelve. I had a friend I wanted to learn how to communicate with. You?"
"Same here. I also have hearing impaired clients. I like to know I treat them with the same respect as I do those that hear."
"Wow! Mind blown!" He tossed and kissed the tip of her nose. "So how come some lawyer, or doctor has not swooped you up?"
"Like I was saying before I was so rudely interrupted. The ratio is 1:10 Kiah. Then you think you've found that great one and his spoilt ass thinks you must be beholden to him and his stupid back-alley ways. Especially if his mama didn't raise his spoilt ass right."
"I would also say females don't want to be with someone whose job is their life. I work hard Nia. I didn't set time for dates, and when I had the time, they would have lost interest." He thought it best not to say a bad word on the opposite sex. It usually was better that way.

71

He was the same with the tabloids. They asked, he simply listened. "Think more. Say less." His parents have always advised.

At one point some speculated he was gay. But he neither acknowledged nor denied. There were too many out there who wanted their time in the spotlight. So, he had long since grown bored with it. He had chosen instead to concentrate on making money.
When he wanted sex, he knew who and where to get it.
"So...You are telling me that no one will be joining us any time soon? As in us I mean you?"
"No Nia. I have not had a serious relationship in almost seven years. Well give and take. I am not a monk after all. Plus, you know how much I love to fuck." He decided to be honest. But as of yesterday, can I be presumptuous and assume also that I am taken?"
She looked him squarely in the eye. She had better not play games. She liked how he made her feel, and she aimed to enjoy the feeling for as long as it lasted.
So, she said, "one day at a time Kiah. One day at a time." She offered, before she turned from him, and took her things to the sink.
"Then again let's just say you are mine for the next month. That is how long you will be here yes?"
"Yes Nia." He decided to offer nothing else. He simply got up and came over to join her. Again, they did the dishes in silence. That is until she decided to continue with the rest of the tour.

She showed him the first room off the hallway that was used as her office at home.
It was complete with seating area to entertain clients, as well as a changing room and podium with mirrors and lights.
There were stunning dresses kitted out on the mannequins; five in total.
There was a sewing machine sketch pads and tables.
Again, there was a mural of her mother in stunning costumes depicting the national bird: The Oriole. He was proud of himself for remembering, and gave himself an imaginary pat.
"Again, may I say how beautiful Nia." He pointed to the mural.
She walked over and explained the one in the middle.
"That was the last costume she wore to play mass. She was so incredibly joyous. She loved this time of year and looked forward to the culture and pageantry and the togetherness of our people from near and far who came out to play revel."
"It's beautiful. So detailed. Your mama was gorgeous. Just like you."
"Thank you." She said. Her eyes stung. "Some still say that festival never truly begun until Carnival Mama came out in her colourful array of glitters and feathers. She embodied the spirit of festival in the way she moved and danced. She mesmerised us all."
"Do you play mass as well?"

"Yes, Kiah I do. It generates income for me and my many causes. I get hired to build costumes for contestants entering the local or regional, and international pageant. Winning is my aim always."
"Can I see you in some of your costumes?"
She searched a stack of books she had on the floor and pulled one. She came back and gave it to him. **Festival 2012**.

He opened it and flipped through. There was a photo of her that was totally scandalous. She was dressed in white and silver strings of beading everywhere. It looked like she needed to be arrested. He could feel himself becoming rampant again.
"The aunties had nothing to say?" He pointed to the book aghast.
"Yes, they did."
She pictured the first time she played mass; 2010 and built a costume just for herself. David was acting like a demon, and she had had enough. She wanted to prove something to him or was it to herself? Whatever... She had constructed an actual bed that she was draped seductively across decked out in a diaphanous two-piece swimsuit that left nothing to the imagination.
Spotlight: Racy & Scandalous it was called. Plus, her songs for that year were called **Selling Something/ I Don't give a %$£&** and **Island Madness**. She won **Road March** and **Soca Monarch**. Her pocket was loaded.

The aunties were dumbstruck and thought she had totally up and lost her mind. Especially seeing that Seba was right next to her, dressed as the devil himself and was flogging her ecstatically. It was so controversial that year and still was to this day.
The costume was still what most wanted to talk about.
She would simply say it was something in her nature that she had to exorcise. They had gotten second place for fairness of festival. She smiled.
"We don't always see eye to eye at times. But we can agree to disagree. I take charge of my sexuality. I make no bones about who I am. It is just a persona I must play until festival is over. In costume I am her. Then she goes to rest until I dust her off again. Carnival Baby keeps the lights on."
"Do you know what you will be this year? I can't wait to see you."
"I would very much like to surprise you. Will you let me?"
Grudgingly he agreed and kissed her lips.
She took the book from his hands and placed it back with the other stacks.
She pulled him from the room. She pointed to the other doors.
"Those are guest bedrooms. Pretty boring stuff. But I have one more room I think you would like."
She pulled him into her workout room. She modelled a body builder pose.
"You had this all along? What a tease! I will make you pay dearly for that you little minx!" He slapped her rear.
There was a Pilate's machine, treadmill, stationery and spin bike, weight benches and even a punching bag... He was mesmerised.

"This room is my go-to after I finish my P&M, prayer and meditation. Then I have a run either on the beach, or in my garden. Sometimes I run on the road depending on my mood. Seba is a certified health and fitness trainer. He also teaches Zumba. Never mind the flamboyance. He has a wealth of knowledge, as well as skills."

"I believe that."

He pictured the fella in his mind and thought he would fit right in with Prada and Gucci, His personal A-team in terms of style.

They had kitted him out for his travel. Even wanting to come along just to make certain he was always **A-list**.

He had to remind them where he was heading, and how he wanted to live. No different than when he simply grabbed a backpack and jetted off for a couple of weeks.

"I have to build the stamina it takes to keep up with this hectic lifestyle."

"I get you. My day starts the same. Well except for today." He teased.

He looked her up like a fox in a hen house.

"Kiah!"

"We made up for it though. Right? Speaking of which you have a debt to pay. For keeping this room as a secret Nia."

He lifted her and wrapped her long firm legs around his waist.

"I am starving again." He teased. Kissing her sensuously.

He loved how her body responded easily to him. He placed her atop the weight bench and pulled her tank top up and over her head, then used it as a resistant band to bind her hands.

She giggled up at him. She was so off her head ready for him.

He couldn't shed his clothes fast enough.

She welcomed him eagerly as he spread her and rammed deep within. She didn't wait for him this time. She blasted to the moon twice; wildly one behind the other.

"We need to get out of this house Kiah. Seems like you are planning to have me barefoot and pregnant by the time you are ready to leave."

She rolled away from him. They had ended up on the foam mat.

He reached out and pulled her back. His hair had come undone.

She reached up to cup his face in her hands.

"Would it be that bad?" He asked looking deep into her eyes.

The words had just escaped. He couldn't pull them back. But if truths were being told he was loving the pictures that popped up in his head. But getting that feat accomplished would need a major interjection by God almighty. But he was not ready to divulge any of that just yet. He was a man, and that dream was something that consumed him most at times; seeing an offspring that truly belonged to him.

"Stop messing about Kiah!" She pushed at his body. He held her still.

"I am being serious Nia... I have fallen utterly and irrevocably head over heels in love with you."

"Don't be silly Kiah." She offered. Feeling as though something had shifted. It wasn't tangible but she felt life as she knew it was never going to be the same.

He had changed something deep within her from the moment they'd met. She pictured herself when the time came; when he had to leave, and she knew she would be utterly devastated.

"I love you...I love you...I love you...! He repeated softly looking deep into her eyes. He felt his naked body tremble deep within its core. It was cataclysmic. Maybe only to him but he knew that when the time came, he wouldn't be able to leave her.

"Kiah...Please." She pleaded. Letting her hands fall.

"Nia don't let go." He pleaded.

She wrapped her arms about him. "Kiah this is crazy. But I think I feel the same way too." She whispered. "I am so afraid... I have never felt this before."

The next thing she was reciting verse 7 from **Psalm 28** that popped up in her head. **The Lord is my strength and my shield. My heart trusted in him, and I am helped**...

She repeated it over and over just to quieten the raging in her head and heart.

He loved hearing her voice as she recited the bible verse, so much so that he joined in a couple times.

"I love you too Kiah." She said unabashedly.

This time she added nothing else. She just kissed his lips and welcomed him as he kissed her back.

Half an hour later they were strolling outside in the cavernous garden filled with trees, flowers, shrubs and bushes.

They were arm in arm, walking like a seasoned couple on their honeymoon under the scorching afternoon sun.

The only relief was when they walked under the huge frangipani trees with huge leaves that fanned them, along with huge ivy leaves from furled limbs that had wrapped about the trees for comfort. While old-man-beard crawled and lingered down to mischievously listen to their words and laughter.

She told him something that blew his mind; the property had a cellar that led out to the huge gates. She had come across it when they were excavating. He told her he would like to see it.

She promised him that on the way back she would. She pointed out the space she would run if pressed for time. It was a paved circular stone path about 400 yards over from the pool. It encircled the netball/ basketball court.

"Your property is beautiful."

"Thank you, Kiah,"

They avoided the elephant sitting in the middle by playing basketball, chasing each other, going for a walk on the beach.

She took him down the flagstone steps as they listened to the birds and the bees, fluttering colourful butterflies, and scurrying animals.
Nia remembered they had cleared clumps of sea grape trees to afford them the beauty of her private beach they wandered down to.
The water looked so inviting. Before she knew what was happening, he was stripping his clothes.
"Come with me Nia! Trust me...C'mon baby it is so damn hot! I promise I will take care of you...Trust me...Trust me Nia..."
He held out his hands to her.
It only took mere seconds before she placed her hands in his.
"Okay Kiah. I have trusted you the past 24 hours let's see what lies at the end of this rabbit hole."
"Take that off."
"Kiah! I have nothing under there remember?"
"This is your part of the beach, right? So, I would not tell...C'mon Nia, take them off! Let's get in. Plus, salt is good for what ails. What if I go first?"
"Kiah you are a bad influence!"
"I don't see it that way. The look on your face says otherwise.
Now take it off and come in with me."
He helped her out of her clothes. They walked to the water's edge where the waves broke softly as they scurried to the black sand shore.
She screamed as the cool water tickled her toes and caressed her ankles.
He stepped down and told her to do the same.
They were standing mid-waist. He held her hands because she looked as though she would jump out of her skin.
"It's ok sweetheart. Just breathe. I will not let any harm come to you...Trust me...Trust me, Nia." He offered and thanked God the water was being kind. For she had a death grip on his hands.
"Trust me." He coaxed until her body slowly began to relax.
"Want to go lower?"
He treated her as though she were a kid learning to ride a bike. She copied him. They were about breast height now.
"See it isn't that bad, is it?"
She gave him a lopsided grin. "It's nice." She offered. Because it truly was.
"God I'm placing my crazy ass in your hands." She sank deeper. The water came up to her neck.
He laughed. She was growing accustomed to the sound. It warmed her heart.
"Look at you beginning to have fun." He came down to join her. She looked so inviting. He started to feel ravenous. He reached over and kissed her lips.
"Come closer." He urged.
She didn't wait for him to ask again.
He made like he would kiss her, but he whispered in her ears instead. "Do you want to try water sex? Not the shower kind."
"Out...out here!"
"Something else you can tick off the list."

"Who said I had one?" She knew full well that she did. In her head she had ticked a few. She tossed him a confused look.

"Bet you're intrigued now... Come closer Nia...Stand on your toes... Feel what you do to me each time I look at you." He brought her hands down to his harden dick.

"Sweet Jesus Kiah! I never even knew that was possible."

"Anything is possible Nia. You should know this. Especially when it comes to you and me." He pulled her into his arms.

He devoured her lips. When they came up for air he said, "It's all yours Nia...all yours...Do what you want."

They sat on the sand wrapped in each other's arms watching ships go by on the horizon and enjoying the late afternoon sunset.

She wished she had brought a bottle with her of something. She was so damn thirsty. But it felt so good to be held up in his arms as his words played over and over in her head.

She had said it back to him. Only it was the complete and utter truth on her part. She loved the way she could talk with him, the way he held her, the way he listened, the way he made her feel safe, the way he seemed able to read her mind.

"What are you thinking Nia?" He asked. For he had been thinking how he could have just divulged his feelings to her. Fuck!!! He was pussy whipped. He had gone and acted like a damn teenager. But if truth be told he really did love her. He loved the fact that she wasn't hung up about her body, that she didn't hold back and gave as good as she got. He liked that she had done so many things not just for self but for others.

She loved her mother and took nothing for granted. She was so freaking talented. Yes, there was no hidden agenda. She came with her own and didn't secretly need him to further any.

"What you said to me earlier Kiah... Not that I am not flattered. Because seriously I thought that God had given up on me. I have been so anal in telling him what I wanted. I think he just closed his ears. I didn't want someone I had to be fake around. Denying who I am to accommodate. I don't want to share my bed Kiah. I don't like being lied to. Constantly second-guessing myself to the point of calling myself crazy."

She thought of all the many times she had walked in and caught David with one, or even a couple of his fans. Then he would blame her and say that she worked to damn much. He wanted a woman that when he came home, she would be there and ready to cater to his needs; be ready to fuck when he was.

He slapped her around a couple times when she spoke up. He called it **talking back**, which he hated.

"Nia...I just like how you make me feel. I am not here to force you into anything...Well I am a damn liar. Especially since meeting you yesterday and sort off forcing myself on you." He laughed. "I acted out of character... But I think I like this new me. It allowed me to feel for the first

77

time in years...I am going to be thirty years old this year and for the first time in a long, long long while I feel as though something has shifted. Perhaps I am in a great place. Perhaps I am ready to want to become a great friend and father just as my dad is to me. I have no hidden agendas here sweetheart. I pray to God that I never disappoint you. That I can grow to be the man you have wished and prayed for. That I can always keep you as happy as when I hold you in my arms and I watch you each time you give yourself so openly and honestly."

"Kiah..." She turned and kissed his lips. Tears had come and were flowing as she reached up and held him to her.

"Nia, I've got you. I will always treasure you because I love you."

The wind had begun to whisper a bit louder. He longed for a tall cool glass of something. He was parched.

"I think we had better head back. The sun has gone to bed."

Without much thought the musical **The Sound of Music** popped into her head. She started singing **So Long Farewell**...

To her astonishment he began to sing.

Her mouth opened but no words came.

"I am a sucker for a musical. My all-time favourite movie to this day is **Grease**." He'd loved the opportunity given a couple years ago to dance with John Travolta. The guy was truly a wonderful human.

"Nia, I love women." He knew where people would go with that information he'd just shared. But he didn't feel like pretending to be something he wasn't around her. He kissed the top of her head.

They decided to head back. They chased each other until they got outside the house. They entered on the other side via the kitchen where she showed him the doorway that led to the tunnel.

He was like a kid in a candy store. He insisted she go get the keys.

"Let's get something to drink first. I am parched."

She ran up the steps and unlocked the kitchen door and ran to the refrigerator. She poured herself a nice cool glass of water.

He poured one for himself.

"I am going to get change. It gets cold in there." She ran towards her bedroom. She tossed her clothes in the hamper and ran to the shower. Moments later she felt him behind her.

"Kiah please baby no more." She pleaded. But it sounded more like begging.

"I promise I will be ever so gentle."

"Will you?"

"Very gentle." He chuckled close behind her ear. Accepting the squirt of soapy liquid that he lathered in his hands and then proceeded to languidly torture her body as well as her mind.

It was downright sinful the things imagined as they languished the moment away.

He taught her to slow her breathing. He placed a hand on her heart and asked her to do the same to him, as they looked deeply into each other's soul.

Her heart quickened and pulsed so hard she could feel it in her ears. Her entire being shook with a ferocity that she had only felt as they'd placed her mom's coffin in the earth. She could reach out and touch what she was feeling and hold it tight.

It was exquisitely heady, as she learnt how to control her breathing and her mind. He brought her to the purest of ecstasy once she got into it. When she finally allowed herself the pleasure of letting go. She squealed like a little girl who had just learnt how to ride her bike without stabilizers. He told her it was called **Tantric** sex.

"I have only given you the cliff-notes." He laughed. "I learnt the art from a good friend."

They dressed together unashamedly after blow-drying, towelling and applying lotion to themselves.

When she reached for the Vaseline, he lifted her placing her atop the counter, and applied it gently, while she looked at them in the mirror.

The man was totally beguiling. She loved the many faces she portrayed. So much so she became totally overwhelmed and reached out to clutch him to her. The feeling was totally enthralling.

"Kiah Corrington I will fucking cut your dick off if you fuck another woman ever again!" She said with such rawness.

"I am yours Nia." He hoisted her legs and wrapped them around him and did the same with her arms.

"I am yours Nia for as long as you will have me. I am hooked on you girl... I love you. I love you. I love you." He said it with the same rawness. "Believe that Miss Nia."

They kissed like battling animals. When they managed to come up for air, he reached for her panty and bra set and helped her into them. Then into a baby-blue drawstring jumpsuit that was a size larger than her size 6 frame.

While she sorted her hair and applied some gloss. He dressed in RL jeans that hugged his frame delectably and topped it off with blue and white stripe button shirt, then pulled a navy-blue sweater over his head. He took blue suede loafers from the case.

"Do you think too much for the cave?"

"You still want to go down there?"

"Yes, I do!"

"Well let's go before it gets too late."

She reached for a sweater and then his hand.

"Don't get too excited. There is not much to see."

She grabbed her mobile in her bag, an apple and a bottle of water.

He reached in and bit into it.

"Hey get your own." She tossed.

She reached for her blue light trench and stuffed her feet into worn Nike trainers. Her blue trench was her go to when she was strolling outside in the evenings. She smiled knowingly to herself. Well, you never know she thought.

She fiddled with the lock, then the combination, before she pulled the door open. They stepped in and lights flipped on one after the other lighting the way before them. She closed the door.
The smell of must, dirt, and paint hit his nostrils. He wriggled his nose and squinted as they walked on in silence. He half expected to see pirates or snakes, or something come scurrying around each corner that took them higher and higher. But nothing. He just simply enjoyed the walk at the pace they were going.
"I have told you Kiah. It is not much. All we did was make the structure sounder, we puttied the many holes, and added a smoother plaster, proper lighting and security."
One would think she was planned to pull contraband through the blasted thing that led to the beach.
Twenty minutes was all it took to get through it going uphill.
"Great work out huh? Seba and I do this once a week."
"No shit Nia." He spat as he took a sip of his water. "Did you research what it was used for?"
"Yeah. Moving liquor and goods they didn't want the authorities to know about back in the day."
"Was anything found when you discovered the place?"
"Not really. Just some guns, a couple casks of whiskey and gin and a handful of dead bodies..."
"What! No! You're kidding me, right?" He caught the look on her face, as she paused to get a swig of her water.
"You bet your sweet-ass I am!" She cackled. "Seems like you kept expecting cowboy and Indians, or pirates or something to pop out around every corner. But honestly there is nothing down here. I found nothing. We found nothing. Come on, another ten minutes Kiah."
He reached for her hand. She took it. He squeezed hers. She squeezed his.
"I'm glad I met you, Nia."
"Ditto." She said glancing over at him. They walked on in silence.
We are here." She offered pointing up at the door.
Thank God he thought. He was about ready to give up the ghost. He was by no means unfit, but after going so many rounds with her, he was ready to just wrap up with her and call it a night.
She punched the set of numbers into the panel on the wall and the door squeaked as it opened.

When they stepped out it was just near the entrance of her gate to the far side. She punched the numbers again and the door closed. A boulder rolled into place to disguise the door.

It was dark now, and her motion lights came on lighting up the exterior of the deceptively beautiful house coloured a creamy grey.

A gentle breeze whipped up around them causing the colourful bougainvillaea to do a little dance. That was when his eyes caught the writing on the boulder...

In loving memory of a great lady Rosa-Belle Francois.

He came up beside her and reached for her hand.

"You've done her well. I bet you've kept her smiling Nia. What a beautiful homage you have paid to your mother." He said and kissed her hard on the lips.

"Call me corny, but I wish you will love me as much." She whispered, not realising the words had flown from her mouth, as they started up the long lighted driveway.

"I will show you beautiful lady." Was all he offered as he reached for her lips and kissed her deeply. He felt as though she would be the death of him. He wondered how he was ever going to find the strength to walk away when the time came.

81

Chapter Three

Something buzzed noisily in the distance. She raised her head like a gazelle. She realised they had fallen asleep on the sofa.

The last thing she remembered was switching on the television after they had polished off the remainder of the food and drinks from the aunties. They had settled on the movie **How Stella got her Groove Back**...

Some way along the line sleep must have taken over. Thank goodness she had designed the sofas ergonomically, to be able to fit sleepers comfortably.

She reached for the phone. It was the choir director. Seemed as though the lead singer had come down with severe tonsillitis. She wouldn't be able to sing on Sunday and highly unlikely for the Extravaganza on Saturday evening.

"Mr Pascal...I can't...I have so much work piled up to get to. What time is it?" Her eyes chased the clock. It winked back that it had just gone seven am. She bolted upright. She had slept through her alarm for 5:30. This time on a Saturday morning she would have already been in the shower.

"Shit! Shit! Shit!"

"If I didn't think you capable Nia, I would not have put you forward. By the way didn't Sebastin pass along the message?"

"No, he didn't." She snapped. Making a mental note to sling him up when next she saw him.

"Shit!" She shouted prancing around to get out of the throw that wrapped itself about her ankle.

"Calm down Nia." He said, untangling her and folding the blanket and putting it back in place.

"Shush!" She snapped pointing to the phone.

She walked away from him over to the kitchen. "Fuck!" She screamed stubbing her toe on the step. Her mind immediately abuzz with the things she needed to do.

She hadn't even unpacked or stored the things she needed to finish or end some of the outfits she had in the works. She wanted a cup of coffee she flipped the kettle on. "Mr. Pascal church is one thing...the Extravaganza...?"

"Again, Nia if I didn't think you capable, I wouldn't throw you under the bus." He said in his sing-song Southern drawl. "You are very capable. I don't know why you didn't accept it in the first place."

"Because I wanted Chenoweth to get the break she keeps praying for." Nia added. "I thought we were clear on that. Mr. Pascal no. No, I can't do it. I don't have the time."

She reached for a cup and dumped a good heaping of coffee in.

She felt his hand on hers. He reached for another cup and made her the coffee. He placed the cup in front of her.

"Please Miss Nia. You know I don't beg. Plus, you are magical on the stage love. You know if I didn't think you capable, I would have cast my net elsewhere."

"Mr Pascal! You know how…"

"Sweetheart c'mon. I have nothing else to offer that I haven't already given. Please do this for me and I swear I will be indebted to you for the rest of my life."

"I will take that IOU." Realising she wasn't winning the battle. "Can I call you back a little later? I just need a coffee. I am running late as is."

"I figured." He chuckled. "Heard there is a darling specimen buzzing on your bush."

"Mr Pascal!!!" she stammered, clicking the phone off as she stood there dumbfounded. What the hell! Did everyone on the island already knew about Kiah?

"Anything I can help with?" He asked coming up to her and pulling her into his arms. He was beginning to like waking up in her arms and having her next to him.

"He wants me to sing lead on Sunday and at the Dance Extravaganza on Saturday evening!"

"What is the problem, Nia? We know you can do it."

"Kiah, I have too many things to do. Not to forget you… No! No no no! Do not even think of it. I am going to work today but before that I must go and sort somethings here in the office."

"I can help. Just tell me what you would like me to do."

An hour and forty-five minutes later they were standing in the shower having a good old steamy make-out session. He had helped to unpack her suitcase and took things down to the laundry room on the second floor where she had given him a quick tour.

They had taken what she needed for work to her white Volkswagen parked in one of three garage spaces.

They also had breakfast; he made omelettes and toast and cut fresh fruits they had eaten al fresco.

He scolded her, "breakfast is the most important meal of the day sweetheart. So, let us start it by eating healthily."

Another forty-five minutes and they were walking out the door just as her mobile started again.

It was Madame Cruz… She and her team were beginning to be a gigantic pain in her ass. She had promised on numerous occasions to toss the towel in for them.

However, they were one of her gigantic accounts. So, she swallowed her pride and promised to be at the academy within the hour.

Shit!!! Nia thought as she pulled the door shut behind them.

Thank goodness she had gone for the dress she had picked yesterday. She added a light pink bolero jacket to compliment it. Then piled her braids high atop her head in a knot. She took great care with her makeup. That done she finished off with adding silver complimentary pieces of jewellery.

"You are beautiful." He said when she walked out of her dressing room. She looked as though she had stepped of the pages of a high-end fashion magazine. He said as much to her. He learnt she produced a catalogue of her fashions in **Belle** with her partner Seba.

"I mean it woman. You are gorgeous!" He swooped down upon her and lifted her high in the air. She tossed her arms about his neck and kissed his forehead. They stayed that way for a moment before he placed her back on her feet.

"You are too." She squealed.

He wore beige ankle length chinos, buttoned down white shirt and tan espadrilles. He could pass for a **J Crew** model she thought for the hundredth time.

Perhaps she could talk him into sitting. Although she was certain she could paint him by heart.

His hair was done and looked quite pleasing in a tidy ponytail. He had used some of her hair products. She reminded him they had different textures of hair.

"Will you love me any less?" He asked smoothing the carotene oil in his hair.

She could not resist. She had walked over to him and kissed him hard on the lips.

"You are my white man. Only mine you got that?"

"Yes ma'am." He said saluting. Then he swathed her back side. "Just you wait until I get you home later Miss Nia."

"Promises promises Mister." She teased. Because she felt bold. So, she pinched his ass.

"I swear... No, I am going to be good and let you get to work. But you will most definitely pay. I can assure your sexy ass of that."

"Oh Kiah. The real world beckons."

I will miss the hell out of you sweetheart."

"I will miss you too." She kissed his lips. She had seen him apply some concoction in a tube to them. "Yum yum yummy." She murmured, smacking her lips.

When they got to the car, he walked to the passenger side because he agreed she would drive. He had an updated license. So, she told him he could have the car while she was at her meeting. Even while she was at the office.

He told her he would stay with the aunties after she met with them.

She told him about Charles and gave him the digits. Charles was her taxi - driver when she didn't want to be bothered; like working late, running in and out of meetings, emergencies...

He asked about the dance academy and the showcase.

She explained that the **Extravaganza** was held every year to raise funds for scholarships, and for students wanting to study abroad.

He recalled his auntie had mentioned something about it. He had contributed.

There was nothing he would not do for the woman. She had taken a chance on him when all the odds were stacked high against him, and most especially with his dad.

"Want to listen to music?" She asked. "You would have to settle for mine…"

He shrugged.

She hit the button. **Third World** permeated the interior. She could not resist. She began to sing along happily. She even forgot after a while that he was sitting there beside her.

This was her thing to do when she was alone. She would have the windows down so the tree lined streets with its dense foliage would caress her lovingly.

Twice she made to do it. Then she caught a glimpse of him laid back against her plush interior and thought why disturb him. Because he looked like he was resting.

"Want me to turn it down?"

"No. Do your thing Nia. I like hearing your voice. It soothes me."

"Flatterer." She tossed. "You are good for my ego."

"Glad I can be. Now keep singing."

Moments later she slowed the car down. He opened his eyes and came up in a sitting position.

She called out to someone who waited to cross.

"Miss D! Miss D! Come… Come!"

She paused for the woman with a basket atop her head and backpack on her back to cross the road.

He noticed there wasn't any stoplights or crossings. Guess this was the life they told him about.

"Beautiful Nia! Lord-have-mercy! As I live and breathe. Glad you back. It been too long. How you do gel?"

"I'm good. I'm good. Yourself?" She asked the woman. Genuinely wanting to know.

She had missed peanut Friday last night. Hopefully she hadn't put a price just yet on what was in the basket.

"I got everything. Whatever you want is yours. I had a late start today."

She brought the basket off her head and leaned it against the door. That was when her eyes collided on Kiah.

"You got comp'ny?"

"Yes Miss D." She offered nothing else as the woman waited. She tossed questioning eyes over into Kiah's.

"Kiah meet Miss D… Miss D this is my friend from the US. He is here for festival this year."

"Good to meet you Kiah." She pushed her hand through the window.

"Hope we do not disappoint for festival. You in from foreign and all."

"Good morning, Miss D. I am here for some relaxation with friends more than anything else." Which was true now that he had met her.

"I'll take all that's in the basket." She said and reached for her purse. She whipped out $200.00 and handed it to the woman.

She beamed just like someone had shoved a lightbulb up her rear.

He looked questioningly at her wondering what the hell was in this magic basket.

He whispered as much, as the lady took the cash and stuffed it into her fanny pouch.

"Nothing sinister Kiah." She laughed. "Miss D sells the best parched cashews and peanuts, as well as spring onions, mint thyme, parsley..."

"Rasta I could get you a bag or two." Miss D interjected. "That is if you want the proper shit."

"Don't you even think of it!" she tossed across to Kiah.

He was fighting laughter. His face had coloured like a strawberry.

"What! I am listening to Miss D!"

"Never mind Miss Nia. Just call me." She rattled off her number to him. "By the way want any sugar-cake?"

"I'll take a bag. They will eat them at the office. Just add the rest to my account. "By the way want a drop?"

"I would not refuse. Even though you know I like my feet planted firmly on Jah's soil." The woman tossed as she clambered out of her laden backpack.

Kiah climbed out and walked around to open the door for the woman.

"Eh eh! He been raised Miss Nia! He is a nice friend. Not bad on the eyes either." She said when she climbed in.

"I know right! Shush!" Nia said as she felt a tingling.

When he got back in the car, they were acting like silly schoolgirls. After she came up for air, she asked.

"How is Tafari doing?"

"He ire you know. I must tell him you back. By the way how come you got them?" She pointed to his dreadlocks.

"I got them by a dare couple years ago. But if truth be told I have grown accustomed to them. People never seem to know what to make of me."

"I see. But for real they suit you. They look neat. I ain't never seen no white boy hair look so tidy with dreads."

"Thanks Miss D."

"So other than Miss Nia you got any family here?"

"Do you know Lady Bellot Corrington? She is my aunt."

"Fire and Brimstone!" She fanned herself with the colourful wrap of her skirt. She looked from him to her and back again. "Well, sah!"

She winked at Nia. "That is good stock. So, you must be too."

"Thank you."

"What business you into? Just tell me it positive and not no shit."

"I'm a real estate broker and developer." He offered.

86

"Mmmmh...I like that. You like anything to develop round here?"

"I sure do." He offered easily looking over at her.

"I see you... You are growing on me Ras Kiah. She is spun gold."

"Miss D do you think I don't know this?"

"Glad you do Ras Kiah. Glad you do. But we must chat again on this estate developer stuff. Because I know a few places that can stand a facelift. Pump some life into this tired relic."

"I like that. It's a date. That is if it's ok with her."

"Miss Nia like anything for the betterment of the island because she is the heart string to so many projects around. She supports **Meals on Wheels;** food is provided 6 times a day for the elderly and shut-in seven days a week."

Nia's phone interrupted. She reached for her headpiece.

Thankfully, he picked it up and plugged it in.

"Thank you, Kiah." She offered. She liked how he saw to the things she needed.

She had forgotten a promise; to meet with Audra the Prima Ballerina on island. She had told her she would meet with her as soon as she got back from her trip. She hadn't remembered.

Now the diva was contacting her. While she spoke to the spoilt brat.

Miss D continued to chat to Kiah who had turned himself in his chair and was focusing his attention on what she had to say.

She told him about **Meals on Wheels**, **Pass it On** and some of the other charities Nia started. She also told him of the **Fun Day** that was coming up. He listened in amazement. Making mental notes.

He tuned back in when she said, "Only she knows why these things are so close to her. But we thank Jah for her. Her mama was my best-friend. When my mama threw me out for falling for the wrong fella and I had nowhere to go, it was her mama that took me in.

We slept on the same floor, atop the same clothes bag, under her granny's roof. To know Miss Nia and her mama is like knowing Jah. They are angels.

"So, what is it that you do?"

"Oh, I run the **Meals on Wheels** program in her mama's name. Did she tell you she left us in a tragic way? I still miss her to this day Rasta. When she exited this world, I wanted to follow her, but I knew she would not have wanted that. Especially when she needed me to be there for her."

She pointed to Nia. "They were so close those two. Saying it, makes it sound so simple. Cause they had a love that was so noticeable. They say parents are supposed to love their kids, but theirs was special. It even transcended mother and daughter." She dabbed at her eyes.

Both picturing the woman and the girl. Each in different scenarios.

They had entered a colourful part of town, where he saw lots of Rastafarians milling about. The colours were so vibrant they dazzled as everyone moved about in the sunshine. It was like stepping into the rainbow.

Stalls were laden with beaded accessories, fruits and vegetables, cloth and garments, mementos and gifts...

"I'll get out here." She tapped Nia lightly.

She wrapped up the conversation about dresses and fabric, saying to the person that had her face twisting into a kaleidoscope of many frowns, she even bit into her lip and chewed on it a few times.

"Miss D I can see that **Safari Square** is hopping. Maybe on our way back we can pick up some Ital for Kiah...Oh gosh come to think of it..."

"Ras Kiah you feel Ital. No problem I get you a bag ready. Let me see if they have."

"No Miss D I have a couple of meetings."

"Then perhaps later, on my way to **Costume Tent** I will drop some off. I will call when I am ready."

"Thank you, Miss D."

"Welcome to **Safari Towne** Ras Kiah... Ain't it a sight? Lots of blood sweat and tears, but we got it this far. My son and his family along with my grand-children Jah bless. They live up dey."

She pointed to a huge gate coloured in red, yellow and green. The symbol of a huge mane lion and a flag at the top.

"By the way Miss Nia. Please tell that nephew of mine a visit is long overdue."

"Will do." Nia promised. She did not enjoy getting involved with Seba's family drama. They were too rigid in their beliefs at times. So, things could get a bit too dicey, and she didn't like it.

"Do you know my nephew?"

"No, I'm afraid I don't."

"So, you've not met her conscience? You've not met her Seba?" "You mean?" He looked to the woman in confusion.

"Yes Ras Kiah. There is no him without her and vice-versa. The two are as thick as thieves. She became his solace when his mama died. God rest her soul."

"Yes, I have met Seba. Interesting person."

"Interesting is not the word that many used to describe him. But because of her he can do all things."

"Because of us." Nia corrected her. "He has always been my strength."

"I know child. You two have always been inseparable."

"Because he knows me and respects me for me. Plus you know he's been blessed with the best eyes ever for fashion."

"Jah!"

"Rastafari." They chorused together. It was Nia's turn to look him up and down."

"Nia, I have friends too."

They all had a good laugh.

She slowed the car down.

Kiah exited the car and held the door opened so he could take her things out.

The two chatted for a while longer and then hugged.

"Miss Nia…Ras Kiah you two take care of each other. I will see you soon with the Ital." Miss D concluded.

They were now in the heart of the bustling town; cars and people buzzed about noisily, as they came upon the crossroad.

He spotted a beautiful pewter fountain with water spouting from the four points and a gigantic emerald balancing from the fingers of a protruding hand, smack-dab in the middle.

"That's interesting." He offered pointing to the sculptor.

"That's our Hand of Hope. Many claims it has brought them good luck when they've offered it coins.

"Like the **Trevi Fountain** in Italy?"

"I suppose so. I have never been. But yes, it sounds like the hot water pond we have here on the island as well. Where a couple veins from the Montserrat Soufriere Volcano have extended her arms in friendship."

She smiled at the recollection of the many healing that most has claimed from the pond. But whatever keeps people full of faith and holding on she had no axe to grind.

"I will take you one day if you let me, Nia." He offered looking over at her.

"I look forward to that." She said, not taking it as gospel. Because she and Seba promised that they would indeed take the trip too one day.

Kiah smiled. He had caught the disbelief that scampered across her face. He would make her belief he thought to himself.

Cars seemed to be everywhere as they went around the impressive structure. He didn't miss the different ethnicity of people as they happily milled about dressed in colourful skirts and dresses, as well as hats and wraps.

Some had bags and baskets atop their heads, or bottles and even an animal…

Music echoed all around when she brought the windows down, and an array of aromas accosted them. It made him so ravenous.

He thought of some of the many islands he had visited and wandered around in.

"To the left is going towards our shop **Belle**. Going straight ahead will take you to **Corrington's,** and this right takes us to the academy. I can run you down, but it will make me late…"

"Don't bother about it. Just keep going. I will wait until you get sorted at the academy Nia. I'm on holiday remember?"

"Bless you Kiah. I promise I will get done as quickly as possible. Well, sort of. Those two can be a blasted handful when they want to be. I can't afford to burn bridges right now."

"You go do you Nia."

Five minutes later after they passed lots of modern and impressive structures, houses, and apartments and restaurants as well as cafes on either side of the road. They pulled up alongside a white pillowed wall being adored by beautiful well-trimmed flora and fauna.

The sign outside read **Emerald City Arts & Theatre.** She called out to the security guard who looked like he was being addressed by royalty.

"Hello Gavin. I have meetings with Madam and Audra. I am running a tad late. So, if you can fast track me, I would be ever so grateful."

"As long as you bring me a nice cool one on your way-out Miss Nia." He said as the wide gates parted, and they drove into a crowded parking area on both sides.

It reminded him of the New York library. Students were exiting cars, running up steps, and disappearing. Some were standing about clad in their eclectic uniforms and costumes chatting, some were dancing routines...

"Welcome to **ECAT** Kiah. Our state-of-the-art dance, theatre and music school. This was a long time in the works, but we have completed it. It took us five years. But we are a rivalled state of the art academy. We have students coming in from all over the Caribbean and oversees to attend."

"Impressive. I can't wait to see the inside. What do you need me to help with?"

"Just the sketch bag in the back."

Thank goodness she had done some major upgrading when she was away on holiday.

He took the huge bag and waited for her while she grabbed hers.

His eyes went to the two lifelike ballerinas flanking either side of the entrance way. Then they took in the emerald meld in the top of the building, where statues in various artistic poses appeared to be pulling you in from the plaster.

A couple of the students called out her name and came over for a hug. Others wanted to know where Seba was, and who Kiah was.

She introduced him.

Some looked to him as though he was a celebrity. Others like they wanted to haul him off to their dens. Some with questioning glares as though to ask what the hell he is doing with her.

Some asked for his photo; he promised he would accommodate as soon as he could because she had a meeting with Madame.

"She is on the war path Miss Nia. So, watch your back." One student called over.

Nia thanked them, and they hustled up the steps and into the cavernous building with its massive sliding door. Inside was even more impressive.

A throbbing restaurant called **Lush** was at their left where the smells wafting out to greet them made him hungrier.

The sun outside had forgotten to play nice. He was sweaty and could go for a tall ice-cold glass of something.

90

Reception was to the right. A lovely Asian female with rouge red lips greeted them.

"Good day Ajanta. Can you please...?" The woman shifted her head and averted her eyes; to let Nia know she would be swooped down upon like a hawk by a tall very slender raven-haired woman, and another with flowing salt and pepper hair.

They wore all black that covered their legs that seemed to have emerged from their armpits.

Kiah half expected to see a broomstick, or two in the midst as they regimentally walked down the steps towards them.

"Madam..." Nia said and offered her hand. "I apologise for being late." The older elegant woman took the hand, as she looked quizzically over at Kiah.

"Let this not happen again Nia." Her voice dripped with tightness, as her predatory eyes took in Kiah. "You are?"

"Kiah...I am Kiah Madame." He offered feeling as though he was the new boy in front of the classroom. He offered nothing else. He wasn't even supposed to be there let alone being introduced.

She had told him about the restaurant, and he had looked forward to slipping away before her people arrived.

"Kiah... as in Kiah Corrington Lady Bellot's nephew?" She asked nudging the younger beautiful girl slightly.

She sprang into action as though she was unwound. She swooped down on Kiah.

"I'm Audra..." She extended her hand artfully. "I'm the prima ballerina here at ECAT. Will you be attending the showcase? Oh, Kiah please say you will!" She purred coquettishly.

So, this is the nephew? Madame Cruz thought as she looked him up and down.

He was quite pleasing to the eye she thought. Remembering that Bellot had mentioned her nephew would be visiting the island.

She had pressed for a date and time; that she'd paid dearly for at the immigration office.

She had also received word that he was seen hanging around Katho's niece like fly to shit.

Well, she was not going to have it. Audra needed this shift in her career as well as her life. Seeing she was always going for many of the dead beats and playboys on the island that had nothing to offer.

She'd said as much to the silly girl. "Get your hooks sunk deep within him and forget all other male on the island. Bag him before he gets back on that airplane to California."

"Why?" The stupid girl asked.

"Because I am telling you to. Plus, he is as rich as God." She shouted at her. "And we will never have to worry about cash ever again, you stupid girl. Because we would be set for the rest of our lives once you hitch your wagon to his."

"Mother!"

"Grow up!" She'd spat at the girl. "Leave puppies to mama wannabes. Bag yourself a real man and stop being a door mat for spoilt assholes." She pushed the conversation to the back of her mind, as she gave her the signal to work her beguiling magic. Beauty only lasts for a short while, and dancer's feet will fail as you get older. So, females like them had to rely on their brains sooner or later to stay viable.

Thank God she'd gotten her claws stuck deep in one of the riches old expat money bags on the island. She smiled at the memory of when his heart finally gave out a couple months after they'd gotten married. Thank God she was pregnant. She never had to have sex again without choice.

She shook herself together, and back to the annoying girl she had poured everything she had into. Stupid girls who grew into even more stupid females who paid no attention to fading youth. It was not for the want of trying. God knows she had tried. But she had drunk from her father's cup of lust and good times.

"Mother... Mother will Kiah be joining the meeting?"

"No! I don't think..." Nia tried to interject. But they had tag teamed her.

"Nonsense!" Madam re-joined them. "Nia let Audra take Kiah around and give him a personal tour of the school. You and I will discuss the changes with Lucien. I am sure Kiah will me in great hands."

She hooked her arms through Nia's and led her away. "Let's make our way to the hall. Lucien is there working on the new routines with his students."

"I hope he remembers the showcase is on Saturday?" Her eyes wandered off to the retreating backs of Audra and her man.

They were heading towards LUSH. She wanted to run after them and punch the skinny witch in her face.

Choose your battle Nia-Belle. She turned half expecting to see her mama. "Come along Nia. Let's not dawdle."

"Yes Madame." Nia tossed as she walked alongside the women whose black kitten heels seemed to summon her attention.

"So, tell me Nia. Have you been spending time with Kiah? Corrington since he got to the island?"

"Yes. The aunties would like me to show him around the island."

"Perhaps I can make it easier for you...Why don't you allow my Audra to show him around the island seeing as you will be rather busy."

Nia wished she could say what popped into her mind, but her mama's words warned her again as she entered the semi dark auditorium, and Lucien's voice bellowed all around them through the microphone.

"Something to think about." She offered. Not missing the look, she received from the woman, as though she was a blockage in whatever scheme she was cooking up.

"Seize the moment, Nia. Believe me Audra would be a great influence on our Kiah Corrington. Let me remind you again of all the free time you will have to sort that calendar of yours."

"Thank you, Madam. I will ruminate on your words."
"You will thank me, Nia. That is if you look at it rationally... Now Lucien wanted to have a last look at the costumes. Did you remember to bring the sketches?"
"Yes. I have them right here."
"Great." The woman pulled her through the door, and they walked into the semi-lighted room with Lucien's voice echoing throughout the room from the speakers.

Nia and Lucien went back and forth on the sketches while he conducted. He had sketches of the stage scenes and held them up to her sketches as he explained concepts.
She quickly nipped and tucked and enhanced...
To the point where all she heard was excellent... bullshit...better... fabulous...
He would pause to yell at the dancers and in another breath back at her. But when all was said and done, she got the concept he wanted.
She indulged him even though his voice was beginning to grate on her last nerve. He had the attention span of a flee. But she pushed through it and changed the sketches.
Finally, they came up with a plan. She promised they would have something tangible by Monday.
She now had to go back to the office and convince the team to redo what was already done. Lord-have-mercy on me she thought.
But she got it. All his insane thoughts. She got them all. Every asinine one. Because if truths were being told she could be exactly like the madman. Bringing creativity to life.

Her head reeled, and her body felt like it was tied in knots. Plus, she was so hungry, and craved a Kiah fix.
She looked around and noticed they still had not re-joined them from earlier.
Neatly she placed things back in her sketch bag and gathered the rest of her things. It suddenly dawned on her that the call from Audra had nothing at all to do with costumes. Seemed it was more about Kiah.
Madam was now leading the class of two ballerinas on the stage.
Seemed the mission was to keep her away from her daughter and Kiah.
At times she asked questions that were already asked, or she had her go over some pointless correction they'd already sorted.
Nia so wanted to tell her to get her conniving-ass out of her face, but she bit her tongue reminding herself that trouble never last always.
That thought now prompted her to take the opportunity to slip out of the auditorium.
She also longed for a chef's salad at LUSH along with a glass of guava spritz lemonade.

Nia walked out into the beautiful eco-friendly atrium with its huge skylight; the sun was shining upon the panelled tinted glass; that served as a shade, so the sun did not obliterate the plants in the pond hanging out below, accompanying the mesmerising fountain with its many features that lighted up beautifully at night.

There were also life-size pewter statues strategically placed in various poses throughout the hallway, along with benches and lovely seated areas that offered one a chance to sit and commiserate with others, self or with the numerous pots of tall plants and flowers.

The state-of-the-art building was truly beautiful and was among one of the islands' treasures for many visitors. It consisted of a museum you could explore along with a gift and souvenir shop.

There were also a beautiful, scented rose and bougainvillea garden with so many unusual colours, along with many indigenous shrubs and waterlilies in a pond.

The academy also offered dorm rooms to accommodate some students and staff along with other amenities. Last, but not least.

A majestic theatre and impressive stage boosting the latest in technology to aid in concerts, stage productions, weddings, balls, or some governmental shindig that the island needed to enhance.

That was why she had thought to host the **Masquerade & Auction** on New Year's Eve right there in the atrium.

Nia sighed and finally forced herself to walk on. She had to get food to replenish what those inside had taken. Then she could singlehandedly take on that beautiful skinny bitch when she returned with **her man**. What-the @&*$! Whoa! Where had that come from? She stumbled blindly towards the smells that were making her dizzy.

A few people called out to her and motioned her over. She was not in the mood. She made the sign for phone and walked to a corner table in the back and seated herself between tall ginger lilies and bird of paradise.

When the waiter came over, she mouthed her order. He returned with her drink. She thanked him and dived in just as her mobile went off.
It was Kiah.

She was tempted to ignore the blasted thing; let him stew for his disappearing act with the fabulous looking supermodel/ ballet dancer. She pictured herself walking up to the bitch and punching her in the face!!! But she could not give into the temptation.

So, she quickly reached out and picked up the thing. She told him where she was. He promised to be with her within the minute.

True to his word. He walked in and came over to her table and kissed her sweetly, and hungrily on the lips.

"I've missed you, Nia." He truly did. He kissed her again. He could feel the hesitancy on her lips at first, but he managed to coax her over to his side. "You have not missed me?"

94

"You know I did Kiah. I hated that you left with that Amazonian beauty. She seemed like she was staking claim."

"I only have eyes for you, my beauty. You know that."

"Yeah right. What were you doing for so long?" She asked knowing she sounded like a jealous shrew. But she did not care. She was not going to give him up without a good fight. Of which she had not done in a long, long, long damn time. But she was certain if the need did arise... What!!! She had come to damn far and worked to damn hard for her sanity. She was not about to hop back into the devil's convertible. No siree!

She reached for her phone.

"Nia...Nia...Calm down sweetheart. I have no interest in her."

"Says the spider to the fly."

"Honestly sweetheart. I only have eyes for you." He hoped he had made it quite clear when she tried to kiss him when they were in the garden. He told her he was already seeing someone. She had seductively tried to coax it out of him by saying all was fair in love and war.

He stepped away from her. He also said to her that he would end the visit if she continued down that path. He reminded her there was someone out there for her, but it was not him.

"Seriously?" Nia asked. "But she is so gorgeous!"

"Not interested. I don't like females who think the world owes them something because they are beautiful."

"But the woman is gorgeous! Those eyes, and her lips..."

"Nia I am not interested in her. Yes, I saw all those things, but I only want you. I don't play games. Plus, my attention span only permits me one woman. That way I can concentrate on giving her all the best of me. Seems like I am lagging though. I've missed you, Nia." He reached for her hand.

She snatched it away. A look of immense crossness marred her face.

"You hungry?"

"For you? You know the answer to that..."

"Kiah please." She spat.

"Nia... You have no need to be jealous."

"I'm not jealous Kiah!"

"Really?" He laughed. "You are wound so tight in its arms."

She kissed her teeth and continued to jab at her phone.

"Nia I only have eyes for you. No one else. I recognise a great human being in you and there is no way I am planning on messing things up. I love you and only you woman. Only you. But seriously she showed me around this impressive place and gave me some of the history behind it. We then strolled the gardens after we had a drink. All boring after the tour really, because all I wanted was to see you, be with you. I just wanted you."

"Kiah..." She placed the phone down. She took his hand. "Thank you." She truly meant it. David the cagey bastard skipped across her mind. She pushed it away. "I ordered salad." She offered, feeling silly for her reaction.

He motioned the waiter over. I'll have a tuna melt and fries. Can I have what she is having?" He pointed to her chilled glass.

"So have you sorted your business?"

"Thank God. I just wanted something to eat before we head out.

He rewrote the piece, and the costumes needed some tweaking. Lucien is such a drama queen. He is a bloody genius though. But I am looking forward to seeing the back of him. Such a contradiction."

She explained that the man had met someone a couple of years ago when he was on holiday. The partner wanted him closer, so he was giving up the gig and moving on.

Thankfully, they did not have to wait long for their food. They ate hungrily and played footsie under the table, like proper horny teenagers.

Then something popped into her head. She paused and riffled through her bag and produced a pen. She used it to scribble and sketched away on a couple of napkins. She did not look up again until she had captured whatever it was that was toying with her.

She then sucked her glass dry and motioned the waiter over.

By the time she paid. He was ready.

He called his auntie when they got to the car. He waited as she delivered a lunch bag to the guy at the gate.

Ten minutes later they pulled into the busy parking lot of **Corrington's.** The four-storey white concrete building was awash with shoppers going in and coming out. It brought back memories of his parents' store, and him helping on the weekends. Getting his first kiss from Charlie; a much older girl who worked the cosmetic department.

It made him smile. Most of his memories at **Corrington's LA** wasn't bad. It's just that he wanted more, and he ran to find out what else he could do before regret took root.

Thank God for his grandfather as well who had diversified and had bought shares in a property development scheme.

So many things had transpired in his growth. Thank goodness for the woman he called auntie; for she had always been ahead of her brother; his dad.

She learnt to concoct lotions, soaps and gels, and even perfume and diffusers from the flowers, fruits and plants from an early age. A skill she was taught by great-grandmother, who learnt from her grandmother...

Nia too went back in her mind's eye of coming to the store with her mama, and then her auntie, who had worked in the shoe shop: Bata then for years. Before it became the world-renowned Corrington's.

Seemed as though she had met Lady B when she was vacationing on the island with her family. They claimed it was love at first sight.

The story was that Lady B went back to LA and couldn't get auntie out of her mind. So, she kept returning until one day she decided she would remain indefinitely.

Many claimed she was disowned by her parents for her foolhardiness. Years later a fatal plane crash saw her inheriting a lump sum; she used to purchase the shoe shop Bata when it came up for sale.

Both women then took the shoe shop and sent it pummelling into the 21st century.

Corrington's boosted a thriving high-end cosmetics and fragrance department, along with fine jewellery on the first floor.

The second floor caters in women's and men's apparel, shoes and accessories for all, including intimates; lingerie for woman and under things.

Third floor held the children's department; clothes toys and shoes, as well as household goods.

Offices and staff quarters were found on the fourth floor.

All this highlighted by an elaborate wooden staircase with lattice railing from floor to ceiling that would stop you in your tracks and slowly stole your breath away as you follow with your eyes all the way to the top.

Not to forget the ostentatious and most intricate crystal chandeliers that extended like serene angels; but was the home of the most state-of-the-art security cameras; that followed your every move, and observed all that happened in, out, and around the ostentatious store.

The aunties deflected yet again, by installing a luxurious glass lift that gave you a 360-degree view, ascending and descending. This was the highlight for many going into the store in. Including her.

Nia thoroughly enjoyed the views from all angles, even now if truth be told.

Air conditioning was later added as a bonus to visitors and even islanders who wished to cheat the sun by popping in when it was sweltering outside.

Corrington's was a work of art and was also on the **'must see'** tourist attractions.

Many shoppers called out to her when they got out of the car. She waved. She promised to pick him up when she was done at the office so she could give him a personal tour of her shop.

They kissed quickly as they spotted his aunt coming out of the building. She was still a remarkable looking woman. She always reminded Nia of shorter version of Catherine Chancellor from the **Young and the Restless**. She was dressed in a sleek and stylish cut lavender suit with white top, finished off with black court shoes. Her raven black hair was pulled back in its usual chignon when she was working.

Sometimes Nia thought the woman should be working as a Vogue editor.

"Hello you two. You are late." She kissed them both.

"Sorry auntie."

"You are not staying?" She asked Nia. "You have the nerve after doing a no-show yesterday. You are slipping. You have never done this before."
"I am so very sorry Ma'am... It would never happen again. I promise we will be here with bells on bright and early on Monday morning."
"You had better. You know time is money Miss Nia." She chided the girl liking how she had her on the hook.
"Thank you, Auntie."
"Hush now sweetheart. I know it wasn't so much your fault. But I will make him pay dearly to overlook this."
"Geez auntie. Have mercy." He leaned in to kiss her cheeks.
"How is that crazy Lucien?"
"He wants us to rework a portion of the costumes."
"Does that over-indulgent fool realise that the showcase is this weekend?"
"I know. But after watching the second act with him today. I can see where his vision is heading. So, I promised I would have something for him by Monday."
"I hope your invoice will be heavier Nia. The man is impossible. Thank goodness it is his last run. Creativity we will miss. All his other shenanigans." She threw her hands in the air dramatically. "Hezekiah Carter Corrington the III.... Tsk tsk tsk... You've done a disappearing act." She wrapped him up in her arms. "But I understand. It's not like I didn't do the same."
"I'm sorry Auntie. But I find myself simply just wanting to be with her. I will visit often I promise. But where she is, is where I will be."
"I understand. I will take you anyhow I can get you. By the way. Has he been a good boy?" She winked over at the girl.
"Yes, ma'am he has." She stuttered. Praying for a hole to just open. The only good thing was that her auntie had not come out.
Only God knows what the woman would have said.
"No, he has not. I do not believe that."
"Auntie B! Gosh somethings are sacred!" He feigned innocence. It made Nia smile. He wagged his finger at her. She turned her back.
"Which is why you had better think of putting a ring on it because Katho will be chasing you with her gun if you hurt her."
"Auntie B!"
"What! I am speaking the simple truth. Now come on in."
She bent to whisper in his ear. "We can find something that suits her. Nia, we will see you later then?"
"Bye Auntie. Tell auntie K I will see her soon. She is, okay?"
The woman assured her she was. She waved them off and climbed back into her car.

Before she could park, Seba was out to greet her.
"Good afternoon sleepy head. This is late for you. We didn't even think we would see you here for the weekend." He wrapped her up in his arms. "Wow! You are glowing girl!"
"What the hell are you on about?" She asked him as he looked her over like he knew something she did not. "You got me in trouble with Madam."

98

"Shit! I forgot all about the old hag. I take it you had to come pronto to the academy." He feigned her uppity accent. "What did they want?"

"To redo the **Oceania Graveyard** sequence. So, a whole new costume line Seba."

"What? Do they realise that the show is this weekend?"

"I swear to you if I hear that question again, I will scream. However, I promised one last redo. That we will have it ready by Monday the latest."

"More freak in-money, right? Think of all the materials we will have wasted."

"Not wasted Seba. I had an idea after he showed me the changes. I get it. Which is why I think what I did will get you on board."

"Fees? You had better charge for the redo Nia. No charity here. He cannot act like an asshole then think he walks away smelling sweet."

"Of course, Kiah. Shit! I mean Seba."

"I bet you did. Think I did not hear how he had you purring like a kitten last night! Bitch you didn't hang up the phone! I heard you!"

"No!" She was shocked. "You heard?" She asked as she felt the colour crawling about her face. "You heard it Seba?"

"You betcha!"

"Oh God Seba!"

"That good huh?"

"Flippin brilliant!" She whispered devilishly. "Seba I never..."

"Dang girl!" He wrapped her up in his arms again. "I am so happy for you. Even though I am jealous as heck."

"Seba he even told me he loves me."

"He did! Dang! That fine ass does move fast. But why are you so shocked? Girl, look how long you been misused. You deserve this! Now enjoy."

"But seriously, did you hear me Seba?" She asked in disbelief as she brought her hands to her face.

"Yes, I did! But I didn't listen for long though. I was so shocked I threw the dang phone down."

"Oh my God Seba! I didn't know you could...I mean...Seba he makes me so so so..."

"Yes, girl it's about time. Glad you getting those dusty shelves cleaned. And just so you know, I will not. Emphasis on not be home for the weekend. I am staying in town."

"Seba! But seriously you don't have to do that."

"Yes, I do. Now stop. I want you to enjoy yourself. Don't worry about me. I will be fine."

"By the way I picked up auntie D and dropped her at Safari City. She says she wants to see you, talk to you."

"When I get a chance. Now come let's get some work done. Ooh! Guess who has been blowing up your phone?"

She stopped in her tracks. "Who?" she asked, feeling like something had crawled along her back.

99

"That vampire bitch Audra. Sounding like you two are besties. She says she would like to take you and Kiah out for lunch. Makes me suspicious as hell. Because you know she doesn't buzz around males unless she could drain their bank accounts."

"You should have seen how she and her mother were buzzing around him at the academy. She even pushed me aside so Audra could sink her claws into him. She even disappeared with him for forever."

"Girrrrl! You had better keep her gnarly claws off that man! He is yours dammit! Come to think of it...There is something about him...You know me and faces. But when I get it, you will be the first to know. Oh! Pascal told me that you are singing **Pleasing** tomorrow in church. He also said you are singing in Chenoweth's place at the showcase on Saturday."

"Seriously that man is another one! I told him let someone else do it, but he insists that I be the one."

"Glad he did as well. It is boring when the others sing. Call me selfish but you make that choir girl."

"You are always good for my ego."

"Glad to assist. By the way, are you coming to Festival Village tonight? I hear there is a surprise artist coming in.

"You don't know?"

"Tried to find out but everyone's hush-hush."

"That's strange... You are slipping Seba."

"Seems so ain't it? But mark my words before the day is through, I will have some info. So, help me."

"I believe you." She clutched him to her. "I'll head up. Hopefully I will have the costumes done. Then I can pick up Kiah and head over."

She paused long enough to greet Hannah and the rest of the team. Some of whom were assisting a few customers.

The shop floor looked spectacular. She knew Seba would always keep the place in good stead whenever she wasn't around. She waved to some of the well-known who frequented the boutique.

She spotted jumpy Anais the full-figured cutie and went over and gave her a hand in picking out a few more flattering pieces. Her dad's platinum gold card was used a lot in her shop because she hated crowds and liked the intimacy **Belle** offered her.

From his auntie's window he spotted the car dealership **Maxim's**; that sold high-end luxury cars. He had the team on it while he spoke to his aunt. One couldn't be too careful.

The crew had followed no doubt on Ama's orders.

William and Terrence were his close body protection team. Some were already dispatched to Heart Island. He spotted William whom he could often be found sparring with when he needed a robust combat workout. They were both ex-militaries.

Terrence had been at the academy. William was at the store.

Kiah would always say detail was not necessary, but they all disagreed.

"The Playboy's Paradise. That man is a disgrace to the youths. He had them dropping like flies every couple of weeks." His aunt said vehemently when he asked after the name.

"What do you mean?"

"He plays fast and loose, dealing substances. Not to forget those drag races on the back roads, and that new track he just installed behind his shop. They started off as a wholesome family dealership. His dad is a good man. But when you allow puppies to lick your face, and not let them toe the line Maxim is what you get. One day he came in from the UK and couple years later his dad had a stroke. He took over and you have his idea of what the children of well-off families needed and should be driving.

Just be careful Hezekiah."

"I will auntie." He kissed her cheeks.

"And don't you dare purchase anything we would have to scrape you off of."

"Yes Auntie." He laughed and took the elevator to the second floor. There he picked up a hat and a pair of aviators. They all now knew who he was in the shop. He didn't have to pay but he did none-the-less. He purchased some perfume; tuber rose and gardenia for her. His auntie created the scents. She was a chemist first and had earned a bit of notoriety for things she concocted. She told him Nia loved the oils, lotions and fragrances. He also purchased a diamond heart pendant; the semi-biggest one in the shop, along with the matching earrings. He rebuffed the engagement ring. He didn't want to overwhelm her just yet.

Plus, from what he learnt about her she was not fussed about to many material things.

The aunties said she would rather give away most of what she owned, which was a sizable amount. However, some of it kept disappearing because of all the charities she ran, at times to her own detriment.

He thought of infusing some capital, but maybe later after some more discussions with his aunt. He promised to speak seriously to her later.

They had sent her flowers; sterling silver roses, anthuriums and birds of paradise. They bought all the shop had. They must have already arrived. He tried picturing her face. She did things to his heart every time she crossed his mind.

The sun was a bastard out there. He walked the street and crossed over and headed down to the shop. He spotted William; he was eating outside a bistro under an umbrella. Kiah knew he would be followed seconds later. He just got on with it. They were like his breathe. They were the best that money could afford.

Inside Kiah was quite impressed by the machines; from bikes to the cars, he saw scattered all around such as **Rolls Royce, Porsche, Tesla, BMW, Aston Martin, Bentley, Mercedes-Benz**, and **Lincoln**…

He owned a **Range Rover** and a **Porsche** as well as a **Ducati** and **Harley**. They were all he needed. He owned shares in many. His reasoning was, how many vehicles can one drive at a time?

He walked straight towards a silver Range Rover. "I'll take that." He said easily. Not asking after the price. "That as well." He pointed to a black Harley Davidson motorcycle.

The young guy seemed taken aback.

"Are you visiting the island?" He became quite friendly now. It was rare they had customers who walked in and shelled out that kind of green. He had to pull out his best salesman pitch. But turned out the dude already knew what he wanted. He didn't even want to try any shit! He seemed to know exactly what he wanted. He hoped he had the fucking mean-greens to back up the cheek.

He tried to get a good look of his face, but he couldn't, only a glimpse because he wore a baseball cap pulled low and shades. He looked quite non-descript, not like some off the asses who occasionally popped in and showed off their stupidity to impress.

This one reminded him of a bodyguard kind of. Maybe he was scoping out the island for some bigwig coming in. He reminded himself to get it together. While he prayed this would be his lucky day.

"Would you like me to tell you about...?"

"No need."

"Ok sir. So, no test drive even?"

"Not necessary."

"Then let me take you over this way. While we get your pieces sorted." He offered knowing Boss-man would be watching from every angle of the cameras. Surveillance was everywhere. The man trusted no one. Which reminded him he had better wrap things up before he sent someone else in to interfere.

"How long have you been working here?" Kiah asked, having searched him out. Because he was the only one who appeared as though he could use a great windfall. He looked eager to make his mark.

"Three months now sir." He stammered. Gesturing to a couple of females. Kiah followed him over to the transaction room, plush black leather and chrome and steel. One would think he had stepped onto a pimps' set. Perhaps that was what the poles from the rafters were for Kiah reasoned. He shook it off. He also refused the champagne that seemed to have magically appeared by beautiful girls in shiny skimpy shorts and strappy beaded tops.

Kiah half expected cameras to be stuffed in his face, and then someone would say, "Smile you're on candid camera!!!"

Cigars and joints were produced after he did the paperwork and handed over his black card.

Suddenly the door parted and the great Maxim; a double for the cartoon character Jaffar from the movie Aladdin strolled...no, sauntered in. Kiah had lost count of the many times he had watched the movie.

102

The man just seemed to have materialised into the room.

"We can get you some blow…ice if you prefer?" He tossed in an upscale British accent. As he brushed back his long black trench so he could perch atop the edge of the desk.

He also adjusted the cowboy hat he wore. He smiled presenting a full set of grills. He was dripping in platinum jewellery.

Kiah recoiled, as he watched the man seductively crossed his legs, and arms when he lounged atop the desk. He displayed the tips of his boots that glittered from all the bling. They also had honest to goodness 'spurs' on the back.

Kiah felt as though he was seated in the presence of the devil himself. He longed for a long hot shower. He told himself he had better hurry and get the hell out of the place.

He spotted the guys. They were making their way over. He stayed them when they got closer.

"I have an appointment in half-hour Maxim." He offered to the man as he pumped his arm up and down and tried to keep him in his chair. Especially when the young salesman brought his card back.

Quick as a flash Maxim snatched it. His fingernails were spikey and well-manicured.

He gestured the females over as he perused the card.

"H. C Corrington…Why do I recognise that name?" He asked and used the card as a fan. "Any relations to **Corrington's** down the road?"

He sussed out that he must be super-rich. Because his card was a 'freaking **Amex Black**. Which was only held by a select few. There was a secret to be learnt Maxim thought as he looked the pretty fella up and down. No doubt trying to deflect attention from himself.

"You can say that." Kiah offered, staying the females. "No thank you beautiful ladies." He wasn't a prude but there was a time and place, and now was not it.

"Are you certain we can't entice you with anything else? How about the track? We have a couple races starting soon." He quickly waved them away. One brought the remote to him.

"I don't think so. I really must make my appointment. But this is quite the interesting place you've got here."

"I aim to please." He flicked the girls away offensively now as though they were bothersome mosquitoes. They left the room.

"But really Maxim. I must hurry." He rose to his feet.

"Thanks Corrington. Maybe we can meet up again. How much longer will you be here?"

"Couple weeks."

"Nice. We can have a chat soon."

"That's a plan." Kiah offered. Feeling as though he needed some sanitiser for his hands.

The man moved with him.

Kiah had the impulse to push him aside. His gut told him to get as far away from the place as possible before he was forced to give blood.

"I still say there is something…" The man continued to look him over in much confusion. "It will come to me."

"Perhaps." Kiah said and snatched his card. "Now the Harley can you make sure that gets delivered to the address on the paperwork?"

"Done. Got PPE; helmet and such? How about we sweeten the deal with those?" He offered like a proud peacock.

"Appreciated Maxim. It has been a pleasure." He offered one last handshake.

Then he turned to the young fella. "Good job. Perhaps we will see each other again soon." He meant it. He shook the young man's hand and tipped the rim of his hat. He was glad he would be scoring the commission. He will check back. Because Maxim didn't seem the sort to share.

He took the envelope he'd seen the young man put the paperwork in. He accepted the keys. He loved Nia but her car was to cramp for him. He needed more space and independence. He liked coming and going at his own leisure.

The car was brilliant. He liked the creamy leather interior and the fresh smell. Granted it was an older model to the one he had at home but never-the-less. It made him grateful.

It was easy driving around in town. The fellas were driving the rental; the black one to his and they were behind him. He drove the long stretch of road until he started seeing and smelling the sea even more oppressively. He drove off the road and into a safe gap, overlooking the beach below. His mobile phone interrupted the semi-silence; he was playing soft music. It was Nia.

She was beaming over the floral delivery. When he hung up, they joined him. One pushed a cool bottle in his hand, he unscrewed the lid and bought it to his mouth. The water was so delirious. The other handed him a file.

Another hour and he was picking up the things at the shop, along with toiletries and a pair of shorts and shirt. He felt incredibly sweaty, and he hated it.

It was not difficult to find the shop. The fellas were in the lead. Before he got out of the vehicle he wiped up and changed. When he stepped out Seba was already heading out the huge sliding glass door.

"Good to see you again Mr. Handsome." He greeted the man. He reminded himself this was Nia's blessing not his.

"I thought she was going to pick you up." He had not missed the ride he had stepped out of. It was SWEET!!!! No doubt he had stopped off at the scheming **Maxim's.**

"Hope he did not rip you off. Price wise?" Seba knew the high-end stuff was kept inside and protected like the Queen's jewels.

"He did not. Good to see you again. How are you?" He remembered what everyone said. So, he allowed the man to link his arm through his as they walked towards the shop.

"We are all fine. Just like you...Gosh you are FOINE." He bit comically down on his hand.

It made Kiah laugh.

He begged his heart to settle. He could see why she dropped her drawers.

"By the way the flowers were a great touch, and gorgeous too. We ran out of space to put them. Now all the workers get to take some home. Her choice."

"I would expect nothing less." He offered easily. She'd said as much to him. Glad he could bring smiles to everyone's face.

He paused long enough to get a good view of the shop. The sign atop was in a shiny black gloss; **BELLE** a male and female in evening wear stood next to it.

The building was a four-storey white modern build. There were huge picture windows home to well-dressed male and female mannequins poised languidly in fashionable and couture pieces.

His eyes wandered up to men's fashion suits tuxedos and casual pieces. Then at the top were elaborate costumes of sequins feathers beads...

They got closer and a few females came out the door and stopped in their tracks like a deer caught in headlights.

Seba said "Ladies say hello to Kiah Corrington."

They sprang to life shifting flowers to shake his hand.

"This is Derris, Kathy, and Alma."

"Nice to meet you Kiah." They became giggly.

Just then a couple more came out carrying more flowers and copied the same looks the others had.

"This is Kiah Corrington!" They continued.

"Miss Nia's Kiah?" The first one to recover asked.

"Yes!" They chorused.

"You are hot. Can I get a pic?"

"Can we all get one?" They chorused.

Kiah obliged them all. He hadn't genuinely done that in a while. Doing things like that just seemed tedious. Thank God he had changed before he came in.

"Are you a celebrity? You look remarkably familiar."

"He was the one with Miss Nia on FB."

"Ooh...But ..." She bit her lips in concentration. "It will come to me.... Thank you for the flowers. See you soon Mr Seba. Bye Kiah." They giggled all the way around the corner.

"Come to think of it. You do look familiar and not because of the Facebook photo. There is something." He said perusing him again.

They got so busy today he didn't get a chance to play detective. But the day has ended, and he sure was going to find out about the super sexy

Mr. Kiah Corrington. Something as fine as him must have baggage and he was aiming to sift through some before he ended up hurting his Sista.

The beautiful huge sliding doors opened, and they walked into sophistication, style and grace.
He wasn't a fashionista, but what he saw he liked. There weren't any customers. The shop was tidy and set up for the next working day.
There were mannequins in black and white, dressed in lovely pieces scattered around on pedestals.
He most especially liked the huge black and white tiles on the floor.
The room was fragrant with some of the flowers she had kept dotted about on tables and shelves.
Wracks were neatly stacked with hangers in the same transparent colour and heading straight in the identical direction. No mass production here or overload.
Seems like customers were offered ease of either shopping or browsing if they so desired.
He spotted dressing rooms with floor length mirrors and curtains that weren't pulled.
"Welcome to **Belle.** She must have forgotten what time it is again. That is our girl. She usually is the first in and the last to leave." Seba said, as he caught the tiny glimpse of disappointment that scampered about his face.
"I understand. We can all get lost in our work at times."
"I can take you to her."
"Thank you, Sebastin."
He followed him up steps. He stopped to read a 3D poster on the far back wall that read, "**All women should be given the enabling and immense right to look beautiful and at their best no matter her size.**"
The words seem to materialise more into view the closer you got up the steps.
Huge frames lined the wall. They were of her mom in different styles and costumes, even in a tuxedo and suit.
It was like museum art. One could tell lots of thought had gone into the design as well as layout of the place.
He liked it and could see her hand in everything. Her mama was an integral part of every nuance of her life. She was all around.
It was as if she had not left.
"My studio and showroom are to your left." Seba continued garnering his attention again. He pointed out the sign **Sebastin's.**
"Maybe when you stop by next time you can pick out a few pieces."
He had a feeling the man would look great in anything he wore.
"Her room is here."
He knocked…nothing… He pushed open the door. Loud music floated out to them. Luther Vandross singing **Ain't No Stopping Us Now.** He gestured him in.

106

The sight was magnificent; she was gyrating and grooving; dancing like a possessed barefoot banshee pulling pins from a pin cushion on her wrist. He folded his arms and took her in.

God she was beautiful. Her hair had come undone and laid splayed against her back and moved when she moved.

She sang out loudly. She was truly in her element as she pinned the diaphanous flowing material about the thing.

"She is a maniac when she is in the zone."

He walked over and tapped her. She jumped and spun around wildly.

"It's me! It's me and Kiah!" He pointed.

"What! Who?" she shouted.

"Kiah!" He pointed again.

"Kiah! I didn't pick him...What? How?"

Seba picked up the remote and switched the music off. "You always do this when you think you are alone. How in the hell can you hear if someone God forbid comes in?"

"Seba stop being dramatic. I am totally safe. You know full well crap like that only happens once in a blue moon here on the island. Plus, we are among the top three island paradises in the Caribbean. Hi you. When did you get here? How did you get here? I told you I would pick you up."

"When was the last time you looked at the clock?"

"It was only 5:00 pm when I said bye to the others. Good God is that the time? I am sorry Kiah. I thought I could do this and then."

"Not to worry Nia. I am here now. Don't worry. Glad I got to see you at work, or was that play?"

He opened his arms to her. It had been too long since he'd had a fix.

"I'm sorry Kiah." She ran to him.

He pulled her close.

"I lost track of time."

"I'm here now. I've missed you." He kissed the top of her head.

"Well, I think this is my cue to say goodbye for now. By the way are you still coming to Festival Village?"

"Kiah? Are you sure you are up for it?"

"I'm yours."

"Ok we will come by for a bit."

"Ok girlfriend. I will see you two soon. Please don't do anything I would."

He laughed and blew them kisses and left the room pulling the door in behind him.

They were hungrily devouring each other's lips when Seba burst back into the room a mischievous look plastered all over his face.

"Don't forget to set the alarm missy."

"Seba!" She scolded, knowing he did what he did on purpose. "Nosey bastard." she hissed. She knew him well.

"What?" He feigned ignorance. "I was just reminding you. Then again as you were." He tossed, giving a wink and thumbs up to Kiah.

Secretly wishing he were in her place right at that moment, as he did a jig and skulked away gleefully.

"He is growing on me." Kiah offered, before he went back for her lips. She gave him as good as she got.

"I hope you do not live to regret it. By the way. How did you get here? Did Silcott drop you?"

"No, I drove."

"What do you mean?"

"I picked up a ride at **Maxim's**."

"You did? Wow!!!" Must have some money to burn she thought. Knowing only the rich and idle, or those who have something to prove shopped there.

"You've been busy. I noticed you've also changed."

"I was so sweaty. I hate that. Now stop distracting me." He pulled her in again.

When they came up for air he said. "I have missed you woman."

"I've missed you too Kiah. I am sorry I was late to pick you up." She truly was. "Thank you again for the flowers."

She gestured towards her worktable that housed a computer, telephone, and lots of books. There were two tall vases sitting proudly there.

"All the ladies felt so special today. Thank you for that Kiah."

"Glad I can put a smile on your face. The ladies as well. I met some of them as we were coming in."

"Hope they didn't put you on the spot?"

"I felt like a celebrity." If she only knew how true, that was. "So, it looks like you got a lot done?"

"We sure did. The academy's costumes are sorted. I just hope they don't want any more redoes."

She gestured to wracks and wracks of garment bags.

"It was a successful day. Now I have got to show my face at Festival Village before the workday ends. But first let me change into something more comfortable."

"Can I watch?"

"You're so nasty Kiah!" She giggled as she slipped behind a changing screen.

"That's what you do to me woman. Now c'mon a sneak peek." He taunted. As he took in more of the room, worktables with sewing machines, scissors and bulks upon bulks of materials in an array of colours and textures. Boxes labelled pins, buttons, sequins, elastic...

There was even a mini runway and couple pedestals and more mannequins.

"Sorry, this is where you would find me most days and nights. It is a bit cramped. Then again if I move a couple things... Nah! It works for me. For my team. When we need more space, we work on the top floor as well, where we have another work area, our factory, rec area, lunch area... What do you think?"

108

"It's brilliant. It's your workspace."

"Thank you, Kiah. Maybe the next time you come we can do a tour of upstairs. Sorry I allowed time to fly away today." She tapped his back. He turned.

"Good God almighty woman!" She stood there in faded jeans and a purple contraption-like bra. She held her purple top open.

"This is what you do to me as well Kiah. I can't think straight at times." He walked to her and scooped her up hungrily in his arms.

"God woman! I am so damn ravenous for you." He bent delivering little kisses from her mouth all the way to hover above her heart.

"I am madly and irrevocably in love with you." He kissed her atop her heart. "You are mine Nia...only mine... Do you hear me?" He asked her roughly.

"Yes Kiah." She purred softly. Loving the way, he made her feel. She kissed his lips. "Kiah, we must go...One more stop, and sweetheart I promise... I will be yours." She tore from the embrace as he tried to unbutton her jeans.

"Later Kiah!" She snapped and pulled him from his trance as one would do a naughty dog set on mischief. She quickly pulled the long straps of the purple halter top together and deftly around her neck. "Down boy." She teased. "We will get back to it later. "Now zip me up...Please... Please... Kiah...!"

"Okay baby." He growled at her. She turned her back and gestured. He obliged. Both panting like derby horses.

He kissed her bare back. God help me. He thought. Thinking he would bury anyone who got in his way. Including himself.

"Thank you, Kiah. Now let's get you a light jacket. Something from **Seba's** shop. The temperature can change at the drop of a hat being so close to the water."

She reached for her bags, giving a long sniff to one of the bouquets on the table. She noticed his eyes had never left her once. It was like that from the first time they had met. She told herself she had to be meticulous otherwise she was certain they would never leave the shop.

She reached for his hand.

"Spoil sport Nia." He said sounding as though he were still off in that trance.

"Never mind. Later Kiah. Now c'mon."

She crossed the hall and punched in the codes, and they waited as the sliding glass door eased quickly into the walls. She gestured for him to follow.

The room was the total opposite of the man. Classy and understated. It was neatly stacked, suits on mannequins along alcoves in the wall, and numerous ones in shades and colours on hangers on the floor.

Fitting rooms in the back of the wide walkway.

Then casual styles artistically put together. Some too flamboyant for his taste but nice none the less along with accessories and some shoes in

109

the pattern that Nia wore as well as what trimmed the fellow's jacket when he first met him.

"I like those." He pointed to Seba's **HaVana Line**. "Auntie sells pieces from both your lines as well. I noticed them earlier in Corrington's."

"Yes Kiah. We both design pieces for **Corrington's**. Especially the holiday and cruise wear section, as well as lower end evening and social dresses.

"Nia that's brilliant." He offered but it was only for conversation because he already knew all there was to know about the woman and her dealings, and all who were in close contact to her.

There was a piece of the puzzle that they could not connect. But team Incognito would get there. There was also a brute called David that he was working on. He would never get his hands on her ever again if he had any say about it all. His time had passed for sure.

He thought the man could give some of the headliners a run for their money.

He walked over to a navy-blue slim cut suit. He had a couple of the exact style from **Armani, Hugo Boss** and **Brooks Brother's**...

He recognised the **Boateng** flair.

He had modelled a couple pieces for him and had a trunk load in his closet. Comfort was key for him, as well as smart and stylish, cutting edge.

"This is nice."

"Told you he was brilliant." She walked over to the casual section and picked him a white linen jacket. This should be a perfect fit."

She helped him into the jacket. He of course looked like his body was designed for anything. "Do you like?"

"It is your choice, Nia. I will wear anything you put me in."

"Flirt."

"Truth." He said looking at himself in the long length mirror. "Nice."

She had picked a perfect fit for him. Why should that surprise?

He had learnt her body. Wise woman to have learnt his. "Anything fits your body magically. Are you sorted for church tomorrow?"

"Yes I am. Auntie instructed."

"Good nephew. Now come along. I need to show my face. Then we can head home, and I can show you how happy you have made me feel today."

She slapped his rear, then headed for the door.

He spun around so quickly; he thought his neck would swivel.

"Rarse! Lead the way, Nia. You do not have to tell me twice."

"What!" She stopped in her tracks. "Did you just say rarse?"

"You betcha!" It made her laugh. He loved it. He thought of the things he had in the car for her. He waited while she locked up and set the alarm. Then they held hands all the way to the car.

The parking lot was clear now except for his vehicle. He spotted them across the road a little way up from the shop.

"Are you up to driving?" He asked holding up the fob/keys.

"Are you kidding?" She exclaimed." Hell yes!" She shouted and grabbed the keys and clicked the switch hearing the vehicle locks slide.
"I would like one of these one day Kiah. But now to many outgoings. Business must be great for you."
"I cannot complain Nia. I am extremely thankful to God and to the universe that I no longer must worry about my wants and needs so much."
"Lucky you Kiah!"
"I like the word blessed more. I notice you use it a lot. So, I think I will porch it and say I am blessed."
"Well good for you."
She opened the door. She spotted the **Corrington** bags.
"You shopped at the aunties. What did you get?"
"Look and see Nia." He waited as she took out the first bag and looked inside.
"Kiah! You shouldn't have. How did you know? Silly me. Those two know a lot about me. Seems like you do now. Thank you." She spritzes herself.
"Smell me." She said like a little girl teasing a friend having just sprayed her mama's perfume.
"Nice." He said wanting to kiss her. She was so infectious.
As he watched her squeeze lotion and massage it into her hands.
"Your aunties' skincare and perfume line are such a hit. Not to forget her diffusers."
"Dad says she can sell shit and make it smell nice."
She busted out laughing.
"What's in the other one?"
"Open it and see Nia, they are all yours."
"Kiah you are spoiling me rotten."
She rummaged into the bag, took out the jewellery box, and flipped it open.
Her mouth opened and closed a few times, and nothing came.
Tears stung her eyes.
"Kiah it's beautiful. You must have spent a fortune today."
"Don't worry about it."
"Kiah this is too much."
She could not resist running her hand along the outline of the heart.
"This is a real diamond! This is 3 carats! I know because some of the girls and I saw when it came to the shop. It needed its own close protection team. Kiah this is way too much. I know she is your aunt, but you spent too much money."
"Let me worry about that Nia." He laughed, "Why don't you turn around and let me put it on."
"No! Kiah you are going to take this back. That is too much."
"Suppose I had gotten you the mama? She is only the baby Nia! Now be a good sport and wear my heart. Turn around, then open the other box."
"You mean there is more?"
"Yes Nia! Open it!"

"Kiah you got me the earrings too?"

"Yes, you deserve them all. Let's take those ones out and put these ones in."

"Kiah are you sure? I mean it's not too late to..."

"Put them on and I want to get a picture now and one of you later when you are naked."

"Kiah!"

"I mean it Nia."

"Seriously Kiah that is a lot of money. Did you win the lottery before you came here? Or are you super rich?"

"Super-rich Nia." He decided to tell the truth.

She looked at him as though he was simply telling porky-pies. Then she reached up on tip toes and kissed his lips.

He kissed her back.

"So, you like?"

"Damn Kiah I love them! Thank you!"

"You are welcome. Now get in. Perhaps if you are a good girl and keep those, I will pick the mama up for you later."

"No way! No more." Shit! What the hell had the fool gone and done? This stuff cost money. These pieces were not chump change. "I mean it Kiah. No more." She admired the luxurious pieces in the mirror. They were stunning on her. "I must admit though I feel like a million box." She said preening like a peacock.

"Wait until Seba catches a glimpse of these. He will flip!!!"

"You look beautiful Nia. Even behind the wheel." He concluded as she started the engine and pulled off like a pro.

"This is a sweet ride. Seba lets me drive his sometimes, but he is too particular."

They laughed. It was a nice sound in the luxurious interior.

Kiah liked the fact that his legs weren't as cramped as they had been earlier.

Nia searched for **ECB** radio and after a bit of tuning. DJ Dread-Up was already way into his grove, which was her thing on a Saturday evening. She could be found dancing around the house to the many artists being played, especially Mighty Shadow.

His songs kept her and her mom together. **Music** was her mama's favourite song and she'd learnt it and would sing it every time in remembrance of her for teaching her the love of art.

"Well, well...Where in de world is **Soca Diva**? Anybody see Soca out dey? Well, if you do, mek sure all-you tell her that **Festival Village** need her to show her face. Yeah man she got to come down. They are waiting. Guess a surprise is in store. Soca-gal whey you be? Whey you be Gal?" He chatted loudly and played a bit of the music and stopped.

"Come to think pan um. Why don't you give awe a call? Yeah man call us! By de way somebady say they see she love up an ting pan de ferry de other night! They say no fly coo pass by! Well, it not me say so. It's what somebody tell somebody who tell somebody!!!" He started to play **Tabu** out of Montserrat's **Somebady.**"

"What!" She spat and slapped the steering wheel hard.

DJ interrupted the song again. She hated when he did that.

"Yes, my dear. Guess Soca off-de-market! Guess lots of us getting our hearts bruk burrruk foo de white-Brudda-Bob! Yes!!! That's what I says! De white-Brother-Bob! Yeah man! They say he got dreads... Neat ones to. All de females going gaga. They say he prettier than some a-dem. Lord have his mercy!!! **Somebady**!"

"Is that fool talking about me?" Kiah sat bolt upright in his seat and pointed to the radio.

"He sure is." Nia said. Caught between being pissed and wanting to laugh.

"He referred to me as Bob Marley?"

"Well, he also said you are pretty."

"Pretty? Kiah gasped. "Nia, he referred to me as the white Bob Marley." Well, he had gotten lots of that if truth be told.

One even had the nerve to refer to him as Bo Dereck. He busted out laughing without meaning to.

Nia started laughing as well. "Well, if we don't laugh, we will certainly cry. I am just going to continue to ignore stupidness. But you know what Kiah? You sure are a pretty fella. For real. You will give someone gorgeous babies one day."

"You too Nia! I like the baby bit. Are you ready?"

"Hell no! I give birth to fabric." But she must admit that a baby with him... Lord have mercy!!! She was dick-whipped indeed.

"But for reals though. Soca, you need to be at the village. They say he is chomping at the bit to see you." DJ Dread Up continued.

Nia almost flew into another vehicle as she tried to park. Someone had just stepped over her grave!!! She didn't know why but her entire being trembled. It felt like an ill-wind just blew by.

"Hey people! News flash!!!" The DJ continued. "Someone say two presidential vehicles were seen on the road earlier today down at Rendezvous Bluff... People we either got the president, or a celebrity. **Somebady**!!! Tell me. Word is they are spotted at **Festival Village** now. Ah whaya-tall!! Somebody!!!"

Nia reached out and switched it off. How many times had she sat at home and laughed when the shoe was on the other foot? She had lost track. Tonight, though she felt betrayed.

His mobile went off. He looked at it...

She stepped out, not missing the way his face crinkled. It looked important.

"Nia!" He called as he tried to detain her. Seems the idiot was there. He just came in on the first ferry and decided he was going to play for the people. He had been on tour for almost two years. He lived in the UK and had a good following playing clubs, pubs and some festivals...

She opened the back door and reached in for her bag and jacket.

The temperature had changed, and it had grown darker. He felt it when she'd opened the door. He hung up and climbed out pulling the jacket with him.

Festival Village was loud, and smoke was rising from the place as though they had forgotten to say someone had set the place on fire and now it was smouldering. All kinds of scents accosted his nostrils. He felt hungry suddenly.

"Hey Soca!!! They are looking for you! Nice ride! You the president or de celebrity?" Somebody called from across the Bayfront wall.

"Hey! Look its Brudda-Bob! Rarse! Miss Nia that you man? He sure pretty! Sweet ride an-ting man."

"Hey Bob! Can we get a picture next to de ride?" They came into the light. Each had a spliff. It was a couple young fellas who were in her troupe.

"What are you doing smoking that ting? You two ain't fraid Babylon roll up on you?"

"Fire bun dem Miss Nia! But seriously that's a sick ride. That straight off **Maxim's** lot, right?"

"A black one park over dey. It pulled up just as you two did."

"Really?"

"See it over dey so." They pointed off to the bluff. "Seriously can we get some pics?"

"It's his, ask him. When you two done come and bend some wires."

"We on our break. Batty-man say we could."

"Hey! Hey, you two have some respect!"

"But it true. He no love woman like we love woman. He prefers man!"

"True star!"

"I mean it Lazar. Respect or you two are out of my troupe. His name is Seba and nothing else. Do you understand?" This she said to him but more so to Daemon aka **Gecko** upcoming wannabe Snoop Dog.

The nickname suited him. He reminded her of one. He acted like he had solved Einstein's Theory when he gave the analogy of why Seba was referred to as a Batty- man.

Thank God he didn't go into the other bit.

"Sorry Miss Nia. We sorry and ting. Nough- respect."

Kiah told them they could get their pics. He stood aside and pulled her to him. People were coming in and some were going. She got a whiff of Ella's goat water. She could sure use one. "Hey you two. You had enough?"

"You two go. We keep an eye on the ride. But seriously Bob. Bling this shit out and you get chicks like that!" Gecko chirped.

"I am totally satisfied with my gift."

"De best Brother-Bob. De absolute best. She's a star."

"I totally agree."

He thanked them and they set off.

"Want something to eat? I am hungry. Let's go get some goat water."

114

"Goat water?" He asked in confusion. I don't want to experiment now. I would like real food. Chicken and rice…"

"Shit Kiah! I forgot to call Miss D. Maybe she is in here. Let me pick up my goat water and we go to her stall. But seriously you need to taste **Ella's.** It's not as ominous as it sounds. Some refer to it as an Irish stew, but stew is thick, goat water is nice and slow, so you can sip, dip rolls or bread, or gently spoon. Don't knock it until you…"

"Soca! Soca!" Someone else called out. Guess who is here?"

"Who Diane?"

"David! David is back! They gonna do a second set again soon."

"Shit! Shit! I can't deal with that fool on an empty stomach. Let's get something." She walked over to a tent where lots of fellas were hanging. "Ella! Ella can I have a bowl please? Couple rolls too."

"Hey gal! Good to have you back." He reached out and pulled her into a bear hug. "You de one that stole our Miss Nia? Damn fellas! He sure a pretty man foo true."

"Rarse!" The Three Stooges commented as they swung into action. Ella went nowhere without them.

"He pretty no rarse! He does look like Brudda- Bob foo real. Say Bob! You gonna try some?"

"Of hers…"

"She no share goat water! We better get you yours."

They gave him a cup. Nia had already dug into hers with the spoon. She swallowed a few mouthfuls before she came up for air.

"What! I'm hungry." She paid them. She dipped her spoon in again.

"Good stuff Ella. Set me up a big bowl for the road. I will stop by on our way out.

"Pretty boy where you from?" Ella decided to be Oprah.

"California."

"Where in Cali?"

"The Hills." He didn't say **Holmby Hills,** and that the Spelling mansion was just a couple blocks from his house, as well as a few other celebs.

"So, you a celebrity?"

"No."

"What work you do?"

"Real estate."

"Property and shit?"

"Yes."

"You must make shit-loads of money when you live in de hills."

"True."

"You don't say much, do you?"

"Sometimes."

"So why you here on de island?"

"Came to visit my auntie."

"Who?"

"Lady Bellot."

"You mean you a Corrington? Shit Nia! You and that auntie of yours sure know how to pick em! That family is loaded as shit!!! Great store right fellas?"
"To pricey foo me pocket."
"True that. So, what you think Rasta-to-de-back-but-not-to-de-belly?"
They made a raucous that ascended to the heaven.
"It's delicious. Can I have another one? For her as well." He noticed her bowl was empty.
"Told you she inhales de stuff. Miss Nia way you put all that food you eat gal?"
"In my derriere boys. Don't it show?"
"In you wha?" They looked confused.
"She means in her ass boys." Kiah interjected. Bringing the cup to his head. "This is some good stuff."
"Rarse clart! Corrington gat chat and shit. You like she ass then?"
"All of her. She is gorgeous!"
"True that. But seriously Miss Nia is good people Rasta. Treat her well or else all de man and dem going come at you. Especially that one up there getting ready to show he renking-ass."

David and his band were getting ready for their set. He called for her.
"Soca Diva! Soca Diva! I hear you in De Park. Everyone let's join in and give Soca a big hand. Tell her come join us in a few songs! Come on Diva! Anyone see Diva?"
"She over by Ella's!" someone called out."
"Wha?"
"She ah eat goat-water over by Ella."
"She sure loves that shit. Now come on Soca." David taunted.
Someone had messaged him to say she had arrived. He really wanted to see her. Make things up to her. He could really use a piece of that ass. As well as get her to do a few things for him. She could never say no when he put on the works.
He remembered the last time he had seen her. He was dick deep in some pussy when she'd walked in. Nothing he said that night at band house could save him. She said she was through, and she seemed like she had meant it.
"He really knows how foo show he rarse, don't he? Well perhaps you should just go and put him outta he misery."
"I really hate that bastard." She wiped her hands furiously after spritzing sanitizer, then using wipes. She then pulled out a mirror and looked at her reflection as well as checked her teeth and applied gloss.
"Kiah please excuse me for a couple of minutes eh."
She gave him her bag and huffed off and over to the stage.

Applause went up all around as people shouted out her name as he encouraged them. She stared him down all the way over to the band.
"Good to see you all guys. What's up?"

116

"We all good."

They started playing their instruments. It made her nostalgic, for just a tad. She glared David down. She didn't have the energy for him and his shit. He looked her over. He grinned the biggest grin; that's how he had won her over at school. Just like he was doing now. She had thought the sun had sprinkled gold dust on him. He sparkled. Then he had left the gaggle of girls that had him surrounded and walked over to her finally. David was **Glee Club's** sexy crooner. He had a voice like not many on the island had. Which meant he was called to sing for anything Ritzy and Glitzy from a very young age. He's sang for prime ministers, queens or kings visiting the island.

Nothing was anything without the singing styles of David. He was good and he knew it and used it. Getting into lots of scrapes and bumps over the years. He was their Teddy, Luther, Quincy, Arrow, Third World and so many more trapped in the one body. No wonder he was so screwed up at times. Musical genius or madness.

"Good to see you again Nia. Did you miss me baby?" He asked in his smooth as silk velvety voice.

"No." She added staring him down. She had to admit next to Kiah he looked cheap.

"Oh, don't be like that baby. You know we always had magic Nia baby."

"Until you blew it sweetheart." She spat at him.

"Have you not forgiven me yet?" He asked in his oh so fake English accent. He chuckled seductively.

He'd try to weasel back in. She wouldn't accept any of his calls or letters nothing. He'd come home for his nephew's funeral and tried, and she still treated him like shit under her shoes. Well, he'd made a vow; before Festival closed, he aimed to be deep within that sweet pussy once again. You can count on that he promised himself.

God she was divine when they were together. But he always wanted more, and she was always too busy trying to rule the world.

"Don't be like that baby." He teased.

"I've moved on. Don't you think it's time you did?"

"Get over you baby? Never happen! You are my magic. I did some bad shit back then. I'm sorry baby. Just give me a chance...One little chance baby, and I swear you'll never regret it."

"Says the spider to the fly!"

"Don't be like that pretty lady. I promise. You and me just like old times baby. You know we had magic. Tell me you remember this? Please Miss Nia. Just forgive me once more... Just one more time and I promise..."

"Music guys!" Nia said cutting him off. She truly didn't want to hear any more of his lies and empty promises. She didn't want no stress. She'd worn that tee-shirt too that read Lego de Stress. So, in her opinion like the old folks say, she done tark.

He quickly got the message. "Guys let's do **Dingolay**. You know whose fav that was right Nia-My-Heart?"

"Of course, I do David."

117

The band started **Mighty Shadow's Dingolay**. It was her mama's favourite song from the artist.
She could be found dancing to him when she wanted a music break. **Dingolay** brought her joy, and she would ask Nia to sing it for her lots of time. Nia learnt the lyrics just so she could. Her mama loved the simplicity of the lyrics.

> *The one who invented music is got to be terrific; got to be one who created the sun and trees, rivers and seas. Music fills the world with happiness plenty sweetness and togetherness.*
> *Music has no friend it got no enemies.*
> *Music is in the atmosphere; sweet music is everywhere.*
> *Even in the dark a blind man can find a melody.*
>
> *Music fills the world with happiness plenty sweetness and togetherness.*
> *Music has no friends or enemies.*
> *Everybody could dingolay*
> *You don't need a bulldozer to become a composer. Every little pock or a tock in me head Could construct a melody.*

She would always say "Our God is an awesome God in sharing out creativity. Isn't he Nia-Belle?"
She glared him down. This underhanded shit was just like David. But when the intro stopped, she got to singing...
Nia did a couple of her songs from back in the day. She had won the **Soca Monarch** crown three times in a row with title songs: **Do What You Do... Selling Something... Bumpa... Bad Gel Nothin foo Prove...**

David tried to dance and whine on her especially when she sang **Bumpa**. Back in the day she would have used him to give the audience a show. But not tonight. She didn't feel like doing it.
Maybe she had outgrown that side of things. Which is why she had stopped doing that secular sort of music... Long story different day.

She expertly side stepped him and did her stuff on her own. He called her a tease. She ignored him.
He free styled on the lyrics making suggestions to his dick and telling the audience it was on lockdown," jus foo she."
She free styled back on his dutti-ass in reggae style; calling him a two-timing ole-hoe who allowed his best friend; Dick to run his life and mess up the best shit with his then wife; who was now over his nasty-rarse. So, he should feel free to go f£$% any ole Janet, Trixie or Mary he please...
The crowd was in an uproar. They chanted, clapped, and encouraged her. She slipped back into the beat of the song easily and finished on a high note. She was not going to play his games tonight.

118

She sang another couple of songs with his organist Briggo; whom she'd collaborated with on a few occasions; two great albums.

They chose **Dutti Heart**. It was a crowd pleaser. Conscious Reggae. It dealt with two-timing, bad mind, shadiness, grudge...

They had written it together. She had to funnel the negative energy from all his shit; the backlash from a couple of his who tried to accost her, spread rumours...

It was a hellish time. But thank God she got over it. And what better way than in song. The crowd was in a frenzy. They wanted more. So, she adlibbed and tossed a couple verses in to coincide with his conniving and trifling ass.

They did **Workie Workie** and **Hot Hot Hot**.

At the end of the set. She thanked him and shook his hand.

He came in for a kiss, she quickly hugged him, and thanked the audience and slipped off the stage.

He caught up with her. He yanked on her arm and pulled her hard.

"What the fuck was that shit, Nia?" He pulled her towards him.

"How many more fucking times do I have to say that I am sorry? I tried calling; you ignore me. I wrote letters you disregarded. What else do you want from me?"

"That's the thing David. I don't want anything from you. I told you that you were free to do whatever the hell you wanted. I don't care."

"You don't mean that baby." He brought his face down and tried to kiss her.

"Stop David! I said no!" She pushed at him. He held her fast.

"The lady said no." Kiah interrupted. His voice was like a snarl. She'd heard it earlier in the evening when he said, **'you are mine Nia'.**

It made her jump full of fear.

"Why don't you get fucking lost white-boy?" David snarled back.

He looked the pretty guy up and down. So, this is the fucker she been laying up with? Well, he was here to put an end to the bullshit. Cause that pretty bitch-ass got nothing on him. Cause everyone knows that white guys can't jump.

"Not until you let go of her. I am not going to ask you again."

"Go fuck yourself!"

He turned his attention back to her. "Is that honky-bitch de one you been seen dragging about with? Why you not giving me de time a day?"

"Leave him out of this. He has nothing to do with me not wanting to bother. Now get your hands off me."

She tried to get free. He held her fast. "David you are hurting me. Let me go."

"No! Fuckin... What the...!" David shouted. He released her; no, he was dragged away with such ferocity.

Nia saw him being flipped on his ass. It was like watching a fight scene from one of Steven Segal's movies.

David was quick up off his backside. He came at Kiah, who side stepped him. It caused him to rush into the barricade. It didn't keep him down. He recovered charged again.

Kiah eased her out of the way and pushed her behind him.

David threw a punch and Kiah caught it and pushed him off.

"We can do this the easy way or..." Kiah ducked and landed a fist in his abdomen that caused him to double over.

"Kiah let's go." She pulled at him. The next thing she saw was David charging like an angry bull.

"David Jeremiah Fenton! That is enough!"

Nia peeked over Kiah's shoulder to see Francy his sister.

"Stay out of this Francy!"

"The hell I will brother. I see that you are making an ass of yourself again. Why don't you go sort yourself with your band mates?"

"And leave my woman in that rarse-hole's hand?"

"Nia hasn't been your woman in years. Why can't you get that through your stubborn head? She is not interested brother." She held unto him. He tried to break free.

"Sis, I need to talk to her. I want her to know how sorry I am. But that mop-head wouldn't let me get near her. Please...Please Nia. Just let me talk to you a moment."

"I said all I needed to the last time I saw you. David do get it through that thick skull of yours. I am done. I have nothing more to say, much less listen to. Thanks, Francy. Kiah let's go."

She pulled him along. This time he moved with her. She noticed also that two other males had joined them in the cordoned-off area. They looked to him it seemed. He put his palm up and they relaxed and stepped aside.

"Nia! Nia! Nia!" David called after them.

She ignored him.

Nia didn't stop walking until a little girl ran over. She stopped her in her tracks.

"Auntie Nia! Auntie Nia! You are here!"

"Hello beautiful girl." Nia said and bent to pick up the child. "How are you doing?"

"I'm fine. I saw you on the stage. You were great." She threw her arms around Nia's neck. "I am going to be just like you when I am old."

"That's nice to know London."

"Who are you?" She asked Kiah. "Are you a prince?"

"I'm Kiah. I'm her prince." He pointed to Nia.

David flashed by in his mind. He thought he would have sent him straight to hell if the other woman hadn't interrupted them. How dare he put his hand on her? Thank God he had followed when he saw her exiting the stage. What an asshole! He could tell he was up to something from the way he was undressing her on stage. He had even tried to get on top of her when they got close. Like he had a point to prove.

120

She clearly was rebuffing him, but the message was clearly not being received. He kept pushing.

"Do you love auntie?"

"Yes, I do." He answered the child whose voice pulled him back from the precipice he was atop.

"Where is your mommy young lady?"

"She is over there. She let me run to get you. Can I get an ice cream Auntie Nia?"

"You sure can." It was their customary thing to do before they left.

"Kiah want to get an ice cream too. I like chocolate. What do you like?"

"I like chocolate as well." Kiah offered. Thinking she looked good with the child in her arms.

"She wants ice cream." Nia called over to a girl waiting by a huge container.

She waved them on.

They walked over to a **Chico's** ice cream van and waited.

"Who are those two men Prince Kiah?" London asked him. Pointing to the guys. They flanked them. She had spotted them earlier. Slightly behind him with every move he made.

She recalled seeing them as she was on stage. They were standing one to either side of him. She thought it strange at the time. But she was pulled to the performance and had forgotten about it.

"They look out for me. Make sure that I am ok everywhere I go."

He decided to just come clean. No doubt they must stick out like sore thumbs on the small island. He gestured them over.

"Nia... London, meet William and Terrence."

"Great to meet you Ma'am." They offered and took her hand and pumped it up and down. Huge grins on their faces.

"Nice to meet you too." Nia offered. As she looked at them keenly. They reminded her of white Blade the Vampire stunt doubles. Like they could wrestle a pack of wolves barehanded. She reckoned her hand must have felt like a twig in theirs. But they looked friendly enough. Quite clean shaven in jeans and stretch white tee shirts.

"Would you like ice creams as well?" She asked out of politeness.

"Much appreciated ma'am."

"Please call me Nia. "She offered politely. Thinking who the hell was he that he went about with bodyguards?

This was not what normal people do. She replayed conversations while she looked from them to him and back again.

He gave the order because she was still lost in thought when it was their turn.

"Can I have a guava juice please instead of ice cream?"

This would have to be her last cold for the evening she reminded herself because she had to sing in church.

She had come to give a hand with costumes. But had ended up on stage instead with that ignorant fool.

Thank God Kiah was no pushover and had whooped his ass basically with one hand.

She looked quizzically up at him. He dropped that gorgeous smile on her. "Put her down. The guys can watch her for a bit so that we can talk. Do you want to talk Nia?"

"Yes Kiah." She spat.

"You don't mind, do you?" She asked them. "Her mama is right over there." She pointed stupidly.

Her head reeled. Just who the hell was this man standing next to her? Her mind went into overload as she took a couple steps away and he followed.

Shit! Hope he wasn't some damn mobster hiding out here on the island. They had had a couple who had done it before. Just her friggin luck jumping out of the fire and landing straight into the frying pan.

But the aunties would have said something! They surely wouldn't have foisted him unto her if he were trouble!!!

"Nia? Are you ok?" He asked handing her the bottle she refused to take. He too had settled on water.

"Just who in the hell are you? Are you in the mob Kiah?" She asked her voice raised hysterically.

"Absolutely not Nia!" He laughed. "I have told you before what I do."

"Then why does a Real Estate Investor need them?" She pointed to the two.

One was taking the child over to her mother. The other was watching them. He was drinking water. He smiled.

"That's protocol Nia. Wherever I go they go. I had a bit of trouble a couple years ago. So, we thought it best. They don't usually show themselves unless they feel it is necessary."

"I still don't get it Kiah! Who the hell are you?"

"I am rich Nia." He led with the truth.

"Yes Kiah. Your auntie is rich. You don't see her walking around with personal security. What the hell aren't you telling me?"

"I am filthy rich Nia."

"Yes Kiah?" She was still confused. Her hands had gone atop her hips. "You're filthy rich, and?"

"I can buy this island if I want to Nia." He said matter-of-factly. "Plus a few more if I desire."

"You're joking with me, right?"

"No Nia. You can call the aunties. Or you can browse the internet..."

"But you are Kiah Corrington!"

"Yes Nia. But I am also Hezekiah Carter Corrington III. I am the **CEO of Carter Inc.** One of the top ten global investment companies out there."

"Yes! And?" She was still not clued up. Things were running about in her head.

"Sweetheart..." He reached for her.

"Don't! Don't Kiah."

122

"Nia, I invest and even own properties globally. Name something anywhere in the world and Carter Inc. has a stake in it. I know and speak with people like Ted Turner, Michael Jordan and Magic Johnson, Bill Gates and even Oprah Winfrey..."

"No more Kiah! My head is spinning." She reached out and dragged the bottle from his hand. She took the biggest gulp ever almost choking herself. She spluttered.

"Sweetheart!"

"Don't you sweetheart me!" She pushed at him.

The guy walked closer. The other started over. Their pace quickened.

He came for her again. She saw they walked quicker.

"Shit Kiah! Does the aunties know?" It was more like a hysterical statement rather than a question.

"Yes, they do. I don't keep things from them."

"You are so freak-in-cool about this shit! How...I mean why me? Shit like that doesn't happen to people like me! I mean you can have anyone you want in the goddam world! You can have Naomi-Freaking-Campbell if you want... No don't tell me. I bet you know her too?"

He nodded again matter-of fact.

"And you want me? You must be goddam high or have just completely up and lost you dog-gone mind." She poked his forehead.

They stood behind Kiah.

"Go back over there!" she barked at him. "He can bloody-well take care of himself. I have no doubt about that!" She shouted over at him.

"Calm down Nia." He had to stop her. She was causing a scene.

Passers-by stopped and were looking on. A couple of them called out to her. She paid them no attention.

"We can go to the car, and you can yell at me there." He saw that some were using their mobiles. He hated it. She looked genuinely freaked out.

What the hell could he do? Short of picking her up and tossing her over his shoulder and run with her to the car. Because the scene unfolding would not be great.

Well, what the hell... He followed through on it.

She pounded and yelled like a banshee.

Terrence got the intention. He took off after he signalled. William took up the rear.

He got her to the car and placed her kicking and screaming in the back. He jumped in beside her and pulled the door closed.

"Let me out Kiah! Carter! What-ever-the hell your name is! Let me out!" She pushed at him. "I don't need this shit! Let me out!" She pummelled him proper.

"Ouch woman! That hurts! What the hell! This is not the reaction I was hoping to get. Most women would be fucking happy to know they were dating a filthy-rich man! You...? You are bloody freaking out! What the hell Nia?"

"Am I the experiment to come to the island and bang the first chick you, see? Damn Kiah shame on you!"

"What the fuck Nia"

"No shame on me for allowing you to fuck me on the first night without truly knowing who you really are! What the hell do they call people like that?"

"Stop it, Nia! Just stop it right now! I did not plan this. I didn't even know I was going to meet you! I would also have you know that I do not go around fucking every woman I see. I am not a bloody whore!"

"That's me! Fuck! Fuck! Fuck! I have become one of those fucking females."

"Nia quit talking shit! I am confused though. Would you have felt better fucking me if I was poor?"

The next thing he felt was a hard slap across his face. It was a surprise! When he recovered, he saw her cowering in the corner. Her hands were raised defensively.

He rubbed the sore spot. He deserved that. It was a stupid thing to say. But she was pissing him off with the shit she was spewing.

"Nia I am sorry... I'm sorry baby.... Shit I am sorry baby..." He reached out to her.

She recoiled into the corner.

He withdrew. "But shame on you for selling yourself short. You are the best woman I have come across in a very long long time." He stressed.

He wanted her to hear it and believe it.

"Take your hands down woman. I will never hit you. Not even in anger. Never...Never ever... But please never hit me again either. We are adults."

"I'm sorry Kiah." She whimpered. Amazed that he hadn't slapped the hell out of her like David would have done. She reached out and rubbed his cheek.

He leaned into her hand.

"Shit like that doesn't happen to people like me."

"You deserve all good things. That is the law of the universe Nia. You give to get. You give so much to the people here on the island. So why would God not give you back something in return?"

"But people like you don't fall for people like me!"

"Who says? What about Marcus Winter and Yvonne Mulcaire over in Star Island? Their marriage is solid. They pretty much started off like you and I. He said he fell for her the instant he laid eyes on her."

"I know Kiah. I have met her loads of time. But..."

"You make me want to give you so much and more. You gave yourself to me before you knew I could buy you the world. I know you've had lots of men who wanted to sweep you off your feet, but you waited, and you gave yourself to me. I am so fucking honoured woman. You are so bloody awesome! You blow my fucking mind every time you look at me!"

"But..." She couldn't find the words.

"Stop over thinking sweetheart. All I want is to make you happier. If I can buy you stuff I will. Because you are my girl. You are my girl, Nia. Do you understand? Now stop this. Be rational. Now no more of that shit you spouted earlier, or I swear to God, I will keep you locked in this car until you come to your goddam senses."

"You can't do that!" She said, noticing that the guys were preventing anyone from coming near the car.

"Trust me sweetheart. No more talking crap. Shush! Or so help me I will…"

"What?" She tossed.

He sprung at her and covered her mouth with his. She bit him hard. It excited him. He kissed her ferociously. He pictured the way she was on the stage earlier. Too bad he couldn't say it to her because of that asshole earlier.

He had to get him off the island and away from her. He wanted to kick his ass way into oblivion. Too bad his sister had rescued his brazen ass.

He didn't lift his mouth from hers until he felt her kissing him back.

"This is what you do to me woman. You drive me crazy! I will fuck your brains out until you realise just how crazy you drive me." He kissed her again. "Now I will let you up if you promise you will not cause any more scenes? I don't think the guys have worked so hard since they got on this island so have pity on them."

Nia kissed her teeth. She folded her arms.

"You promise to behave yourself Nia? I mean it Nia, one more scene out of you and I will whisk your beautiful ass off of this island." He pointed his finger at her like a truant child. "I mean it. Now play nice."

She wriggled under him.

"I mean it! You do not get out of this car until you promise to behave. I am very very good friends with Richard Bronson…"

She opened her mouth.

"Yes, you heard me. So, stop testing my patience and behave your sexy ass. Yes Nia. You absolutely blow my mind. You were so phenomenal on that stage by the way. Sorry I didn't get to tell you earlier."

He kissed her again.

"Now are you ready to get out of this car?"

She nodded.

"Behave Nia, or so help me I will make love to you right here, right now. Got it?"

She nodded obediently. She realised she acted like a damn lunatic. She had even hit the man and he didn't hit her back! David did!

How come this crazy stuff is happening to her? God must have fallen asleep on the job. Because she could not believe that someone like him could be genuinely interested in her. She knew she sounded like a broken record in her simplistic views.

"Always overthinking things Nia Belle. Sometimes it just is what it is." She thought her mama's voice whispered.

Suddenly there was a raucous. She looked past him and saw that William had lifted Seba clean in the air. Her hand came up to her mouth and she pointed.

125

"Nia! Nia sweetie! Kiah Corrington you let her out! You damn-well let her out you hear me!"

"Shit Nia!" He spun around. "Look what you've done. Why couldn't you be a sane female?" He asked through laughter as he pushed open the door and climbed out.

"Kiah! Kiah where is Nia?"

"She is there Sebastin." He gestured to William. He placed the writhing banshee back on his feet.

"You!" He jabbed at Kiah. "Sweetheart! Sweetie are you ok?" He ran to her and wrapped her up in his arms when she clambered out. "Did he hurt you? I swear to God
Kiah Corrington if you..."

"Sebastin, I simply told her the truth and she became deranged. Not what I was expecting."

"What did he tell you baby?" He turned back to the girl inspecting her up and down.

"Rarse Nia! Is that the...?" He pointed to the necklace.
She nodded.

"That is the bitch we saw at **Corrington's** the other day! We were daydreaming about the mama and her babies. Now you are wearing her! You bought that for her?"

"Yes Sebastin. She is my girl."

"You gave her a flipping 3 carat diamond necklace? Even earrings too? Bitch! Forget you!"

He snuggled up to Kiah in all his **HaVana** glory; loafers and fitted trousers, biceps bulging in his tight white tee.

"Can you buy me one too pretty please? I like the ring. Shit! You must be loaded Kiah!"

"You don't know the half of it." Nia mouthed.

It made Kiah laugh. He pointed his finger at her.

"You had better not forget your promise, Nia."

"Oh, be quiet Kiah."

"Nia-Belle..."

"Seba like I was saying. I am sorry I have not made it to the tent. I just got a shock and reacted badly."

"Girl, I heard all about it. That fool didn't hurt you, did he?"

"Depends on which one you're talking about." She spat.

"Not that one for sure." He pointed to Kiah. "Girl you are wearing bloody diamonds in de damn park! Bitch that is just uncivilised. "You are wearing blasted 7 carats worth of diamonds!" Seba whispered in her ear.

"Focus!" Nia snapped. Clicking her fingers in front of his face.

"Kk! By the way who are those hotties?"

"They are with him. Apparently, they go where he goes."

"You mean they are bodyguards?"

"Uh huh." She murmured folding her arms. Seba looked confused.

Much like she had done when she was enlightened.

"But what for?"

126

"Apparently, he is…" She bent to whisper in his ears. "He knows people and shit."

"People? What people?" He blabbered.

"Does Oprah ring a bell?" Nia asked him.

"No-he-doesn't!" Seba said stupidly. He looked Kiah up and down. "Seriously Kiah who do you know?"

"President Barrack Obama. I had dinner a couple of months ago at the White House."

"Shit Kiah! I knew there was something about your pretty-ass!" He pointed his finger at him. "You are a real dark-horse, aren't you? But seriously do you really know the blasted President?"

Kiah nodded.

Seba screamed like a girl. "Do you know anything about Necker Island?"

"I vacationed there a couple times."

"Take the bitch! I mean I will be your bitch if she doesn't want to." He waved her away flamboyantly.

Kiah laughed loudly. "I only want her though." He pointed to her and smiled. "So, tell her to behave."

"Behave sis! Behave your beautiful ass! Do you hear me? By the way great performance earlier. You didn't even pick up your phone. I was calling you to tell you he was here. The bitch-ass came to the tent. He claimed he wanted to apologise. I chased him. I heard you kicked his ass Kiah. Good on you."

"Glad to be of service. I will always put her first Sebastin." His eyes never left hers.

"Good. Because no matter how strong those two are I will always find a way to bury your pretty-ass, okay?"

Kiah saluted. "Yes sir."

"We are done for the night sweetie. I am too damn tired. I promised the aunties I would be in church tomorrow." He blessed himself. "Plus, you know when you sing, I am there with bells on. Pascal says you need to be there an hour before to run through the numbers; Brooklyn Tabernacle Choir's **I love the Lord, Pleasing and Psalm 34.** That should be a piece of cake. You've done em before."

"Thanks, Seba. Sorry again." She reached out and hugged him. Feeling a warmth spread up her body at the way Kiah was looking at her.

"No apologies sweetie. You deserve all the good things there is. God is blessing you, so you had better not allow fear to piss on things. Now give me a hug and behave your damn self. By the way are you up for giving London and her mom a ride? I would, But just that…" He bent to whisper. "I am staying in town." He turned and winked to Kiah. "She is a bit rusty and has trouble being on the receiving end."

"I understand."

"Smart man." He turned to Nia. "I mean it sis. Just behave your damn self. Pay heed to the verses of **Psalm 34** while you are at it." He kissed her on her cheeks. "And you. Come here."

127

Kiah went in for the hug.

"Turn her ass out tonight. Make her forget that asshole. By the way my clothes suit you. We'll talk soon."

"You don't have to tell me twice." He laughed. "Your clothes are brilliant. Feels fantastic too." He said to the guys, who sashayed over to the two guards looking at him strangely.

"As you were fellas. You! You are pure candy!" He rubbed his fingers along the outline of Terrence's lips and licked his. "I've got my eyes on you. Jesus! I am surely gonna burn in hell for the things I am thinking!" He blew kisses. "Keep up the magnificent work all of you! Mostly you Kiah Corrington!"

They all looked at Seba as he retreated.

Terrence and William busted out laughing.

"Freaky as hell." William said.

"Scarier off paper... But he's cute. I like him." Terrence said looking at Seba until he disappeared.

"Boss, are you ready?" William asked.

"Nia?" Kiah turned to her.

"Let's get London and her mama." She gestured over to Georgie and her daughter; she was cradling her in her arms.

William ran off towards them. He took the child gently and brought her back and placed her attentively in the back seat. Her mom got in beside her.

"Shall we stop by the shop for your car? One of the guys can drive it back."

"That sounds like a plan. By the way Georgette meet Kiah.

"Nice to meet you Kiah. You are the talk on everyone's lips. Even Miss London. She says she is going to marry you soon."

"Bless her heart. I will have to have a talk with her to let her know I only have eyes for her auntie." "Good choice Kiah."

"Those two are Terrence and ...."

"I've met William." She said all giggles. "By the way Miss Nia Ella gave me your bowl."

"Thanks Georgie. I so forgot about it in all the scuffle."

"Nice to meet you, Miss Georgette." Terrence said. They waited.

"Do you want me to drive?" Kiah asked.

"No! I will! You can drive me tomorrow in broad daylight."

"Smart woman." The men said.

When they closed the doors. They took off running towards their ride.

In the car Kiah reached for her hand. She moved it and placed it atop the steering wheel. She knew she was in her head thinking about what he'd said to her earlier. But who could blame her? It was a lot to digest.

"Nice ride Boss." Georgette said infringing on her thoughts.

"It's his." Nia said absentmindedly pointing across to Kiah.

"**Maxim's,** right?"

"Yes Ma'am." He offered easily.

128

"Maybe I can shop there once I win the lottery. In the meantime, I will bum a ride, flag a buss, and let us not forget **M11**. They will be my modus operandi if you please."

She wanted to ask about the two guys but cautioned herself. She didn't think it was the right time because her boss looked pissed. That was a rarity. But they have all learnt over the years once she got that way to just allow her to ride it out until she came down.

So, she left her alone. Perhaps she will learn who they are later.

The tension was thick. She longed to know what had gone wrong though. Especially when she had seen him pick her up and toss her over his shoulders and took off running.

She ran to Seba and told him to go and make certain she was ok. Because what could possibly have gone wrong in such a short time? Maybe it had something to do with her cousin David.

Seba came back and said they were just having a squabble and that they were going to be fine.

She hoped so. Especially because she hadn't recalled her boss being so cheery and full of smiles in such a long time. She looked as though someone had plugged her up with electric wires.

Georgie knew around this time of the year she was beaten down and sad because of the memory of her mama. She made the sign of the cross and whispered, "God rest your sweet soul, Mama Belle."

"By the way Miss Nia I am so sorry about David. He promised us he wouldn't pull any crap when he saw you. But Francy told me what happened."

"Don't worry about it Georgie. David will always be David."

"True-that. I am sorry none-the-less."

"What's done is done. No use crying over spilt milk."

"Kiah I am sorry too."

"Not to worry." He offered. His fingers tapped distractedly on his thigh as he thought, **so long as that idiot kept his distance and responded decently around her and keep his hands to himself**...

His heart pumped furiously. He lowered the window a bit to calm down.

The night-time scenery was electric. He didn't miss the many noisy and colourful umbrellas, along with makeshift stalls and bars with laughable names like **Moose, Hairy Bush, Knuckle Dem, Love Shack, Daily Bread, Alpha & Omega**...

Some appeared to have only been erected since they were inside beckoning to all as they drove by with sights and smell.

People were sporadically milling about buying, eating, or selling something.

He smiled as he recalled one of her songs from earlier.

Some interestingly dressed and diverse group of people tried to get their attention; by waving or hailing them over, or showing lots of skin and thing...

It was hard to determine male or female at times as they drove out.

In town there seemed to be no difference. It overflowed with the miscellaneous groups who seemed infused with the spirit of celebration as they hung around out at quayside bars and restaurant, sitting or grouping in the front of shops, standing and eating, shouting and dancing, singing and greeting, some even arguing heatedly...

Scented smoke wafted about and crept in and swirled about them from grills, barbeques and frying.

It made him ravenous as the smells accosted his nostril. He ignored it.

He could go without food for hours, a day even when he was working on a tedious project.

His eyes took in the passing buildings; concrete and wooden. Finished and unfinished. Beautiful as well as modern, while some showed off a sense of garish theatrics.

Some were painted in white and some in a pastel fusion.

People were sitting and chatting loudly or dancing to loud music on their balconies. Some waved as they passed by.

Along with animals; cats and dogs who would not be forgotten.

"There's Gene and Dinah boss. Wonder whose pockets they looking to finish off tonight? By the way. They looked gorgeous in their showpieces they picked up today. Impressive job on the plumes boss."

"Great paying customers. I don't care what anyone says about them."

"I hear you."

Kiah looked at the two females or were they males? They were unloading cases from their vehicle outside what looked like a nightclub called **Frivolity.**

"Great song choices for tomorrow as well. Mr. Pascal said he didn't want to add any more pressure."

"You conspired with him too Georgie?"

"You know it is boring as hell when you are not singing."

"Georgie, you know we are booked solid for this month."

"I know boss. But you still need to learn to delegate."

"Are you calling me a control freak?"

"The hat fits boss?"

They laughed.

"I also told you I am willing to work a full shift this month on Fridays. Because **Safe Haven** has space and can keep Lonnie a full day."

"I told you I will think on it."

"I mean it. I can be an extra pair of hands."

"Stop trying to convince me Georgie! Shit I am sorry. I am in my head."

Nia apologised to the girl. She was a brilliant assistant. But she believed Christmas time was meant to be with family. She preferred her spending the time with her daughter. Children grew very quickly, and when all was said and done didn't remember trinkets, but time spent with family. Mamas especially. Her eyes stung.

They pulled into the back parking lot to collect her car. As she rummaged through her bag her mobile went off.

It was Seba. He screamed in her ears. "Jackpot bitch! Booyah!! Do you know he is among the fucking top ten riches men in the US? His estimated worth is 70 plus billion. I mean fucking billions Nia. I googled his ass! He is nasty rich bitch! I sent you the file. He was telling the goddam truth about President Obama. He got pictures to support. He even knows the fucking Dalai Lama!!!"

"Seba calm down before you give yourself a heart attack."

She held the phone away from her ears.

"It is too much Seba. I still haven't wrapped my mind around it yet."

"You had betta! I am warning you Nia. Don't play fool and mess this up girlfriend."

"Later Seba. I will speak to you later." She hung up the phone.

She kept her eyes straight ahead. She didn't trust herself to look across at him. Even when he took the keys and their fingers brushed together. She felt as though someone had hooked her up with jumper cables. She quickly put her hands back on the steering wheel.

Kiah hated it. He did not want to cause a scene. So, he reasoned to just let it go. She looked wound up tighter than a yoyo. He reckoned the shit wasn't over. He could feel it. It made him smile. She sure was a spitfire.

William flashed the lights and they started off again.

"So, I take it you're not gonna attend Omar's Beach picnic tomorrow boss?"

"Let me get through tonight, Georgie. Church even. Then I will let you know."

"I wouldn't blame you if you didn't show up. His crazy ass will probably be there. You know they are good buddies."

"I thought he wasn't coming back this year. Why is he here? What happened to this big thing he had in the works?"

"David is a hot head with a diva complex. Probably played his ass and the deal went south."

"I just don't care anymore. My head hurts."

London snored loudly. It made them all laugh.

"What I wouldn't give to be doing what she is doing right now." Georgie said.

"You'll be home soon." Nia offered.

They had now entered her village. She took the next turns carefully. Because '**Limers**' were out enjoying the night. They were playing cards and dominoes, drinking, listening to music or gambling at **Lord Hayes, Pica, and Rice Na Packet...**

Then some would be stumbling home blindly in the street, having started their drinking since last night.

Thank goodness they finally finished installing more lights over on this side of the island.

They had long since left the loudness and buzz of the limelight behind them.

131

Kiah reached out and their hands touched. They were going after the radio.
She recoiled as though he were contagious.
"Look at that fool." Georgette said sharply. "Mas Pete get you drunkin backside outta de road!" She called through the window.
He brushed her off. It was his regular thing to do.
"Crazy ass! I don't know how he ain't dead yet. Since Miss Ellen left him, he has gotten worst. Men, they get what they want, and they don't behave, and when the woman finally gets tired and decide to walk, they act like that. When most of it is their own damn fault. His fault to be exact."
"He has no one to blame but himself. But bless him. Hopefully he gets it together before it is too late." Nia said as she thanked God, she wouldn't be the one to put him out of his misery tonight.
Two more turns and they were parking outside her development.
Clusters of pastel-coloured houses with neatly trimmed hedges, bushes and trees, low gates and walls.
She had helped the girl to buy a partial in the government scheme.
Eventually she would be able to pay it off and become an owner.
It still was a rollercoaster dealing with Boots, her abusive partner.
That was why she had used **Safe Haven** for a brief period until she could stand on her two feet.

"Home sweet home ladies." Nia said as she looked at the two men bounding up. Before Georgie could reach back in to scoop the child up William was there.
"I'll get her ma'am... You get the door."
"Thank you, William." Georgie giggled again as she led the way up the walk.
"You home now Georgie-gal?" It was her elderly neighbour, Miss Evers. She had taught them at primary school.
"How was the village? How Miss Nia?"
"Yes Ma'am. It was good, everything and everyone is good. Miss Nia is good too. London is asleep so I am going to try and get her in."
"Ok darling. Glad you home. Be safe. See you at church in the morning. By the way I hear Miss Nia will be singing. That girl could always make our hearts bleed when she opens her mouth."
"So true Ma'am. So true. Night night. See you in the morning."
She opened the door and walked in. William went in behind her.
Couple minutes he was out. She was standing looking at him as though he had wings.
"Night night Georgie."
"Night boss. Night Kiah. Night guys. Bye William and thanks again."
"Don't forget to switch your security system on Georgie. I mean it."
"Yes boss."
The once pretty girl promised as she showed off busted teeth and a wonky eye. Trophies from her Boots relationship.

132

She waited until they all got back in the cars, then waved them on.
She thought of William; he was cute and so strong and helpful. She' had
stuck her phone number in his pocket.
He smiled and simply said, "thank you ma'am."

In the car he decided to bite the bullet. The silence was ripping at his
heart. He took a chance to break it.
"Why were you so adamant about her security system Nia?"
"She was one of **Safe Haven** recipients."
"Georgette?"
"Yes Kiah. She only has partial sight in her left eye. He beat her within an
inch of her life..." She shook herself from the memory. "I would also like
to help her get a perfect set of teeth to match that 100watt smile of
hers. There are other things. But those are starters."
He bit his tongue before he could say done. He didn't want to add
anymore salt to the obviously festering wound.
"Is the guy still around who did that to her?"
"He's behind bars. Where thank God he needs to be. Serving a
lengthy sentence. Stalking and attempted murder. Kiah he almost killed
her."
"Serves him right."
"Kiah... I think you should..."
"Don't you dare! I am not going anywhere."
"Kiah I can't do this. I don't know how." She could feel tears stinging the
back of her eyes.
"Then we talk, and we fight. But I am staying. Do you hear me,
Nia?"
"Kiah please. I need to think about all this."
"I asked you earlier would it have been better if you didn't know. You
never answered. So, I will ask you again. Would it have been better?"
"Kiah...What will your people say when they find out about me?"
"Why are you worried about that Nia? All I am concerned about is you
and me. I love you."
"But how? Why? How is this going to work?"
"Nia, we have 28 more days to figure it out. But how will we do it if
you want me to leave? Please be logical."
"But Kiah..."
"Let's cross that bridge when we get there. Please Nia."
"Sit back in your seat."
"Why?"
He found out couple seconds later when they came over this drop.
Kiah was certain his heart was now located in his mouth.
If he opened it, he was certain it would surely jump out and run.
"Shit Nia! Why didn't you warn me?"
"But I did." She said and laughed, for his expression was priceless.
He began speaking another language.

133

"I hope this makes us even now. I think you did that on purpose."
"I did not. This is just the quickest way to get home. That back there is called **Slavers Gully** and over there pass that gate is known as **Betrayers Point**. That was where 15 slaves lost their lives in 1833 when they rebelled against their plantation owners who treated them abysmally. Some say this part of the island is haunted. They go as far as to say on the odd occasion you would glimpse them crossing the road being chased by a couple headless plantation owners atop horses.
"That isn't true is it, Nia? You are pulling my leg."
"Many claimed they have seen it. I have never. I don't want to. But I must admit my hair does stand on edge when I drive through here late at night."
"Just think what a mecca this place could be for Halloween."
"We do go all out for St. Patricks. Just like they do in Ireland and New York."
"Slavery was an abomination. Pity it took so long to get it abolished."
"Damn straight. But I guess it worked for the money makers otherwise it could not have lasted this long."
"True. A shame that one race dominated another for so long."
"Greed pure and simple."
"Stupidity too." He finished. Thankful that she was speaking to him again.

Couple minutes later they were driving down her road. She stopped the vehicle outside the gate.
"Can I have my bag please Kiah?"
He handed it to her.
She riffled through it pulling out the remote. The gate opened and they drove in.
"Does that mean I can stay?"
"Yes Kiah. I am too tired...Plus knowing me I will not sleep well. I will be up worrying."
"Thank you...Please just give us a chance. I know it's a big mouthful. But just let's deal with it one day at a time."
"Come on. Let's go in. By the way where do they stay?"
"Where I stay Nia."
"What do you mean?"
"Are you gonna freak out again? Because if you are. I will not say anything else on the grounds that I may incriminate myself."
"What are you saying Kiah?"
"Not one word from me Nia... Thank you William." He took the keys the guy handed him.
"By the way William where would you two be heading now? Will you be going up to the manse?" Nia asked.
"No ma'am."
"What do you mean no? There is no place around here to sleep other than the... Kiah!"
"What?"

134

"I am too tired for this shit!" She walked away and towards her door.
She could feel him behind her.
"Kiah they can use the second floor. I will get the keys. They can come in and grab something to eat."

She left the keys on the table and them in the kitchen and went to her bedroom. She longed for a shower.
She stripped taking everything off down to the necklace and the earrings he'd bought her. She left them on the counter. She promised she would give them back in the morning. She ran her fingers along the necklace recalling his face when he'd given it to her.
She pulled herself away and covered her head and walked into the shower stall.
Images of the entire day jumped mischievously in and flashed about in her mind's eye. His confession and all that Seba said reverberated like a messy stew in there. She didn't know how long she was standing under the warm shower until she felt him behind her.
She jumped right out of her skin.
"It's me Nia!" He reached out. He didn't know how she would react. Her body stiffened. He held himself together and respected her space.
He waited and prayed like he had done so many times in the evening since he had told her his identity.
"No Kiah...I can't do this..." She pushed back on him. Fighting the immense urge to lean in.
"I find myself apologising. But I don't know why Nia. I have worked hard. I have made money lots of it. Now you are making me feel as though it's something I should be ashamed of. Honestly speaking I don't get it."
"Kiah I am tired."
"I know baby." He went to her again. This time she allowed him to hold her. "Let's just table it. Because honestly, I don't see the problem." He buried his face in the outline of her neck.
She allowed him too. Just for a bit. Then she sprung to life.
"I'm going to bed." She offered and stepped away from him.
He reached for her. She dragged her arm out of his. He watched as she grabbed a towel and draped it about herself.
She walked away and headed to her dressing room and dried herself. She applied lotion, then walked to her bedroom.
He finished his shower. By the time he made it to the bedroom she was already in bed with the covers up about herself.
"Nia...Nia...Nia..." He ventured softly. His heart was truly aching. He still did not see the big deal in what he had revealed. But she was angry, and he just had to give her the time she needed to wade through it.
He tossed his towel and climbed in beside her. She did not acknowledge him. He switched off the lights. Even when he nestled up beside her, she still did not respond.

Chapter Four

Nia turned... She was wrapped up in his limbs as though she were a fly in a spider's web. She hadn't recall falling asleep. She had pretended when he came to the room. Even when he laid next to her and reached out. Thank God he didn't push. She had breathed a slow sigh of relief when his breathing changed. As she laid there caught between a rock and a hard place.
She turned to look at him; he was asleep and breathing easily. He didn't snore. What a surprise. David was the complete opposite.
She couldn't help herself; she reached out to touch his beautiful face. Her hands brushed back a couple of his neat locks that had tumbled about his face.
God help me she thought as her fingers ran the length of his face. They lingered at his mouth roaming around his lips.
He was right; nothing about him had change. She thought. He was still the same amazing Kiah Corrington that had swept her off her feet from the moment their eyes had met. The other persona she would ease into...
But this one lying there beside her was the one she loved.
She couldn't help it. She felt starved. So, she bent to kiss his lips. She missed his warmth...touch...voice...
Her hands ran the length of his body.
He shifted. He whispered her name. It made her pause in her exploration. Tears stung the back of her eyes once again.
"Kiah Corrington...God help me...I am totally head over heels in love with you." She whispered.
She bent to kiss his lips. She was starving for his touch. Her entire body quivered. She had never felt like this before. Come to think not even David. Yes, she loved him, was quite besotted by him. But never this bold yearning. This man, even his presence made her ravenous for his touch. She bit down on her lips fiercely as tears streamed down her face in earnest.
"What am I going to do about the way I feel about you? God help me. I need your help to deal with this because I am handling this so badly. Help me God."
Nia hadn't realised she was on her knees. She was talking to God like her mama had taught her to do.
Suddenly she was being lifted and flipped unto her back. He was atop her. His beautiful eyes buried themselves deep within hers.
"Kiah!" She groaned. As her heart thumped away in her chest.
"Nia I am head over heels in love with you too. I love the woman I have come to know. I am so proud of all the things you've accomplished. I too thank God for you. I believe in the way the universe works. We get what we give to it. So, woman I am not going to apologise about being filthy rich. I am never ever going to apologise for wanting to give it to you when

you want me to. Fuck Nia! You are the first female I have met to react to my money as though it were contagious. You are rare. So let me remind you that I am never giving you up. Nod if you understand Nia Belle Castle nee Francois."

"How do you know?" She whispered stupidly for his eyes held hers in a trance.

"Understand you beautiful women. I know everything there is to know about you. My team is bloody brilliant."

"See Kiah that is the thing that sticks in my craw. You are like a character we watch on television or the big screen."

"Never mind about any of that stuff. You can get accustomed to it. Like I had to. It wasn't easy. I wasn't born with it per say. But that is my gift for working as hard and as honestly as I do. Unfortunately, there are people out there who will always try to take advantage. Which is why I need them, Nia. Not to show off but to give others pause if they entertain the idea of coming at me. Now you sweetheart. I will never ever allow anyone to hurt you ever again. But we will cross that bridge when we get there. For now, please… please… please let us enjoy each other."

He held her gaze and forced himself not to even move.

"Nia, I don't get to do this often. Just take a breather. Maybe it's because I don't do idle. But dear God with you I think I am entitled. So please just allow me to show you that you mean the world to me." His voice cracked. He felt the sting in the back of his eyes. He had her attention, and he aimed to keep it, to keep her.

He never wanted another night like what he had endured last night. He had earnestly prayed to God and promised a lot of things. Thank goodness he was not like us.

Sleep had finally come.

Without much thought and more out of an instinct for the way he made her feel she reached up and took his face in her hands.

She was overwhelmed about the feelings that washed over her body.

"I'm sorry Kiah…I am so very sorry…I will try my best because I don't want to lose you. You have become so damn important to me in the brief time that I have known you…"

"As you have become to me Nia. I am head over heels in love with you gorgeous woman. Yes Nia. I love the hell out of you. Do you hear me? Better yet do you believe me? Do you believe me Nia? Because we can't go any further unless you believe this. I am serious. I will ask you one more time. Do you believe that I Kiah Carter Corrington 111 is head over heels in love with you? Your answer will determine my next action, Nia."

"What do you mean Kiah?"

"Just think about the question. Do you believe that I am totally head over heels in love with you woman?"

He had concluded last night that if she couldn't believe it, he would indeed leave. It was going to be the fucking hardest thing he would ever have to do, but he wasn't going to stay.

He told the team to get ready just on the off chance it went haywire. They had also convinced him finally they weren't going to the second floor. He had left them in the living room watching television.

"Yes Kiah." She said after the longest period in each of their lives. She genuinely believed he did. She would be a poor judge of character if all they had been through in the shortest of time since meeting had her believing anything else.

"I do Kiah. I do. I missed you so much." She reached up and kissed his mouth. He didn't kiss her back. But she could feel his body responding like it had done the moment he had climbed atop her.

She kissed him again. He still did not kiss her back. She repeated it a couple more times until she thought she would lose her mind if he didn't kiss her back.

"That's for all the crazy shit you made me think Nia."

It took all the strength he had to resist her. He cupped her face in his hands.

"I love you." He whispered. "So, damn much. You drive me insane." He breathed raggedly.

"I love you too." She whimpered. Before they lost themselves within each other.

When they came up for air they ran towards the bathroom and sorted themselves. Then decided to head out for a run.

They exited through the sliding doors where they grabbed a couple bottles of water from the refrigerator, she kept out there.

After a period of stretches they took off for the beach. They ran the length up and down, side by side.

Occasionally they would ask each other, "how are you?" But that was it. She was not a talker when she ran. Neither was he.

They were so hot and sweaty by the time they completed the run.

In the cool down he said, "Your place is so beautiful and serene. So much detail went into it. The layout of the land as well."

"Thank you, Kiah, and thank the ancestors as well who had the good sense to parcel some of theirs out to my mama."

"So, you inherited all this?"

"Stop asking because you are being polite."

"So, we are good then?"

"Kinda... But tell me something. What would your next action be if I had said no?"

"Dear God Nia! I never ever want to go there again. I was scared shitless. Thank God for the answer you gave."

She laughed. He consumed her. "By the way did those two get to the apartment?"

"No. I couldn't convince them."

"So where are they?"

"I left them watching television in the living room."
Please don't let her freak out again he begged God as he glanced across at her.
She stopped in her tracks.
"You mean? Oh my God! Oh my God Kiah!"
"Not again Nia. I swear to God my heart is getting worn."
Shit! He thought. "What is it? Talk Nia! Please don't hit me again." He cowered comically when she came at him.
"They must have heard this morning!!! Gosh they must think me a damn skank!"
"Who gives a fuck what they think? We all fuck each other, Nia! It's natural woman."
He rushed to her and scooped her up. "They had better get accustomed to it woman. Because that is all I aim to do for the next month. I'm addicted to you."
She screeched out loudly.
"That's exactly how I want to have you, Nia. I love to see you enjoying yourself when we fuck. You don't hold back. I love the way your body fits mine. The energy you transmit. I swear we could light up a couple islands if we wanted."
"Kiah you make me blush! I am like an addict when I am around you too."

They were now hidden amongst the many indigenous trees and plants that grew wild on the island now.
She had managed to clear a pathway without destroying much of the vegetation.
She pulled him into a decent grove. They would be hidden. She had mischief on her mind.
"Nia!" He warned. Kissing her back.
"I want you again Kiah!"
He kissed her just as hungrily as she was doing to him. She felt that burning trail coursing through her body. Especially when he managed to get her top off and reigned ravenous kisses from her mouth all the way down to her breasts.
He unclipped her sports bra in the front. He took each straining to the tip hardened nipple into his hot mouth.
She was certain they would pop like berries on the vine under a hot sun, as he devoured them hungrily.
She moaned feverishly.
He continued the lava like trail down her belly and paused teasingly at her belly button; there he flicked his tongue like a hungry alley cat to a bowl of milk.
She whimpered softly.
He continued until he got to the opening between her legs and buried his face like a sniffer dog deep within her.
"Kiah! Kiah! Kiah we can't do this! Not here! Not now!" She panted like a racehorse.

139

"Says fucking who!" He snarled looking hungrily up at her. "I am going to make you regret tormenting the fuck out of me Nia. You have been a very naughty naughty girl." He ground out.

He eased her out of her shorts. Then her panties. He spread her wide. He teased her savagely and watched as she handcuffed herself to the tree and balanced achingly on her toes.

He tongue-lashed her violently until she began to howl sickeningly.

The next thing he felt was an onslaught on his head as she grabbed fistfuls of his hair and shoved his mouth like a clamp unto her clit and screamed. "Right there! Right there! Right there Kiah!"

He eased her up with his hands and shoved his tongue deeper.

It caused her to meld into a fit as she moaned and hummed in pure delirium.

The sound egged him on. It seemed like he couldn't get enough of her. His tongue and little nips of his teeth was her rod of correction.

She started to explode. He tasted her.

"Not yet naughty girl." He teased. "I'm not through."

He came up swiftly and she helped him to get free of his bindings. She threw his clothes wildly as she reached for his lips and suckled them like a hungry baby.

When they came up for air, she called his name as though from the depths of deep despair. The sound goaded him on even more.

It was as though she was a siren from the oceans' depth.

He devoured her lips, then swiftly and deftly he flipped her around and pressed her hands into the trunk of the tree. Before he slipped in and disappeared deep within her. It was so easy.

He rode her like a lead pony. He followed her movements as he pushed her lower so he could dive deeper.

She cried distressingly and sickeningly as her body writhed devilishly.

"Oh God Kiah! Kiah I am losing my mind! I am losing my fucking mind Kiah!"

"Me too Nia. Me too." He chorused. As he tried to cling to her.

Task unaccomplished. So, he sought between her legs with his hand.

His thumb and forefinger played maliciously with her clit before he gently squeezed... She lowered her squat, he plunged deeper.

She thought he would rip her apart; completely splitting her down the middle.

Her body swerved, or was it her legs? She had completely lost her damn mind. She blubbered in delirium. So did he. As she hunkered down upon him for what must be the last stretch. She believed she would die. It was pandemonium now.

Animals made their presence known.

She thankfully hugged the tree trunk for having pity; to bear her up.

"This is what you do to me Nia! Oh God!" He lifted her off her feet.

His body raged as he unplugged himself just long enough to shift position; he pushed her up against the tree. She brought her leg expertly up into his hand as he gripped the tree. He was amazed by the action. He slipped back into her and pumped mercilessly. Her body was dynamite. Sweat streamed from his raging form.

"You are fucking mine Nia! Mine do you hear me? Mine!" He covered her mouth unceremoniously. As images of her on stage with that bastard flashed through his mind.

He didn't think he could plunge any deeper without breaking his dick. But she was so fucking volcanic, and he felt febrile. She was his and his only. He raged on tumultuously until he couldn't hold it any longer...

He released all he was deep within her.

Seconds later he felt her shattering hotly ferociously like molten lava over and over unto him as their screams exploded into the surroundings.

They tried to cling to each other. They gave up collapsing in a heap, panting and clawing for every breath.

When they pulled up outside the church building and parked. Members were already gathering in the parking area. He stayed her a while longer. He did not want her with them just yet.

The boys had sorted breakfast, fruit salad, pancakes and bacon along with eggs and made pancakes.

"Typical home-grown American right?" She asked when they presented her with a plate. "Thank you, guys. But not before my coffee."

William presented her with a hot mug. She was surprised. They had used her coffee grinder. It was a perfect blend.

"I added a touch of cinnamon and pinch of nutmeg."

"How do you know? Seriously don't tell me." She meant it. She held up her hands to stop them.

They laughed like they were a real family. Like she had three big brothers who stopped by to raid her refrigerator.

They complimented her on the house. They were beginning to grow on her. Especially as she watched them clean up after themselves meticulously.

By the time she left to get herself sorted for church she had eaten two strawberry pancakes and bacon and drank two cups of coffee.

When she emerged from her dressing room, he was just walking out of the bathroom a towel haphazardly placed about his waist.

The man was so amazing to look at whether he was naked or clothe. She was certain her teeth sweated each time. It should be a crime for someone to look so dog-gone good so early in the morning she thought.

"Hello again." He said cheerfully as he came over to kiss her possessively. He wrapped her up in his arms.

She was wearing sexy lingerie in black lace and thigh high stocking with little red bows.

"Are you attending church or going on stage?" He asked her, loving the picture she presented.

"It's between me, you and God Kiah." She teased.

141

He swathed her behind.

"I have a confession." She teased. Lost again in his mesmerising violet eyes. He smelt of her rose oil. She kissed him lightly. She didn't want to redo her make up.

"You know we can talk about anything right?" He asked his eyes lost in hers.

"Yes, I know Kiah."

"So?"

"I liked the way you thoroughly spoke to my body in the bushes this morning. I enjoyed your class immensely." She whispered in his ear. She felt his arms tighten.

"I aim to please sweetheart. You got an A+! Nia, you blew my mind." He kissed her sweet, glossed lips. Pictures of earlier flew through his mind. They'd cum unashamedly in front of each other in the shower stall where he'd jerk off just drinking in her wet body.

"Nia, woman you gaslight me every time woman." He spoke his truth as his hands ran the length of her body. "I have a secret of my own as well." He whispered in her ear like she had done to him.

"What is it?"

"I want you." He pushed her bottom into him. He had a woody.

She wiggled and giggled. She too wanted more. But common sense prevailed. She knew they would be late to church.

The house phone interrupted their kiss. She went to get it. It was her auntie; she had heard what had happened in the park.

"I am doing fine auntie. Don't worry about it. I am... I mean we are getting ready for church. We will be there with bells on. I love you too. We will see you soon...Yes auntie I will speak to Kiah about coming up later. Yes auntie. We will see you soon."

He looked to her. "Someone messaged her about the park." She relayed. "She wanted to know if we are ok."

"Are we Nia?"

"After I took your class Kiah? I can still feel you deep within me." He laughed loudly filling the cavernous room.

"You had better behave your damn-self Nia. Or I will not spare the rod." He wagged his finger at her.

She flounced back to her dressing room to get ready, swishing her hips at him.

He laughed loudly again. "You are going to be the death of me Nia-Belle."

She froze in the spot. Then the next second she was running back to him and stood on her tiptoes to embrace him tightly.

"I love you too Kiah. So very much." She did not finish the rest of the sentence. But it scampered across her mind's eye.

Please please please don't ever make me regret this.

He brought his arms up tightly around her too.

That is until she whimpered, "can't breathe...can't breathe."

The team pulled up on the far side of them. The journey had taken fifteen minutes.

They parked on a massive tarmac in front of a two-storey white building shaped like a warehouse. The sign on it read **Faith & Hope Ministries.** Two huge open palms were the symbol above the door.

They chatted a bit about the place. She told him the pastor was a female who came highly recommended from Joel Osteen's ministries nearly five years ago.

Pastor Sarah Seaton was quite the visionary and had taken the church to new heights. The doors were always open for anyone.

She was approachable and her ethos about 'change' for the world as well as the vision for the church was well known.

She held yoga and meditation classes and serve as a psychiatrist; she was certified.

"People are seeking another way of acknowledgement other than the old archaic way of seeing and doing. They did not want the ordinary fire and brimstone preaching. Lots more wanted to do more, help more."

Nia agreed. She recalled something the aunties said.

"If God was love, why would he punish them for loving each other just like a heterosexual couple do? No one is perfect. Everyone wants to be seen, be recognised, feel worthy for the positive things they do for self and for community and the world." She repeated it to Kiah.

"Faith without works huh?" He was not a church goer. But his faith was strong especially in the things he believed and did. The big guy was pleased and still worked in his life. He paid attention and was very grateful. His light source was high through his yoga and meditation. Life was great.

"Exactly. I had become very disillusioned with the churches. Seems like you couldn't question the leaders about anything. No room for thinking outside the box. But the straw that broke the camel's back was the treatment of Seba. He was beaten up a couple times and robbed. Yet he continues to do so much. They took from him under the table yet not stand with him in public. Kiah, I hated the hypocrisy. Same for the aunties. **Faith and Hope** changed that for most of us."

"I hear you sweetheart." He thought how remarkable she was yet again. Which was why he had to speak to her before she got out.

The team reasoned that trouble was looming. Because David had unfinished business. He was a member of the same church and no doubt he would be attending. He had been calling her mobile basically all night until she simply just switched it off. She had not gone looking for it today. He had kept her very busy.

His auntie telephoned. He gave her the cliff notes but told her they were back on track. She asked if he had told her the important bits. He said not yet because he did not think it was the right time. So, he pushed it to the furthest regions of his mind.

He thought perhaps when they were a bit more solid, he would tell her. But not right now. She asked, well it sounded more like a command that they be over at the manse later. That much he owed, seeing he had skipped out of staying there.

He promised they would have an answer for them by the time they met at church.

"Kiah I will have to go in soon. We usually do one last rehearsal. You can come in with me."

"Nia...Have you looked at your phone today?"

"No. I am shit when it comes to that. Especially on weekends. If it is urgent most know my house number." She felt him squeeze her hand.

"Is there something else I need to know Kiah?"

Her heart started to beat loudly in her chest. The look on his face was severe.

For the hundredth time today, she thought him drop dead gorgeous. Especially when he emerged wearing a slim fit honest-to-goodness Hugo Boss grey suit with white fitted top and grey Gucci loafers.

She swore she could hear the **007** intro.

"You look gorgeous."

"So do you." He said to her.

She looked so regal. He knew it was cliché' but the woman was mesmerising. She appeared to glow.

Nia had chosen an homage to Carolina Herrera; crisp white wrap blouse with asymmetric layered ruffling at the elbows, over a flowing ankle length A-Line mauve-grey skirt with ample material to be worn as a sexy halter if she needed to be someplace else later.

The aunties usually hosted a brunch; an afternoon luncheon that could run late into the evening. It was open to anyone. Hosted the first Sunday of every month. Which was exactly what today was. She had forgotten. She grabbed a diaphanous silvery 5-meter length shawl; it was her signature piece for the festival season this year.

Instead of lugging along weighty sweaters or jackets this was the piece to have. It was supposed to be shown to the aunties yesterday along with the formal wear designs.

"Do you have it with you?"

"Kiah please." She said as she tuned back in to give him her full attention. "What now?"

"Get it out, turn it on. I turned it off last night. He was ridiculous."

"Who? Ooh." She kissed her teeth. "I seriously don't have time for him."

"He will be coming here today no doubt. He has unfinished business Nia."

"Mine has been long concluded Kiah. Forget him. He is an asshole."

"On that we agree. Nia...I know he has hit you before. Not once...I seriously want to kill him." His hands became fists.

He pictured driving them into his smug face. He was so damn cocky to think that as soon as he strolled back on the island, she would drop everything for him. But that was what he seemed to be banking on because she had apparently done it a couple times before. "Kiah it's

144

over. I have you now...I don't even want to hear that fools name. No dampers on our brilliant morning. I am still thinking about it. Good God I am gonna burn in hell, aren't I?"

She reached across and kissed his lips. "Now you are all the man I need. Let's go in and get this day over with. Then we can go home and snuggle up. I do not want to talk about him anymore."

She reached for the door handle.

The aunties' car pulled in. Silcott parked a little way from the entrance. As soon as they stepped out of the car Nia felt like hiding. She also felt like running over and yelling, 'I got a man! As well as "thank you for keeping him for me all these years!

She felt him behind her.

"Are you ready for the firing squad?" He asked laughing.

His hand followed the outline of her back and came to wander across her full round perky rear end. His heart stirred.

Was this a natural phenomenon; to absolutely adore someone in such a short space of time?

He had heard a lot of people talk about '**love at first sight**'.

He was one of the scuffers for years. Now it had bit him in the ass.

I warned you to be careful what you put out there, his thoughts seemed to jeer.

"They make me feel like such a little girl. Like they must always protect me."

His breath tingled the back of her neck.

"Glad they could Nia." He reached for her hand. He did not care who saw or wanted to write a goddam thing. She was his woman, and he was going to show the hell out of her.

"Hello you two..." It was Auntie B. She ushered them over.

They hugged and kissed. Nia had to admit they were two beautiful women, and not only on the outside.

They were both wearing her designs; auntie B was decked out in a creamy green skirt suit and white silk tank her statement pearls; sea foam and chunky three strand, with big round earrings to match. Her hair was loose and flowing held off her face by a gorgeous fascinator.

Nia knew the designer of their jewellery and accessories. Her name was **Bonswa**. She was a young female who migrated from Haiti via a small prostitution ring.

They had discovered her selling some things she made on the side of the road. They had bought a couple pieces. She looked dirty and beaten down at the time. She had stayed with Nia on her mind.

Then she had worked late one night and when she was leaving the shop she came upon her sleeping at the door. She was badly battered and bloody.

Nia took her to **Safe Haven** after they checked her out. The rest as they say was her story...

The woman now has a thriving business and her own studio aptly named **Bonswa.**

Nia recalled the outfits. They were from the **Pastel Line**. Another hit. More ticks than crosses. She had a great feeling about the line.

Auntie K had chosen a milky purple in a flared V-neck pantsuit. Gorgeous amethyst and sea glass stone necklace and earrings complimented the outfit.

Her hair was in a neat chignon atop her head. Simple elegance.

Other cars were pulling in with some of the famous faces around the island.

Guess many liked to snuggle up to God on a Sunday, it made them feel important and worthy for the rest of the week.

They fed on each other's strength as they held hands.

Just then the Premier George Brade and his wife Mary elegant as ever stopped by. She was a frequent shopper at **Belle**.

Once she recalled having to go around before church begun and readjust some of the females; they were wearing the same style but different colour. Small Island. So, she made certain the island élites who shopped at her store were never seen in the same styles at any event. Which is why she always travelled with her 'box' of tricks.

She had to explain it to Kiah when she had them put it in the back of the car. She never left home without it. Just in case she had to think on her feet.

She also told him to take a change of clothes. They might do a bit of sight-seeing if the mood strikes.

So, while introductions were being made; Kiah being proudly paraded around. Nia took the opportunity to slip away for choir practise.

In the back hall majority were enquiring as to how she was. But it was more like being 'farse'. Because some had posted videos on Facebook.

Georgie showed her a couple of the videos...

A couple of her on Kiah's shoulder... Being sequestered in the car... Some of the team protecting the car...

Others posted pictures of the two cars with captions like **Soca Diva and her new man...Soca Diva Horn the Horner Man...Diva and her new man...**

There were pictures of her and Kiah at Ellas'...

"I don't want to see anymore."

Thankfully Pascal came in and they had their run through of the songs. Couple times the man yelled at her and told her to get her head in the game.

"By the game sweetie I don't mean the hottie parked in the audience." He fanned himself dramatically for effect. They all busted out laughing.

She acquiesced and sailed through it. But she was indeed thinking about Kiah truth be told. She was all tingly still. Every time she thought there was nothing else, he could do to make her body squeal he always surprised the heck out of her.

"Congratulations Miss Nia. Glad to learn that you are finally succumbing to the power of love. You are now learning that you do need to take care of yourself for a change. Otherwise, there will be nothing left to give to others, right?" Pastor Seaton asked interfering with her thoughts.

The woman always got straight to the point.

"Yes Pastor." Nia offered. She liked how easy the admission rolled off her tongue.

She smiled as she remembered how many times they had spoken. David had been problematic.

She had reminded Nia that she too had to keep her husband happy. She had taken the sex workshops.

Her husband was the islands first professional scuba diver and instructor. He operated a diving school that gave expedition tours to the many reefs around the island.

He too was another categorised as Bob Marley, but his name is Samuel. **Sammy** for short if you knew him well. It was also the name of his shop.

"Have fun sweetheart. To be in love is simply sublime."

"Thank you, Pastor." Nia said. She liked the woman who too liked her service. She embraced her lovingly.

Georgie helped her into her uniform, and she zipped it up. One last look in the big mirror and an extra dab of gloss and she was ready.

The little butterflies started flitting about in her chest. It always happened no matter how many times she walked onto the stage.

She thought of her mama, and she repeated the mantra "**Do good... Do good... In all you do...Do do good.**"

Church began. She could hear the organ, as well as the church bells as they peeled out to welcome all. They started the walk out.

Then the commencement and processional hymn begun as they got to the entrance. They proceeded into the choir loft.

Nia chanced a look into the audience. Their eyes met and he smiled. She was certain that she had risen from the floor and floated up to the ceiling. He was sitting between the aunties.

The guys were in the back of the church. They looked like sore thumbs. Because everyone knew everyone who knew everyone.

Services was being live broadcasted and videoed. The Oprah wannabe had her camera crews panned the audience from every angle.

Her eagle eyes kept the camera to long on Kiah as he beamed light it seemed into her.

"Do they go everywhere he goes?" Georgie asked from beside her.

"They sure do!" Nia said all too quickly.

"I like him. He is so cute." She waved sweetly over to William.

He gave her a cocky grin.

147

The choir was up. **Pleasing** was the first song. It was a piece of cake for her. She loved singing it. She sang to him.

Her eyes hardly waivered as she gave praise to the Creator for bringing him into her life. When the song was ending her eyes shifted into the audience. David came through the door...

Kiah immediately turned. When he looked back at her the tightness came back on his face.

Seba and of his friends were there as well. Even Jean and Dinah and some of their friends. They were videotaping.

Bonswa and her family; her husband Glassford and their daughter Esther. London was sitting with the neighbour. She waved up to them.

"Mama! Auntie! Kiah is over there!" she called out. They shushed her up. But levity scampered about the church; it was a packed place today. Ushers were still putting seats in the corridor and along the back.

The pastor's message: **When prayer becomes your habit. Miracles become your lifestyle.**

The phrase stuck in her head. She finally understood when the junior choir assembled. They sang **Psalm 34.** The lead male vocalist Joseph was singing with Nia.

She became truly overwhelmed which served to strengthen the entire presentation. They received an immense standing ovation.

The closing song: **I Love the Lord** got everyone on their feet. The Holy Ghost was no doubt being felt in the room.

The church was alive, and God's name was being praised for an exceptionally long time.

At the end of service everyone congratulated her. Even Pascal called her a soul stirrer. Many said church hadn't felt like that in a long time.

Pastor Seaton gushed. "Perhaps you need to rethink who you sing for Miss Nia. You have been missed."

It took so long before she could get to him. He was speaking with the aunties and the Premier and his wife. He spotted her and he opened his arms wide.

Without hesitation she ran to him.

He caught her and kissed her lips. "Nia you were magnificent!" He enthused. Thinking again how utterly amazing she was.

"Well, I guess the secret is out of the bag now huh K?" Lady B turned to the other woman and asked.

"I guess so." Her auntie said, not able to contain the excitement.

"Hello everyone." They heard. The air stilled.

It was David. He looked them over.

"Good morning, David. How are you?" Auntie asked him politely.

"I'm fine Auntie Katholeen. I just came over to congratulate our girl. She was magnificent, wasn't she? Congratulation's sweetheart." He reached for her.

"She is not your sweetheart." Kiah spat. He gestured to the team.

William placed London on her feet, and he inched forward with Terrence beside.

"Why don't you let her speak man? Are you her new keeper or something?"

"Please don't make a scene David." Auntie Katho reminded him.

"I don't want to. He just wouldn't let me have a moment. I wanted to talk with her last night, and he popped up like some damn ghost."

"Just go away!" Kiah snarled. Putting a death grip of force on her hand.

"Kiah my hand!" Nia whimpered. He relaxed his hold.

"Why do you insist on wanting to talk? I do not have anything else to say to you David."

"I want to apologise… Nia. You mean the world…"

"Enough!"

"Hezekiah Carter Corrington. Maybe you ought to let him speak to her." Auntie B said as she held up her hand to him.

"David, you have five minutes and no more. Do you understand?" She turned to Kiah. "Come with me. We will wait over there. Five minutes David." She pulled a reluctant Kiah along.

"Bellot might be understanding to you. I don't have to be David." Auntie K spat. She showed him her purse. "I will remain right here while you say what you need to, to my Nia." She squeezed out tightly.

David remembered the rumour; that she always carried around a loaded palm pistol in her purse.

"Baby I just wanted to say sorry. You ignored all my messages…"

"David fine. I accept the apology. So, what else?"

"Nia, please baby don't be like that."

"Please stop calling me that. It is not sincere. Especially coming from you."

"I'm sorry Nia. Baby…I mean Nia I truly am sorry."

"Okay David. Apology accepted. So please no more calls. No more trying to get me on stage. No more messages on the radio. Just stop. I don't want to be with you. So just cease and desist. We are over. I have moved on." Nia said truthfully.

"I haven't." He offered stupidly. Feeling completely trapped. He just hated to see the way she was looking at him. They seemed unable to keep their eyes off each other.

He reminisced when she used to look at him in that very same way. He had no doubt she could again. But in the meantime, he reminded himself he had to play nice.

"Nia, we didn't part on the best of terms. I acted like an asshole. Please forgive me Miss Katho. But you know I love her. We are meant for each other."

"No David. Not anymore." Auntie Katho said. Wishing she could just flick the idiot away. He was too damn late in what he was doing now. Typical she thought.

"David once upon a time I thought you hung the moon. Even when you did me wrong, I gave you chance after chance. I allowed you to treat me like a doormat. But not anymore. There is a saying once you know

149

better you do better. Now stop this. I have finally recognised that I can do all things. I got over you, and by God's grace I have met someone who sees me for me, and I am so damn grateful. So, I am not going to allow you one step in. Just go away David and have a great life because I am aiming to enjoy what is left of mine. And I will do it with him." She pointed to Kiah.

He looked as though he was smoking. Like he wanted to come over and rip the idiot's head clean from his body.

Auntie B was the anchor. Because he truly looked fit to be tied.

She reached for her aunties' hand.

"Come on Auntie. Let's go enjoy the rest of the afternoon. Bye David and be well. I truly mean it."

"Nia please. C'mon beautiful. You don't mean that. I can be better."

"Time given, so gone David. " She spat.

"I am so very proud of you my Nia-Belle." Auntie K said a touch above a whisper. For the first time in a very long time, she realised she did not have to worry too much about the girl anymore.

Everyone knew she would go to the ends of the world for her.

May crossed her mind yet again. She wondered how she was.

The girl hadn't touched base in a long while. She figured they needed to get together and have a chat about the girl.

"Thank you so much Auntie K." She wrapped her arms about the woman. "I know at times I did not make it easy for you to love me." She felt tears running down her cheeks after they stung her eyes. "But I thank you so very much for sticking by me and believing in me all these years."

"Sweetheart we are family, and that is what we are supposed to do. I would not have it any other way." She hugged the girl to her.

She saw Kiah bolting over towards them. His face a mangled mirror of emotions. She gave Bellot props for containing him for that long.

"I must look a mess. I have been so emotional lately."

She felt him behind her. She turned to him.

"You are my mess, Nia. But what a gorgeous mess you are." He wrapped her up in his arms.

"Nia... Mr. Corrington."

They turned to Indiria the island's Barbara Walters/Oprah Network. She was the media sweetheart; in charge of **ECBC** the Emerald City Broadcasting Corporation. She dealt with the social media side of investigative journalism; **Farsing** simply put in Nia's opinion.

But say what you will, because she went fiercely after what she wanted. Since coming home and joining her father's telecommunications business. She had started a couple well sought-after magazines and hosts her very own programme; **In the Hot Seat** which airs at 2;00 pm every Sunday afternoon local and regional.

"Let me just jump in and say I've heard you two are an item?" She chirped.

"Excuse you." Kiah offered as he turned to the woman who reminded him of a younger Angela Basset in all her beauty and fierce personality.

150

"I'm sorry. Let me introduce myself. I am Indiria Osbourne of the Emerald City Broadcasting Corp, Newspaper, Television and online medium. It is quite the mouthful I know.

"Nice to meet you Indiria. How can we help?" He tossed. Not wanting to be bothered anymore.

"Miss Nia! You were fantastic. Always a show whenever you pick up that microphone." She felt like she needed to flatter the woman to get to the man. She had a knack for that observation.

She also noticed how fierce he was of her. She hadn't missed the look of complete hatred he had bestowed on her long-time love interest.

Indiria recalled interviewing the two a couple years back when she had started here on the island. They were infectious in their banter, but she also noticed he had a roving eye.

"Thank you Indiria. Trust, you have been well?" Nia asked.

The woman was a contradiction. She was brilliant in her job role sometimes a bit to tenacious. She and the team she led.

She would bet top dollar that it was never easy for the likes of Barbara and Oprah and the many other females who delve or made their living as television personalities; whether investigative, reporting roles or otherwise. So, she always gave her props.

Indiria was another champion of **Belle**. Even now she was wearing a massive floral print asymmetrical dress from her **Flora and Fauna** line. Nia recalled how many hours she had lingered on the tasks of painting and printing the flowers. It was tedious but the outcome was glorious. She looked fantastic in the dress that was designed for all body types. It was something her mama always reminded her she must do. She heard her voice even now.

"All women should be given the enabling and immense right to look beautiful and at their best at all times."

Nia smiled. She never left her image or words far from anything she did.

"Yes, I have been. We are waiting with bated breath for the **Tis the Season** line this year. We are front and anticipating the reveal tomorrow at **Corrie's**. Which you are a member we are told Mr. Corrington?"

"Call me Kiah, Indiria. And yes, Lady Bellot Corrington is indeed family. She is my aunt. Nia..." He turned back to her. Forcing the woman to turn her microphone back to her. He didn't need cameras.

"That is true. **Tis the Season** is ready. I may give you a sneak preview later at the manse if you play nice Indiria."

She hoped her meaning wasn't lost. Because she didn't feel like being in the spotlight just yet. Her face must truly be a mess.

"Well nice to meet you Kiah. May we ask how long you will be with us?" She continued. Her thought was to get the lovebirds in her studio ASAP for a sit-down interview. Also giving her time to digest the info she had dug up. Gosh they had an honest to goodness fucking multi-billionaire visiting the island. Her mind was so blown!!!

"For the entire month of December and a little while longer..."

"A little while longer you say. Could this very talented and beautiful island Sista have anything to do with this decision?"

"Very much so." He kissed her cheek and gave a naughty chuckle.

"Wow Miss Nia! You are truly blessed, aren't you?"

"Indeed I am. But I am certain you would like to have a chat with others." Nia added. Giving the persistent woman an annoying stare.

She ignored.

"Indiria darling. They are gesturing for us to come inside. Brunch is ready to be served. Please do not let us keep them waiting." Lady B admonished sweetly.

She also reached out to Kiah. "We usually have a little something to eat and a community presentation Kiah. I know you will like this. Seeing as it was started by our Nia and has blossomed into something our people look forward to on each first Sunday."

"Lead the way auntie. Thank you again Indiria."

"You are welcome. I hope I can get a proper interview from you two soon?"

"It's up to her Indiria." Kiah offered looking to the woman that made his heart skip each time he looked at her. She smiled. His heart soared.

"Soon Indiria. Please let us talk soon." She turned and walked with Kiah and his aunt back towards the church hall.

They greeted Bonswa and made introductions. She told him that she was s originally from Haiti. Kiah easily switched into creole.

"Impressive." Bonswa said with a huge grin. She made the introduction to her husband.

The men seemed to hit it off immediately and promised to meet up later in the week.

Nia reminded Kiah who Glassford was. He was over the moon. He also liked meeting the pastor's husband who promised to take him down to see some reefs.

"Without me." Nia said matter-of-factly when he invited her yet again. "There must be a reason I was never given fins or gills. I like my feet planted firmly where I can run if there is danger."

Nia unfurled her arm from his and gestured towards the restroom.

He made a signal for Terrence to follow.

"Kiah that's not necessary." She whispered. As she looked to him in annoyance.

"Humour me, Nia." He said, because he had no intention of allowing that man close to her again. Thank God he had skulked back to the mire he crept from.

"Ok. Ok." She relented and disappeared inside all too quickly. Thank goodness it wasn't too full. She accepted the praises of the few and gestured to a stall. By the time she came out the place was empty. Tasty food didn't keep islanders idle.

She washed her hands and dried them. Then she gave her not to bad looking face a once over, blotting fresh powder and adding fresh gloss. She wasn't a huge fan of lipsticks.

"Girlfriend...Girlfriend!" Seba barged into the room. He scooped her up in his arms.

"Since when has the ladies-room become a free for all?" She asked as she wriggled from his grasp.

"To hell with all of that. You were dynamite earlier. You had me praise worshipping and shit in my tired ass."

"What time did you get in?"

"I was googling and Wikipedia-in your man and shit! Nia he is so goddam rich. He can buy 5 of these friggin islands or more. He knows so many celebs. I think he is God's son!"

"So are you Seba." She offered easily. "You know I don't care for all of that. I am just as happy doing what I do."

"Girl please. You don't have to wuk another day in your fucking life ever again."

"Seba! I am no gold digger."

"Gold, black, white. I'm just saying. You can lay on the beach and have me fan shit and stuff."

"Seba! Seriously. Do you see me as that kind of person? Plus, his money is his. I think I would love the man even if he were poor as a church mouse."

"Well, the reality is he is not. Just think all the things he can help you to do for this island girl."

He had so many ideas running around in his head. But off the top of his head; meeting Ozwald Boateng. Because he wore suits made by the man himself. They knew each other. There were pictures to prove this. He almost had a fucking coronary when he came across the photos. Wonka and Tang his Asian homeboys came running when he screamed the condo down.

"Seba, he has only been here two days. Let the man relax. Give him a chance to spend time with his family before you overload him on all the things he needs to do. We are not beggars."

Which was true. They had gotten along just fine without Kiah, and they would do so after. Her heart began to palpitate. "I am hungry. Let's go get something to eat." She tossed before panic set in.

"You are always hungry bitch! But believe me I am going after his ass. Because I have my eyes set on meeting the Big O. Let him drape my skinny-foine-ass like he did Will Smith and Keanu."

"Yeah! Yeah! Your shit can rival his any day. Then again, we need to get our hands on some proper materials. "

"There you are." It was Terrence. He was standing outside the door. A look of constipation marring his Tom Cruise face. He too looked smart in his fitted black trousers and grey buttoned short sleeve shirt, emphasizing his muscles.

"Down boy. I told you she ok. Now c'mon in your cute self. Let's go grab a plate." He tossed his arm around the guy who smiled ever so easily for him.

The hall hummed. It smelt heavenly. The stylish buffet was complements of Natasha and her team. She was legendary and a well-known chef who many claimed was taught by God himself to wield her hands.
First Sundays belonged to her and her team of 40 and counting.
She no doubt would be cooking at the manse later.
She greeted Nia and Seba as they entered with a glass of chilled mango and mint juice topped off with a lemon slice and cherry.
"You are the best Nat." Nia said as she took the glass and thanked the woman. She took a long swig. "Everything smells divine as usual. No doubt you have out done yourself."
"Thanks Miss Nia." She offered nicely. "Which is why you had better grab a plate before it all disappears." She gestured to her workers.
Nia went over and got stewed salt fish, Johnnie-bakes and eggplant and fried plantains.
The aunties gestured. She started over.
"We will talk later." Seba said. He grabbed a bowl of fruit salad. "You had better work that shit off later." He tossed gesturing to her plate. "Where the hell do you put it?" He asked as he scurried off to find his friends.
She took the seat next to Kiah. He seemed much more relieved than when their eyes had met earlier.
"Why aren't you eating?" She whispered to him. Loving his scent. He was wearing Gaultier; smooth and powdery. She just wanted to curl up in him and lay there, with her eyes closed as she listened to some smooth Jazz; Gregory Porter would be nice.
"I was waiting for you. But now I know what kept you." He knew it wasn't the punk. For he was sitting at a corner table shooting daggers into him.
She had taken almost the identical things the aunties took.
He settled on eggs, bacon and waffles. Along with seasonal fruits. Compliments of his aunt no doubt. She had gone for the traditional breakfast/brunch.
"So, let's eat. Speeches will be coming soon." She dived in.
"I love to watch you eat. Do you not ever pretend?"
"With food Kiah? Never! Do you know how many people are starving out there? Then again don't answer that. Seba was regaling me again as to how rich you are. He is aiming to bend your ears on meeting the famous Ozwald Boateng. So, you had better prepare yourself. The fool thinks they are brothers from another mother." She laughed.
"For you I would do anything Nia." He chuckled. He loved looking at her as she enjoyed her food. Her eyes lit up like orbs. Especially if it was something she truly enjoyed. Just like they did when they were having sex. He promised to ask her if she ever faked. Because she would be worthy of an Oscar.

154

"Kiah! What the hell are you thinking?" She knew that look. He chuckled cutting and popping some waffle into his mouth.

"You are going straight to hell in a hand basket." She whispered.

"You two!" The aunties berated.

"You are acting like fleas. Get your mind out of the gutter." Auntie Katho tossed as she admonished the girl.

"Now Kiah eat your lunch. How are the waffles sweetheart? B said all those were your favourites."

"All second best after meeting her." He gestured. "But they are delicious." He looked at her when he said it.

Nia lowered her eyes. She was most certain she had wet her panties right then and there. Thankfully she had slapped a liner in before she had exited the stall. She was a ripe horny bitch since the man had started to turn her out. She never believed one could have so many orgasms so consecutively in all her years of existence. He had certainly proved her wrong.

She shifted. Then she felt his hand on her rear. She warned him with her eyes. More like pleaded.

The food, him being so close, touching, her thoughts everything it seemed was conspiring against her.

"Have a drink, Nia!" He gave her the glass and winked deviously at her.

"I mean it you two! Not at the table!" Auntie B warned.

Nia brought her hands to cover her mouth. Or else what food she had in there would have scampered out and landed on them both. Thank goodness she had nearly finished her plate.

"Are you ok?" He asked. Thinking what nerve! Because she looked like she would have gotten them both in trouble. He knew she had cum; the look on her face was epic!!! He grinned with delight.

People were mingling again. Nia spotted the Asian twin tigresses. They had zeroed in like heat sinkers and were on their way over to him. They were knock-outs and seemed to tag-team at times saying the identical things when their mouths opened. It could be so annoying especially when they sounded like cats in heat on a feverish night.

Picture Eartha Kitt's Cat Woman.

"Kiah Corrington." They seemed to sing. "Finally! We have been dying to meet you. We heard you were on the island. I'm Amina and this is my sister Anaya."

"Armenians?" Kiah asked nicely.

When they agreed. He spoke to them in Armenian. He watched them meld seductively into each other. They sounded as though they were under water. He thought it neither seductive nor alluring.

They continued in their native language. He pulled Nia closer.

"Nia darling." They switched back to English. "We have a fitting scheduled for the end of this week, don't we?" They just hated that he was drooling all over her.

"Yes ladies." She stated matter of fact. Their family was among one of the top 10 richest families on the island. They were marrying into one of the other rich families. Again, she said to herself bite your tongue. Because once again they could have chosen someone else. Plus, they had already paid their hefty commission fees. They were over the moon at their last fitting. She aimed to keep them that way until the last payment was collected.

"You are fantastic! Whitney Houston! Yeah, you were like Whitney! Wasn't she fantastic Kiah?" They purred noisily.

"Ladies! Ladies!" It was Seba. "Hello Kiah, I would like you to meet a couple friends. He flicked the bothersome two away, gesturing for his boys to come over.

"Kiah these are my boys. This is Wonka/Lee...That one is Tang/Park. They are two of our best realtors on the island. They have been dying to meet you."

"What's up Kiah Ma-man?" Wonka piped up.

"Nice to meet you Wonka. Do I detect a bit of Korean?" He sussed out the underlying nuance of the accent. He diverted to the language, greeting him. Trying to grasp a hold of the hand and the freakish handshake or twitching he was doing.

He was loudly dressed, way to baggy black top and trousers. Spiky asymmetrical tousled gel-hair and clunky jewellery and red round tinted spectacles.

"Kiah My-man you are fantastic." He guffawed. So, it wasn't a fluke. He could speak the language. The man was cool. He was also a sharp dresser. That suit he was wearing was a **Boss** Original.

"How rude." Tang interjected. He flicked his brother away with much elegance. He offered Kiah a proper handshake.

"I would like to show you around the island sometime." He continued to speak their language. Kiah spoke it back. "An immense pleasure to hear you sing again Miss Nia. The voice of an angel."

"Thank you, Tang." Nia said. Taking the proffered hand. He was always impeccably dressed. All white baggy trousers, vest and long military style blazer, even white trainers. Their outfits were all compliments of Seba. They were two of his favourite models.

"Auntie Nia! Auntie Nia!" Little London called out trying to wriggle free of David's grasp. "Put me down Uncle David."

Nia turned to see him place the girl on her feet. She ran over to them. She tossed her arms around her leg.

"Hello again Lady London." Kiah greeted her and reached for her picking her up.

"Hello Prince Kiah. Did you like Auntie Nia's singing?"

"I sure did."

"Uncle David says he did too. He's always saying he sang with her. He says he wants to make music with her again."

"I bet he does." Kiah said frostily. Looking over to where David was standing. Willing him to stay over there where he belonged.

156

Nobody moves nobody gets hurt. Kiah admonished him telepathically. He prayed the fool listened.

Just then the announcement came. "Can we all please take our seats? I promise we wouldn't be too long winded. Please take your seats everyone." Pastor Seaton said again.

"Also, we would like to invite Mr. Hezekiah Corrington to stand with us and kindly share in the immense honour of **Gift Giving** today. Let us welcome him again to the island. We hope he has a wonderful time with us for the remainder of his vacation among the people he loves and will get to meet. We pray for his safety. Amen."

Kiah placed the child in her mother's arms. He left bestowing upon her that drop-dead gorgeous smile as he went to oblige.

"Hezekiah, we wish that you will visit with us here as often as you can." Pastor Seaton continued as she pumped his arm in recognition.

"I promise to." Kiah said.

"What do you think of our island so far Hezekiah?"

"Please call me Kiah. From what I have seen so far, I think it is amazing." He looked straight at Nia when he said the last word. She smiled. His heart stirred.

The **Gift Giving** commenced and he shook hands and gave envelopes and got his photo taken. He also made a mental note to seriously talk to the woman seeing his aunties said she was the one who started the program.

The honourees were a Mr. John Slim Nanton and his chirpy and petite beautiful wife Veronica.

They were outstanding members of the community and around the island. They contributed by being of service to the children.

Slim drove the school bus and was kind and caring to the children. Many wrote to her about why they thought he deserved his envelope.

His wife prepared meals for the children at the Maple Leaf School. She went beyond by having brown bags ready for some who came out of homes where poverty was ripe. So that at the end of the school day they had something to eat in the evening. Even on the weekends for children in her village.

Nia also learnt she had branched out further to neighbouring villages. Her husband personally drove and delivered meals on her behave.

The last was Daniel Vammo Weekes. He could be found with his ukulele playing for the elderly at the Golden Years Nursing Home where he worked. Even on his days off and on Sunday afternoons he would visit just so he could play familiar songs for them. He even visited the shut in and played for them.

After the applause and picture taking and a bit more chatting and introductions. People started to say their goodbyes.

They changed in the restrooms of the church before they left. Promising the aunties, they would attend dinner later.

Nia also told Seba before he left that she would not be attending Omar's Beach Picnic. She was not up for any more drama.

He said he understood.

Nia emerged wearing an extra baggy khaki jumpsuit with large side pockets and white tank. Her hair was bundled up in a scarf. White trainers clad her feet.

Kiah and the boys were waiting outside, they were chatting amicably with Sammy and a couple other fellas. All eyes descended on her.

She suddenly felt self-conscious.

"What! Do I have something on my face?" She asked.

"You are simply breath-taking Nia." He took the clothing bag.

They said their goodbyes and promised a meet up soon. Then they were on their way.

He wore brown baggy drawstring trousers, white tee, cap and sunglasses.

"Do you ever not look good in anything?" She asked as they walked to the car. He was driving.

"Are you trying to say I am hot Nia?"

"Super-hot Kiah."

"So are you baby!" He reached for her hand and brought it to his lips. "You were dynamite today. I am so very floored by all the things you do for your people. Why did you start **Gift Giving**?"

"Simple. Because we just want someone to say I see you. I know what you are doing, have done. We know it is not easy, but you do it. So, thank you. Just a little acknowledgement. It can get a lot of things going because people know that there is someone paying attention. Plus, it all started when I was approached a while back by a couple of students who wanted to do something nice for their teacher. They wanted to buy her one of my couture dresses. It was a dream of hers to wear one. So, for her 40th birthday they came to me with what they had. You know me. I had them go back and device a plan as to what dress their teacher would like. She drew what she wanted, and I made it for them to give to her. The money they raised I had them throw her the best birthday party they could and buy her presents. Honestly... must have started from there."

"That is so awesome of you Nia. How about **Live & Learn**?"

She laughed. He truly listened. "My mama started that one. I am simply carrying it on by providing uniforms for children from different schools every term. I also make certain that those who cannot get to the library have a way to get the books they need by providing a mobile lending library. This way they can get books of interest and books for learning. Mama taught me that to increase wealth one must start with educating the mind. So, she made certain I knew that. She was an avid reader and shared her love of books. She could be found reading to children on a Friday evening under the biggest and sweetest tamarind tree there is on our island. I placed a plaque there a couple years ago. Just so she would

158

never be forgotten for all the things she has done for others around the island."

"Wow Nia. That is some legacy."

"Kiah I can afford to buy the things I need thank God. I don't want for much. But so many others do. My cleaning crew are so trustworthy and do one heck of a job, but they have families who have families... I give so much at times I must work twice or three times as hard so I can continue it all. Eventually I had no choice but to start asking for help. I can tell you a few more stories."

"I am all ears' woman."

She laughed. "I was leaving my office late one evening and this young girl offered me her baby Kiah. She thought I could provide better."

"Good God Nia!"

"I even had an intern, where in her household, they were struggling so much. She didn't even have money to buy sanitary napkins. Her home life was so chaotic because her parents were alcoholics who physically abused her and her siblings. Kiah my heart bleeds. It is bad enough when you are an adult when someone hits you. But a defenceless child. I cannot go around and shoot these perpetrators who hurt or prey on children. But at least if I can supply a place for them where they can come and feel safe for a couple hours, or a night, or until they can take care of themselves. I would have done my duty to mama and to God."

"Amazing! That is why I love you, Nia." He mouthed. His eyes stung.

"As you must know already, today was supposed to be a fundraising event to sort things out for **Iya's Place**. I did not know that idiot would come home and rain on the parade. But despite him. So many people are doing such amazing things each day that go unrecognised. They are my angels, and that is why I do the things I do."

"May I ask why the name Iya?"

"For my best girlfriend."

"Do I know her?"

"Unfortunately, no. She drowned. We were very young. It happened around Easter time in 1996."

"My family and I celebrated one Easter here. I think it was 1995 or 1996. I became a local hero. I tried to save two little girls. Seems like they were trying to reach their bucket. I only got one. I kept calling out. I was on an inflatable. I reached out and grabbed one, but the other got washed out with the tide. She was never found."

"Kiah!" She realised that he had finished the story. Iya had gone after her bucket when a wave washed it out and under the pier. She ran in to help her friend and lost her footing. She was thrashing about as she tried to save her. She lost hold just as she felt a hand reach in and yanked on her...

"Kiah that was you? You were the boy that saved me?"

Chills ran the length of her body. Tears stung the back of her eyes as she looked over at him in shock.

The vehicle swerved. It pulled him back to the task at hand. He had to concentrate on the road.

Those eyes...her eyes... those were the eyes that had haunted him all his life. Disturbing his dreams. He would wake in cold sweat and clawing at anything. That was why he never slept with anyone.
"Nia, are you saying you were that girl?" He stole a chance and glanced over at her.
"Take the upcoming right."
"Fuck me, Nia! That was you?"
"Yes Kiah! That story you just recanted was exactly what happened!"
"Fuck!" How the heck had they not pieced that puzzle together?
"OMG! Oh my God Kiah!"
"What the fuck is happening? What is the universe trying to say?"
"God Kiah! You saved me!"
"Yes Nia. I could only grab on to one. I was little...Oh fuck!" He slapped the steering wheel. "OMG indeed!" His body trembled. This was fucking phenomenal! Mind blowing!
"Kiah! That is why I don't do huge bodies of water. Iya died that day."
"I know. It all happened so quickly. One minute she was there and the next..."
"Kiah, I have missed her so very much."
"I can just imagine."
"I have often thought of how I could honour her. I could not save her that day. Which is why I will try to save as many children and young people in crisis as I can." She cried. She hadn't even notice she was.
He took her hands in his. He brought them to his lips.
When she brought her head up and their eyes met. He realised that those eyes were the eyes that had looked to him on that horrible day.
They morphed into hers. No wonder he was always held captive. They reminded him of that little girl. No wonder he felt this undeniable pull towards her.
"Kiah you saved me." She whimpered.
"Somehow, I did Nia. What the hell is happening?"
"Kiah, I don't know. I just know I was praying so awfully hard the best way I knew how. I wanted to save her."
"You fought hard. You almost pulled me under...I am so deeply sorry I could not save your friend."
He reached out and wiped her tears.
"I am so very sorry sweetheart."

When they parked up. He stayed the boys. As he unhooked his belt and then hers and pulled her to him.
The Dalai reminded him that the universe works in mysterious ways. We must train ourselves in becoming aware when it shifts on its axels to allow us a glimpse as these cataclysmic atoms pop to reveal what is around or

inside to help us make connections. Well, this was a baseball bat to his knees. This was phenomenal! He clutched her tightly.

"I am so sorry. I am so very sorry Nia. But sweetheart I am so glad I saved you. The universe is giving us a second chance Nia... Wow!" His mind was totally blown. Nia I am going to seize it. I am going to hang on to this ride and go all the way. " He murmured as his heartbeat strummed wildly in his chest.

"Now tell me Nia what would you like me to do so you can get your Iya's Place sorted?"

When she finished blubbering. She riffled through her bag for tissues. She mopped her face.

"I am being serious. Tell me what you need Nia."

"A new building first of all because we have been using **Safe Haven** as a base." She whimpered as she dabbed at her eyes. Then she wiped her face.

"It is done."

"What do you mean Kiah?" She looked at him stupidly.

"We are going to get Iya Place sorted."

"We are?"

"Yes Nia! We are."

"But how?"

"Leave it to me sweetheart."

"Are you real Kiah?" She snivelled. She recalled her prayers to the universe; she would always bullet point her desires.

She knew what she wanted this time around to compliment her life.

He had to be **God fearing, self-motivated, patient, unselfish, determined, unwavering and kind-hearted. Someone who is very sure of himself but not arrogant...**

"Yes Nia, and so are you. But just on the off chance... He brought his lips hard down on hers. He kissed her suddenly as he gave praise to whatever deity had brought her back to him.

She laughed unexpectedly when she recalled speaking her truth. At times she thought it too long-winded. She even wrote a letter to the universe. **Psalm 34 verse 4;** I sought the Lord and he heard me... came to her mind.

"Yes, I am. So are you, Nia. That is why we will do this together. Tell me more."

"Kiah I would like them to have their own place. Feel safe and help to make their own rules. I want to incorporate a summer camp programme as well. I mean the government establishment is there and bursting at the seams. Some feel like it's a jail. I don't want **Iya's Place** to feel institutional. I want children to come there and feel like their wellbeing and mental health are at the root of the place. Iya loved life and she loved to see me happy, as well as others. I want her to be remembered. I want her to feel proud."

"So, a new building? Anything else?" He would give her any amount she asked for.

"Yes Kiah. But I will sort it. I have other irons in the fire. We have other fundraisings, an auction and masque ball and raffle coming up. I just had an interesting thought. How about this? We need a couple fine male specimens. Would you like to help me out?"
"You should know by now I will do anything for you." He said. What the fuck she did not ask him for money!!!
"Will you be one of our men?"
"What on the chopping block?"
"Do you know how much money we can rake in? Just think off all those females who would give their eye-tooth to be with one of the worlds sexiest bachelors?"
"Not anymore Nia. Get this straight I am yours. You are mine. So, you had better pay dearly. I have shown you what I am capable of."
"Kiah Corrington get your mind out of my pants." She scolded him. Thinking she couldn't love him anymore.
"Never Nia. But seriously you know if you need anything I am here."
"I know Kiah. But let me try my way first."
He shrugged. But he was already cooking something up in his head. But seriously he admired that she didn't come right out and asked for cash. Like so many have and would have done. She was using her initiative. But he was going to speak to the aunties. Her friend's legacy would get sorted.

They climbed out of the vehicle after she sorted her face and stuffed her makeup bag back into her purse. She grabbed the backpack before she exited.
She had stuffed a couple bottles of water in it before they had left church. Hopefully they were still chilled. They were. She quickly tossed one to each man. She was still reeling over the information that had transpired.
She looked to him in awe as she reached for his hand, and they started off and out towards the Emerald City lighthouse in the distance.
It could be reached from any point in the island. Its surroundings looked desolate and was very bushy, but the islanders had paved a well-worn path on the huge slabs of concrete steps.
The terrain was home to lots of wild cows, goats and birds. Even wild dogs. That were mainly seen at night. They have taken to calling them wolves. They have never hurt anyone. But many have sorted the goats for delicious curries and stews.
The lighthouse and its beam offered a panoramic 360-degree view from sea to shore. Last night on their way home it had beckoned them. She made a mental note to bring him over for a visit.
The lighthouse was built in 1910 and was renovated a couple times in 1945 and 1989. The latest was to the revolving light in 2001. There were 1000 steps going uphill in a spiral. But the view was the thing that made what some say was torture worth undertaking.
Nia told Kiah of the Race for Life charity Fun-Run that was done on Easter Monday. Where they raised $25,000 for breast cancer. They had also

done a meditative walk; no communication as you walked the steps for Mental Health and Well Being only this year. They reckoned it would become a yearly commitment.
It was an idea she had formulated a while back when a bunch of them were having lunch.
They discussed the root cause of so many problems. Many deduced that it was silence. So, by doing the walk it puts you in the shoes of another who had been abused and felt like they had no way out.
In the end so many said it was the hardest thing they had ever done.
Nia reasoned that many wanted to talk but were just too scared of consequences; hurting or humiliating family and friends' also church and community as they battled with their troubles and even disabilities.
So many are still living by the rule '**never let your left hand know what your right hand is doing.**' To the point where so many are dying in their traumas or dilemmas.
"You do so much good work Nia."
"Because for some cosmic reason I get to see the need. Maybe because God sees that I am trying to clear my aura each day. Kiah, I want to be pleasing to our Creator. What is the use of having shit loads of money and you do absolutely nothing to support others?"
"True that."
"How many shoes can I wear? Cars can I drive? Kiah, I do what I do so I can help others who need the help and support especially here on my island. Don't get me wrong, I would like to travel all over the world, but only on short breaks. Because me navel string bury yah."
He laughed.
"But who knows? Maybe when I retire? But even then, once I am in good health, I think I will still be battling for my people. I know for sure that my home will always be here. I honestly don't think I can live anywhere else."
"Rock on Sista!"
"Are you saying my diatribe was to long winded?"
"Let me think... No woman. I got that you are never going to be comfortable living anywhere else but here on Emerald City? Did I decode it right?"
"Dam skippy! Emerald City is the blood that courses through my veins. But well-done Kiah. You have been listening."
"Yes Nia. I do listen. Just like you I happen to want to do many good things. But to be able to do so one must have the ability to listen and discern. To be able to support well. I too enjoy speaking with the universe and asking for her help in everything I do. So, I pay attention my love and I am always helped."
"Amen Kiah." She stopped. It was her turn to embrace the man. "I guess I must pay attention to why this." She gestured amongst them. "Is happening between us. At times it just seems so surreal."
"You feel it too?" He asked incredulously.
"That is why I don't want to screw it up. I can get very anal about my work, and we live on two different continents so how are we gonna make

163

this work? That is what drives me crazy. Because how am I going to say goodbye to you when..."

"Nia, we promised each other we would do this one day at a time. I do not think we are the only ones who are in this situation. Like I said before Marcus Winter is a very good friend. Why don't we meet with him and his wife for dinner and have a chat? What do you think?"

"Ok Kiah." She reasoned. Then she released him and started running up the steps.

"You little minx!" He tossed and chased after her.

They were nearly to the top. They had sips of water and continued.

At the top they ran to the window and cast their eyes as far as they could see. Both near and far.

The view never failed to cause her heart to be still. Their island was truly breathtakingly beautiful.

She pointed out the Wetlands in the far distance and the many nature trail walks, and so many other things.

This was a usual thing for her and Seba. She loved to come to the lighthouse when she was stressing. She did not do it alone though.

Because a couple reports had come in of rapes occurring.

So, people; mostly females were reminded not to wander by themselves.

"Great advice." Kiah offered. He did not like the thought of females being prey.

Nia thought about some islanders as well as the tourists who lived in the concrete jungle that so many investors were building up as they buy these prime pieces of land off the locals.

You see them as the roamed about over here. Disregarding most of the warnings.

Numerous times, the news was filled with those who came to use the lighthouse and its surroundings as a pit of mischief.

She said as much to Kiah. He winked at her. She told him not to get any ideas.

She had learnt from Seba that he had joined the experimenting masses. She had called him a duttiness.

They collapsed laughing.

But come to think of it, what she had done with him in her back yard!!!

The pictures of the two of them scampered across her mind. She fanned herself heatedly.

"Are you ok?" He came to her.

"Uh huh! She assured him as she avoided his gaze.

He playfully slapped her behind and chuckled. He loved being in her company.

They continued to enjoy the day and each other's company and took lots of photos. She conveyed the informative history behind the place when they asked.

Thank goodness she had paid attention in class, and what was said by the many elderly people she visited. As well as what was written in their history books.

They seemed to like the history, and she thoroughly enjoyed sharing the love and opulence of her island with them.

Soon it was time to head back. On her way down Carmen sprang to mind. The woman had worked as her personal assistant for years.

She could not forget the day they had telephoned to say there had been an accident; a drunk driver had run into the school bus her child was on. He died instantly.

Carmen went into shock on seeing the body. She was never the same. To say the child had been the light of her heart was an understatement. Some would say she woke because of him.

For anyone who knew her and was familiar with her, always saw how much she worried. The child was autistic. So, her entire world crashed and came to a standstill that day. Some say she is lost on the path to reaching the child.

Nia loved her dearly. She was someone who always went beyond her duty. Everyone loved her. She promised that when she was ready to come back her job would always be waiting.

It had been two years.

"Penny for your thoughts."

"Huh?"

"What is troubling you?" Kiah asked. She had gone quiet.

"Just thinking that David is keeping me from yet another commitment. I usually visit with a colleague and particularly good friend. I check in to make certain she is ok. But he is back and no doubt crashing there. So, I can't visit." She kissed her teeth. "Asshole." She spat.

"Nia, you know you can talk to me, right?" He stopped and reached out for her hand. He hated that the guy was just causing problems for the woman on so many levels.

"It's just that I have not seen her in a couple of weeks."

"Seen who Nia?"

"My friend Carmen. She is my PA. That was until she tragically lost her son in an automobile accident. She went into severe shock and is lost somewhere. We can't reach her no matter how hard we try.

"That is tragic."

"I know. I usually visit her to keep her up to date and to let her know that her job will always be there no matter how long it takes."

"What do you mean? Are you saying you still pay her salary?"

"Of course, I do Kiah. She is a friend. Plus, she has always been there with us through thick and thin. So, I wanted to be there for her just like she has always been for us."

"Good God Nia!" He looked to the woman in utter amazement. Every time he thought he had a handle on who she was she threw a curve ball. "You make me sound so fucking selfish woman. How do you do this?"
"By the grace of God Kiah. Mama used to always say that God never gives more than we can bear. But when I see her, I must admit I do lose my way. But I regain it when I see her husband with her. The love between them is precious. The way he takes care of her Kiah. So much love and patience. I prayed for such a love. Now... Kiah I just wanted to stop by and make sure she is ok."
"Then let's do it. I mean I don't want to cause you any problems. But I don't want you to put your life on hold because of me. Or him for that matter. I will just have to walk the landmines. We are adults. We can do this."
"He is her brother Kiah."
"I know Nia. But screw him! Let's go see your friend. If he is there, we will work something out. We must learn to co-exist. It is a small island. You cannot hide from things you love or your obligations. So come on let's do this sweetheart."

She directed him. He was a great driver. He took directions well. She even said as much to him. He laughed and winked over at her.
"By the way I like your company, Miss Nia." He offered, for it was the truth.
"Same here Kiah." She offered easily, spotting **Sips & Bites** in the distance. She loved popping in to see Miss Ruthie.
"Kiah let's stop over by that shop on the right."
"Your wish is my command my lady." He didn't ask any questions.
"I am thirsty. Let's go get a couple of cold drinks. We can get some food as well."
When he parked. She hopped out and walked to him.
"Come on Kiah. I need a top up."
"Where do you put it all?" He asked as he reached for her hand and they walked down large concrete steps to a painted emerald, green shop.
It was filled with lots of potted plants, tables and chairs.
The sun glistened off half opened white louvered windows. The smell coming out to greet them was intoxicating.
"Miss Nia! Gal you back! Come in! Come in! What you want?"
The elder woman wrapped her up in her arms as she eyed him up and down from under her shoulder length black bobbed hair hidden under a hair net.
"You looking well me dear. Sebastin tells me you found yourself a man. Is this him?"
"Yes ma'am." Nia offered. "He is." She looked to Kiah. She was certain anyone who looked at them could tell how much they loved other.
She truly did not mind anymore who knew. He smiled to her quite pleased.
"You had better tek care of our gal you hear me? Cause you found you-self the best this island has to give. So just remember no hole will be deep

166

enough to climb into unless we put you there if you don't take care of her."

"I aim to Ma'am." He offered. Thinking he had not been threatened so much since he had come to the island.

As he looked about, he realised the inside was a carbon copy of the outside. Except for the darts board on the wall and jukebox in the corner. On the other side there were lots of photos in picture frames and many island artefacts.

The smell overpowered him. His stomach rumbled. Everyone laughed.

"You had better. Pearl...Pearl...Bring Miss Nia and she man some cool drinks. I hear you related to Bellot. So, you can't be at all bad. Dem two wid you all?" She asked pointing over to the guys who entered behind them.

"Yes, they are. Wherever he goes they go."

She bent to Nia. "Sebastin tells me. They he bodyguards. Tell me he rich lek blood."

"True to it all Miss Ruthie." Nia offered easily.

"Ah Ghad! See I tell you Miss Nia, good tings sure does come to them that wait! Ghad you good and we thank you foo she loaden gifts." She threw her hands to the heaven. Then she asked him "true you relation to Bellot?"

"Call me Kiah. And yes, I am her nephew."

"Well nice to finally meet you and them. What you fellas want to drink?"

"You don't happen to have sorrel?" Kiah asked. He had forgotten how much he liked the drink. He had discovered it in Jamaica, and he was hooked.

"What you know about sorrel white boy?"

"Half black. I had it a while ago in Jamaica. I loved it."

"That is a staple drink foo us most around dis time. So, any way you go they will always have it. Whey de hell is that girl? Pearl...Pearl. Whey you be? Must be loss in that damn cellular. Leh me go get you you drinks. Miss Nia, you usual guava? You two what you want?"

"Water please." They chirped.

She looked them over suspiciously.

"Can I use your rest room ma'am?" William politely asked.

"It over there. And pay very close attention to dee sign. Cause I will call you back to clean it if you mess it up." She tossed before she disappeared behind the counter.

"She will too." Nia chimed in. Knowing full well that Miss Ruthie did not play. She kept a cricket bat behind the counter. She was still to this day the best batswoman on the island.

Stories had it that a local tried to rob her. Many said she was still beating the daylights out of him with the bat when the police came.

"By the way we have fried chicken, or even stew if you want dinner Miss Nia. And stop being nuf and pret-up and come get de drinks."

"Yes ma'am." Nia offered quickly and jumped to her feet. She ran over feeling like a little girl again.

She remembered when she and her mama use to stop off at the woman for fried chicken and chips some Friday nights as a treat. Habitually her mer mama would help when the place got too busy.

Nia took the tray and brought it to the table and set it down just as William came out and Terrence gave the signal. He too was off.

"Did you leave it clean for the next person?" Miss Ruthie called over.

"I sure did ma'am."

"Good on you."

"We are on our way to see Carmen. I haven't seen her in a while. I just want to see for myself how she is. Then we are heading back to the aunties for dinner. So, we will take chicken. I will have breadfruit salad with mine. Kiah what would you like?"

"I will have fried chicken and fries."

"We will have the same." The fellas said as they sat at the table with Kiah.

Other people started popping in. Some greeted Nia and even came over to hug her. Some said she was brilliant at the park last night, that she should bring her voice back to the arena.

She promised she would give it some thought.

Some congratulated her from church and said hello to Kiah. He said hello back.

"I don't think anything change. Cause Paul woulda say something."

"I know. But I just want to see her."

"I know. Poor unfortunate soul Miss Nia. But it is a good thing you do for her...Pearl get you backside in yah. We got customers! So, you had better get off that damn phone before I throw it ass in de rubbish. Now come and help me."

"She is very scary." Kiah said above a whisper. He liked the fact the place was filled with ceiling fans the sun had decided to put its hat on. Soft spiritual music played in the background. Kiah took a sip of his cold sorrel and looked around.

The place was neat and tidy, very colourful and smelt like heaven. He couldn't wait to sink his teeth into what she was clattering around to prepare in the back.

A lanky teenage girl with braids in a bun came out and brought their tray over.

"Hello Miss Nia. Glad you are back. You were fantastic in church today."

"Thank you, Pearline. Joseph (her boyfriend) was brilliant as well. Hope everything is ok with you two?"

"We good Miss Nia. You know what is on his mind most these days. He is determined to win ECGT (**Emerald City Got Talent**) next year. He thinks he's the next Bruno Mars." The girl chided.

"Remember what I said to you?"

"Yes Miss Nia. While there is life, we should all hope. Hope brings possibilities."

"Well done. Never give up on Miss Hope. So, are you ready for the showcase?"
Nia explained to Kiah that Pearline attended the dance academy, and that she was studying modern ballet.
He congratulated her.
They waited until she placed their plates in front of them.
"Please enjoy. Grandma is happy you are back on island. She doesn't like when you are away for too long."
"I know. By the way Pearline this is Kiah, William and Terrence."
"I am so pleased to meet you all. Do enjoy."
"Thank you. It was our pleasure.
The shop got busier, and every so often someone called out her name to say hello. Introductions were made and they buried themselves back into their succulent dishes.
Nia told Kiah she believed Miss Ruthie's hands were bewitching.
She had added coleslaw and toss salad.
They had all cleaned their plates.
Kiah insisted on paying. While he did that, she took the opportunity to disappear to the restroom.

When she returned, he was chatting comfortably with a couple people.
Suddenly she could not believe who strolled in and swaggered over to them.
"Miss Nia." DJ Dread-Up chuffed. "I finally meet the man of mystery. Small world."
"Don't you small world me!" Nia tossed.
He was great at his job. He gave good laughs. But she didn't enjoy the ambush last night. She let it be known.
"It's just radio Miss Nia. I didn't mean anything by it. Oh gosh man.
A bit a levity is all."
"Nia sweetheart. It's all good. I just need to tell him that if he tries that shit again, I just might become his new boss."
"Mr. President we cool and ting." He guffawed. Not doubting the guy for a second. Because Indie (his woman) had told him exactly who he was.
She had done her homework. She was also dying to get him on her show.
So, she had told him in no uncertain terms to cease and desist.
"Miss Nia oh gosh forgive me no."
"I will think about it." She said folding her arms across her chest.
They had attended the same primary school. He was very shy and not a looker growing up. His head was always stuck in comic books.
He disappeared to the UK after leaving grammar school to study Broadcasting & Media.
When he returned, he looked like he stepped off the cover of **Ebony** magazine.
He sported long dreads, and he was free of glasses. He wore grey contacts and sported a smile to die for. An attribute that many islanders were blessed with.

169

Some said it was because the water flowed straight from heaven. Because the island boosted its own heavenly spring: It was called Runaway Ghaut.
Where many claimed if you took one sip you would never want to leave the island.
Nia aimed to test the theory: she planned to take him there for a huge mouthful. She smiled deliciously.

They said their goodbyes. She gave her apologies when he asked if she was heading over to Omar's. She told him she wasn't and that he should pass along her apologies to the man and the gang. He promised he would. They set off fully loaded once again.

Soon they pulled up outside Carmen's house and parked under the huge hibiscus tree. Junior's swing was still there attached to the breadfruit tree. It swayed back and forth in the breeze. It was as if he had only run off to the house to get an ice-lolly.
Nia remembered dropping them home and she and Carmen would sit on the porch and watch the boy swing back and forth laughing heartily.
"Would you like me to come in with you Nia?"
"If you don't mind. I would like her to meet you. I am sure she would love it. She was always certain God would send me an equal. Kiah she is a wonderful individual."
"I believe you Nia."

The door opened and Paul came out atop the porch. She sighed a relief. He waved to them. She waved back. They continued going up the four huge stone steps.
The child's toy boxes were still there. They had tried to remove the things and Carmen had gotten so upset. She screamed so much they just left the things where they were.
"I told her you were coming Miss Nia. I think she is waiting because she usually goes down for a nap, but she is refusing." Paul said. "Do you want to come in or should I bring her out? David isn't here."
"We will come in then." Nia offered.
She made the introductions, and the men shook hands.
The guys decided they would stay outside. They thought it was best.
Nia knew why.
The house smelt like coconut cake and tart. It was her favourite. Paul was a baker and worked part time as a sous-chef at the Wade Inn Guest house.
It was always Carmen's thing to bring bake goods in on a Monday for the team.
"Paul, I smell coconut tart." Nia said jovially to the man.
He laughed, he loved her for the love and care she took of him and his family.

Many times, she recalled saying to Carmen that she would start a relationship again if she found a man who would treat her the way her love treated her.

Carmen would say, "Miss Nia he is on the way. Just keep trusting God. He has a plan. He works on his time not ours."

Carmen was propped up in her husband's chair and the television was on. She liked to watch soap operas.

The Young and the Restless and the Bold & Beautiful were her favourites. So, Paul would record them and play them later for her.

Sometimes when Nia stopped by, he would be combing her hair, or giving her a shower, or feeding her, doing her feet or her nails.

He never seemed to complain. His favourite thing to say is, "I made a promise to God to protect the woman for better or for worse. Cause I believe with all that I am if the shoe was on the other foot that she would do the same for me."

Nia totally believed it. The two had a love people say was so very rare. He was once a recipient of the **Gift Giving** ceremony. For the man was a prince among men.

"Can I get you two something to eat, some cake and drink?" Paul asked. He went over to kiss the woman gently. "Honey Nia is here. She came to see you. We know how much you missed her."

Carmen smiled. It was so fleeting that if you blinked you would have thought it simply imagined. Then her eyes went back to the television. Nia was accustomed. She had rare moments of lucidity.

"No thank you Paul. We popped in to see Miss Ruthie and we got something there. But I would not refuse a takeaway."

"She is well?"

"Yes, she is. She sends her love."

Nia kept to the tradition; never insult an islander who offered food in their house on a Sunday.

"Carmen sweetheart. It's me. I have missed you." Nia offered.

Her heart swelled at the sight of the woman. She went over and planted a big kiss atop her neat braids. The woman smelt like a mixture of ginger and oranges.

"I brought you something." She dug in her bag and pulled out the tissue paper she had wrapped at the office. She placed it on the woman's lap. "This is your very own piece from the Corrington's Christmas line. Speaking of Corrington. This is Kiah. He is Lady Bellot's nephew." She ushered him over.

"Nice to meet you, Carmen." He squatted down before her and kissed her hands.

She allowed him to hold them. As she briefly pulled her gaze from the television and looked him straight in the eye.

Couple minutes later she looked back to the television.

"I have so much to tell you." Nia said as she seated herself in the sofa across from her. She missed her so very much.

171

"Let's open it so you can have a good look. Then tell me what you think."
A slight shuffle. Then Kiah said, "We will give you two a chance to visit."
He turned to the man. "Let us allow the females to have a moment."
He led Paul from the room.

When they left. Nia opened the wrapped tissue for the woman. Then she spent the time talking to her about the many ways she could wrap the huge square piece of cloth.
"If you tie it this way... you can wear it as a bolero jacket over a dress, a halter top, or dress. You can also tier or layer it and use a flower at the neck. It could be used as a head tie, and a scarf when you are in the park and it's cold. You can also layer the scarfs." She laughed out loud.
"No pun intended my dear. You can also use it as a bag to carry things."
Nia smiled. Carmen shifted. Her eyes lit up and Nia thought she glimpsed a huge smile as it scampered across her gorgeous face. Exactly as she would have if this tragedy hadn't taken such a great deal from her.
Nia dropped the material and rushed to wrap the woman up in her arms and held her tight.
"Carmen darling please... Please come back to us..." Her voice cracked. Her eyes stung. Tears slid down her cheeks. "Carmen, I need you. I need you to see to see how good Kiah is to me."
She looked about as though she expected David to spitefully appear. Even this house she had given to Carmen. It was on the list of many assets from her grandfather.
They had remodelled and updated. She was extremely happy she could support so many by what God has blessed her with. She prays that her cup overflows more so she can continue to be of service.
Carmen reached for her hand. She squeezed it tight. "Sorry Nia." She said softly, slowly.
"You are doing great! You are doing great!" Nia cried. "Keep coming back sweetie. Keep on this path. That is all I need. I love you Carms. I miss you so much. Please come back. I have so much to tell you."
The woman shook her head. Tears streamed down her face. She clung to the best friend she had. Pity her idiotic brother had spoilt things. Thank God she never held to any of the shit he pulled with her against the love they shared. She loved her brother. He knew it. But she always told him how wrong he was in his treatment to her. He was always making lame excuses. Traits he inherited from their dad. Who treated their mama abysmally. She ended up in an early grave. Heartbroken and ill mentally. She took it out on them most times. She had maintained her sanity for a long while. But she lost her boy... She had to find him. She had to apologise that she was not there in his last moment. She felt helpless. The day they had placed him in the earth she had lost all hope.
She missed her and she missed her boy even more. She was caught between a rock and a very hard place.
"Nia... Sorry...Sorry."

"Carmen I know sweetie. I know. I am sorry too. Its just that I selfishly want to scream to my best girl just how wonderful Kiah is."

The woman pushed against her. When Nia looked into her eyes, they seemed to say tell me.

"I know you are in there. I can see you fighting."

Carmen shook her head. "Tell me." She whispered. Her teary eyes bright and sparkly.

"He is amazing Carms! He has taught me so many things. Especially about lovemaking." She grinned down to the woman. She squeezed her hand. Nia reciprocated the squeeze. She brought her hands to her lips.

"Carms, wait for this! I slept with him on the first night."

"You...!" The woman mouthed.

"Yes! Girl I was a hoe! The man turned my ass out!" Diana Ross's **Upside Down** came to mind. Nia started to sing.

"Happy." Carmen mouthed.

"Ooh Carmen I feel like a silly schoolgirl with a crush. Imagine me. Imagine me having a crush at my age. Carmen we did it outdoors. We did it on the beach... in the bushes... buck naked like wild animals. Yes girl! I screamed so loud all the damn animals took off running."

Carmen smiled.

"You told me a woman can have multiple orgasms. Carmen, I never believed it until it happened to me! You told me about squirting... Carmen I did it!"

Her smiled widened.

"I finally experienced this phenomenon. Girl I am so happy... Oh the biggest thing that will blow your mind. Do you know he is the one the aunties had been harassing me about? He was even the one that saved me when I almost drowned. He reached in and pulled me from the water!"

She gave Nia a look of shock. It was comical. Just like the ones she used to give when she was told something spontaneous and funny.

"Yes Carms! He saved me."

"Thank...Thank God." She stammered. She meant. Death had made a huge enemy of her. She longed to kick her ass.

"Thank God indeed." Nia continued. "He bought me diamonds! He also filled the entire office with flowers." Nia hugged her. "Sweetheart I know it is selfish, but I want you to come back. Because I am going to need you. Especially when the time comes when he must leave. I need my friend to sit and eat ice cream with me and lie to me even. Honey please. We miss you so much."

"Nia. Love you."

"I love you more."

Nia placed her head in the woman's lap. Carmen rubbed her back gently.

"I miss you so much... Please Carmen I am going to need your help... Please...Please come back to us."

The woman simply rubbed her back continuously.

173

Couple minutes later the men walked back in. "How are you two?" Paul asked.

"We are ok." Nia said lifting her head.

The woman took her face in her hand. "I…love you…Sorry."

"Ditto Carms. I love you more. It was good to see you sweetie. But I must go now. Kiah and I are heading up to the manse. We have dinner with the aunties."

She got to her feet and planted a kiss on the woman's cheek. She draped her with the red diaphanous scarf slash shawl.

"Bye sweetheart. I will see you soon pretty lady." She kissed the woman one last time. Immediately an accusation David had made flashed across her mind's eye.

"You don't want to fuck me because you want to fuck her."

No matter how many times she had denied it. He never believed.

She smiled ruefully. What an asshole!!! How the hell could she have wasted so much time on such an idiot?

"It was a pleasure meeting you, Carmen. I look forward to seeing you again." Kiah offered as he lifted her hand and brought it to his lips.

He could have sworn he felt her squeeze his when he replaced it. Their eyes connected. He tried to release her hands. She held them a bit longer.

"Nia." She whimpered. Tears slipped from her eyes.

"Yes sweetie." She reached for her hand.

She watched as the woman linked her hand with Kiah's.

"Love…Love her…Love him…" She mouthed. Looking deeply into their eyes.

"I promise you Carmen, I will love her dearly." Kiah offered, as he felt the tears stinging the back of his eyes.

In talking with the man, Kiah had learnt of how they had met. How much he loved her and wanted for her. How difficult it got at times to grieve for his child and still take care of her.

He told him she had moments of lucidity where he glimpsed the woman he had fallen in love with. Then just as quickly it disappeared. But still he kept the faith. He believed she was in there. He knew it and he believed it. It was what gave him the strength to get up and fight for her daily.

He would not have it any other way.

When the man broke down. It aggravated his heart. So, he promised himself that he would do something to help.

He had also learnt that Nia had her cleaning crew come to their house and sorted things, laundry and cleaning twice a week. She would also come over for a couple hours and keep the woman company so he could go about and do whatever he wanted, even if it was simply to go to a quiet spot and just be.

He praised the woman so much for being an integral part of their lives. Moreso since their son died.

174

On their way-out Paul said, "Miss Nia this is the most coherent she has been all week. Thank you. I think she was waiting for you to come back to us."
"Thank you for sticking by her. For loving her and caring for her Paul." Nia said to the man. Because in her book he was tops. She deduced that at times it was the simplest things people did that endeared them most to us.

They sat in the car for a bit before they took off. Kiah reached for her hand and brought it to his lips. When he placed her hands in his lap he said, "Nia I will do something for you in the next couple of days. Please do not look at it as me interfering in what you are doing here. I know you need a great influx of cash...No...Please Nia...Let me help...Let us do this. Let me help. Let me show my love for you by being your Christmas angel."
"Christmas angel?" She laughed. "Only you Kiah would come up with something like that."
"But I am serious. You do not want jewels, clothes and shoes. So, what else can I do to show how much I love you other than supporting you with some of these things you hold so dear to your heart? Take for instance that couple. Nia, he needs time away. He needs to grieve his child. But he is putting all he has into supporting Carmen."
"I know Kiah. I commend him for sticking by her."
"Sweetheart he needs to grieve. Better yet speak to someone. Nia, I know a wonderful grief therapist and psychiatrist. I can give them a call. We can fly them out if you want us to."
"Thank you, Kiah. Don't get me wrong. I want to say no, but common sense entitles me to hold my tongue. I need the help. But I am worried that others will say..."
"Nia! Stop! I have told you before what we have has nothing to do with others. I believe I know your intention. I trust in the work you are doing. Nia, I have the means to help, so woman let me help."
"Okay Kiah." She said after a long time.
"What?" He asked in shock.
"I said OKAY, Kiah."
"You mean you will accept my help?"
"Yes Kiah. No one has ever accused me of being stupid."
"You are doing so much great stuff."
"I have one condition."
"Shit! I knew it was too dog-gone easy. What is it?"
"That whatever you put in goes towards the **Belle Foundation Fund**. Not to me."
"Nia no one has ever accused me of being a rarse."
"Kiah!"
"Don't Kiah me. You think I did not know you would say that?"
Her laughter echoed about in the car.
"I want to see more of that, hear more of that. I just want you happy for however long we can keep this good thing going."

"Kiah, I hope we can for an exceptionally long long time. Cause my heart would shatter." She was telling the truth. She no longer played with words when it came to the man.
"Kiah, can I say this to you?"
"That you love me. Aaaah."
"Shush Kiah. But on a serious note. I do love you too. But Carmen taught me this phrase. May you live as long as you want, and may you never want as long as you live."
"Thank you, Nia." He had heard the words before. They were poignant. So, all he said was, "I've got this . We've got this woman." He reached over and kissed her lips. "Now let's push on before the aunties have our heads."

When they pulled up outside the house. It was aglow in lights. The aunties telephoned. They apologised for being late. The two accused them of being like rabbits.
Her auntie told her to get her heated behind up the hill in no uncertain terms.
They promised to. It was the quickest shower they had ever taken.
They were out of the house in half an hour.

He had chosen an Ozwald Boateng three-piece navy blue slim fit suit and matching waistcoat with white shirt and black tie and shoes.
"Kiah you are so dashing. I feel like a peasant standing next to you."
"You are royal Miss Nia." He said as he waited for the guys to get his cuff links sorted.
His hair was sleeked back in its elegant ponytail.
She tried to picture him without the locks; that she had totally grown to love on him.
She enjoyed when they touched her face and her body when they made love. It added to the sensation.
Nia still remarked as to how neat they had gotten them done. Not like the clumpy mess (bongo) that many white guys seemed to boast and pass for dreads.
His were small single stranded almost like invisible braids painstakingly mastered.
He told her he had them done by a wonderful hairdresser called Dawn who had Jamaican and African roots. She had studied the art of interlocking hair of different ethnicity.
He had funded her program as well as her products. Glad he did.
She said his hair was easy because he had traces of African which made it easier to manage. He visited her salon twice a week privately.

He asked after a hairdresser. She told him about Beverley. She was the only one on the island she trusted her hair to. Islanders can be quite picky about who messed with their mane.

But all joke aside. Beverley was quite good. It's just that she could get quite busy, and the wait could be a killer. But it was all worth it in the end. However, she promised to call and arrange an appointment for him.

She had chosen a free-flowing sparkling white knee length sequined strappy sweetheart halter dress; her interpretation of Marilyn Monroe manhole photo-op.
She wore her hair free flowing down her back. She added the necklace and earrings set he gave her. To compliment the look, she chose silver sling backs.
"Hubba! Hubba!" He exclaimed when she walked out of her dressing room.
"Do you like?"
"What are you wearing underneath?"
Nia quickly lifted her dress and gave him a sneak peak of her stringy thong.
He swore raggedly.
"Don't blame me if I make you pay for that later Nia."
"Well, you asked Kiah." She tossed, bending teasingly to pick up her purse.
"You little minx." He ground out and pulled her up against him hard and buried his lips in the crevice of her neck.
She loved the spot he seemed to like kissing.
"You smell divine."
"Compliments of your auntie."
"Nia!" He groaned. "If only we didn't have to leave. I would teach you a lesson."
Nia laughed, loving the way he made her tingle.
"The sooner we go and honour our commitment the sooner we can get back home. Now come on." She pulled his hand. "Boys, are you two ready?" She had grown accustomed to them.
They had refused the apartment downstairs. So, they each had a bedroom on her floor.

Nia's mobile went off. It was Seba. He was giving her a blow by blow of how the scene was at the beach.
Apparently, it was jam packed, mostly by young people. He put Omar on speaker.
Nia apologised. She told him she had forgotten she had to be at the manse for dinner. But she thanked him for all his support.
He told her David was performing with his old band members Hammer International. They were **mashing up** de place and the vibes was tight!
So, they would take it up to near midnight if she still wanted to pop down.
She told him she would not. She had an early start. Seba was her representative. She was not ready for round two with his pal.
He said he totally understood. They said their goodbyes.

The grand entrance door opened, and the aunties came out to greet them as soon as they stepped up under the huge portico. Held up by two huge pillars.

They were both wearing jumpsuits. Her auntie was wearing the white half shoulder number; embellished on the top by a huge jumbo diamante tuber rose.

Kiah's auntie wore the cream one with quarter length puff sleeves.

Both their hair was down and flowing freely.

"Well, it's about time you two showed up." Auntie B said. She gave them a tiresome look. "Hezekiah Carter Corrington you know I detest tardiness."

"Yes, Ma'am I know. But we do have a legitimate excuse..."

"Yeah, yeah! Bedtime romping?"

"Auntie Katho!"

"Well, there is nothing wrong with that. Just do it on your own time. Because I am the one who ends up getting blamed for you enticing him. Just look at the way you are dressed. Isn't she beautiful Hezekiah? But that is no excuse for your tardiness of course." She winked at auntie B when she gave her the eye. Then she winked at them.

"Oh, B they are young. Have you forgotten what it was like for us back in the day?"

"Katho don't you dare encourage them. They are late and that's that."

"But seriously we had an enjoyable time. Nia took me over to EC Sturges Lighthouse and we visited with some friends. Really, we had a nice afternoon exploring the island."

"Well, I am glad you did. Now come in and meet the guest. By the way K is right you two are absolutely gorgeous."

"Thank you, Auntie."

They walked into the hallway illuminated by the biggest and grandiose of chandelier Nia had ever seen to this day. It was spherically shaped in varied sizes ranging from biggest to smallest in four layers. Its siblings lined the lengthy hallway for company.

"Hello Lumiere" Nia whispered. She smiled imagining that he welcomed her back. When she first came to live at the grand house the majestic thing had become like a friend and bosom buddy, a confidant of sorts. it was the first and the last thing she spoke to at the start and finish of every day.

Lumiere was loyal and kept all their secrets, spilling none, as he stood guard over everything, down to his siblings.

Nia loved to watch when they were bathed, massaged and dressed. They shone royally now as they welcomed everyone from the ceiling that drew your eyes when you entered the superbly cavernous and elegant house.

Huge wall mirrors lined the hallway on both sides to doors leading to restrooms on the right and a massive walk-in cloak room to the left.

178

She glanced at her image as she walked atop the red carpeted floor that ended just before you descended six granite marble slab steps into an elegantly decorated living room.

"We are congregating in the atrium Hezekiah. I bet you don't even know where it is. You disappeared so quickly the other night."

Nia knew the atrium was where they held grand and lavish balls and dinners. She loved playing with May in the beautiful place.

She wondered how she was yet again, and prayed she was doing well. They had not spoken in what seemed like eons.

The atrium was gorgeously decorated. The crème de le creme of island society milled about and chatted amiably to each other.

When they walked in all eyes zoomed in like heat sinking missiles upon them.

Madame Cruz and Audra's eyes especially caused her to recall the saying, **if looks could kill**.

The Premiere and his wife, Pastor Seaton and her husband, speaker of the house, Iayana and Desmond Buffonge (Indiria's parents) plus Indiria; she was on duty milling about the room.

The underwater twins along with their parents; Muna and Sanjit, Wonka and Tang's parents; Lei and Pak they had bought land off her to set up View Pointe Hotel; one of the island's most luxurious hotel; that offered dignitaries and movie stars spacious and elegant accommodations.

Pascal and a couple members of the choir, a couple well known doctors, lawyers, athletic figures, Simone the Mezzo-soprano on the island, Joyce Mason the head of the library. The islands' governor David Dawson and his wife Daniella, the head of DFID (Department for International Development) they came out of the UK and are responsible for administering oversees aid. They promoted sustainable development to eliminate world poverty.

She could see why they were there. She will approach them later.

Amanda and her flower power team from Prestige Flowers, and the philharmonic orchestra; were playing joyfully off to a corner. The Yacht Club owner Cyril and his wife Buffy…

Gosh Nia had forgotten for a split second that first Sunday dinner was usually a soiree of the highest calibre on the island.

The room looked heavenly and smelt equally as divine. Stringed lights and an abundance of flowers. No doubt the many roses and tall orchids and ginger lilies, as well as birds of paradise and so many more flowers came from her infamous horticultural garden and green house.

There was a huge glass conservatory off the room that lead out to the beautiful gardens. People were mingling about inside.

Nia absolutely adored the room that was very versatile; the roof or blinds could be opened; to allow huge gulps of air or sunlight in. It was Nia's magical room. She had created many sketches in that space.

Natasha and her team were there again. The woman waved to her. She waved back. People were engaged and sampling little plates of some of the decadent things the woman and her team had put together. Again, introductions were made.

Audra slid over to Kiah. "Darling. You never called. I hoped you would. I would have showed you around."

"Nia and I did some sightseeing today. That is why unfortunately we are a tad late."

"Mommy and I were late as well. But it is great to see you again. Hug me darling. You look positively scrummy." She wrapped herself about Kiah like a hungry anaconda.

"Aren't you forgetting to say hello to Nia. She is my date for the evening."

"Oh darling." She slapped at his shoulder playfully. "Because you look so scrummy, I only had eyes for you."

"Audra my nephew is spoken for. Nia is with him... Kiah come be a dear and let me introduce you to someone." Auntie Bellot said as she extricated the gorgeous vampires red talons from about Kiah. Even though it resembled more like peeling.

"Coming Nia?" He asked, as he reached for her.

"I need a quick word Kiah dear." Audra purred. Her eyes cutting Nia to the quick.

"I'll find you." Nia said and watched him go off with his aunt.

"Nia darling so good to see you...Does it mean that you and Kiah are official?" She asked. Feeling the sudden urge to rip her to shreds.

Just think what a waste of the beautiful red low-cut ankle-length halter she had specifically chosen to wear. He hadn't even looked at her a smidge.

"You look divine Audra." Nia said changing the subject. The dress she wore had put a tidy penny in the kitty. "Great colour against your body as well."

"It's one of yours dear." She snarled. Wishing it had not been lost on the man she wanted. He made her so horny with desire each time she was that close to him.

Audra hadn't forgotten how she had devoured Simon, who just seemed as though he could not get enough of her tonight. They had had a quick one in the car before they had entered the house tonight, with her mind filled with images of Kiah Corrington.

"I know Audra. I am simply saying you do the dress justice. Thank you."

Nia liked to play the game. But thank goodness her man; the on again-off again Simon came over and whisked her away after a quick hello.

Nia sighed thankfully, and wandered over to the flowing fruit punch fountain, nothing but the best.

It was topped off with lush strawberries, pineapples, and kiwi. Her eyes wandered.

She had forgotten just how beautiful the place was when it was taken out for a swing. The house team had outdone themselves.

Nia recalled somethings as she sipped her punch.

The aunties saying, they would get rid of the grand house because they were getting too old. Perhaps get something less grandiose. They had reasoned since neither she nor Hezekiah had any intention of ever giving them any grandchildren.

At the time she had not realised who he was. Because she never felt the urge to speak to him except a hi, a quick bye and she was off.

Most times when she dropped by the house, she was always eager to be off.

The last time she had spent a full night under its roof she was at the age of 19. She had come into her inheritance when she turned 18. Her auntie was the one in charge of everything.

Seems like her father inherited lots of land on the island; even all the acreages her property sat on and much more from his great great-grandfather.

Somehow her clever mama had managed to get him to put everything in a written will. Down to the little house they lived in and so many more around the island.

She had come into it all when Mis'ta Zacharias passed. Turns out she was his only heir because he never had any other children other than the man who sired her.

So, when his wife died, and he did. Nia automatically inherited everything. With the immense support of the aunties who she felt totally indebted to, she had managed to obtain so much.

She sold a couple acreages off to some investors, who wanted to build lots of condominiums around the island. Down to where they built the dance academy and other places owned by the government...

They were all hers. So, asset wise she was set for the rest of her life.

She pulled herself from her reverie when Pastor Seaton and Pascal came over for a chat.

"You didn't tell us that he was on the Forbes top ten list?" Pascal purred.

"Get the money signs out of your eyes." She spat at the man.

"Who me?" He purred and hugged her to him.

Pastor did the same. "Enjoy your blessing, Nia. Scripture reminds us, what you sow, so shall you reap."

"Amen." They all chorused.

"But seriously Miss Nia you hit a good foot!"

"That is all he kept saying. Do you know how many times today he reminded me that we needed a new piano?"

"Well, we do dammit. If Mr. Money pants can help, then I don't see why not. I have just the darling thing in mind."

"Mr. Pascal don't forget that you still owe me."

"Spoil sport. You!" He turned to pastor. He wagged his finger at her. "You should be encouraging this. Just think if we got that beautiful Steinway..."

"Pascal we are not charity cases. We will fundraise for what we want..."

"But in the meantime, Miss Nia here can use her wiles..."

"Pascal De' Monet I will not be a part of this you heathen."

181

"Amen pastor."

"You two I swear are going to be the death of me."

"Miss Nia...We trust that you enjoyed those beautiful flowers?" It was Amanda.

"Yes, I did. They were lovely." Nia offered. Wanting to copy the woman's up-your-nose English accent. She was beautiful, even though her skin was so pale.

Nia thought often that she should be working at a funeral parlour instead of a flower shop. She longed to tie her in the sunshine. But bless her heart she was a carrot top with freckles to boot.

"Nothing but the best he said and proceeded to buy the entire shop. How darling of him."

"How darling indeed." Pascal copied. "Yet I cannot get my Steinway."

"Excuse you?" Amanda tossed to the man.

"No excuse you...and you...and you. I am off to get drunk." He sashayed off in the opposite direction. Then he remembered where he was supposed to go and twirled away again.

"I think he is already there." Pastor Seaton said. They all laughed infectiously.

Nia spotted the twins one on either side of Kiah. They seemed to be pulling him along to meet their parents. He looked over pleadingly at her. She laughed at him.

"I pray blessings Miss Nia."

"Thanks pastor." Nia said when the woman gestured.

The bell rang for guests to be seated for dinner. It was to be held in the conservatory, off the atrium. They started piling in.

The room was now aglow with lights from strings as well as electric and candlelight.

People wandered in from the garden, and to her immense delight she spotted the dynamic-duo, Marcus Winter and Yvonne Mulcaire.

She waved shyly over. They waved back.

The woman looked so elegant. He still looked at her with so much love. It was a fairy tale affair when they had gotten married. Thank goodness they were seated next to them. Kiah came over and both men embraced. Like they were indeed old friends.

"Marcus this is Nia." Kiah made the introduction.

"So pleased to finally meet you, Nia. My wife speaks about you quite often. Nice to be able to put a face to the name." He pumped her hand up and down. "Glad also that you snagged the heart of this slow poke. He had us worried for a while there."

"Glad to meet you to Marcus." She said looking at him and at Kiah. He was an older version but still just as handsome. He was a renowned photographer. He had come home to his island and met Yvonne and fell madly in love. The fairy-tale version that was well known.

182

"A hug please." Yvonne said. "We have walked the same path my dear. Trust God Nia. He never makes mistakes." She whispered in the girl's ears. They took their seats across from each other.

Dinner starters; a selection of mini aubergines and tomato tastes, shrimp and avocado garlic bread delights, or plantain cheese and bacon bites.
Soup: Carrot and Pigeon Pea, Pumpkin and Kidney Bean, Leak, onion, thyme eddoes and Christophene/chayote.
Salad course; lettuce and ham salad, macaroni salad or bean salad.
Main's course; salmon or red snapper and asparagus foil, roast beef and sautéed sweet potato, or Caribbean fried rice and tofu meatballs.
Chicken: fried, jerk, baked.
There was always something for everyone. No one went without.

There was a mini break. For everyone to stretch their legs and mingle, while listening to the orchestra.
Kiah and Marcus agreed to go scuba diving after they had lunch at the Yacht Club and mariner on Tuesday. Because the power couple were leaving after the Extravaganza. Marcus had a photoshoot in Antigua.
Yvonne had to finish classes at the **Mulcaire Fashion Institute.** She had started the school of Fashion and Technology.
"Not all of us can afford to jet off to Paris or New York. Thank God Marcus had taken her to all these places, and she had met so many interesting people. But she to loved living on the island because she felt safest there.

Nia and Yvonne left the men briefly for a chat on the patio, while they sipped their fruit punch.
She learnt that she too had fallen in love with Marcus very quickly because of the way he was with her siblings; that she had to become parent too when her parents died. She said it was the hardest period of her life, she would not wish it on anyone.
It had taken all her strength. She had to dig deep; wake every morning just so she could take care of them and their self-destructive auntie.
Nia had to grab the answer to the bothersome question. So, she bit the bullet.
"How did you manage the long distancer relationship?"
"Nia darling, wake up! There are endless possibilities. I learnt to do internet chats, even phone sex...Oh yes! I have become quite deft at it. He and I had to find a way to make our new life work. It was difficult at times but what we had was worth fighting for. Sometimes he would fly in and whisk me away for mini breaks. But you know being a designer and keeping crazy schedules. You just learn each other's grove. The biggest of all is the innate ability to trust not just self or each other, but God. Nia when you cannot speak to anyone else speak to God. So many of us place him high in the sky and leave him there. I don't see him/her/it... that way. My God is everywhere. So, I speak as though to my best friend. Nia, I have faith that he sent Marcus at a time when I desperately needed him. He has

become my best friend. When things bother or worry me about my best-friend I talk to God. He is at the centre of us. Nia don't be too rigid in actions and thoughts. Communicate with each other always. Learn likes and dislikes especially when it comes to sex. Do not be ruled by fear. It is the number one crusher of most relationships. And another thing before I stop my sermon sweetheart. Don't overdose on social media. Use it sensibly. Kiah can tell you much more, but please do not use it to look for stupid stuff about yourself or your significant other. That place is a hot bed of mischief."

"I know. I don't have much time for it anyway."

"But sweetheart you are now in a relationship with Kiah. Especially if he gets super busy and has not had a chance to check in. We are all human and the devil is there listening to prayers as well. Oh yes, a lot of us don't realise this. We have forgotten that he was cast out and is still building his army every day. Nia there are many who will not be happy about the decision he has made concerning you."

"That is the part that makes me worry Miss Yvonne. It scares the be-Jesus out of me."

"I know. It can be very debilitating. But that is just the way fear works. If you invite it in and give it a home and feed it. It will be your moocher. We don't need that, and I am telling you right now it will not work with Kiah. Nia, I have had to use my head to fight fear. It wasn't easy. But you must find that space within yourself where you can go and engulf yourself in, I can do all things through…" She waited and gave the girl a chance to think. She had heard her sing via the church broadcast earlier. One had to know God to be able to express themselves in such a way Yvonne thought. She had said it to Marcus.

"Christ." Nia added. For the umpteenth time she thought of how gorgeous the woman still looked. She liked the way she never kept the Creator far from what she believed.

Nia had flown over to Montserrat where she was a guest speaker in their **Alliouagana Festival of the Word** week. They had spoken briefly.

Her platform was on **Women in Fashion** and **Ways to Move Further**.

She had opened her own Fashion House and academy on her island. She too was a household name.

Nia had quite a lot of her fashion pieces in her closet. Corrington's' also carried her brand, **Mulcair Fashions**.

"Yes, my dear. I know I said I had one more thing…But on this last thing; you must always remember that things are not always simply black or white. There are lots of other shades like sides to a story; **theirs, his, yours and Gods'**. If you feel it there… question it. Even here."

She touched over the young woman's head and then her heart. She liked her very much. Women need to stand in their strength and lift each other up.

"God has made us so unique Nia. He has blessed us with great receptors to tune into the movement of the universe and each other. They are not just for greed, selfishness and pain. Or for throwing shade at each other."

"Amen." Nia mouthed. She waved to Kiah. He was still chatting with Marcus and a few other people who had joined the circle. He blew her a kiss. So did Marcus to his wife.

They sat for dessert, guava ripple cheesecake with mango coolie, sweet tamarind cream pie and lemon curd mousse, coconut yoghurt panna cotta and fruit salad and minty ice cream.

When the dance floor opened, Kiah danced a Foxtrot with his aunt and the Waltz with auntie K.
Nia was floored. She had no idea that he was such a great dancer. He was trained in Ballroom dancing; his mom taught him.
The aunties mentioned it. They were looking on. Because Audra of course, had to test the theory.
She decided on a Tango and chose the music from her playlist. They were spectacular to watch. He was mesmerising. Nia's eyes were peeled once again to the way he moved his hips.
She saw herself butting in and running like Baby for the lift like they did in Dirty Dancing. Shit!!! It wasn't that scene.
Amidst hand clapping he came over to her and kissed her neck.
"Come with me to the garden Nia." His voice was very husky.
He swept her out of the room and whisked her away. He reached for two glasses of chilled cocktails that the waiters were carrying about.
The guys followed. He stayed them.
"We'll be fine." He growled.
"Kia are you ok?" She asked anxiously as she followed almost running behind him.
"Nia, I want you." He brought one of the glasses to his lips and swallowed the liquid quickly. "You know this place better than I do. Where can we go?"
"You mean? Good God Kiah after what just happened in there you must…"
"Exactly." He swallowed the other glass. "Now come on before I take you right here."
"Good God Kiah! I want you too. But my shoes…"
"Fuck-em! I will buy you more. Now come on."

Nia knew a short cut to the potting shed. They got there in breakneck speed. Thank God she hadn't broken an ankle, worst yet her goddam neck for being such a trollop.
Thank God too that the door was not locked. They slipped inside.
His trousers were already at his ankles. He grabbed her and yanked the thong she was wearing aside and slid deep within her.
He sighed languidly.
"I couldn't stop thinking about you woman." He offered as he wrapped her long legs about him and loved how warm and welcoming, she felt.
They hadn't realised Audra had followed.

Back at the house they noticed some of the guests were starting to leave. Others were still dancing and stuffing themselves with the rest of the desserts; scones, biscuits, tarts, cakes, coffee or tea...

Nia felt heady. Some would cast aspersions. But whatever! She was happy and satisfied. A huge grin stretched across her face.
"Are you ok?" He grinned down at her.
"Are you?" She asked.
He pulled her up hard and squeezed her firm backside. "To be continued beautiful lady. To be continued." He kissed her quickly.
She felt intoxicated as he reached for her hand. She tingled again where she had only just wiped before they exited.
Thank goodness she always carried wipes. She had taken a handful from her wrist-let purse and extended some to him.

Just before they stepped up to the patio, he helped her to wipe her shoes and then his.
"You are a prince among men Kiah."
"Thank you, Nia. But just so you know. I could not keep my eyes off you all evening. I am so sorry my attention was stolen but I aim to make it up to you."
"Kiah, I didn't know you could dance like that! Gosh you were magical."
"I had to learn. My mom was a dance instructor, and she competed for years in ballroom dancing. Pops was always too busy with the store, plus he had to left feet. A bonus skill that always came in handy because I could score lots of females."
"I bet you did Patrick Swayze."
"I also got teased too."
He recalled briefly as a teenager walking to his mom's studio and a couple guys jumped him. His dad immediately sent him off to learn self-defence: boxing and karate. He still got his ass kicked in the early stages but each time he got better.
"Poor baby." She kissed his lips.
"Lots and lots." He teased.
She understood and kissed him. "No more you pretender or you will get us both in trouble. Now let's get back in there before they notice. But you can bet your sweet ass we will pick this up later. By the way you were right. I spoke to Yvonne, and she gave me quite a lot to think on."
"Glad she helped. I too had a chance to catch up with Marcus.
Nia, I want what they have."
"Me too." She kissed him. "Me too you devil."
"I thought I was a prince."
"My devilish prince. Kiah you make me want to..." She whispered in his ear.
He laughed loudly. He didn't think he could want the woman anymore. He slapped her rear end playfully just before they entered.

"You were delectable." He whispered against her cheek. He couldn't resist. He was salivating again.

"Kiah we are going to get into so much trouble with those two."

She pointed to the aunties.

He waved and shrugged over at them. They tossed him a questioning look, then laughed before they turned back to their guests.

The two still did not realise that Audra had followed and had looked on spellbound as her sharp talons scraped the wall because she imagined herself on the receiving end.

She still could not see what he saw in her. She pounded the wall furiously. She pictured herself charging in and grabbing a fistful of hair and yanking as she tossed the lucky bitch across the room. She fumed as she stewed in her wantonness.

She melded herself against the exterior when she heard them exit, and wilfully glared at their retreating back.

His aunt tried to get his attention. He stayed her. He wanted to take his woman for a spin on the dance floor.

He wrapped her up in his arms for a very long time and kissed her longingly each chance he got.

It was nearly 11:00 pm when they finally said their goodbyes. Nia liked that they had chosen to go over. It was long overdue. She had danced with her auntie like they used to. She danced with Kiah again and then they all danced. Everyone was having a good time.

Even Silcott; danced with the aunties. It was long rumoured that he had the best of both worlds because he was sleeping with the two women. Nia had indeed caught him leaving their bedroom a couple times when she lived at the manse. But he had never confirmed nor denied anything.

Even the boys: Terrence and William were busting moves on the dance floor. The aunties were using their playlists. They danced the night away.

Audra was drunk and tried to cause a scene. Her mom made apologies and gestured to Simon.

They tried to get her out quickly before all hell broke loose. But clearly, she was determined to speak. She screamed.

"Call me Kiah...We need to talk... I saw you two in the shed by the way! It... You... You were fantastic!" She spat as she broke free and came back to beat his chest and claw viciously at his clothing.

"Audra! Please get a hold of yourself." Kiah squeezed out as he tried to extricate her arms.

"Why her?"

"Simple Audra. She isn't you."

"Your loss Mr. Handsome. Your loss."

"You are drunk Audra."

"All because of you."

187

"I do apologise." He offered. He hated scenes such as this. He disliked when Jordanna did it.

He gestured to her mom. Scene sorted. They got back to enjoying the rest of the evening.

"She followed us?" Nia asked incredulously.

"Forget her. Let me concentrate on you." He whispered in her ear and kissed her neck lightly as he twirled her about the dance floor.

Chapter Five

The alarm sounded. It woke Nia from a deep sleep. She was naked and wrapped in his arms. His hair was strewn across the pillows. The covers hovered about his thigh. He was a glorious sight.

She couldn't resist. She reached over and kissed him.

He pulled her to him.

"Good morning sweetheart."

"Good morning, Kiah." She snuggled in. "I love waking in your arms."

"Nia, I didn't hurt you, did I?"

"Why?" She asked, as she tried to erase sleep.

"I don't sleep with others in my bed. Nia, I have not been able to do so since that accident with your friend."

"What do you mean?"

"I do not sleep in a bed with females Nia."

"But you slept with me."

"We all have our secret proclivities. That was mine. I have sex. I fuck. When I want to sleep, I go to my own bed. Since meeting you again it has been the only time."

"Really?"

"I had nightmares. I would thrash about basically all night and wake reaching out to grab at things. I woke one night with my hands around someone's neck."

"God Kiah!" She reached up and kissed him. "You have never been like that with me."

"Thank God. But that has only happened it seems since meeting you."

"You sleep like an angel. I like to watch you."

"Stalker! But honestly, I don't think I have thrashed about not once since I found you."

"No Kiah. You have never hogged the covers or thrashed out at me. Come to think of it. I too have slept very well. I did not even remember falling asleep."

"You remember this don't you?" He flipped her deftly and climbed atop her. She laughed loudly. He loved it.

"I am going to give you what you were gaging for last night."

"But you punished me then. Not fair. I should be the one to punish you."

"Then go right ahead Nia."

He rolled off her and back unto the bed with the sheet poking high in the air where his cock was straining.

"Ok lover. You asked for it." She challenged. She felt bold. She loved that she could bring her sexuality to the forefront and not be criticised.

She cackled and reached down into the drawer under her bed. She tingled with excitement. She was back brandishing a pair of handcuffs. She held them up high.

189

"What the fuck Nia!"

"You didn't think I had it in me did you Kiah Corrington?" She teased boldly.

"Woman I don't deny that you can do anything." He tossed. For it was the truth.

"Are you ready to play?"

"So, fucking ready!" He squirmed as she eased over him and cuffed his hands and clipped them to the head of the bed. By the time she was finished with him. He was truly wasted.

However, he was never one not to play fair. So, he summoned up the strength after a short break. When he returned, he reciprocated and fucked the hell out of her for that stunt she had pulled.

She whimpered to the bathroom.

Halfway there he ran over and scooped her up in his arms.

They walked around the property a couple of times for exercise. Nia wondered how Audra was. She voiced it to Kiah. She still could not believe the woman had followed them.

"Kiah, she saw us!"

"So what?"

"Dear God!" She moaned, as she pictured them as they had been in the shed. It was hot, fast and sinful.

"I hope she didn't video us!" Her hands came to her face. "Kiah you see the trouble you get me into. I can never keep a clear head when I am around you."

"You aren't totally blameless you know you little minx!" He laughed. "But she is trouble. It will do us good to avoid her."

"Amen!" Nia piped up.

"But did you like it though?"

"You really have to ask?"

"Humour me." He said and reached out and hugged her tightly. He truly was having a grand time being here with her. He was enjoying her company, as they chatted and laughed.

"Tell me. I am a guy. I don't mind positive input." He grinned.

"You truly are an imp Kiah Corrington. But honestly, I have no complaints. Can't you feel I am always ready? I am open to it all when it comes to you. You bring me joy."

"Say it again Nia."

She obliged.

He kissed her hungrily.

They carried on walking and talking. He spoke about his parents.

She learnt the statistical things, names and ages.

His dad was auntie B's sister. His name; Denton William Daniel Corrington 11. He followed in his father, who followed his father...

They had started off as haberdashers in the 1950 and grew from there.

In its hay day Corrington's Department Store could rival chains like Bloomingdales, Macy's, and J C Penney's and so many more all over the American states.

Corrington's also had a store in New York as well which was sold in 2009 to upkeep the California store. Which they sold in 2012 earning a tidy penny.

His mother's name is Elena Marcelle Bardot Corrington. She is as beautiful as she is kind. She reminds me a lot of you. You two will get along like a house on fire.

Last night at the dinner party she had gone to the wall and looked at the photos. Kiah was there for sure, but he did not have dreads. Funny she had never paid any attention because he was indeed a great looking guy. She had said as much to him and to the aunties.

Kiah spotted the same dark-skinned girl on the wall. She sat with Nia and Seba, the aunties, with Silcott, and even by herself in the garden. She was on the beach, by a hut in the woods.

She seemed to be everywhere here on the island. But they did not speak of her, and he could not find anything about her anywhere in the dossier. He would ask Nia, or the aunties. But tonight, was not going to be it.

So, he tuned back in and listened to them as they continued to chat about the past.

"She only had eyes for that no-good brute." Auntie Katho teased.

"You thought that lout hang the moon."

"He could not do anything wrong." Auntie B tossed.

"You mean she had her head to far up his ass?" Auntie K fired as she reminisced.

"Young folks." Auntie B mouthed. "Ooh! Ooh! Remember that troupe she and that devil Sebastin created?"

She kicked off her shoes and plopped down on one of the thick plush sofas in the living room.

"Good God who can forget the image of those two!" Auntie K croaked.

"Auntie I was only expressing myself. I had a lot to say back then."

"Still do. I was worried for a while. But when you left that David, I just wanted to climb up on the roof and shout halleluiah."

"Well thank you God is all I will say on that subject." Auntie B chorused.

"Back up. What troupe?" Kiah asked inquisitively.

"Oh Lord Hezekiah! She was dressed in dardi-oh! I can't even say it! Sebastin was the devil. They looked like something straight out of the Heathen's handbook. He played the part with whip and chains to boot. Jesus-have-his-mercy! The mischief that came out of those two! I swear my heart would just up and give out." Auntie K tossed and dramatically held her chest.

"Tell him about the sheik."

"There was a sheik?" Kiah asked enthralled.

"There was a sheik from Iran visiting that wanted to make her a part of his harem." Auntie B continued. She was dying with laughter.
"I think he was planning to kidnap her?" Auntie K guffawed.
"Auntie K!"
"Don't you Auntie K me. Lord have mercy! I can sit back now and enjoy being old." She brought her feet up and stretched them out on the table, as they continued to share stories and laughed and chat.

She curled up in his arms. She loved how they felt wrapped about her. He kissed the top of her head.
"So, your birthdays are coming up soon." Auntie B reminded. "Do any of you have any plans?"
Nia thought, because according to the aunties his parents were hoping to be in to celebrate with him.
"Not really." They both said together.
"Finishing each other's sentences already? That's a good sign." After the shock. They all had a laugh.
"You sound whipped." Silcott teased.
"I know right?" Auntie K smiled to the man.
"I don't deny it." Kiah tossed, kissing her again, amongst many oohs and aahs.

Kiah's birthday was on the 15th and Nia's was the 17th of *December.* He would make 30 and she 25. Landmark birthdays.
He aimed to make hers memorable. "I don't want any fuss. I was thinking of a barbeque for close friends and family.
"Sounds nice. Maybe we can do our birthdays together."
"I don't want what they do Kiah. I like my birthdays quiet."
"What did you do last year?"
"I worked all day and into the night. I came home had a glass of ginger wine and went to sleep. What about you?"
"I was in Maui sitting on a beach."
"Well, we can sit on my beach together. I am rather looking forward to my birthday this year."
"Me too." He turned and scooped her up. "By the way. I am glad I am here with you."
She threw her arms about his neck. She kissed his lips, then threw her arms wide and shouted. "I am so glad to Kiah! You bring me joy!"

When they walked the path back to the house the guys were waiting. They greeted him. William told him there was a call he needed to make. By the look on his face Nia thought it must be serious.
He excused himself after planting a kiss on her lips.
Coffee greeted her. She enjoyed two cups and ate fruit before she disappeared to her bedroom.
She stepped into the shower and hoped that whatever it was that had them bothering him was not going to cause him too much grief.

She tried getting something from those two, but they were like guards of the Holy Grail.

She was dressed in her black power suit when he walked into the bedroom.

"We will run you in to the office. Then I must take a flight out…"

"Flight! But why? Kiah you just got here!" The jacket she was holding slipped from her hands.

"Nia I will be back."

"Kiah what is going on?"

"I need to fly over to Heart Island."

"What's over on Heart Island?"

"A couple snakes who are trying to fleece more money out of me."

She looked confused and very worried. He didn't want another melt down. So, he decided to tell another truth. He prayed for support.

"Nia, I bought the island."

"You bought the island? But what for?" She was still stuck at the words **bought the island**.

"Sweetheart I bought the island off the previous owners. I thought everything was sorted. But now it turns out they want more money. I am not giving them another cent. I paid them too much as is because I thought one was a friend. Anyway, I am just whizzing over, and I will be right back."

"Kiah are you sure? I mean I don't like this…"

"Me neither sweetheart." He kissed her.

"Don't do that." She stepped away. "Kiah you bought Heart Island?" She spat.

"Yes. I thought it was a great investment."

"Kiah you bought an island." She said more like a statement as she tried wrapping her mind around the word.

"Yes, Nia I bought an island. That island. I thought it brilliant for what I have in mind."

"You bought Heart Island? You bought an actual island? How in de hell… Dear God Kiah, you bought Devil Island?"

"Yes, I did. So, I guess that makes me the rich Lothario…"

"Don't! Don't you try that shit! I mean what in de hell does one do with an entire island?" She asked stupidly.

"Nia let me shower." He tried to kiss her again. She threw up her hands. "I promise we will talk some more on the way in."

It was 8:30 when they got to the cars. Her heart was still drumming loudly in her chest. She had waited in the bedroom until he was sorted with his shower and even when dressed.

He still tried to convince her he would zip over and back.

Something kept screaming at her to not let him leave. She didn't know why. All she could do was pray.

She begged and pleaded with God. Even while she was seated in the car next to him, she prayed.

She reached for his hand and brought it to her lips.

"Nia I will be fine." He offered. He could feel the distress pouring out of her. "I will walk away if we cannot come to a resolution."

"Seriously Kiah. Why do you want an island?"

"To develop sweetheart. It is what I do. I have always wanted to do this. I bought the island. It is mine. I even told the guy he could stay until the New Year. Now he wants to renege. I am not having it. He wants to play hard ball. I will grind his in a vice."

"Kiah please. I am worried. He sounds very untrustworthy, and I don't want you alone with him."

"Nia…Terrence and William aren't my only detail. I have a fleet if I need them. Even as we speak, they have that entire island surrounded. So, you see I will be perfectly fine. Now come on. I will be back before you even miss me."

"I miss you already. I don't like not seeing you Kiah." She pleaded.

"Same here baby. But I promise I will be ok."

"You had better be. Because I don't know what the hell you need an island for. You can live with me. That entire part of the island is mine. I can give it to you if you want to develop something that badly." She was serious.

"I know that, Nia." He laughed loudly. She truly owned lots of the island for real. But he wanted Heart Island it had great prospects. "Let's change the tone of this mood sweetheart. Why don't you tell me what you have planned other than meeting with the aunties?"

"Kiah, I mean it. If you want to develop something…"

"Nia, I have never been fearful when it comes to making deals. I am a great businessman. This is a great venture. So, let's be positive. I have chartered a helicopter. We will fly in and out. You would not even get the chance to miss me. Now c'mon cheer up. Tell me what you have got planned."

"Other than missing the shit out of you? Kiah, I don't even know if I can concentrate."

"Oh yes you can. I have every faith in you."

"Make this right." She interrupted. Pointing. He had done well in remembering the route. Plus, it is usually one straight road into town from her house until you get to the crossroad.

"This is Parliament Street to your right straight into town."

"Yes Boss. You look gorgeous by the way. Sorry I was too distracted to say it earlier."

"Sweet talker." She laughed, "I am telling you now Kiah. If you get hurt in anyway, I will seriously hurt you more. I swear to God."

"Nia, I promise I will be careful."

She was tempted to tell him to stop the car when she spotted some of her team. But she did not feel like having anyone in their space. She was being selfish.

God knows if she hadn't rescheduled the meeting with the aunties, she would have cancelled and jumped on that damn helicopter with him.

194

That asshole over on Heart Island had better not entertain anything or even harm a lock on his head or there will not be any holes on this earth for him to crawl into.
Nia, Nia sweetheart, isn't that one of your workers? She just came off the bus. Do you want us to pick her...?"
"No!"
"Okay." He knew why she said it. He was beginning to be able to read her expression. She was worried as hell. They had better not pull any shit if they knew who his Nia was. He pictured her as one of Charlie's Angel. He smiled.

He parked outside the shop easily. They sat for a while until she unbuckled her seatbelt and reached over for him. She folded him up in her arms.
"I mean it Kiah get hurt and I will hurt you. Do you understand?" She squeezed him tightly.
"I will miss you too. Just think the sooner you let me go the sooner I can get back to you."
"Kiah, I don't like this." That was not what she wanted to say. She felt teardrops as they crept from her eyes. She wanted to tell them to get lost.
"I don't like this either Nia. I would much rather be here with you." He reached up and flicked the tears away, then buried his mouth on her trembling lips. He kissed her hungrily.
"It's just for a little while sweetheart. Now pull your beautiful self together." He kissed her one last time. "Now c'mon. I will see you soon."
He got out of the car and went around to get her door. She came out. They stood on par. Her heels made it possible.
"You are stunning. Knock-em dead sweetheart." He swathed her rear. She started walking away. Her chest felt like someone had opened it and fitted it with heavy rocks.
Halfway across the parking lot he couldn't stop himself as he watched her go. He called out her name. She turned. It was like the last scene in **The Bodyguard**. They ran towards each other and embraced and kissed like they each needed the other to breathe.

Just then disorder descended; they were startled apart by the loud blare of a car horn accompanied with loud music.
"Good morning you horny people! Get a room!" Seba called out.
It made his heart flutter to see the girl being loved the way she was supposed to. They made such a fetching couple.
He stopped and quickly reached for his cell and clicked a couple pics of them. He snapped one as they turned to wave.
"You two look so beautiful together."
They waited until he pulled expertly into his space and hopped out. He ran to them. He had to get his smooch as well. But he was forced to stop in his tracks when he got to them. Because her face crumpled, and she reached for him.

195

"Kiah Corrington what have you done?" He asked poking at the drop-dead gorgeous man. "What have you done to her? Come here baby." He wrapped her up in his arms. "I warned you. I warned you Kiah."

"Sebastin, I did not hurt her. I would never hurt her. I must go on a trip. She is worried."

"What trip? You just got here!"

"She will fill you in. I need to get to the airport. I have a flight to catch. I told her the sooner I leave the sooner I can be back. I love you sweetheart." He bent and planted a kiss on her lips before he turned and ran towards the guy's vehicle.

There he stopped and turned. "By the way I left the remote in your bag. She is yours if you need her." He shouted. He was going to miss the fuck out of her.

"You had better come back." She called out to him.

He waved before he disappeared into the interior. His heart was roaring loudly in his mouth.

They waited and waved until the men pulled out and disappeared. Then she fell back against Seba.

"You-beautiful-lovesick-fool...Come on let's get you busy." He bent and picked up her bags. "Nia he will be back soon."

"I know. But I just have this feeling."

"Stop it! You stop it right now! Stop thinking crazy shit girl. God would never do some fucked-up shit like that to you ever again. You know how long we have waited for some good shit like that. So, girl bite your tongue and let us go put some serious prayers on your man."

He guided her to the building. He paused long enough to unlock the door and entered the code.

Nia allowed Seba to host the staff meeting because she was not in the mood. The faint smell of dying flowers followed her everywhere and tickled her nostril. The sight of them was all over the place. They had her thinking she would simply just burst and let a scream out. She felt utterly depressed and missed the man so damn much.

She turned on her heels and slipped away. She walked to her office upstairs in the costume room. There she tried anything and everything to distract herself until the only thing left was praying. She opened her mouth and started whispering to God to watch over him and his men in their undertaking, and please keep them safe.

Her mobile went off in her pocket. It caused her to jump. She yanked it out and cast it with a look of annoyance. But when she saw his name, Sinner Man. Her heart soared. She had entered it like that from the instant they had exchanged numbers. She saw herself entering worship lots of times. She answered quickly.

"Kiah! Kiah are you ok?" She asked breathlessly.

"Hello sweetheart." He purred. He pictured her beautiful face. She was Angel in his phone.

He loved the many nuances of emotions that scampered across it. Most times he could pick out consternation such as why me, or what does he want, or will he be, or how will we...?

"I am still cross at you." She said into the phone.

"I know you are." He paused just to hear her voice. "I miss you." He offered.

"I miss you more." She spoke her truth.

"What are you up to?"

"I ran from the staff meeting. I wanted to scream just to get rid of this feeling of worry and frustration that is threatening to eat me alive."

"I'm sorry baby. Just think I should be back by the time you are finished with the aunties. We are already ten minutes into the journey."

"I hope so. By the way did you call them?"

"They were like you. They were not happy." He said as a smile played about his lips. He pictured her face for the millionth time.

"Kiah please be careful...I don't think I can survive this world..."

"Sweetheart...I will be ok. Let's not think ominous thoughts. I am taking care of business. As soon as it is finished, I will be on my way home to you."

"I like how that sounds Kiah."

"What?" He asked. He liked to play word games with her. Just to get her to hear and believe what they had was solid.

"You...You said you will be home."

"Yes, what else? Finish it, Nia." He teased.

"Kiah, I heard you."

"So, finish it."

"You said you will be home soon."

"Say it again sweetheart."

"You will be home."

"I will be home to who?"

"You will be home to me."

"Good girl. Now stop slacking off and get back to work. I will see you as soon as I am done."

"Okay Kiah." But she could not find the strength to click off.

"Nia sweetheart, please hang up."

"Kiah I can't. I am afraid."

"Truth is...Me too."

"So how are we going to do this?"

"Sing for me."

"What do you want me to sing?"

"Anything sweetie. I just want to hear your voice."

"Okay Kiah. She thought of Etta James' At Last... She opened her mouth. She sang for him as though he were sitting right there in front of her. Her voice messed with his heart in ways he simply couldn't put in words. He clicked the recording button as tears streamed down his face. He too pictured her singing just for him. His heart swelled and did a crescendo.

"Fuck Nia." He said when she finished. "I will be home as soon as. Now get

197

to work so we can spend the afternoon together. Just you and me woman." He prattled with conviction. He prayed he didn't have to maim anyone to beat a path back to her. He missed her something awful. "Okay Kiah. See you soon." She whispered with bated breath.

Seba walked in to say the van was all loaded. "You look better." He stated. "Stop worrying my friend. God has your back. He will take Kiah to his meeting and bring him right back to us. By the way where is he off to?"
"Heart Island."
"What's over there? Does he know that island is Satan's playground?"
He shook himself at the recollection of the place. He and a couple friends had snuck unto a ferry to the island pretending to be entertainers for a weekend a few years back.
He had never seen so many drugs and shit in all his life. But of course, you were threatened when you were leaving in the nicest of ways. But to an islander simply pointing your finger in their face was a serious threat.
So, he had gotten the message. Especially when a couple months later a member of the group was found floating in a pool. It was declared an accident. Seba didn't believe it because the idiot could not stop talking about all the things he had seen.
There were young men and women so wasted out of their heads and ripe for the picking of anyone who desired. It was ridiculous. There were all kinds of fetish shit going on some of which made Stanley Kubrick's Eyes Wide Shut movie child's play.
Let's just say if he could have swum back to his island he would have.
He was not squeamish about his sexuality even though many thought and said he should be. However, he would immediately put a stop to anything that made him truly uncomfortable; bestiality, fisting, knife and gun play, strangulation... lions tigers and bears oh my!

He had wandered out to a far side of the terrace and had witnessed an orgy happening that blew his mind on so many levels. He had made a stupid comment that "white folks were just nasty and depraved."
But in the true light of day, he had to reason it wasn't just white people, people on a whole can be very corrupt and ooh so despicable.
He also reasoned that whip cream was one thing but shit and piss? Hell no!!! Some people were just FUNKEE!!!"
So, he had curled up in a far corner. That is after someone had said to him, "try this."
He begun to feel like he was being twisted in a kaleidoscope; everything swirly and dazzling. God had sent guardians no doubt. Because the next Thing he knew it was daylight and everything was normal again.
That was when he rationalised that maybe he had not seen what he thought he had. But he never longed to find out again.
He shook himself out of the clutches of Déjà vu.
"He bought the island Seba."
"Bought the island? Girl what do you mean?" He squawked.

198

"You heard me. His crazy ass bought that damn island. Now it seems the men he bought it from wants more money that he says he is not paying. Seba, I didn't get a good feeling about it. You yourself once told me of the crazy shit you saw going on over there. What about the people that have been rumoured to have disappeared? Seba, I don't like this. Maybe I should charter a copter! I am going completely bonkers."

"Now wait! Wait a damn second here Jessica Fletcher! Let's just think about this rationally. I am sure he didn't go over there by himself. I am sure Jet Lee and Jackie Chan went with him."

"He says they are not all. He told me he had a whole team over there."

"See? So, what the hell are you gonna do? You will only be getting in the way. So, let's just keep our commitments. We go to **Corrie's** then to the academy. Then we grab some lunch. He should be back by then."

He held her fast. "Nia Kiah is a big boy. He has been doing his stuff before you. Heck, he bought an entire island. I mean how the hell do you do that?"

"What? You want to buy one too?"

"I need to fuck a few more frogs before that can happen. But why did he buy Devil Island?"

"He wants to redevelop it."

"Into what?"

"Seba, shit I don't know. I...we didn't get that far. I only found out about it this morning. Dang Seba! I even offered some of my lands."

"Dang girl! "He looked at her in shock. "I hope it was to buy?"

"I don't care about that. I just want him safe."

"But you have to do some of that thinking with your head honey." He poked her there.

"Aaawh! Fool I know that! It's just that I was scared. I got a bad vibe, and you know me I can be quite emotional. But let's go and sort business. I will give him until 1:00 pm. Then I will be on him like fleas."

"I will be right behind you sweetheart. Now let's go make some more money. We have a lot of envelopes to fill for Christmas."

The van pulled up outside **Corrington's** and Auntie K came out to meet them. "Bellot is on the phone dealing with an over-seas matter. Hello my beautiful niece. Kiah called. He said you are worried about his trip over to Heart Island...Hello Sebastin."

"Good morning auntie." The two chorused short of curtseys.

Nia curled up in the older woman's arms. She smelt of lavender. It reminded her of her mom. "I will be better once he is back here Auntie. I got a bad feeling. I pray he is ok."

"He will be sweetheart. You'll see. Now come along and knock the socks of the buyers. Sebastin you are looking quite spiffy." She kissed his cheek.

"You smell so good. By the way you owe me a Sunday dinner. It was good of you to cover for Nia at Omar's yesterday."

"Family help family. You taught us that."

"Good man. Very proud of you."

199

"Thank you, auntie. I promise I will repay dinner." He offered as he looked her over and complimented her suit choice. It was quite flattering. He loved the pumpkin orange against her warm brown ripe coconut coloured skin.

"You are such a flatterer Sebastin."

"Truth teller Auntie K. You are a dynamite looking female. In my next life I want to be like you."

"There can be only one Sebastin. God broke the mould after me." She cackled as she embraced the two, who had become her children. She gave thanks every day and pray for their protection as she does for May. Today though it was for Kiah.

The team pushed the racks of clothing through the docking area and unto the merchandise lift for the fourth floor.

A couple of their models should have already gathered. She asked her auntie after them. She was informed they were already assembled and getting sorted. Kiah crossed her mind and she wondered how he was getting on.

She whispered a prayer before she left the lady's room. She had slipped off there to pull herself together.

The conference room was buzzing; the summit would soon begin. Nia was so nervous; like she always got every time she was centre stage. After she greeted everyone, she went to the backroom to make certain they were all ready. She would always choose a range of body images so they could see the clothes on many.

Ayanda; a beautiful endomorph girl with big boobs (no enhancement) and wide hips.

Sharma was an ectomorph who was lean and long.

Wendy was a mesomorph who was muscular and well built.

They wore the outfits with such elegance. After the first few entries everyone begun to relax. Especially when they showcased the huge multipurpose scarves in sequins and beads. Some were plain or painted, diaphanous and even feathered.

There was such panache and intrigue. Even the buyers were excited to come and give it a go. The meeting went on longer than expected but everything was sold.

Nia praised God.

They were all having such a great time celebrating when Nana the secretary burst into the room to tell them to turn the television on.

The mobiles phones in the room started to hum and buzz. It seemed like chaos simply ran in and held everyone captive.

ABS and **ECBS** were now on the scene, and from what they could glean seems shots were fired in a stand-off on Heart Island.

Nia's heart immediately sank to the floor. The aunties motioned her over, but it seemed she had forgotten how to move. She felt Sebastin's arms go around her.

"Baby it's nothing. He is ok." Seba didn't know whom he was trying to convince as he guided her over to sit next to the aunties.

Indiria and Domini were broadcasting, "Seems like the millionaire brothers: Derrell and Jayden Kassem, who owned the island has taken multi-billionaire Hezekiah Carter Corrington 111(Kiah to most who has met him on Emerald City) and some of his men hostage. This has apparently occurred over prior sales negotiations of the infamous island. It is alleged that Jayden was dissatisfied with the outcome of the sale and wanted to renegotiate. He has allegedly brought a group of militias to the island to make certain things swung his way."

The aunties picked up their mobiles and so did she. They dialled his number. He did not pick up. They were just hoping.

Nia tossed it back to the table. She took up pacing just like the aunties.

"The devil is a liar." They kept repeating.

"I told you I was going over there." She spat at Seba "You told me he was gonna be okay. I told you I was going."

"But Nia...Sweetie thank God you didn't. Look at what is happening. You would have only served as a distraction. Worst yet bait. Then instead of just him he would have been worried about you. Now stop this."

He pushed her back into her seat. "Let Kiah do what he has to do without worrying about you."

"He is right darling." Her auntie offered. While Auntie B was on the telephone with police headquarters. When she replaced the receiver, she informed them that police officers were already dispatched as well as the Defend Force.

"See sweetie anybody who needs to be there is there."

"I know Seba. I just feel so helpless."

"So, what did mama teach us when we felt like that?"

"To pray."

"Then that is what we will do."

"How about we do Psalms 61? I say you sing."

"But..."

"Shush girl!" He started the psalm... " Sing Nia...C'mon sing..."

Ten minutes later Nana told Auntie B that Kiah's parents were on the phone.

She took the call and reassured them. When she hung up, she walked over to Nia and knelt to her and said, "Kiah will be fine sweetheart. I have every faith in a positive outcome. So, we are going to sit tight and wait on God for deliverance. Am I right?"

"Yes ma'am." Nia mouthed, whilst her eyes were peeled to the picture that jumped out at them from the television of the beautiful island. She had to admit that albeit it grudgingly.

Domini was giving a history lesson about the island. Nia tuned out. Seemed they were as much in the dark as they were. Indiria was broadcasting the present.

Nia and the others tuned back in. There were men in similar plain clothes patrolling the beach. She could spot some of their police officers and defend force in green.

"I am calling that woman right now." Auntie B said pointing to Indiria. She walked away and leafed through her rolodex and picked up her telephone.

"Indiria this is Bellot. What else can you tell me as to what is happening on that confounded island? Okay then. Please keep me posted the minute anything changes."

"What is happening auntie?" Nia asked jumping to her feet.

"We are waiting just as she is. No one can get into the house."

Everyone looked back to the television as shots rang out from it. Nia thought how surreal; because it seemed as though they were looking at a scene out of **Hawaii Five O** or **Miami Vice.**

But the reality was starring them in the face because the main character she knew most intimately. He had only just kissed her a couple hours ago. She doubled over. She felt as though her head would explode. She rationalised that she couldn't simply just sit there idly twiddling her thumbs. But where could she go? She was just about to hightail it from the room when she caught a glimpse of him on the screen.

She pointed dumbfoundedly.

"Auntie! Auntie look! He is ok! He is ok!" She ran towards the screen and touched his face. Even in a crisis the man was still absolutely dashing. She ran her fingers along his visage. "Be alright sweetheart. Please be alright." She whispered as the tears that were struggling to consume her came pouring forth. Someone seemed to be saying something which caused him to turn slightly…

"What! What is that on his shirt? Is that? Auntie that is… Oh God! Kiah! Kiah! Kiah!" She screamed. Seba caught her just before she crumbled to the floor in a heap.

"Seba he is bleeding! He is hurt! He is hurt!"

"Jesus Kath! How in de hell is this happening?" Auntie looked from Seba to her love. She didn't know what to do.

"Sweetheart let's not jump to conclusion…"

"He is bleeding Katho can't you see his shirt?"

"Yes, but he does not look stressed. Maybe someone else…"

"Shush!" Her auntie ordered.

Indiria and the Domini were speaking all at the same time.

The next thing they saw from the screen was chaos as shots rang out. Nia brought her hands to her face. He was dead for sure she reasoned. Because no one could survive in all that. A lifetime passed before peace ascended on that island.

It was half past three when the first call came in. Auntie B beckoned her over.

"He is all right! He is ok Nia! Come and say hello." She offered as tears escaped like a fountain from her eyes.

Nia ran and grabbed the phone.

"Kiah! Kiah! Are you ok baby?"

"Sweetheart." He exhaled. He could not continue because all the pent-up emotions came pouring forth at the sound of her voice.

He pictured her face and how devastated she would be if he got himself hurt. He could not put her through another tragedy. Neither could he go off to Hades knowing he was leaving her behind. He reasoned he would be the biggest pain in their ass because he would not be able to leave her behind.

So, when he spotted an opening, he had given the men the signal and they had laid siege.

It did not take long for the idiots outside to fall, for they had the support of the neighbouring police and defend force teams.

Kiah relented and offered more money, but not the amount the idiot brother wanted. So, he demonstrated by displaying the countless reams of footage.

He did not want bloodshed, but a decent conclusion looked like it would not be, because Jayden would not acquiesce. He died for his greed.

Kiah continued to explain that the blood stain on his shirt was from a bullet that one of his men took in his shoulder.

Thank God for great favours they all thought in the office

"So, you truly are not hurt?"

"No sweetheart." He breathed raggedly.

"Thank God... So, everyone is, ok?"

"Yes Nia. Raphael is being flown out in a couple of hours once we get the clearance."

"Then you will be home soon?"

"Yes sweetheart. We are just tying things up with the officers. Making certain everyone is ok. Then I will be home to you."

"Please hurry...My heart hurts Kiah. I want you here. I want you home." She pleaded.

"I will be sweetheart. Just a couple more hours."

"Kiah? I love you. I love you so very much. Please hurry."

"I love you too sweetheart. I will see you soon." He said, with the phone pressed up to his ear. Because all he wanted now was to be with her and wrapped up in her arms. He hated circumstances had gone so horribly wrong.

Nia thought it good to cancel the meeting with the academy. Her nerves were too raw. She wanted to see Kiah. She would wait with the aunties until she did. She could not take any more mindless chit-chat.

203

The aunties ordered a late lunch, and they sat about just picking at it. The team had left after she thanked them for their arduous work. They had done extremely well. The styles would be in the shop as soon as possible. "Eat something Nia-Belle." Her auntie encouraged, even though they themselves were just picking at theirs.

Then auntie B excused herself to take another call; more of the family wanted to know what was happening. She had to reassure them.

Indiria was talking with Kiah now. She had her microphone stuck in his face. He looked bothered as though he wanted to be any other place but there with her.

"Good to see that you are ok Mr Corrington. I mean Kiah. We heard that one of the brothers has died?"

"Unfortunately, yes Indiria. Jayden Kaseem has died."

"We heard that you are the owner of this island?"

"Yes I am." Kiah offered with such annoyance. Thinking Dominic Lazar had better hide in the deepest hole. He was the brothers' lawyer and had assured him that everything was copacetic to go ahead with the sale. Guess he had his eyes more on his commission.

"So, the sale is official then? Because we heard that the brothers were trying to renege. Anything you can share with us?" "Yes, the sale is official. But on anything else please let's hold off until the officials have done their investigations."

"So will you be staying on the island?"

"No, I will not." He barked at the woman. He had had enough. It was a long tedious day. He wanted to head home and see his family.

"Kiah! Kiah! Do you know who those other men were?" She heard they were his team.

"Like I said Indiria when there is something to tell I will. In the meantime, please. I really would like to see my family."

"By family you mean..."

"That will be enough. I will speak to you again and soon."

After he was told he could leave he seriously had thoughts of walking away. His gut was annoying the hell out of him now even though he still felt this was a viable investment. He wanted to convert the mansion into luxury apartments.

He reckoned he could get about forty or so. The island was slightly bigger than Necker. He had not known he would meet Nia. He thought he would develop the island and maybe when he desired, he could come home and simply chill. He was getting older, and he did not enjoy the hustle and bustle anymore.

His phone distracted him. It was his parents. He reassured them he was fine. His mom told him they would cut their trip short and get to the island sooner rather than later. He did not even fight. He longed to see them, and he wanted them to meet Nia.

204

When the helicopter landed, and they cleared immigration he couldn't wait. He spotted her and took off running. She was waiting with the aunties.

He welled up like an angry volcano about to blow its top from all the pent-up energy. It came bursting forth; he felt the wet trail on his face. He brushed them away frantically.

He scooped her up in his arms and covered her face with kisses. She kissed him back with so much intensity.

"Are you two going to allow us to get between you?" Auntie B asked as she wiped the tears that gushed from her eyes.

"Aunties." He breathed softly. They wrapped them both up in their arms.

"You too Sebastin." Kiah offered opening his arms. He had no doubt the man had stood by his woman and gave comfort when he couldn't.

"That was quite a scare you gave us Kiah." Sebastin said as he jabbed at him and wiped at his cheeks.

"I am sorry. I did not mean to."

"You had better not do it again." The aunties admonished as they folded them back up in their arms.

"I promise... But please can we not talk about it anymore. I just want to grab a shower and get something to eat and just lay around and hold her and thank God that I am back here with you."

"We understand sweetheart. We just wanted to make certain you were ok."

"Thank you, aunties. I am fine now." He offered, as more tears stung the back of his eyes. He fought to keep them at bay.

"Your parents will be in sooner than. They were worried sick." His auntie said.

"I know. I spoke to them. They will be docking in Antigua on Thursday."

"Thursday?" Nia asked stupidly. "So soon?"

"Nothing could have kept them away Nia. But that is okay. You have nothing to worry about."

"Easy for you Kiah. But let us go home. I want to take care of you." Nia offered. Not leaving the confines of his arms.

They gave the aunties hugs and promised they would call when they got in.

Seba and the guys disappeared. It gave them time together. They showered and changed and held each other for a bit before they emerged for food; vegetable paella and roasted chicken. Compliments of Rosario and her kitchen.

Nia had forgotten today was cleaning day with all the chaos. The house was spotless when they walked in and smelt glorious. She always cooked on a Monday.

"This is delicious." Kiah said as he dug into his. They were sitting around the island.

"I will pass your message along to Rosario. She is my housekeeper, and she cooks for me on a Monday when she comes. She says I do not take care of my eating habits."

"Aren't you going to have some?"

"I am very happy just to watch you eat and make certain that you are ok."

"Wow! I think a hurricane will be passing by. You! Refusing food?"

"Kiah you gave me such a scare."

"I am sorry baby. I honestly did not think something like that would transpire. The sale had already been wrapped up."

"Then tell me again what happened."

"One brother thought the other was weaselling him out of pocket. So, he wanted more. He came to the island and held him hostage. Then he made him call me to say he wanted to renegotiate. No wonder he was so insistent. Jayden showed himself while we were negotiating. He had a couple of henchmen and guns..."

"Kiah, I meant what I said this morning. You can have Bransby Point or even Isle's Bay Bluff if you want to develop something. I was contacted by investors' a couple of months ago. I turned them down. But you can have one or both. I do not like that damn island."

"I had second thoughts about it after today... But please let us sleep on it and we'll decide after a couple days. Thank you for trusting me and wanting to share with me."

He reached out and touched her cheek and caressed it. He did not think it was possible to love her anymore.

"You would do the same Kiah I have no doubt." She believed it. She kissed his hand and whispered a thank you to God once again.

"Kiah please just think about it. Those lands can be yours if you want them."

"No more now. Please just let me enjoy you. Come, eat with me."

He picked up his fork and fed her. "Thank you for caring for me and for looking after the aunties. How was the buyers' event?"

"They absolutely loved it. They bought all of it."

"Wow that's brilliant Nia."

"I know. They should be in the store by the end of the week. Christmas festivities have started."

"I am so happy for you." He fed her again. He loved to see her enjoy her food.

"Kiah, I am worried about meeting your parents. You think they are going to like me?"

"What's not to like about you? I think they will adore you."

"I hope so Kiah. Because what will we do if they do not?"

"Don't forget I own an island, Nia."

"Bite your tongue Kiah Corrington! We will just have to barricade ourselves here is all. Uh-oh! Does that mean you are going back to the aunties?"

"Heck no!" He pulled her off her seat and propped her on his lap.

"I live wherever you live understand? I am your man. Got that?

Now tell me you understand this, Nia."

"Yes, I do Kiah. I am your woman and wherever you live I live. But not over on that blasted island."

"Are you back on that again woman?" He asked laughing loudly. "I never got off it. I will be hounding you until you leave that devil place to someone else."

"Oh Nia. I missed you something fierce."

"I missed you too Kiah." She wrapped her arms about him and thanked God for watching over him and bringing him safely back to her.

Chapter Six

Kiah's sleep was troubled. He woke repeatedly. The last time she sat up and cradled him between her legs and sang softly to him.
They had not made love even though they had turned in early.
She must have fallen asleep before him. Now the alarm was babbling annoyingly. She turned and slapped at it.
He was sitting up in bed in a meditative state. He reached for her.
"Morning." She snuggled into his arms. It was pointless to ask if he was ok. She could see in his eyes he was not.
"Let's go for a run Kiah." She said as she reached up and gave him a kiss.

They ran in the tunnel for core strength. When they emerged, they strolled about the luxurious property before heading inside. Both were genuinely shattered by the time they entered the house.
However, that did not stop him from kissing her delicately as he stripped her of her clothing for the shower.
She copied him and before long they were enjoying each other on the cold bathroom floor.

They sat in the kitchen having coffee and eating toast with butter and her favourite sorrel jam; Rosaria must have purchased it. He loved it as much as she did.
When the guys; Seba included wandered in after their run or workout; it looked as though they had punished their bodies unceremoniously.
"Hello you two." Seba greeted. He came over and kissed the top of her head. "She was mine first my brother. Nothing has changed."
"I know." Kiah said easily. "Thank you for taking such good care of her all this time." He genuinely liked the guy.
"You are sweaty Seba! Yuck."
"Love you too." He grabbed water from the fridge. He tossed a bottle to each guy. He winked over at Terrence.
"Anything on the agenda today boss?" They asked Kiah. They had been in contact with the others last night. Things were calm. Derryck was still on the island. Raphael had left.
"Take a break guys and enjoy the island. I will be fine." Kiah said to them.
He had already concluded he would shift the island. It was not worth it.
He knew he would not get the full cost of what he paid but fuck it!
He had already checked his mobile. There were so many people who wanted a piece of the action.
Greta said she was on her way, even Ama.
He told them directly not to come. They capitulated in the end.
Greta admonished him once again not to say too much to the press.
"Just keep it short and sweet as always Kiah."
He promised he would. They said their goodbyes.

208

"Thank you for always taking care of him." Nia said to the guys. "I forgot to say that last night. I swear I truly did not understand what it is that you do. But I am so damn grateful." Nia said to them.

"A pleasure ma'am." They responded cheerily. For they genuinely liked her. She was so different from the those who tried to grab their boss's attention.

They were always rude and did not even acknowledge them.

Not Ms Nia. She would always say please, thank you, and checked to see if they were ok, or had something to eat.

They noticed how much their boss had changed in the brief time he had met her. She was good for him they surmised.

"Seba, can you open for me today? I think I will avoid the office for a bit." She asked not wanting to leave him today. She had just gotten him back.

"Nia I will be fine."

"Shush Kiah. I have got this. We have got this. Now finish your breakfast. I would like to take you over to Isle's Bay Bluff."

"Nia!"

"Just keep an open mind Hezekiah Carter Corrington III." She copied the way his auntie spoke his name. "Plus, it is a win win.

You buy my land I can get a couple of my projects up and going. Right boys?"

"That was really very good Nia." Seba said. "Brilliant idea. We can get some more high-end visitors here on the island. Then international boutiques..."

"Not too many Seba. We as local vendors still want to remain viable. We still want our island to be in the top ten of safest islands in the Caribbean." She had to reel him in. That was why she had not sold to those who came sniffing. She did not want local trade disappearing.

"True. But one must balance out the other. With high-end customers coming in the government would be urged to put a proper mode of transport in place so it is not so bothersome getting into the island. Come to think of it, Kiah how about you buying us a proper ferry?

"Seba!"

"Don't you Seba me Nia. Just think since we lost the Jayden-Son we have not had a proper means of transportation. We all cannot afford to charter flights in and out. Plus, our airport is not big enough to sustain a major airline that can transport our damn luggage, or even the barrels that family members send to sustain their family. Which means we must rely on a ferry system that may or may not run. I am just saying he has the means to invest. You are here, his auntie is here. So why Heart Island? When he could do it right here?"

"Brilliant ideas coming from you two. Leave it with me. We will speak in a couple of weeks. I promise."

"Kiah we are not a charity case. I mean we would like to do so much. But I don't want to risk the safety of my people because we want to improve tourism."

"Nia it would improve the job markets. Get our youths off the street and working. Mas Joe is still talking about this bridge that we could build to link the different islands. He says put a toll booth on either end, then charge for crossing over, add a footpath even that pedestrians or cyclists can take advantage of. Look at the George Washington Bridge or even the Dartford River Crossing. These bridges would be viable for all. The toll booth fees can go towards road maintenance and help fund construction."

"Seba people do not want to die in building these bridges. I am thinking the government is thinking this also."

"Nia, you can call me cruel. But how do you think scientist prove their theories? Or these drug companies their drugs? Some will have to die so the majority can live."

"Seba, you sound so cold. I do not think I would ever accuse you of altruism."

"Nia, we need this to keep our island sustainable. We need to provide work for our people. How often are we expected to go to Great Britain for handouts and expect them to give? The well is going to get dry and what will happen to our people?"

"Dammit Seba I do hate when we call asking for support from the UK a handout. We are a part of their colony so we should receive support when we require it. Do you think St Thomas consider themselves beggars when they need support from the US? We have the right to aid not a handout which makes it sound increasingly like begging my friend."

She took a deep breath.

"It sounds like you are throwing your hat in for parliament. The next Premier."

"They would not vote for my rainbow-coloured ass. Darling Kiah because I am considered an abomination. Especially to these bible-toting assholes. I use the latter lightly. Nia, you see how hard they fight me to obtain a permit for Gay Pride on the island every year."

"Ok you two. Time out. I can hear the passion coming out for the love of the island. It gives me a great deal to consider."

"But seriously Kiah. Mas Joe has a point. We would need staff to maintain the bridge, as well as toll collectors..."

"Dead people, dead marine life because we are messing with the eco-system..."

"And you wonder why the government is always so slow in implementing these things. You are damned if you do and damned if you don't."

"Seba we always fight when it comes to this. But I will always ere on the side of caution."

"And the island goes nowhere Nia. Just at a slow pace. Youths are getting bored and want quick money to buy all the shit that these celebrities are peddling. So, what are they going to be doing huh? Begging, robbing, and killing even? Nia, we need to get them interested in other things. So many have IT skills that they only use to check out negative videos of all kinds of degrading shit towards women. Some have even started on children, grooming, and using them in the most heinous of ways. Nia, we need to increase work here on the island."

"Seba, I know this. But small steps. I say the ferry is a better more viable option."

"When the water is a motherfucker then what? Just think how many get trapped in Antigua on their way home to us, to Montserrat. What little they have scrimped and saved to spend in their island they must spend there on food and lodging especially if they don't have relatives there. Nia it is not right."

"So, let's see if we can build a proper airport."

"We got monies for that Nia and they ended up beautifying instead of upgrading. Sweetie, we need to be able to accommodate bigger airplanes without having to stop off in Antigua. I am sure you have a **Lear**, right?"

"Yes, I do."

"You could not even fly it in. You had to layover in Antigua, right?"

"Yes, that's true."

"Wouldn't you have loved to simply fly into the island directly? Then catch your ride and be on your way home?"

"Sebastin we can visit that plan because I can see all sides especially for convenience."

"Kiah I am not saying you should. I am just saying that coming from you a proper investor you can bend their ears."

"I have a lunch meeting scheduled with the premier and a couple of those DFID members I met the other night. Let us see what we can implement so I have enough to get a serious project started. "

"Kiah, I have no doubt that you are here for a reason. Yes, you met our princess whom we love to pieces. However, the bond that you have forged with her means you will now be spending more time on the island. So, would you not want it to be more convenient coming in and out? For you Nia, just think, you would not have to set foot on another ferry if you didn't want to. My man here can land his **Lear** in and out just like that."

"Oh, shush Seba! Go clean up and head off to work and leave Kiah alone." She tossed at him. Knowing full well he had raised enough valid points. She always admired him for his tenacity. He was like a dog with a bone when he wanted something bad enough.

"Food for thought right Kiah-my-man?"

"Well stated Sebastin. We will have a talk again. Definitely."

"Love you princess."

"Love you too you hound dog."

"BIATCH!" He chimed before he disappeared. If she was afraid to speak up, he was not because he had nothing to lose. Plus, so many islanders live by the motto; **you no ask you no get.**

Nia spoke to a considerable number of people before she switched off her phone. She had had enough, and it was taking her attention away from him.

Pastor Seaton, Pascal, and Ms D... also called. She assured them Kiah was doing fine. He spoke to her briefly. She had forgotten his Ital because she had an emergency. They told her it was ok.

Ms Ruthie and a couple others, even Audra and her mom telephoned. Kiah spoke to her briefly. While she laid atop his legs across the bed. She could feel a migraine coming on. She told him as much when he hung up. He got her a pill, and she took it, and they laid back against the pillows.

When she turned later. He was not in the bed next to her. She wandered out, she could hear them on the veranda.

Kiah was speaking in another language and there was an Asian man talking to him from his computer. She waved to William and wandered back to the kitchen to grab herself a drink. Her tongue felt like she had chewed on cotton wool.

She grabbed a bottle of lemonade and poured a glass. She sat down and sipped at it. Her headache had not totally disappeared, and she had not heard when Seba left either.

But looking at the time the shop should be already in full swing. She dialled the number and Georgie answered. They chatted for a bit.

She told her Seba was in, and the store was 'hopping' because so many people had wandered in.

"Boss I think they might even be reporters from visiting islands because of the kinds of questions they asked. But I told them if they were not shopping; spending we had nothing to say. Boss they seem like sharks circling blood. But if they spend money we do not care."

"Thank you, Georgie. I appreciate it. So sorry I cannot be there. But thanks for stepping up."

"Shucks Boss just doing my a job. You sound funny."

"Bless you. You know me so well. I have a migraine."

"Get some much-needed rest boss. We are sorting things on this end. You do the same there. We are glad everything worked out with Kiah. We give God the praise."

"Thank you, Georgie. I will come in for a bit later. Let us see."

"Do not push it. Just take the day off. Seba will keep you updated."

By the time she hung up Kiah was standing behind her. She thankfully leaned into him.

"How are you feeling sweetheart?" He asked kissing her neck.

"A bit better. Glad you are here. Do that again. Distract me a bit." She said loving the feel of him against her. She turned and kissed his lips. "You seem rather busy out there."

"We were. I think I may have a buyer. Two to be exact. But we shall see how it pans out in a couple of days."

"A buyer?"

"For the island. Devil Island as you so poetically put it."

"Well, I'm glad. So does that mean you will take me up on my offer?"

"Yes Nia." He said truthfully. She had made a valid point earlier. He wanted to support her as much as possible. He kissed her longingly. "You taste good. What is it you are drinking?"

"Lemonade. I just felt so thirsty. I thought of having tea, but I wanted it quickly, so this is my next best thing."

"Nia you are funny. I want to go for a swim. Would you like to walk down to the beach with me?"

"Yes Kiah. If that is what you want to do." She wrapped her hand around his neck. He came to kneel in front of her. Their eyes locked and held.

"Nia don't poke a hungry dog." He teased.

"Kiah I just want you." She offered up sexily. Every time I think I could have lost you yesterday. I just feel like I should hold unto you more."

"Is that so?" He teased, kissing her breathlessly. "You are going to be the death of me." He teased and lifted her in his arms.

"I know how you feel. Take me to your lair." She teased pointing to the bedroom.

"Don't you mean that the other way around?"

"Whatever. I just want you. Now off we go." She giggled all the way to the bedroom.

When he lifted her dress over her head and tossed it, she was more than ready.

While he stripped hurriedly, she eased out of her panties and used them as a sling shot.

"I guarantee you Nia-Belle you will get what you are gagging for." He said sliding swiftly into her. She giggled loudly. He loved that.

He started a slow rhythmic beat inside her. God at the thought of him never being able to lay with her like that. He hiked her legs higher and dove deeper.

"Nia... Marry me." He pleaded. Lost in the garnet depths of her beautiful eyes, and the slow melody they were creating. Pounding out a sweet rhythm of their own making.

"I will Kiah. I will marry you!" She whispered burying him up tightly within her.

"I love you so much Nia." He gasped as he emptied his essence deep within her and she exploded hotly upon him.

Japan...The news interrupted her work out. Pictures of Kiah's face flashed over and over on the huge screen.

"We were told that the CEO Hezekiah Carter Corrington the 111 is held captive on a beautiful and secluded Caribbean Island known as Heart Island..."

She jumped off the treadmill and reached for the remote and turned the volume higher. After a couple seconds, she reached for her phone and dialled.

Her legs felt like jelly as she tried to stand. She finally gave up and sank to the floor. She listened as her best-friend's groggy voice in California picked up.

"Why didn't you call me?"

"About what?"

"Kiah! Kiah Corrington bitch!" Jordanna screeched. "Who the fuck else!"

"Why would I do that?"

"Because I just saw on the fucking news that he was held captive on some tiny Caribbean Island."

"Oh that. He is ok. I called Ama and she said he is fine."

"He is fine?"

"Yes, he is fine."

"I want to see for myself. Now get yourself sorted we are heading to the Caribbean."

"We are? Aren't you in Japan?"

"So what? Shooting wraps up in a couple of days. I have a shoot in Barbuda soon. We can be in this Emerald City for Christmas."

"Wait a minute! Why we?" She asked wiping sleep from her eyes.

"I don't want to go. I am looking forward to a nice quiet Christmas with my daughter."

"We can all be together for Christmas. You know he loves being with his daughter. We can be there to cheer him up. Leave it with me. We will be on a fucking plane soon as we can click our heels together."

"But seriously Jordanna I don't want to be anywhere..." She mumbled sleepily.

"Jasmine listen I will contact you in a couple of days."

"Jordie you are not hearing me. I do not want to go. Aren't things over between you two anyway?"

"Just shut the fuck up Jasmine! Just do as I say. Just get yourself and Jourgette ready. We are heading to the Caribbean." She slammed the phone down.

What! What the fuck! Jasmine thought. What does that fucking- crazy-hurricane want with me and my child? She wondered flopping back against her pillow. But she was too damn tired for her shit right now.

She tossed the phone unto the floor and snuggled up to Christopher her new young stud.

"Kiah?" Nia whispered.

"Huh?"

"Do you think a person can be addicted to another?"

"Why are you asking?"

"Because I have never had sex so many times in my life. I am always so horny for you. Seems like I cannot get enough."

"I feel the same way too. Yesterday when I was facing all that shit all I could think about was you. Touching you, smelling you, fucking you.

Nia just the thought of not being able to see you made me want to kill those two so badly."
"Let us not go back there. I am glad you are home. By the way are we still meeting with Marcus and Yvonne?"
"I cancelled. I do not want to wander around with people in my face asking me all these questions. I heard there are reporters gathering on the island as we speak. Some might have even found their way here.
Terrence and William will be keeping an eye out."
"Thank God they cannot get in so easily. The beach though is another. So, swimming needs to be done in the pool."
"I figured as much. So, what do you say?"
"Kiah you know how I feel about that."
"You will be with me Nia." He laughed, pulling her along with him. "Ok Kiah. I will come down and sit with you while you swim. Be your cheerleader."
"Ok. I will take that. By the way. You did say yes to my proposal, right?"
"Yes Kiah. I did say yes." She kissed his lips. He held her fast.

Nia laid on her lounge under an umbrella and watched as Kiah swam laps in the pool. He looked like an Olympic swimmer as he sliced through the water a couple times. She wished she could be that comfortable. But truth is she was not.
He did not press.

The men decided on barbecue. They brought down a basket of things they found in the freezer. They had steaks and chicken. They made a salad using sweetcorn and coloured peppers with lettuce.
They had cold beer and a variety of juices.
"Nia come join me." Kiah called over to her. Reaching out.
"Do I really have to? I like watching."
"I like watching you too. But from closer."
"Ok Kiah. I did promise that today is all about you." She got up and plodded over to him. She had chosen a discreet two piece in black with boy shorts.
He had chosen a pair of black speedos; that had her blushing each time she peeked. The man looked like a God. Each glance got her worked up in a nice lather. She bit her lips to stabilize herself.
He gestured a come-hither to her, tossing in a suggested wink, and blew her a couple kisses.
She jumped from the lounge and ran towards him. She crouched down on the edge and allowed her feet to dangle in the water.
"You look delicious." She whispered in his ear.
He laughed out loud.
"You are such a breath of fresh air Nia."
"I love when you are like this." She threw her arms around his neck and plunked a kiss on his lips.

215

"Come swim with me before I devour you right here Nia." He reached up under her armpit and lifted her in.
"Relax Nia. Relax I have got you. Just hold on tight."
She did as he instructed. They wandered around in the pool just cuddling.
"Can you swim at all?"
"I can. I learnt privately."
"You are amazing." He chuckled. "So, let's swim. Are you ready?"
"Yes Kiah. But only in the shallow end."

They swam around for a while, and she truly started to enjoy herself.
The guys found Seba's water volleyball net and hooked it up.
They enjoyed a couple matches. Then they got out and had a nice meal.

Nia learnt William had two sisters one was an RN and the other was a middle school teacher. He had four nieces. He had known Kiah from school and use to beat him up on a regular basis for taking away his girlfriends. He was dating but nothing serious.
Nia told him Georgie liked him. He told her he liked her too. She learnt they had been talking to each other on the phone. They had exchanged numbers. More like she stuffed her number in his shirt pocket.

Terrence was an only child raised by a single parent, who cleaned houses to put him through school. She had died a couple of years ago of ruptured aneurism.
He threw himself into his job when he got a second chance; being employed by Kiah's firm. He was with the team for three years.
William was four.

They enjoyed each other's company and swam a bit more.
Kiah and the boys fell asleep under the huge awning. While they slept, she quietly cleared the table, took the dishes up, stacked them in the dishwasher, and switched it on.
She then remembered the cake and tart she had brought from Carmen.
She sliced fruit mango, pineapple, kiwi, oranges, and guava.
When she went back down, they were stirring, and came to help.
"I brought drinks, cake and fruits and some more fresh plates if you want to eat again."
"I'll have some fruit punch it reminds me of the sorrel."
"I like sorrel too. I will get a couple bottles from Ms D she makes it very well."
They ate cake and fruit and lazed about for a bit more. The guys went swimming again. Kiah joined them. Nia began to feel a bit cooped up, so she suggested going for a walk. It was semi-dark now, but she liked walking about and enjoying her island.
She usually did it with Seba; he was home. He called out to them.
Holding up bags. "Peace offering." He called out.

216

When he came out to join them, he had **Sylvie's**. Once again Nia felt ravenous. Going for a walk now long forgotten.

They tucked into succulent fried chicken and fish fillet, coleslaw, pigeon pea or cheesy biscuits, potato salad, and toss salad.

They lighted the tall citronella bamboo candles, brought fresh beer and Seba put music on.

They ate, danced, and had a nice time.

Seba told them other reporters had come to the island.

Kiah knew because he had turned his mobile on mute.

CNN, Sky, and countless others were calling. Greta had even telephoned again. He told her he would ride it out by laying low. She did not wholeheartedly agree but she had learnt not to push him when he got stuck in.

Kiah also had a bone to pick with Indiria for making the decision to go live. But then again, she was a strategist. If she had not, it meant that someone else would have taken the headline. So, with that said he had to applaud her. He had no doubt that had this incident taken place in America it would enhanced massively.

Seba said he was certain he had been followed home. Thank God no one could enter without permission.

"Told you that damn-gate would come in handy one of these days huh?"

"You have been tolling your own bell a lot today, haven't you?"

"But seriously sugar. I would not put it pass them for someone to scale those walls. Maybe we should borrow some big dogs from Boogie..."

"No Seba!"

"Suppose a few of them decide to climb...?"

"Seba we are not that important."

"He is. Nia he is an American Icon. I am certain they know now that he is here on the island. So, they are already on their way. Kiah what is your press people saying?"

"I will be a turtle for a few days." He offered and laughed.

"Lay low then?"

"Sharp Sebastin." Because he knew what the man said was truth. But he was not going to give fodder to the fire.

The reporters had found the aunties. But security at the building kept them at bay. He apologised with a promise to check in when they left for home.

"Nia honey. Sebastin is right. Perhaps working from home will be the best for the next few days."

"But Kiah I have so much that needs to be done." She suddenly felt a panic coming on.

"Can any of the primary stuff get carried out from home? If not, you will need an escort."

"You mean bodyguards?" She snarled. She could hear the panic rise in her voice. What was happening here? They had gone from peace to chaos. "Bodyguards Kiah? I don't need them!"

"Then are you prepared every time you leave here to have a camera shoved in your face? Because darling, that is what will happen. At least if he provides some protection, you will not have to be cooped up here." Seba reasoned.

"Dear God in heaven! What is happening here? Do you mean I have now become a prisoner in my own home? All because I fell in love with you?" She jumped off his lap. Her hands came up to cup her face.

"Kiah, I have so many things to do for the season. Seba, you know this is our best time for the fiscal year."

"So, accept the man's offer then. You do not want to work from home. So, the next best alternative is him providing security for you."

"But that's insane!"

"Sweetheart calm down." He urged. He could hear the hysteria laced in her voice. "I am sorry." He wrapped her up in his arms. "I truly did not mean for all this to happen. But the press will be out there. We cannot escape it. Well short of me whisking you away..."

"No! No! I am not allowing anyone to chase me from my job or take me away from here. No Kiah."

"Then let me call a couple of the guys. You can resume your workload if that is what you genuinely want."

Nia knew what they were saying would be the only way, other than to be held up at the house. So, after an eternity she said,

"Ok Kiah. Call them. But I have two conditions."

"Yeah?"

"One you are paying not me." She loved him. In for a penny in for a pound. She was not walking away. "Two we visit those lands I offered. Cause I warned you about going over there in the first place, and you didn't listen."

"Deal." He offered. Filling the evening with a melodious raucous.

"Seba, you turn coat, you are witness right? Terrence, William, you heard him, yes?" She started walking away.

"You drive a hard bargain my Nia." He chased and scooped her up, she squealed with delight.

Before they turned in for the night. They called the aunties. They said a couple of reporters had followed them home when they left.

A pair asked if they knew where he was. But they gave them nothing. They remained outside the gate and as far as they knew they were still there as per Silcott's report.

The aunties wanted to know if they were ok. They told them they just had an easy day at home and that they are working on how to proceed in the ones to come.

The guys were still down by the pool when they went to bed. Nia was out like a light.

Chapter Seven

He awoke before her. For the first time in a long time, she slept like a baby.
It was 9:00am by the time she stumbled out of an empty bed.
She sorted herself and went out to join him. There were four new guys
sitting at her table. They were even more ripped than the two she had
come to know. Thank God she had dressed in her joggers before she
went out.
"Hello sleepy-head." He greeted and came over to plant a kiss on her lips.
She looked questioningly up at him. "They are your escorts if you are
thinking of going into the office today... No Nia we had a deal. Whenever
you go out of this house, two will always be with you. The others will be
with the aunties."
"And they agreed to that?"
"With a bit of gentle persuasion. It will not be for long sweetheart. I promise
only until this crap I created settles down."
"Ok Kiah. And do not forget your promise either." She pointed at him.
"I won't."
"Good, and good morning to you all. Which two of you will be my
bodyguards?" She asked, accepting the cup of coffee that William
offered.
They were always so attentive.
"I am Onrey." An equally handsome and dashing one offered and rose to
his full height of six feet. He had a deep-set voice. He was clean shaven
and looked like he could toss her with ease. He
The other was Russell. He looked exactly like Matt LeBlanc. Then there
were Daniel and Dimitri. She gave up with description because they all
looked like they spent days in the gym, then prepped for a stud
catalogue.
"Nice to meet you. I hope I will not give you cause to worry." She
offered. "I usually don't require all this fuss."
"We understand Ma'am."
"Nia. Call me Nia." She said to them. Then whispered to Kiah.
"Where are the females? Don't you hire females?"
He laughed. "I have four. But they are off having quality time with their
families for Christmas. "You will meet them soon."
"So, when did you guys get on the island?"
"Late last night Ma'am."
"Nia." She insisted. Thinking most did not 1look older than she was.
"Yes Ma'am..." They looked to Kiah. "Nia"
"Here's your fruit Nia." William placed a bowl on the counter.
"Nice place you've got here Ma'am. I mean Nia."
"Thank you. Please make yourselves comfortable."
"Thank you, Ma'am. Nia."

They seemed to move like military. She watched as they excited the room and moved to the veranda where they had their computers opened atop the table.

"Why didn't you give me a heads up?"

"Figured you needed your beauty sleep." He wrapped her up in his arms when she placed her cup on the counter.

"You have had a lot to process these last few days." She wrapped her arms about his waist.

"I like waking next to you Kiah." She placed her head on his chest.

"I am sorry for disrupting your life, Nia." He truly meant it. But short of walking away which he couldn't do, providing aid was the other.

"It has been a rough couple of days."

"We will get through it Kiah. You know the saying what doesn't kill you." She tiptoed and kissed him. Then she tucked into her fruits.

"Great woman. So have you decided on what you will be doing today?"

"Did you see Seba?"

"Yes. He says to tell you not to worry about the office. They have everything under control."

"Seems like I have not been running the day-to-day operations of the place. He had been taking on the brunt of it."

"That is not how he puts it. He said you needed a holiday."

"I just came off of one Kiah!"

"He said you would say that. Even though you were working even while you were on holiday. Buying fabrics brocade all the stuff for costumes and clothes. Checking in, enhancing this…"

"That man talks to damn much if you ask me. But I am working on a dress for the showcase. I almost finished it. Now this."

"Do you want to go in then? Or I can have the guys go in and collect it."

"Kiah it just seems like so much fussing. I need to call the academy. I promised a last fitting before the show."

"Seba said he had that under control. He will be taking Mandy and Tara with him. I do believe that you know what that means?"

"That I am not required in the office today. Kiah, I hate that we had to cancel with Marcus and Yvonne."

"When is your dress rehearsal?"

"Tomorrow evening."

"Maybe we could meet at a private location later. Mom and dad will be in early. We have chartered a flight for them. We are meeting at the aunties for a late lunch. I did say I will run it by you. What do you think?"

"Kiah I am so nervous about meeting your parents. Suppose they…?"

"We have been through that before sweetheart. They know how I feel about you already. I am happy, they are happy. They will love you like I love you."

"We will see. But just know I will stalk the hell out of you if they decide they don't."

Kiah laughed loudly. "I was thinking the same damn thing. I will have to lock us away somewhere until they come around."

"Ha-ha. It is usually easier for a man to be loved by family members rather than a female. Suppose she asks if I can cook? Clean?"

"Well, can you?" He teased. "I certainly did not fall for your cooking skills. I can cook for myself. I can clean. I can iron. I am generally good with things domestic."

"That's not all." She said and winked at him. Finishing the last of her fruit. "They have to move downstairs… Or else we can't…You know what I mean Kiah?"

"What?"

"No booty." She whispered. "It was bad enough with two. Now six! Good God! People might start to think I am running a stud ranch."

"As long as I am the only stud you want Nia. I don't have a problem."

She laughed aloud and started singing Whitney Houston's **All the man that I need.**

Then she headed over to her piano. She played and sang and even did a version of **I'd Rather Go Blind**…

The men gathered at the door and clapped at the end.

The four who had never heard her sing were quite congratulatory. They likened her to Whitney and asked how long she had been singing.

She told them from the time she could string two words together. But her voice was nurtured in church and Glee Club.

She discovered that Dimitri could play the piano quite well and that he sang a bit of Jazz in a band. He hopped on the stool beside her, and they played and sang a couple of songs together. He was dynamite.

She made a mental note to speak to her band. Especially when he told her he was great with the technical stuff and had a little studio back home in California.

Nia suggested they go out for a walk. But she knew what she had in mind as they dressed and headed out.

They walked down to the beach, where she noticed the motorboat moored in the cove.

"Yours?" She asked.

"Yes Ma'am. Nia. It is a catamaran rental."

"We can give you a…"

"Hell no! Sorry boys. Guess your boss did not mention that I was made for dry land." But she had to grudgingly admit the vessel was nice, sleek, and looked quite inviting.

They laughed and walked on, and up to the bluff, hiking for an hour and a bit through unworn paths, and through thick flora and fauna that offered shade from the sun's rays.

They interrupted and scared foraging creatures, and spotted indigenous birds, as well as exquisite iguanas, butterflies, and insects.

Their journey led them on the yonder side of her place on the island. It offered them another panoramic view of Emerald City because they were about 1500 feet above sea-level. They also got a backside of the illustrious Heart Island that was quite deceptive; it made it appear as

221

though you could simply swim across or reach out and touch it. She had painted it several times. It was breathtakingly scenic. As if you could step out and an invisible bridge would take you all the way across to the gates of heaven.

"My God Nia are we in heaven?" Kiah asked incredulously as he reached out for her waist. The sight was mesmerising.

"You like it?"

"I...God Nia it is breath-taking! I love it! Nia it is like God's hideaway out here." He whispered. "I am totally smitten. It makes me want to set up camp for a while. Why didn't you tell me?"

"I did Kiah." She laughed. "When we were at the Lighthouse. So, you think you can build whatever project you were hoping for over here?"

"You little minx! Is this what you had in mind all along?"

"Yes Kiah. This is Isle's Bay Bluff." She spread her arms wide. "As far as the eyes can see. If you walk over there you can use that place for rock climbing. You Americans are hook on that daredevil shit. Go have a look. But I am not going." She said and stepped further back. "You guys like parasailing and water skiing. Shit that beckons you to an early death. I like staying on dry land."

"Nia you are funny! Boss she got game!" They guys laughed. "I am serious guys. I love my life. But seriously you can have a jetty with your own boat, do that snorkelling thing. I hear it is beautiful down there. You guys like that shark bait thing on the board when the water has a point to prove. Getting wiped-out. Hell no! Not for me! What did you want to build?"

"A luxury holiday villa and an occasional get away for myself. I never factored that I would meet you. That you would change my life so completely."

"So have I sold you on this place then?" She shouted over at him.

"Are you going to marry me?" He shouted back at her.

"Yes Kiah. I did say that." She shouted back.

"Then will you live here with me?"

"Hell yes!"

"Then you have a deal, Nia!"

"Don't you want to see the other piece? Even though I think this one suits you. It is more hilly and rugged over on the other side, and too close to the luxury condominiums, and the Lighthouse. Get the drift?"

"I like it here." He came back and cuddled her. "Do you like it?"

"Yes, Kiah I do. Very much. I come here to paint sometimes."

"Then it's settled." He said kissing her deeply.

They walked back the way they had come. It was a bit more treacherous coming downhill than going up. A couple times she had to reach out for support. Daniel found sturdy branches and quickly made walking aides.

"Boy scouts ma'am. I mean Nia." He corrected when she gave him a look.

She wondered what else he had in that bag. Other than water and a sheathed hunting knife.

She too had her fanny pack with her trusted things from her jacket pocket: pepper spray and her stun gun.

They went for a swim when they got back down. They swam, she stayed close to the shore. She and Kiah left them swimming and headed up to the house. They wanted to start dinner.
Just before they got inside his cellular rang. He looked at it, then answered and switched to another language.
"Gamsahabnida Mr Park."
She left him to his call and went inside. She headed straight for the shower. Five minutes later he joined her. He had a huge grin plastered on his face.
"It's gone Nia. Devil Island is gone." He said stepping in with her.
"Thank you, God." She gushed. Wishing whomever it was the best of luck with the place. She would never forget that episode for as long as she lived.

Dinner was simple. He made a spaghetti carbonara and she put together a tossed salad. William did garlic bread. They said it was Italian.
The closest she had come to any of that was spaghetti and sautéed tomato garlic onions and peppers, and a toss of parmesan cheese.
It was quite delicious.
Someone suggested turning the television on.
Indiria was hosting the 6:00 pm news.
"Good evening, ladies and gentlemen. Welcome to the ECBC news. Following on from the story that we broke on Monday afternoon concerning the elusive Hezekiah Carter Corrington III who is nephew to the owner of the Corrington Department store here on the island Lady Bellot Amanda Corrington."
They showed a picture of his aunt from church on Sunday. The woman is quite stunning Nia thought. Very similar to her nephew.
"He is a multi-billionaire who recently made Forbes 10 richest men in America."
They showed a picture of him on the Forbes page.
He pulled her up on his lap.
"Seems as though he celebrated with on-again off-again flame Supermodel Jordanna…"
They flashed a couple images of him and the one-named--world-renowned troublemaker.
Nia always thought her extraordinarily beautiful. But she came off as quite obsequious. She seemed like she always had an agenda.
She sat frozen!!! The images swirled about before her. The words dated Jordanna!!! Flashed before her.
The woman did not even need a second name for anyone to know who she was. She was Jordanna the 6-foot Californian beauty who looked quite athletic with long super glossy blond hair. The fiercest blue eyes you have ever seen. She has graced the covers of **GQ, Vogue, Sports**

Illustrated and **Victoria Secret** just to name a few. She had had a couple of run-ins with rival Naomi. They have been dubbed 'The Superpower Duo' whenever they stepped out all over the world.

Nia only heard the rest of the news broadcast on her peripheral vision because she was still stuck on the images of Jordanna and Kiah.

She turned stupidly to look at him.

"Nia... Sweetheart... Fuck! Fuck! Fuck!!! He hated shit like that.

A few of those photos were simply for furthering her career. She never seemed satisfied when she was not in the glare of the media. But fuck Jordanna. It had been over for eons now. He was just always lazy in dating.

"We have been over for so long now. Nia, sweetheart, we have an understanding..."

"But that photo was just this year. It does not look like an understanding. You were kissing! You two looked!"

"That was simply just for the camera's sweetheart. I help her she helps me." He tried to encircle her waist, she wriggled away but sat there stiffly. Thoughts bombarded her vision. Jordanna is...! She was his goddamn woman! Dear God! Look at her compared to plain old her! Jordanna! She was stick thin, no ass, big boobs, blond haired, blue-eyed American bombshell!!!

She seemed stunted as she sat through the rest of it staring off.

She wanted to ask more, but she did not want to cause a scene.

"Hezekiah the **CEO of Carter Inc.** purchased the playboy's playground on Heart Island where unrest unravelled a couple of days ago. Seems like younger brother Jayden Kaseem was not happy about the monies paid for the island and demanded more by luring Kiah as he is affectionately known to many who has met him about the island over to Heart Island. Kiah was unaware it seemed that he was walking into a trap. But after lengthy and exhaustive negotiations, we understood shots were fired. One of Kiah's men sustained minor injuries. Jayden Kassem on the other hand was not so lucky. He ended up losing his life in the malaise that ensued after ECPD and ECDF surrounded the island.

Kiah thankfully left the island unscathed. However, since his return to Emerald City no one has seen him. Some are speculating that he is held up with his new girlfriend Miss Nia-Belle Castle Francois in her home."

She flashed a picture that was taken of them on Sunday at church, then a picture of her house.

"Some are saying he is head over heels in love with her, he has even purchased her diamonds and bought out an entire flower shop for the woman. Kiah has promised us an interview. So, we await this. However, in the meantime we have regional journalists, and I have word that BBC UK and CNN US are on their way here. We are all awaiting word from Kiah."

They flashed pictures of Heart Island, the brothers, Corrington's, the aunties, Belle, her home, her and Kiah, Kiah, Terrence, and William.

Nia jumped off his lap as if she were ejected. She went to the kitchen and poured herself a glass of water. She swallowed it and shakily placed it back on the counter.

"Talk to me Nia."

"I'm just trying to wrap my mind around Jordanna...Then me."

"What is wrong with you?"

"Absolutely nothing. Damn I want to have an arrangement with Jordanna too." She spat.

"I didn't think you were into females like that Nia?"

"What? What the hell!"

"Do you see how silly it is?" He started laughing. She started laughing.

"Nia I am here with you. I love you. I don't want her. I want you."

"Kiah you dated Jordanna!" She held up her hand "Fellas...Me? Or Jordanna?"

"Oh no! No ma'am!" They gestured to each other to get the hell away from this one.

"Men. You stick together no matter what don't you?"

"Come here you little minx." He dived over and picked her up and threw her hanging over his shoulder. He slapped her behind playfully and started off to the bedroom.

"I will show you my choice Nia. Guys see yourselves out." He shouted out to the men.

"Don't you dare try to distract me Kiah Corrington! How come you never said you dated Jordanna?" She asked when he tossed her squealing on the bed and dived between her legs kissing and nipping her sweetly.

"Nia it was not important. She is not important. I don't even want to talk about her. I want to concentrate on you right now." He continued the heated trail pausing at her midriff. Then he kissed her roughly near the opening.

She grabbed his head. She pictured him with the leggy blond-haired person, as he yanked her panties off giving her opening a doggy lick.

"Kiah...Kiah I...curious...is all." She panted.

He was making sweet music between her legs. He hiked them higher.

"Oh God Kiah! She!" He rammed his tongue deeper.

She grabbed fistfuls of his hair. She long forgot who Jordanna was and what she was to him. More like he made her forget as he gave her a whipping with his tongue. By the time he sneaked into her the bombshell was a distant memory.

Chapter Eight

Nia turned. She had to go to the toilet. When she got back her alarm started to kick up a storm. She ran over and switched it off.

He reached up and pulled her back down to bed.

"Good morning beautiful." He said kissing her lips. Her neck. Her breast. She was naked and so was he. They agreed this was how they would sleep. He loved feeling her body next to his.

"I was dreaming of doing just this…Nia I am so addicted to you."

"I am totally head over heels for you too." She kissed him back. "Do you think we will ever get tired of doing this?"

Her hands ran the length of his athletic hard and smooth as a sea-stone body.

"I hope to hell not. Nia even when I am old and grey and my dick doesn't work, I will still find a way to make you go wild."

"I am sorry I got freaked out when I found out about the '**bombshell**'. But that is what we as women do. We compare ourselves to the exes. And it does not help that she has the body and face of a goddess."

"So do you woman. Your body drives me delirious." He eased her atop him. "Sometimes I just can't seem to get enough of you." He slipped his dick inside her. He loved how she was always ready for him.

Her motion matched his.

"Nia, I love the heck out of you. I told you before I will not intentionally do anything to hurt you." He held her ass cheeks firmly. "If I do, please let us communicate like rational people. I don't do well with scenes, and I don't like underhanded people. I try my best not to badmouth anyone. If I am with you, I am with you. I do not go around fucking women just for the sake of it either. And I do not intend to fuck anyone else by the way."

He flipped her. "I am totally whipped by you woman. So, I don't give a fuck who or what Jordanna is or how she looks. I love you. Only you. I want only you Nia-Belle. Only you baby. Only fucking you."

He slowly moved with her as she moved with him. She clenched him tightly by locking her legs about him and laced her hands about his neck. They held eye contact as he balanced himself on his hands.

"Promise me Nia that no matter what happens we will always be like this with each other." He loved when they made love just that way. She said as much to him as well.

Nia's heart was heavy. How could he feel the same way she did about him? How come she loved the man so openly? She felt no guilt when she gave herself to him. The simplest to the most complicated of intimate things they did she was always open to it. However, most of all she loved listening to his voice in their moments like this.

She felt this immense tickle as though someone had hooked her up to a machine. How was he so incredibly different to David? He seemed so in

tuned to her body. To know when she wanted him, when she was nearing her peak, where she wanted to be touched, what she needed to hear...
"Ooh God Kiah..."
She came up to join him and entwined her long legs around his waist.
"What will I do when it is time for you to leave?" She gripped his ass and pushed herself into him. She was certain her nails had left an imprint on his firm ass.
"Nia! Nia!" He cried out to her. He was putty in her hands.
She pushed him back on the bed. She covered his body with hers.
"God help me Kiah...I want you so much it hurts at times."
It was the most intense feeling she had ever had with him yet. Her chest felt like it would open and swallow him whole within her.
She rode him like a needle in the grove of a record. He screamed like a wounded animal. It tore at her heart. It caused the tears that stung the back of her eyes to spill over and down her cheeks and unto him.
He came up to join her after an eternity, as he touched her and tried to caress her feverish body clumsily.
Sweat poured from them as they plodded on until finally neither could hold on any longer.
Nia felt lighted up as though she had popped a handful of mood enhancing pills. Her mind exploded in a kaleidoscope of shapes and colours.
Kiah moaned and writhed as though someone had tossed him in a pit with about twenty diverse and deadly types of reptiles.
His head exploded from the pain. He groaned out her name so loudly. He was certain his men could hear him from wherever they were. He didn't give a FUCK! This was his woman and she had taken him to heaven.
They both fell on opposite sides and laid there for God knows how long before they could utter another word.

Strategy today; breakfast first. It was nice to have more company. She felt like a queen. They always had her coffee sorted.
When they wandered out from the bedroom arms around each other and smiling like Cheshire cats, the scent was glorious.
Bacon and eggs filled the air. The smell of fruits when she sniffed was intoxicating.
Mental note: more mouths to feed more groceries.
Dimitri and Daniel had already left to start their new job of securing the aunties. This according to William who seemed like he oversaw the operation here on the island.
Seba called last night to say he wouldn't be home. She only picked messages up after they had peeled themselves out of bed and sat to meditate for a while on the floor, then prayed.
The intensity of their earlier lovemaking had wiped them both out, but a secret bond had formed. She felt it.
She reasoned; she no longer wanted to live in regret. She vowed she was going to enjoy all that the universe seemed to have dropped in her life by

227

total accident. Because these past few days had brought purpose, whereas before she was consumed by work; leaving at the crack of dawn and coming back to simply kick off her shoes and lay across her bed or the sofa, even at the kitchen table... and simply fall asleep. Consumed by all the things she needed to do for others and not for herself. Consumed by thinking life and living in fulfilment authentically had nothing at all to do with her.

Good love and great loving were an elusive dream for her. She mouthed her mama's mantra again.

He repeated it with her. She stopped and pulled him towards her.

"You bring me joy Kiah Corrington." She said and kissed him sweetly.

"I hope to do it for the rest of our lives together Nia." He said as he wrapped her up in his arms.

They were meeting his parents at the airport for 12:00. Seems like a couple press people had stationed themselves outside her gate. When the guys left, they were followed.

Just like they did when the vehicle came out the gate.

They also had to call the police department to have the beach patrolled. Because a hired fishing boat; one of the locals had brought reporters over.

A couple helicopters were also spotted flying above as well.

"Is this how it is with you?" She asked in awe. Recalling the many clips of Michael Jackson and other celebrities who constantly had microphones stuffed in their faces.

Even the way they had hounded Princess Diana to an early grave.

A couple of the reporters jumped at the vehicle. One slapped at it as they exited the gate. They shouted and called out his name.

"Goodness me! You are an honest-to-goodness celebrity, aren't you?" She asked as her heart settled back in her chest.

"Ignore them, Nia. They will get tired eventually." He reached over and pulled her to him.

"You look gorgeous by the way."

"You do to Kiah."

He wore three quarter length white shorts, white boat shoes, and white buttoned shirt and a sky-blue sweater draped over it. His hair was tied back.

She had chosen a candy-floss pink midriff ankle length dress with huge side pockets and a white asymmetrical sleeved bolero jacket.

Her hair was in a beautiful, neat chignon that she pinned with pearl tipped bobby pins.

A set of big forefinger and thumb circular pearls adorned her neck with matching earrings. She had chosen the same tone pink kitten heeled shoes, underwear, silver strappy slippers and the white version of the dress in a bag along with a huge silver scarf for contrast later.

228

They were meeting Marcus and Yvonne at the yacht club where they were staying.

Terrence drove and William sat with him in the front. She and Kiah occupied the back.

It brought back memories of driving in the aunties' car with Silcott. It made her smile. She thought be careful what you ask the universe because she is constantly listening.

He squeezed her hand. "What are you thinking?" He turned his ultra-violet Ray-Bans lens towards her. She turned to him. She wore huge black out round lenses.

"Why don't you simply give a statement? Say something. Then hopefully they would just go away."

"I will Nia. I was waiting for the deal with the island to be sorted. Now that it is I will."

"Then hopefully things will go back to normal. I mean our people are not interested in stuff like this. It is your American and international counterparts."

"We give thanks to Indiria and her team." He said, knowing she wasn't as cruel as the other media bodies. She had respected their boundaries.

"She wants to be the next Barbara Walters, or is it, Connie Chung."

"Ambitious."

"I can't say I blame her Kiah. We all have our dreams. I mean why allow someone else to run with a story that happened here?"

"Clever woman. It is only fair. I will call her."

Nia's heart was a mess by the time they climbed out of the vehicle. "Please let them like me. Please let them like me." She prayed.

Kiah had shown her pictures of the couple. She had even spoken briefly with them. They had sounded pleasant enough.

His mom kept calling her darling. It was one thing over the phone another in person.

When they got to the airport building, Nia wanted to run in the opposite direction, but she was forced to hold her ground. More like Kiah had her trapped with his hand around her waist.

She thought he got his great looks from his mom. But as she got closer, she kept going back and forth.

While Silcott and the guys loaded the luggage. The greetings commenced. There was lots of hugging and kissing between the aunties and then Kiah.

Then all too quickly it was her turn. She felt as though she was now being rocked, and that at any moment she would just keel over from the way her heart was pounding in her chest.

"Nia darling. So nice to finally meet you." The woman gushed and pulled her in. "My son has been raving about you non-stop."

229

"So nice to meet you too ma'am." Nia muffled from the confines of the tall and slender woman's arms who reminded her of a coffee with plenty of milk Melody Thomas Scott: Victor Newman's wife on Young & Restless. Her eyes seemed mischievous and twinkly like her sons' when she lifted her Cocoa Chanel sunglasses.

When she smiled her teeth were sparkly and white. Nia was certain the sun peered out each time she did. Her laughter was so infectious, and she seemed to dance instead of walk; like she should be standing in line to come to the podium for Q&A in a Miss USA Pageant.

Her raven black hair was pulled back in a tortoise shell clip. She wore white shorts that emphasized her long athletic legs and pink sweater set. Her feet were encased in white Gucci loafers.

Nia thought she was totally in-love all over again, as she prayed to the heaven's yet again that they would like her.

"Hello Nia." His dad said. Taking her off his wife. "My son didn't tell us how beautiful you are." He gushed, holding her aloof.

He looked like a lighter in the body Eric Forrester on the Bold Beautiful and sounded like Laurence Fishburne.

She thought that when they spoke, but in person it was even more of a dulcet tone.

"Dad do stop flirting with my girl." Kiah warned him, as they embraced yet again for what seemed like the hundredth time.

"I am so happy you are safe Hezekiah. You made my poor heart ache."

"Here here." His mum chorused. She hugged him again.

"I am so sorry for worrying you mom."

"I am getting too old for drama son."

" True son. The old ticker can't take much drama... Have you seen my phone dear?" He asked patting down his white polo shirt, and khaki shorts.

"It is in your bag sweetie. I told you I would put it there."

"See what I mean son. Thanks, dear. What would I be without you sweetheart? " He turned back to Kiah. "But like mom says I am glad you got out unscathed."

"Me too dad. But as you can see over there. They aren't through with me." He pointed to a group of reporters with their lenses trained on them as they called out his name.

"Hezekiah...Kiah...CNBC...Kiah BBC...Kiah ABC...Can we have a moment? Is it true that you bought Heart Island? Did anyone else die Kiah?"

"Well seems like you are on their radar once again son."

"Kiah, can we get a photo-op?"

"I don't see why not." He stood with everyone and pulled Nia in closer."

"Kiah stop feeding the fire. Or they will not go away." Nia warned.

"Clever girl." His mom offered.

"Now that's enough." Kiah tossed over to them. Then he turned to his parents and the aunties. "Are we ready to head home?"

They were still calling after them as they walked to their cars. They even followed again when they started off for the manse.

In the vehicle Kiah asked her, "What do you think of them Nia?"
"They are ok. Your mom is quite stunning. I love her dancer gams."
"You love her son too, right?"
"Stop fishing for compliments Mister." She slapped at him. He pulled her close and reached over to kiss her.
"I told you; you had nothing to worry about."
"The day is not over yet. I am still under the microscope."
"She already told me she likes you, Nia."
"What about your dad?"
"He is easy. He likes you if she likes you."
"Let's wait until the end of the day for a true judgement."
"You've got this sweetheart."

At the manse there was more clicking of camera lenses until they disappeared into its sanctuary.
They decided on a late lunch outside by the pool after a brief show round. The parents complimented the aunties on the structure and beauty of the house.
They also shared pictures on their phones of places they had been, and people they had met. Also of some experiences of the trip at sea.
His mom said she had had the opportunity to participate in a handful of ballroom competitions and had won a few trophies and even money.
"Nia, Hezekiah tells us you are a fashion designer?"
"Yes ma'am. I have my own store **Belle**. You can come by one day soon for a personal tour."
"I would love that very much. He has been singing your praises. Speaking of singing we have heard you also sing?"
"Yes, I do. We have our annual **Extravaganza** coming up this weekend. I have been asked to sing. Will you be attending?"
"I did say to Bellot and Katho I would love to. That one on the other hand." She pointed to her husband. "He falls asleep quite conveniently when we go to the theatre."
A round of laughter rang out around the table.
"Hezekiah perhaps we can do something while the ladies go off for the evening?"
"Oh no dad. I will be front and centre supporting my woman." Kiah offered popping a forkful of salad in his mouth.
"Well done son. I have raised him well haven't I Nia?"
"Yes, yes ma'am you have."
"Show off." His dad said. "I guess you and I will be in the front row then."
"Bellot we will need a muzzle." Kiah's mum said. Cutting her chicken and putting a piece into her husband's mouth.
A chorus of laughter went up about the table.

231

Nia found herself relaxing a bit. Then she felt Kiah's hand on her thigh. She reached under the table and took it in hers. He smiled.

She smiled back at him.

"I forgot how absolutely beautiful this island can be. We have been away for far too long. I see why you wanted to buy Heart Island."

"So, what's next son?" His dad asked. Looking up from his plate.

"I am working on another project with Nia. When it gets sorted, we will tell you some more."

"Do we hear wedding bells then? Auntie B asked. Looking over at them eagerly.

"As a matter of fact, she said yes. I have asked her a couple times now."

"Kiah!" Nia spat, astonishment lacing her voice.

"You said yes?" Her auntie asked. "Nia–Belle why didn't you tell me. Tell us?"

"Because I still can't believe it myself Auntie."

"So, you said yes to my son Nia?"

"I...I..." Nia stammered. Looking at him then at all the other faces.

"Congratulation's sweetie."

"Now we can get some real grandkids eh son?"

All eyes descended on him like heat sinking missiles.

Nia did not miss it. Even a blind man could as well. As a deadly silence settled.

The man shrugged. He knew his foot had absolutely got stuck in his mouth. They would give him grief. He blamed it on stress on jetlag.

As he recalled when the shit had gone down with the boy. He had been so devastated.

They had spoken deeply just a couple of weeks ago. He deduced that something was amiss, even after all the accolades he had amassed.

But when he checked in a few days ago, he had not missed that vibe that had laced his voice. He sounded genuinely smitten.

One could feel it when he mentioned her name. This one he knew had shifted something in his son. He liked it. He looked forward to getting to know her more. But in the meantime, who was he to pass judgement?

Because it had only taken him a week before he had proposed to his mother.

He had taken one look at her; he had gone to her studio to pick up his then girlfriend who was taking dance lessons. She was doing a Samba with her partner. He could not peel his eyes off her.

When their eyes met it was as if the world had stood still... He had become her partner and she was in his arms, and they were dancing...

Then the music screeched to a halt and his girlfriend pulled him out of his dream state.

Introductions were made and he held her hands a bit too long. She noticed that also.

"You are leaving me, aren't you Denny?" She asked.

"Why?"

"You have never looked at me in quite the way you looked at her."

He had simply admitted to it. Because he could not lie or forget her face. He thought she was the most beautiful woman he had seen. Well next to his mother that is. Still to this day. He had vowed then and there he would do anything and everything to win her over.

So, after a bumpy couple of days: ending things with his girlfriend, he signed up for private lessons, and then made his move.

Within a month she would become his wife. They eloped because his father refused to give his blessing. In his words, "she is not fit to wipe his boots. Then again that was the only use for a nigga."

He had had her investigated.

He kissed her cheeks. It had not been easy back then. But they had made it. He loves her still as he did the first day his eyes had rested in hers. She had given him a wonderful son who had made their lives bountiful.

It was bumpy during certain periods, but he made good on becoming the greatest son ever.

"Yes dad." Kiah said, as he bestowed upon him a look of annoyance. He prayed that Nia had not grasp the '**real** ' bit.

His dad pleaded with him. Thank God his aunt changed the subject.

"So, you said yes Nia? Then we need a ring Bellot offered." Chastising the man. Who at times allowed his mouth to run while his brain played catch up.

"Don't forget she tried to get you to buy a ring the other day." Auntie K interjected. Not missing the stare Kiah tossed the other man.

"I want Nia to pick out the ring she wants." He offered tightly. As he ignored the apologetic look his dad gave.

"That is not a problem . She can come down to the store when she is ready."

"After all that mess is over. Seeing I can't even get to my office."

"So, you two are engaged? Darling someone has captured your heart?"

"Yes mom. I didn't think it would ever be possible. But dad said it was. He said it happened the same way with you two."

"It sure did. But it is not about us. It about you two. Congratulations my darlings." She was up and hugging her son, then she hugged Nia tightly.

"Take care of my baby Miss Nia. I will not be forgiving if you ever hurt him."

"I will not Ma'am. I love him."

"Call me Elena my darling. Or better yet you can call me mom. You will be marrying our son."

"Do you know how long we have been trying to get them together? They kept resisting. Always coming up with some excuse not to meet, to talk even." Auntie Katho said looking towards Auntie B.

"Nothing happens before its time Auntie." Nia said. She popped another piece of the chicken into her mouth.

"Wise woman. Beautiful too." His father offered. "Congratulations son and congratulations Miss Nia."

"Thank you, Sir." Nia offered. Not missing the look that had passed among them. Most especially Kiah. She aimed to ask what it was all about. But she tuned back into his dad's voice.

"Nia please call me Denton, or you can simply call me dad. You will be our daughter soon."

"Thank you, Sir...I mean Dad." She chewed the last word. It felt strange saying it.

"That's my girl. "

"You mean my girl dad."

"That too." His dad laughed. "But on a different note, son you have a birthday coming up. Do you have any plans?"

"Nia's birthday as well." Auntie Katho said. "I don't think she's had a proper celebration since we gave her an 18th birthday party. She works like a beast of burden always doing to help others."

"Then let us change it this year aunties. I already asked if we could celebrate together. Nia told me she wants a barbecue for close family and friends. I like that. So, I thought we could do it together."

"Then let's do it here Hezekiah." Auntie Katho chorused. "We hardly ever get a chance to celebrate our Nia. It will give us an opportunity to spoil her rotten."

"But I don't want to be spoiled. I have everything I need. I don't want anything. Please I would much rather something low key not too much fussing."

"Fuss. No fuss. Just time spent with each other."

"I mean it. Please I don't want more things to have to find a place to put them. Kiah you promised. Aunties please."

"Just family and friends Nia." Auntie Katho chirped as she tossed Auntie B a warning look.

"Why are you looking at me dear?"

"Because small to you means the entire island." Auntie K accused jokingly. It made them all laugh.

"Bellot is like our parents. A party is a soiree."

"Oh, shush Denton. It is productive strategy. You cannot afford to piss off Peter and Paul when you require them to frequent your store."

"You taught me that aunties. But honestly, I have received the biggest gift ever already for Christmas." Her eyes sort his. "I don't want to tempt the Fate's and be greedy."

"So, barbecue it is then Nia."

"Just a couple friends and us. I don't want anything like what you threw here last Sunday."

"Ok sweetheart." Kiah said. "Small affair here at the pool." He was looking at his phone. "Soiree...I mean barbecue on the 17th since this Saturday is already taken."

"Sounds like a plan."

"Mum, dad. I did say we are meeting with a couple friends in town. Then Nia has rehearsals. So, it means I will not see you until tomorrow evening."

"I understand son." His mom offered.

234

"I am feeling my age. So, I think I will lay here and grab a nap." His dad said as he stretched out on a lounger. "I am totally shattered."

"Me too darling." His mom said, fighting back a yawn. "Please be careful out there, sweetheart. Nice to finally meet you, Nia. I look forward to your performance tomorrow evening." She wrapped the beautiful woman up in her arms. She liked her already, and the rapport they seemed to share. It wasn't easy dealing with her in laws, and to say they made her life a living hell was a vast understatement. She had threatened Denny she would walk away a couple times... Different story for another time.

So, she had promised she would be more understanding with the woman that her son would bring to her. She recalled all that Bellot shared, so she was certain Nia would be a lovely match compared to that hellion-viper Jordanna.

Images that caused her to flinch. Flashed across her mind's eye. He had brought her home once for Thanksgiving one year. She really tried to give the vile thing a chance. But she was so crass and rude to everyone. Even to the household help. She was so raucous when they were having sex. She must have woken all the ancestors.

She never considered herself a prude by any stretch. But she would have muffled her screams out of respect.

The garish girl never even apologised. She just walked about like she owned the place. She always got her son into heaps of trouble.

She was not one to form an opinion so easily about someone, but she had with Jordanna. Hence the name '**the viper.**'

She just hoped he had come clean to Nia. Having secrets like those was not a good thing. She must remind herself to speak with him about it again.

They left after a round of hugs and kisses. The reporters were still at the gate when they pulled out. They took photos and followed them once again.

He reached for her hand. "So, what do you think of my parents Nia?"

"I like them. Your mom is so beautiful. But she seems so unaware of it. It is obvious that your dad loves her a great deal."

"Like I hope you will come to see how much I love you."

"Oh Kiah. I do believe you love me. I love you so much too. But..."

"No sad talk. This is the 21st century. We can do this my girl. We got this." He pulled her towards him. He buried the top of her head and lips with kisses.

"I like their ease and openness Kiah. Call me naïve but I would like what they have."

"There is nothing naïve about knowing what you want. You must be willing to do the work to maintain it though. Nia, they have had rough patches. Especially when the company was drowning. But dad told me what kept him sane was the promise they had made; to never walk away from each other without giving it a healthy fight. They have kept that promise and did not abandon each other. No matter how rough it got. Nia at times I must put my hand up and readily admit that I did not make it easy either. Children and testing boundaries. But thank God that we persevered and withered the storm."

"I am glad Kiah. Because anything worth fighting for ought to be fought for. Plus, anyone with eyes can see how much they love each other. You have a great family Kiah."

"Thank you, Nia." He kissed her lips. "I am glad that you will be able to spend time with us."

"I look forward to that too."

"So, are we going ahead with this soiree on the 20th?" He asked chuckling. Loving the look on her face. She had popped her shades atop her head. "Will you stop with this soiree thing Kiah? I mean it, and frankly I only just want to celebrate with you. Honestly, I do."

"And I with you."

"Then stop the aunties from doing anything on a massive scale." She tossed. "Please don't encourage them." He pointed to himself a questioning look in his eyes.

"Yes Kiah. You. I am serious, I do not want any of it. Please."

"Yes Nia. I will calm them. I don't want any of it either."

Couple minutes later they pulled up outside **E.C Mariner & Yacht Club Hotel** and parked in the busy well maintained parking lot.

An eclectic blend of people milled about. Some casually dressed as they entered and left accompanied by children and young people dressed to the nines, getting in and out of limousines and fancy cars.

This part of the island was where so many with the money lived and hung out. It was set out like a carbon copy of a 'Rio De Janeiro' mariner, or one of those other extremely rich yacht and boating destination scattered around the world.

When they climbed out of the vehicle, the reporters called out. They obliged wearily for photo taking. They poised for proper pictures. They knew they would be broadcasted all over the world. That is why before they exited, she had refreshed her face, ready for battle.

"Good poses equal great pictures. Just give them your best side and you will see." Kiah whispered in her ear. She smiled continuously.

A few said thank you, others tried once again to get him to answer questions. Thank goodness they could not enter the mariner.

Plus, all six bodyguards escorted them as they entered the building, and into the picturesque lobby where Yvonne and Marcus were already sitting in the lounge and enjoying a drink.

They waved them over.

"Mr President! First Lady!" Marcus greeted. They embraced each other. Laughter rang out.

"It's only for a little while until all that shit dies down." Kiah said.

"I hear you, my friend. Annoying as heck. But so be it." Marcus re-joined.

236

They ordered cold drinks; Kiah his usual sorrel and Nia a guava and lime spritz. She totally loved the combination. It was her go-to whenever she held meetings on this side.

"I understand my friend. Hope it hasn't been too difficult?" Yvonne offered as she hugged Nia again. "This too shall pass another thing will happen and before long you will be a distant memory. So just remember to be gracious. Some are simply trying to earn a living, Miss Nia."

"Well said. So far, they have been decent." Kiah offered. "I am thinking of speaking to them, but on my terms. Now that I have off-loaded that place. I look forward to becoming a turtle once again."

"You? Never! You are too Rico Sauvé for that to happen."

"Says the pot to the kettle."

"You look gorgeous Nia. Your creation?"

"You betcha. I am like you Miss Yvonne. I hardly wear anyone else's design. Except for you, but I am my very own walking advertisement, right?"

"Hell yes!" Yvonne copied. The woman was dressed in a magenta halter sundress. Hair free flowing and held back with a white headband. Her jewellery was **Bonswa**: magenta and brown glass tear drops. Nia pointed it out.

"We wandered around in town the other day. What gorgeous pieces. I bought a couple."

"Understatement! She meant she nearly bought out the store Nia. She is happy with pieces like those instead of diamonds and other precious stones." Marcus said bending to kiss her sweetly.

"I feel the same way. Just think how many of our sisters and brothers have lost their lives in these caves mining for diamond and cobalt just so we can prove something to others that we are worth a look or a listen. I don't care for them. I will be happier with something like that or this. Plus, we need to embrace our islanders' creativity. I have a lot of her pieces as well. I like that she creates from what we discard. I like that it doesn't get into the oceans and damage our reefs and our seafood chain."

Amen Nia!"

"Like minds brother. They are ready for the revolution."

"We are indeed. Like King Short Shirt sang in his song Nobody Go Run Me." Nia sang the chorus lyrics. **Tell them I say. I was born in this land Nobody go run me. From where me come from. Nobody go run...** Yvonne joined her in a nice little rendition.

"Look at you two patriots." The men applauded. "Perhaps we can take this show on the road."

"Loyalists to the core." They raised their fisted right hand.

"Yes I." Yvonne finished. She hugged the younger woman to herself. Thoughts formulated some more in her head. She reasoned she would share later.

"But seriously her husband does some fab work for the eco-system. Just like your son. I heard he has created his own line of spices to combat hypertension and diabetes. He and your brother's **Afro-Carib Fit & Grill.**

Heard the restaurant has become a hit on the island. They are also gaining regional as well as international acclaim. I like watching their live grill shows on television and social media."

"Snappy and Marcus Jr are a dynamic duo in their healthier options meals. Their mission is to produce a healthier and more fit generation."

"I know. Brilliant! I caught the terrific duo on **Caribbean Chef**. They are both alumni of the Culinary Institute of America."

"Yes, they have both done so well. **True Flavours** offers a healthier alternative with low sodium and sugar, as well as no preservatives or MSG. They have also become full time farmers/gardeners. They teach children on the island who are interested in learning about agriculture not the back-breaking kind. They plant their provisions upwards in Ferris wheel growers or pods that gets turned manually, but if you are working alone, you can operate them electronically: by a switching mechanism from anywhere. I think. All these gadgets he keeps investing in. They have 70 wheels right dear?"

"Eighty to be exact. It started off as a hobby for Marcus Jr. who always loved mechanical things: wind turbines and Ferris wheels. He is quite sensory; he loves the feel of the earth as well as sniffing and smelling thing out. He has a stellar nose. I must admit when he first started this I did not know where the hell he was going. But as he explained it made sense. Why should the fun be taken out of farming by one constantly doing back breaking work? He always says. But it's worked. Thank God."

"It sure has. He has been featured in so many agricultural and eco-magazines. He received a couple grants as well. I am so proud of him."

"He has made being young and a farmer so very sexy."

"That is my boy that she gave me. The apple does not fall far from the tree, eh?"

"Talent as well honey."

"Thank you for our life sweetheart." He kissed her again.

"You are welcome sweetie. But seriously I love talking about their accomplishments. Because I know it works. I have seen it. You can stand to irrigate, plant, and weed, as well as water. Giving the seeds and plants sunlight is a breeze. The pods are on a timer. I know he is our son. But he is an amazing human."

"Genius! I saw the pictures that Marcus highlighted. Fantastic job also."

"They are also involved in teaching the youngsters the art of cooking and grilling. They have completed two seasons of the island's version of **Master Chef**. They have even begun shipping their brand of seasonings globally. They just hit Dubai, Canada, and Australia."

"Farming and its sustainability for the future. We had better love to eat from the land instead of the can." Nia said. "We have become so lazy and jump for the instant instead of the long term that our fore-parents taught us."

"Amen Nia. Just like we must keep our craft going. It does not help that these oversees influences keep taking over. Our youths and even the adults do not think they are fully dressed unless they are wearing their designs. Some people have even had the audacity to say they did not design their clothes for us. Many don't even give a shit about us, or the struggles that we face on a daily basis." Yvonne added. Becoming quite heated.

"I have often said this in my talks to a lot of the youths. I had to explain to a couple of them that while I am out there bending over backwards to make certain that they have books, clothes, shoes and stuff. These so-call brands are doing absolutely nothing for them and their family here on the island. You can call me any hour of the day or night directly. But can you call any of them? Especially when you don't know where the next cent is coming from to keep your electricity on. I ask $50.00 for a top and many would fuss and say oh that's too expensive. Meanwhile they would commit heinous acts; rob, kill, prostitute self and even their children, or maim even to be seen in these other brands." Nia spat.

"I feel you. Which is why I stopped trying to be up there with some of them who are so damn rude, pretentious and think that because you are from a smaller island that you don't know jack. Some think you ought to kiss their ass. One even snapped at me hey you, go fetch water and be quick about it." Yvonne finished hotly.

Marcus laughed because he knew who had done it. He was the featured photographer, and they had not realised she was his wife. He had tried to step in, but she had stopped him, and just went off to fetch the water. Later the designer had bent over backwards when she realised that she had magic fingers; she had spotted a potential problem and fixed it on the spot. Stunting the growth of a major disaster. The brand had to eat crow in their apology. She is on the board of their design team even now. She had sung all the way to the bank.

"Do they realise she is ranked high in the **Caribbean Fashion Awards** show many times in a row?"

"Some think we are novices Nia."

"When our stuff can rival theirs so many times over. Plus, we are not using slave labour. But do we get credit for it?"

"Whoa! Whoa! She was looking for this kind of discussion to sink her teeth into." Marcus said to Kiah. "I totally support my wife. I can see where she is coming from. Which is why I said to her don't give up. Find other like minds and get together and make a difference."

"Amen. But I find at times that we as women collectively do not support each other ... Oh no! They are here!" She spotted the underwater twins. She gestured to Kiah. "I really am not in the mood."

"Say no more. Let's go." Marcus tossed.

They were up and hightailing it out of the lounge. They pretended not to hear as they called out to them.

Upstairs in their suite: a lovely sea-foam green and beige lounge area complete with a wall mounted massive flat screen, mini bar, and a couple of her huge, overstuffed sofas and colourful throw pillows... They continued to enjoy the simplicity of each other's company. The atmosphere was packed with so much laughter and admiration. A new friendship was formed. As they held quietly up amongst the many potted palms and plants that greeted them.

Kiah told the guys to go and chill, they would call when they were ready." The couples wandered out to the huge balcony separated for privacy.
It offered them a magnificent view of the busy swimming pool in the distance and a great sight of the busy mariner where so many boats and yachts were anchored.
They could see all the way down to the jetty.
Nia had a feeling the beautiful sunsets would be the bonus.

They ordered dinner: lobster and prawn salad and veggie burgers and jugs of local fruit juices.
"So, Kiah what is your plan for this beautiful princess?" Marcus asked. Looking over at Nia.
"I have already asked her to marry me."
"You turned him down right Nia?"
"Absolutely! Not!" Nia laughed. Liking that she could be herself around them. She followed suit with Yvonne and him kicking off her shoes and stretching out on a stripy soft and comfortable lounge.
"Wise woman Nia. Congratulations you two! But please don't allow anyone else to get their claws into him." Yvonne said clapping her hands gleefully. Especially since Marcus told her he had dated the Supermodel Jordanna.
She recalled that she herself had to fight like hell for Marcus. In the end she had won. They needed to prove to others that as a couple they were viable; long distance relationship, racial divide, as well as class could survive if you infused it with authenticity and communicate effectively.
It was not easy. It was hard as hell but they both realised they treasured what they were fighting for daily. She also recalled that once while in the UK a well-known Caucasian reporter had the nerve to scorpion bite: by asking Marcus if he thought he was missing out on culture, and all the amenities that a bigger country had to offer by settling for a simpler diaspora; meaning her as a black Caribbean woman and living part of his life away from the glitz and glamour as well as his life with his then supermodel.
She had taken the microphone and called him out for what he was. A passive aggressive idiot that was spoilt by the short-sighted masses. Then again, he thought he was fighting for the right of his supermodel friend, winning huge favour.
In Yvonne's reasoning it was just plain stupidity. She shook herself out of that reverie…
"I aim not to. Especially since I only learnt last night who I was in competition with." She remembered the bombshell.

"Believe in yourself Nia. You are worthy of him as he is of you. Hopefully, your life does not depend on how many times people see you on the news. Stay true to yourself and always do what you do for the universe. Everything else will truly follow. Plus, Kiah chose you."

"No one else holds a candle to her Yvonne." Kiah tossed. He kissed her softly. "I aim to keep reminding her just how much she means to me."

"I had a challenging time convincing her. But I fought like hell too. I realised what I found, and I had no intention of ever letting it go. She was it for me. Still is. I can't picture my life without her. I am telling you my friend just be prepared for the frequent flyer miles. I gave up work for nearly a year."

"He sure did Nia. He could not get enough of me then."

"Even now baby." He kissed her again. "These two women seem to be the same. They love their islands dearly. They don't mind going out for a bit. But their heart will always yearn for their homeland. So, to keep her happy we sometimes do half and half.

But as I get older, I have realised that I do not need to chase work. I allow it to call me."

"I love you Marcus for never once trying to change me."

"Nor you me sweetheart. Nough respect my heart. I believe this age-old saying that behind every good man stands a great woman."

"Here here!" They all cheered.

They played tennis on the game console and had a wonderful time. Nia thought she could stay and listen to the two for the rest of the afternoon. But she had to get to the rehearsal, then get home and grab a little rest, and tend to her voice and not overdo.

They chatted for a bit longer, and even invited the couple back to the island for their birthday barbecue. They said they would try and shift somethings around and let them know before the end of the week. They congratulated them again on their engagement.

Nia excused herself and headed to the bathroom to freshen up leaving them for a bit.

When she emerged, she had changed into her new dress and refreshed herself and her makeup. She felt on top of the world when they sat to watch the 6:00 o'clock news.

Indiria stated, "To recap our news for the day. **ECBC** is happy to report we have had several sightings of Kiah Corrington and his new love interest Nia here on the island today. First, they were spotted leaving her home in the beautiful unspoilt Palm Loop."

They showed aerial pics of her home, and of them going to the car, getting in, and heading out the gate.

"They headed to the airport. No! They did not catch a flight out folks! They met his parents Elena and Denton Corrington who has now cut their world tour vacation short to fly here to make certain their only son is doing well."

Pictures of them when they had given them the photo-op.

241

"The parents will now be vacationing here on the island with his Auntie Lady Bellot Corrington to his right. She is the head of the last existing **Corrington's** store."

They showed pictures of Corrington's today: Customers piling in and coming out laden. Then they showed the new line and the scarves on display on the mannequins.

Nia's hand came up to her mouth. The line had received the entire western side; where the mannequins can be seen from all angles entering and leaving the store. Looks like once again Seba and the team had done a wonderful job without her.

Nia reached for her bag and took out her phone and dialled up the man.

"Seba I just saw a preview on the news of Corrie's! Seba, it looks gorgeous!"

"Glad you like sweetheart. I just followed your script. Plus, the aunties thought this was a fantastic way to cheer you up. The entire floor team worked on it. Glad you like."

"Seba, I love it! It looks amaze-balls!"

"This is the first reveal for our Ms Nia's **Tis the Season** line. As you can see it is already a hit. So many have already been putting in their orders for the fabulous fashions. Not to forget those scarves; this is where the emphasis lies for the season I was told. Just look at the many ways one can use the scarf: not just a scarf anymore. As you can see it can be transformed into a bag, a scarf, a jacket, a halter, a top; two scarves knotted on each shoulder, on its own criss-crossed, a sun-shade: your personal one over a straw hat to protect your face and body, and still a scarf wrapped artistically to show-off heritage when you don't feel like being bothered by a hairdo, and even to protect your style in the wind; during the day and even at night.

But wait for this one. Look! The scarf can be transformed into an accessory; a cluster of floral petals that can be pinned and worn in any direction you fancy."

They showed a clip of Kimberley as she demonstrated the different styles like Nia had shown them.

"Genius Ms Nia! Why don't you give us a call so you can explain where this concept of a piece of material came from? Ladies as you saw, we technically no longer need to take a bag when we are heading out, or even a jacket. By doubling two identical scarves that we twisted together earlier, or any colour you fancy, if you are like me, and look! Voila! A lovely little jacket that goes with anything!"

"Nia darling! That is genius!" Yvonne said to her. Giving her a tight squeeze. We need to get together. We need to change a few things here in the Caribbean. We need a movement. Something to leave our mark. We need our own Glastonbury here in the Caribbean!"

"Count me in anytime Yvonne." Nia tossed excitedly. She did not know what to do with herself. So, she just jumped into Kiah's arms and shouted out, "I love you!"

"I love you too woman!" He kissed her back. "I am glad they could do this for you. They told me they were working on it earlier."
"You knew?"
"Of course, I did. Anything to keep you happy darling."
"See. Guess he is trying to show me up darling. But good on you mate. A happy her and an even happier you. Get my drift?" Marcus asked as he winked over at Kiah.
They high fived like co-conspirators.
Yvonne and Nia hugged one last time with a promise to stay in touch on a regular basis.

The building was brilliantly illuminated when they finally pulled up. The drive over was manic because the traffic was ridiculous. Seemed like no one was using their feet. A couple times the men had to swerve to avoid collisions. Someone even had the audacity to shout, "pussy!" as they flew by in a flashy sports car with the top down.
They had their window down just so they could enjoy the trade wind breezes.

It was Friday evening and islanders had already started to **Lime:** hanging out on the street, at bars, the Bayfront, outside under trees, on sidewalks, local eateries listening to music, cussing about their week, seeing girlfriends, committing adultery...
You name it good or bad, these things were done leading up to late Saturday evening, or exceedingly early Sunday morning. Just so they could set foot inside a church. Perhaps for purification or abjuration from all sinful obligation.
Loud laughter, music, shouting, crowding, cussing, or chasing skirts or trousers, along with a few petty crimes, were no doubt happening even now. Because people no longer craved nights under the tamarind tree singing or listening to old time stories. Seems of late all they ever wanted to do was hang out on their hand-held devices looking at **You Tube** and yearning for a life that was terrible difficult: first off without much discipline to accomplish what they see on those living out loud on **Facebook** too.

Nia reminded a couple of youths at the centre that they should emulate people like her, their parents, or their teachers...
One said, "my teacher doesn't have no money."
Another said, "Mr. Caesar got too many mouths to feed. I think someone should teach him about sex education."
Another said, "Why you think I am here Miss Nia? My mama sits around and let my daddy beat on her like a kettle drum. So how you expect us to pick them as role models?"
The things said had her heart at breaking point. Because some of it was true. But she could not let it go.
"Are you telling me that Beyoncé or Snoop Dog, or even Will Smith... That they do not have their share of problems? How do you know what their

243

home life is like? Do you think they just wake up and are the way they are? Not even I wake up and look like this. I must work at it, just like we all must do. Hopefully, someone along the way will extend a hand. Just like many did to me, and I will do for many of you. But please do not think that I don't have my fair share of problems."

"Like what?" Lynette one of the teenage girls at Iya's challenged. Her mama's nickname was **Ganja-head.** She got pregnant at an early age and lived her life in a weed induced coma that left the child prey to anything. One day someone saw the child wandering on the side of the road. Following much hisims and skisims, **Iya's** took her in because the state-run institute had no room.

"I have been slapped around Lynette." She decided to tell the truth. The girl's mouth opened and did not close for a while. But her ears perked-up.

"Yes, Lynette like I said, I was slapped before."

"But why? How come?"

"Because I dared to speak louder and annoyed because I spoke up for **my** right. My womanly right. But no more. I refused to allow him to hit me ever again. Just like you all get to decide what happens to you from here on in." Nia said to them.

Thinking the girl was doing better each day. Which was why she would never ever entertain the idea of going back to David. She had girls who looked up to her, and will become women sooner than she wished, so she had to teach them daily to be strong and respect themselves.

Learn to recognise their integrity and what makes them blossom and bloom. She loved to see them thriving getting stronger and more confident each time she checked in.

"You are quiet." Kiah said to her. "Are you nervous?"

"I usually get that way, but it goes away after a while. I am just thinking of all the wonderful things that has happened in my life. Maybe it is because I am cosying up to a milestone age that it is causing me to wax philosophical."

"You mean getting older?" He laughed and pulled her to him.

"Could be." She loved being in his arms. It's as if she belonged there.

"I am no longer bothered by the number. Nor by my health because I feel great. In terms of wealth, I have been blessed and feel highly favoured. But I just feel like I should be doing even more."

"More than what you are already doing?"

"I feel idle Kiah. I feel as though all I have done these last couple of days is twiddle my thumbs."

"And I have not helped the situation, right?"

"Well sort of."

"You don't mince words do you?"

"It's time-wasting Kiah."

"I guess I should sort myself so you can get back to work?"

"Please." She said in a matter-of-fact tone.

244

"Ok Nia. I will give Indiria a call."
"Thank you. I feel so grateful having you here and in my life. But I need to get back to work."
"Ok Nia. I hear you sweetheart."

The auditorium was alive when they walked in. They had stopped in at the restaurant **Lush** to buy a cup of herbal tea. It was terribly busy. She waved or said a quick hello. Some now knew who Kiah really was and wanted their photos taken with him.
He obliged politely.
Indiria and her crew were waiting by the door when they finally came out.
"So nice to finally get a moment with you Kiah. Nia." She said liking that she had them cornered. She usually covered events like this all around the island. So, tonight was no different.
"Hello Indiria." Kiah said and pulled Nia closer. "If you put the microphones and cameras away." He waited.
The woman gestured to the team to lower their gear.
"I would like to give you an interview. If you can have a think and give us a day and time…"
"How about Sunday?" The woman jumped in. Her mouth salivating. Her head began to swim. Two birds' one stone.
"As in day after tomorrow?" Nia asked stupidly.
"Yes Nia. There is no time like Sunday at 2:00 pm."
"You mean for **In the Hot Seat**?" Nia gasped.
The show was the equivalent of Barbara Walters 20/20. They all looked forward to her in-depth interviews with a large number of local and regional persons of interest.
Nia herself had been on the show a couple times. She had even done one with David. They were considered the island's Romeo and Juliet at the time.
"Oh yes Nia! **In the Hot Seat** it is." Indiria almost purred.
"It's up to you sweetheart." Kiah said looking to her.
"You win Indiria." Nia mouthed taking a sip of her lemon and hibiscus tea. "The sooner I can get my life back." She mumbled.
"Pardon?" Indiria pushed.
"Ok Indiria. You have a deal. We will meet you…?"
"I can come to the house Nia. I would like to finally get a glimpse of your lovely home. Deal?"
"You have a deal if I can get you to purchase two couture dresses." Nia tossed in quickly. Loving how she had her on the hook now.
"C'mon Nia!"
"Tick tock Indiria. You are lucky I said two." Nia teased knowing she could easily close her eyes and purchase four. It was her turn to eye the woman up over her cup.
"Deal Ms Nia. Two couture gowns it is."
"Glad to be able to sort this. We will see you at our home on Sunday." She eased into the woman and whispered in her ear. "Buy another and I will

245

tell you something that no other reporter knows." She had to reel the gigantic fish in. Her heart pounded.

"What do you mean Nia?"

"Write me a check for those gowns by the time I am finished with rehearsal, and I will give you a sneak peek."

"What! That is highway robbery Ms Nia."

"It is for a worthy cause. Remember **Iya's Place**? Have a think Indiria. Let me know what you decide after rehearsal." She tossed and winked over at the flabbergasted woman who thought she had them by the balls a while ago. "Come on sweetheart." She said to Kiah and pulled him on beside her.

"My God Nia what was that about?" He asked as he looked down at her smug face.

"She thought she had us. She forgot that I too have a cause. By the way you need to get me a ring, and you will ask me to marry you on Sunday afternoon again."

"You truly are a minx Nia-Belle!" He gasped laughing loudly.

"I fight nasty for what I want Kiah. I want to sort **Iya's Place** and her money will help me get one step further."

When Nia and Kiah walked into the theatre Pascal and the choir members were there. The atmosphere was tight and hopping as everyone busied themselves with the things they needed to do. Georgie ran over to give her a hug and say how much she missed having her at the office. She finished by whispering in her ears.

"Seba told us he was rich, but we never knew just how rich boss."

"Guess the secret is out then huh?"

"Hi William." She chirped. "I see there is more. Who are they?"

"Behave yourself Georgie." Nia teased.

William said hello and reached for her. Then introduced her to the rest of the guys. "How is London?" William asked holding unto her a bit longer. It did not go unnoticed.

"She is ok." Georgie chirped. Then turned to her and asked, "Why didn't you pick up your messages boss lady?"

"Why? What is going on?"

"David is here. London is with him over there." She pointed to the far corner. She spotted the smiling fool. He waved over at her. She turned away and kissed her teeth.

"Kranston is not feeling well. He asked him to help him out apparently…"

"What! How convenient." Nia tossed smelling a rat. She rolled her eyes when he waved passionately again towards her.

"Anyhow he is singing Kranston's parts with you. Pascal informed us a little while ago."

"Shit! Am I never going to be rid of that nuisance?" Nia tossed with so much annoyance creeping about her voice. But honestly the songs were easy for her and David. He had borrowed a little bit of Luther Vandross's suave when it came to soulfulness. She just did not long to share the stage with him anymore. She no longer wanted to be his Diana Ross or Mariah. Gone were those titillating teenage dreams, when he had convinced her to forget about doing her and following him.

He teased that they could become the next big duo out of the Caribbean. Thank God she had come to her senses.

"You are better than all the crap he tosses your way boss. Just do you when all is said and done. He cannot blame anyone but himself for how things turned out. He was always to damn greedy."

"Sweetie! Sweetie!" It was Pascal. He was sashaying up the aisle.

"People! People! I do not want any drama." He pointed straight at her.

"David has graciously decided to fill in for his cousin."

"Bet he did."

"Sugar he is unwell."

"I bet he is. I wonder what David promised him to step down and relinquish his moment in the spotlight."

"Let us just say you two are magical on stage. Just think when the crowds out there find out you two are back on stage together…"

"Mr. Pascal I bet this is justice for the piano." Nia did not miss driving the point home.

"Touché' darling. We will talk semantics later. But for now, let's just play nice. Nice to see you again Mr Multi-Billionaire. Hope you have been enjoying our hospitality very well?"

"I have. Thank you." Kiah laughed ruefully as he cast the cunning man a weary look. He remembered him very well. Especially since he tried snookering money in aide of a new piano.

He had dropped Nia's name several times on his silvery tongue. He had a fleeting thought; perhaps if he gave him the piano… He could kill two birds with one stone. Because he hated that the guy was going to be up there with Nia.

He so wished that he could scoop him up and throw him into the depths of the ocean. For he was once again proving to be a goddamn terrible pain in his ass.

"We are on in ten minutes." Pascal hollered. "Ten minutes people. These are the songs. We have done them all before. **Change** by Sam Cooke, **Impossible Dream, Home** and **The Prayer.**"

Nia kissed her teeth.

"You are a pro Miss Nia. Ooh, and Miss Audra's **Freedom** finale's song has been changed to the **Colour Purple** theme song. You missy, will be doing it with her." He pointed to Georgie, before he walked back down the aisle.

"Oh, and one last thing everyone. Do leave the fireworks out there. If you want to sizzle, do it up there." He pointed to the stage.

"It's just like old times in Glee Club." Georgie cackled to Nia as she smiled like a giggly teenager. "Piece of cake! The gang is back together again."

247

She caught the look on Nia's face. "It is just for a little while Boss Lady. I missed us being like that on stage. **Changes** is back!"

Nia recalled when the name came about. It was after a great summer run singing aboard cruise ships and appearing in lots of shows in and around the Caribbean.
At first, they were simply David's backup singers.
Then Kranston came along selling a big dream. They became **David and the Dreamers**. Then Kranston (the hottest club owner to date on the island of club (**La Cave**) decided he should feature as much as David.
So, an argument ensued. Then David being the blasted hothead he is, told him they did not need his mic-grabbing-scene-stealing-ass. So, there will be some '**changes;**' never rigid always flowing.
A lesson he has never learnt apparently. So, they became a group called **Changes.**
He later told her the name was for anyone else who had any other idea of changing anything. Someone could be added to or taken away whenever 'he' decided.

"You can do this Nia." Kiah said pulling her back from her memories. "You are the ultimate professional. Get in do you and get out. You have nothing to prove to him. I will be right there. When it gets tough look into my eyes."
"I hate this Kiah." She said finishing her tea.
"We can do this Boss."
"You had better warn him not to pull any shit. Or I swear I will have '**them**' take his ass to a far side of the island and bury him." She pointed to the guys.
"You got this baby." Kiah laughed and pulled her towards him, and squeezed her tightly, kissing the top of her head.
Once again thoughts of evil played in his head.

Pascal gave the signal and called for them to make their way up to the stage.
"Get those voices together people. Warm up songs are not going to be the traditional. Let us have fun. We are singing **Loving You Always** and **Ain't no stopping us Now**. We have a full orchestra and band. David has honoured us with the latter. So, let us have some fun."

The auditorium was jumping by the time they got through warm up. David sang as though he had only performed with the choir just only last night. He picked himself up at every cliff she took him. His voice was just as silky smooth as the first day she had heard him sing on stage.
Pity he didn't know how to honour her and the love she had for him.
During the songs, she could feel the old feelings as they reared their head. Throughout certain parts she could hear their voices melding coercively together, as a syrupy warmth spread throughout her body.

248

The magic had indeed returned, and she was certain everyone could feel the intensity. She had to admit they had not lost this innate chemistry on stage they always had whenever they took to the podium. It was tangible, especially when he sang truly from his heart.
She did not think there was any genre of music that he couldn't do or would give a dynamite try at.
He was also an extraordinarily talented musician as well. He had taught her to play the electric guitar. She was great. He on the other hand was a super-star. Even on the piano. He had learnt from the best here on the island.
David was a prickly-musical-genius. He had configured mixing falsetto with reggae and had done it with **Seals Kiss from a Rose** and **Kissing a Fool by George Michael**...
Those two quickly shot to the charts in the Caribbean. She loved when he sang her **Brown Sugar by D' Angelo** and **Stevie Wonder's Man of Many Wishes**...
Talented was a poor word when it came to the artistic so-and so. Even down to his showmanship.
No one could take it away from him, she had to grudgingly admit. She even became teary eyed during certain parts of the songs as the memories came flooding into her reverie.
At the end of their set, she allowed him to hold her closer. A bit too damn long. Which prompted him to pull the next stunt; he hopped on the piano and started singing **Barry Manilow's Mandy**. But he changed the name to hers. It was always a crowd pleaser.
He liked to sing it to her especially when she caught him flirting and was cross with him. Another was **Luther Vandross' Circles.** He knew just where to stick the needle deep in her chest. It stopped her dead in her tracks. His sultry and mellifluous tones haunted her all the way home.

When they walked through the door, the items she had asked Seba to bring home were hanging on her work room door. She took them down and went inside and closed the door.
Kiah did not bother her. He simply left her to her thoughts.

Nia sat and thoughts of David dominated her head. She reasoned that she did not want David back. It was the gospel truth.
She had printed slogans on some tee-shirts and vests and had worn the blasted things that read, **been there and done that,** as well as **Can't lie. Don't want you back, Lies destroys and truth hurts...**
But all the memories; good and bad came flooding back.
A few made her want to scream, others made her want to hit something, throw something. Her entire being was in a tailspin. She didn't want to talk; an argument could ensue. To say his name out loud, or think it caused her anxiety. The more she tried to resist the troubling thoughts of him, the more they kept coming.

Nia recalled their time at school, their first kiss, the first time he had walked her home and given her her first gift; a hibiscus he had picked from their neighbours' yard and placed it beside her ponytail.

Numerous girls were cross and gave her a tough time for days after. She also recalled the first time they had had sex; it was a couple days after her 16th birthday. She was over at their house. He had told her he was tired of waiting, and that she needed to prove how much she loved him, and the only thing he would accept was her virginity.

Stupidly she had given in and handed the most precious thing she held 'dear' over to him. It was over so fast. It was painful, and clumsy. Down to the way he had hiked her legs and dug deep within her, as her heart pounded away in her chest.

All her pleas were ignored. He only stopped when he finished and rolled quickly away. Leaving her to wonder if this was what the great sex-hype was all about.

Was this how she would feel for the rest of their time together. She felt frustrated and disappointed. She tried to say it to him. He held her tight and promised that next time it would be better. It still was not.

He'd tossed her a towel and barked, "Clean up down there."

When she did, he was all sugar and spice, and forcibly had another go. She cried and pleaded all throughout. But she was ignored.

"What? What is wrong with you? Why did you come here? You knew what I wanted Nia. Plus, we love each other. That is what people do when they're in love. You do know I love you right girl? You are my woman."

"But I don't think I was ready."

"The timing was right baby. You were dynamite."

She still insisted she wasn't ready. She felt genuinely like an idiot. But she had allowed him to control her.

Days later she revealed what she had done to Seba. Thank God he knew someone who could get their hands on the morning after pill.

David had come again wanting another go-round, but this time she had told him directly that she was not comfortable.

He had flounced off and didn't speak to her for a few weeks.

She followed him once and found him making out with another girl behind the school building. She thought she would die for certain. She had even absentmindedly stepped out into traffic one afternoon.

Once again Silcott to the rescue. She had told him everything and he had made her promise to speak to the aunties. She did. They were extremely disappointed. But they allowed her to stay at home until she felt comfortable enough to return.

Couple weeks later. When she felt well enough to return, she had to vehemently promise that whenever she felt like she was in a pickle she would come to them first. No blaming. She promised. But to many times she had broken it for him. Even after they had accompanied her to get condoms and birth control.

In desperation she had told him. He tried to convince her she should not take them.

"It's either condoms or nothing David." She had challenged.

For her conviction she had received the hardest slap to her face. He then apologised. Somehow, they had ended up having sex again, and yes without a condom.

This time it was better, especially when he held her and kissed her tenderly, and promised to love her endlessly...

Her period was late the next month. She told him. He accused her of sleeping around because she had been seen being way-to friendly, chatting up other guys. He became livid.

He called her stupid and told her if she believed she was pregnant, she should get rid of it. He told her he didn't want to become a father and be responsible for anyone else at such an early age.

She told him she would not, because she didn't believe in abortions.

He once again refused to speak to her. He stopped calling and coming by and even moved on with someone else for several months.

The action once again left her to spiral near out of control. It seemed she would never stop crying.

But when she finally did, she tossed herself fully back into fashion and costume designing. She enrolled in fashion school and even participated in the **Caribbean Style & Culture Awards and Fashion Showcase** and loved it so much she made a commitment to participate every year.

She placed on numerous occasions and was now even an alumnus.

Thank God for his graciousness; her body soon reacted, and she started having a period again.

Somehow, she was still blinded to David and all his shenanigans. She was caught up again after he swept her off her feet; in the pretence of needing help with songs.

Then one thing led to the other and she was back to having sex with him. But not before she had accompanied him to the hospital to be tested for HIV and other sexually transmitted diseases.

Then reality crept in. She realised she felt increasingly unfulfilled sexually again. Most times it was all about him. She chanced to ask him to slow down once so she could catch up. He called her many nasty names, but the one that stuck when she attempted to ask for another go round was 'nympho.'

He embarrassed her if he caught her speaking with a member of the opposite sex. He would constantly call her a whore.

She realised she was the one who had given him the power to repress her sexuality, down to the clothes she should wear.

He also told her with great conviction that he did not believe in cunnilingus, but he said wholeheartedly he expected to receive 'head' when he desired. Which was always.

She refused him, but once to stop him from leaving, she decided to try it. In her hesitation he grabbed her head and shoved her mouth down hard. She gagged and threw the contents of her stomach up in his lap.

He kicked her hard and away from him. Then hurled nasty insults over at her. Then he grabbed a fistful of her hair and tossed her out with no clothing.

"What you can't do someone else would bitch!"

Thank God there was no one was home. So she borrowed an old tablecloth and draped herself until Seba came to her rescue.

Truer words were never uttered. Because she would always find someone happily obliging. She even found his hypocritical selfish ass in flagrante. He was such a massive contradiction when it came to sex and sexuality. But still he was always the one having pleasure.

How many times had she asked or wondered how in God's name he was not rotting away with some groin-infection? It was truly beyond her.

She pushed the negativity away...far away. Before she started working on the dresses, she would need for tomorrow evening.

She worked late into the night. Kiah had not come in. She sketched way into the morning. By the time she emerged she had finished the dresses and the jumpsuit and sketched two of the couture dresses she promised Indiria.

The other she could choose from the vault if she desired.

She walked from the room. Except for the dim light and the low hub of the television, there was no one else around. She spotted him asleep on the sofa, with his head thrown back against it. His hand rested atop his forehead, as though he was nursing a headache. His hair was loose and flowing. Once again, he captured her breath. Her heart battled in her chest.

As she got closer, she spotted an abandoned glass with brown liquid on the floor next to his feet. He was wearing different clothes: drawstring striped pyjamas and white tank.

She suddenly felt ravenous for him. She touched his hand and he moaned and shifted, but he did not open his eyes. She remained feasting on him with her eyes for a long while before she turned and headed to the bathroom.

There she pulled out her pad and sketched him as she had seen him. She reckoned she couldn't touch him with clothes David had permeated. She felt unclean.

She also recalled not seeing any of the guys either. They must have left him and gone to bed.

When she emerged from the shower and sorted her nightly rituals and dressed in drawstring shorts and tank, he still had not come. She was now feeling the call for her bed snuggled up against him.

252

She had not totally gotten David out of her system, but he wasn't front and centre dominating anymore. She had managed to put him back to lie in his grave. She would be damned if she were going to allow him to stand in the middle of that beautiful man sleeping on her sofa outside. Because he had not done anything wrong to her. So why should he suffer for a conman like David?

She kissed his lips. He stirred but did not wake. She knelt between his legs and kissed him deeper. He tasted like stale alcohol. She had never seen him drink before.

"Kiah...Kiah sweetheart. Wake up."

"What? What's wrong?" He mumbled, as his eyes drifted in from sleep.

"Nia? Are you ok?" He brought his head up.

"Are you? You were drinking?" She said not moving from the position.

"I know, and I am sorry. I just had to."

"I'm sorry."

"Me too sweetheart." He wrapped her up in his arms. "It's either a drink or I go back out there and find that guy..."

"Not worth it Kiah." She said and kissed his lips. "I am sorry I was wallowing. It's just that I haven't had to deal with him in such a long time, and tonight there he was reminding me of how totally stupid I had been. To always allow him access to my life with all his complications."

"Nia please tell me you didn't buy any of that shit he pulled tonight, did you?" He used his hand to brush the locks that had fallen around his face back.

"He just took me back to places that had me going mental. I needed to let off some steam. When I get like that, I like to bury myself in my work."

"I understand. So, are you ok?"

"Now I am." She kissed him again. "I am right where I belong Kiah. I don't want David. He's hurt me badly. Do you know I thought I was pregnant at one point, and I told him? My reward for it was getting slapped. He called me a stupid bitch for not taking care of things."

"What! I will fucking kill him for sure. He has some balls. I will cut them off and ram them down his fucking throat. How dare he?"

"How dare I Kiah? Because I gave him chance after chance to do it all to me. All in the name of some crazy idea of love."

"Oh God Nia." He wrapped her up in his arms. His heart was beating wildly in his chest. "I do not want that idiot anywhere near you. God, I knew there was a reason why I didn't like him. He is such a fucking Jekyll and Hyde."

"That's David. When he gets what he wants he is sweet as pie. Go against him and all hell will freeze."

"Well let me tell you now that his reign of terror will end. I will not give him another opportunity to hurt you. Ever again."

"Kiah please. He is not even worth it. I promise you my eyes are open now. I will never be deceived by him again. Because people like him don't change. Only their tactics. I am through. I know now that real love should never hurt. It uplifts."

"God Nia…I thought he had you. I came this close to going back out there with the team."

"By the way, where are they?"

"They are downstairs. I told them to go earlier and not come back for the evening."

"All of them?" She asked kissing him wantonly.

"Yes. Why?"

"If you are asking why Kiah, it means I am not doing it right." She snaked her hand into his trouser waist and found what she was looking for.

He ground out softly.

She rubbed him delicately. He purred.

She devoured his lips in her mouth. When she came up for air she said.

"I don't like alcohol Kiah." She squeezed his groin a little too forcibly.

"Okay Nia. I am sorry." He whimpered. Watching as she helped him out of his pyjamas.

She kissed him on his dick. It buck and reared. She looked up at him. Those eyes will forever etch themselves in his soul.

"I am sorry baby." His heart began to beat wildly in his chest.

He wiggled with her as she helped him out of his clothing. She kissed the tip of his shaft and licked it like a lollipop. Then she popped the tip into her mouth and flicked her tongue delicately around it. Her name burst forth from his lips.

She took hm slowly…slowly and teasingly into her mouth… He strained. He tried to touch her. She brought a finger up and stopped him, as she applied pressure with her tongue.

He swore loudly. What she was doing to Johnson was absolutely fucking unlawful. It was putty in her mouth as she taught him a lesson.

When he thought he would let off fully loaded in her mouth she paused briefly to take her bottoms off. In the dim light he could tell she was wearing nothing else. He loved that. He reached for her.

She allowed him to touch her now. He turned her around and brought her down on Johnson from the back in a sitting position. He slid inside like a worm…

He hiked her top up as she laid back against him. He brought his head down to suckle and bite and blow on her nipples. She moaned and groaned…

They shifted position. She held to the back of the chair. He entered her again… She called out his name in agony.

"I can't hold out for much longer baby." Kiah moaned deeply.

"I want to see you Kiah. I want to look into your eyes… Please baby…" She pleaded. "I want to do it with you."

Kiah paused long enough to oblige her. He sat on the edge of the sofa and allowed her to climb over him.

When he was deep within her; his shaft buried like a drill. For a moment he suckled at her taps of glory. It got to be too much. He nipped.

She screamed and threw her head back in delirium. He snaked his hand up her back and brought her head back to centre.

When they were lost deep within each other's eyes, he squirted like a gushing tap deep within her. Her twin peaks were still straining like ripe raspberries. He suckled hungrily like a nursing child on each until he felt her warmth all over him.

Before going to bed she felt like a cup of tea. She walked to the kitchen, and he followed. While they waited for the water to boil, they cuddled and kissed; little pecks that eventually turned into deep kissing.

The kettle roared and they ignored it. She wrapped her hands around his waist, and he did the same. He kissed her over and over. She gave as much as she received. He held her ass in a vice like grip as his lips wandered down her neck, her throat and stopped over her heart where he kissed it softly.

"Kiah… the water… Kiah… getting cold." She ground out.

"Screw the water."

"I love you…what you are doing…."

"So, let's keep doing it."

"Kiah… my throat."

"Dang woman."

"Sorry baby. One cup and I promise…"

"Okay, okay." He slapped her ass. One cup."

"Can I make you one?" She asked as she sashayed over to the kettle.

"Okay Nia I'll take one." He said as he leaned over the counter and his eyes fixated on her. "You are so beautiful Nia. I feel as though I am getting a massive do over at being a teenager. Loving on one beautiful girl."

"Kiah Corrington." She crooned. Pausing to look at him and his dreamy countenance. Thinking how in the hell did she get so freaking lucky. Then she heard Miss Ruthie's voice in her head, "Ah Ghad gel!" It caused her to smile.

"Right there Nia. I love that on you."

"What?"

"That smile. You are so damn beautiful to me woman. I still cannot believe it took us this long to get together."

"Nothing happens before God says so Kiah."

"I honestly believe that. Can I make a total ass of myself and say that I think you have been that other side of myself that I have been ignoring all this time?"

"Lord-have-mercy!" She paused. "I feel the same way too. I just didn't know how to put it so simply, so beautiful…" He was on her, and he scooped her up.

"I can't say goodbye to you ever Nia."

"Dear God Kiah." She clasped his face in her hands. "I adore you." She kissed his lips. "I thank God for you Kiah."

"I do too Nia. I love you so damn much."

Couple minutes later they sat to sip their tea: hibiscus and ginger. He refused sugar. She offered honey. He refused that too.

"I don't really like tea. I am just having it because you are."

"I can get you something else."

"Tea is fine." He said looking deeply at her. "Nia... I have something to tell you."

"Fuck!" Her heart started to kick-up in her chest. "Those words were never...."

"Please baby don't freak out!" He jumped off his stool and came to her. "You are leaving again, aren't you?"

"Heck no! He wrapped her in his arms and kissed her. "I told you I will never leave you woman. You are mine. For life. For life, right?"

"Kiah please." She felt a fierce stinging in the back of her eyes. She fought them to stay back.

"Just have an open mind please Nia."

"Are you gay Kiah?"

"Fuck no!" He placed her on her feet and laughed loudly. "I am AC all the way. Even though many think that I could be DC. I have neither confirmed nor denied. I try not to judge... But let's not get away from what I need to say to you because I may lose my nerve... It's just that you trusted me earlier with one of your deepest secrets so now I feel I have to do the same."

"You aren't dying right Kiah? How long do we have?" Her hands flew to her face. She breathed heavily into them.

"For god's sake woman! I have a child!" He blurted out and waited for her to...

"You do?" Was all that popped out. She screwed up her face. "You have a child?"

"Yes, I do Nia." He waited as she looked him up and down incredulously.

"Only one?" She asked stupidly. Thinking he should have more for the way he wielded that damn stick of his.

"I'm not a man-whore Nia." He laughed. Reaching for her.

"Heck no! But you sure can swing that stick!"

"You think so?"

"I've got first-hand knowledge."

"You' are so great for a guy's ego. But please let us not digress. I need to tell you before I lose my nerve."

"Then tell me Kiah."

"I am sorry I lied before... Well technically. I know I told you before that I did not have children."

"Kiah stop fucking about! It's either you do, or you don't."

"Hear me out please." He begged and watched as she threw her hands in the air and tried to jump from her stool. He stayed her. He knew this would happen. He thought he could always tie her ass to the chair and force her to listen. He looked around for something to accomplish the task. But thankfully she sat back down and folded her arms.

"I have a daughter." He waited. She looked pissed. He thought he had better go on before she went into third degree shock.

"Nia I am not her biological father. But I went through a period of thinking I was. But long story short. I had a threesome, and while we were at it the condom, I was wearing broke. Anyway, a couple of months down the line one of the females told me she was pregnant. I was glad Nia. Ecstatic. Then she got into a car accident and the baby was in trouble. She needed a transfusion. That is when I found out I was not the father. I couldn't be."

"Oh... Oh my God Kiah!"

"Please listen... I was also told I would not be able to father a child. The chances are slim."

"What! Dear God Kiah!"

"I went through a dark patch then Nia. In the end I took a trip to Tibet. I spoke to the Dalai Lama. He taught me not to zero in on words. To redirect my energy. Clean up my aura. Entertain that there is a higher being who holds all our destinies in his hands. Nia I never thought in a million years I would travel halfway around the world and meet someone like you. But I did. So, when the time is right who knows? In the meantime, just know that I have a daughter."

"You know the Dalai Lama?"

"Yes Nia. I lived in Tibet for a couple of months." He offered. Thinking her mind was wired strangely. She picked up on him knowing the DL rather than on him having a kid. He shook his head and took her in, fighting the immense urge to burst out in laughter.

For a couple of years most thought he had lost his damn mind. His parents were worried. He assured them he was fine. He just needed time to sort things: put it all in perspective.

Especially when the story broke a couple of years later because the lab technician leaked the report to a paper.

Greta was a genius. No one got an interview if they wanted to focus on the paternity of his child: who he reasoned had not asked for any of it. She would never be subject to anyone's ridicule.

So, If one wanted an interview, you would have to leave his daughter out of it. Simple as.

"I keep forgetting that you are like Jet Li or Jackie Chang. But seriously Kiah. No babies?" She asked disbelief lacing her voice.

"Would you like us to have one Nia?" He asked as he felt hope jumping about in his chest.

She was off the stool, and rational seemed to have returned. She walked to him and placed her arms atop his shoulders, then she cupped his face.

"Eventually my handsome man." She said as a picture of a baby; their baby popped up in her head. She shook herself together.

"But not right now. I still have so much that I need to accomplish."

"I understand." He kissed her.

She kissed him back.

His heart settled in his chest as he wrapped her up in his arms. Suddenly she came away from him.

"It's not Jordanna is it Kiah?"

"No Nia!" He laughed. "It's not Jordanna."

"Then who?" She asked ears opening wide.

"It's her best-friend."

"Kiah! You fucked her best friend?"

"Yes Nia. Jordanna and I have, had an open relationship."

"Wow! I don't think I could be that open."

"I fucking hope not Nia! I do not want to do that shit ever again."

"See that you don't Kiah." She offered firmly. "But seriously. Two women at the same time? How did that come about?"

"She asked who of her friends I would fuck, if I could? I told her truthfully. Then for my 23rd birthday I was blind folded. When it finally came off, I was in bed with the two. Her and Jasmine. Nia, I didn't ask for it. Jordanna asked me a question and I gave an answer. I got an experience I thoroughly enjoyed. But to some extent."

"So, if I wanted an experience like that…"

"Fuck no Nia! Your pussy is mine and no one else's. Do you hear me? So don't think I would ever forgive you if you fucked someone else. Do you hear me?" He jumped off his stool. At the thought of another man touching her…His heart started a prancing in his chest. "Do that Nia and I swear to God we are through. Got it?"

"Kiah I was just asking!"

"I mean it Nia. You and me. No one else, ok?"

"I do not want anyone else Kiah. I told you I am stuck on you." She kissed his lips. "By the way are there anymore secrets you're keeping?"

"Those were the big ones." He kissed her lips. Wondering how he had gotten so damn lucky. "So, you aren't mad?"

"Since you entered my life Kiah, I am learning so many things. Most of all that if you open up yourself to God truthfully, he will bless you in ways you can't even begin to wrap your mind around. So, with that said I am open. So, what is your daughter's name?"

"Her name is Jourgette and she is 6 years old."

"Wow Kiah! Will I be able to meet her anytime soon?"

"Yes. We can give her a call over the weekend. I miss her a great deal. I know it was silly to keep it from you. It's just that some females don't do baggage."

"It works both ways Kiah."

"I know sweetheart. I wanted to tell you the truth, but I got scared of fucking up this wonderful thing we have."

"Well, I am glad you finally came clean. I don't know how I would have reacted if the child was yours biologically and you waited until now to tell me. Kiah just like I had a life before you. I don't expect you didn't have one. But I want us to be honest with each other going forward, okay? Even if I blow my top just tell me. Like in sex we need a safe word when we need to be serious with each other. Yvonne told me that she and Marcus has one." "I like that. Let's get one."

"Ok. Why Jourgette...Did you choose it?"

"Her mom got first choice. I got second. She is double-barrelled Elena-Bellot."

"For your mom and your aunt? Wow that is nice. Do they know about her?"

"Yes Nia! My family knows all the important bits about me woman. Now you. But honestly, they urged me to tell you. Mom whispered it in my ear earlier today. I promised I would. Then that shit happened and messed things up."

"For a little bit. But we are back on track now. Now let's finish our cold tea and head to bed so I can show you how awesome I think you are. Because I know a lesser man would run for the hills and wash their hands of the entire situation."

"Nia I could not walk away. I fell in love at the first sonogram. I made a promise then, that I would be the best dad I knew how. Yes, I was broken when I learnt she wasn't mine but when I held her in my arms and looked into her beautiful eyes..."

He recalled Jasmine and the caesarean... Jordanna was on a photo-shoot, and she had no one. They didn't. So, he couldn't walk away.

"I'm glad you didn't as well. We as women need strong men to love and support us and show us that we are loved royally."

"How the fuck did I get so lucky?"

"Ah Ghad!"

"Huh?"

"Our ancestors and most of the elderly still say this. It simply means its God. That it is all God Kiah."

"I love you so damn much it hurts my heart, Nia."

"Same here Mr. C."

"God Nia. You consume me." He said kissing her.

"As you do me." She said as his hands disappeared between her legs and she eased on her tippy toes for him to explore deeper.

"God, I want you soooo badly." She cooed as she allowed him his exploration.

She moaned softly when he found that ticklish spot again that drove her red-hot blindingly mad.

He tickled her body until it became feverish.

Her body trembled sickeningly. She screamed his name in agony. It never took long when he found her itch-spot. She kept his hand right where she wanted it for the intensity it created. He itched it mercilessly churning her up into a frenzy. She rode it until his name echoed and crescendo on her lips and she collapsed into him. When he finally extricated his fingers, she helped him to lick her deliciousness off them.

"You are so fucking yummy." He moaned looking hungrily over at her

Chapter Ten

Her phone woke her. The last time she checked was after her shower. David had been calling. She tossed the phone and headed out to Kiah. It seemed like he had finally gotten the message.

The sound was coming from the floor. She reached for it. It was Beverley her hairdresser. An appointment for 9:00 am had opened, and she wanted to know if she would like it.

She quickly sprang to life and accepted. The woman was a godsend. She turned to look for Kiah. He wasn't there. She scrambled out of bed and ran for the toilet. She was dying for a wee.

She called out his name and got nothing back. She wrapped herself in her robe and went to brush her teeth. When she started out, he appeared at the doorway with a cup in his hand.

"You rang?" He offered, looking like an Adonis. He was wearing his pyjamas from the night before. She loved the sight of him. The presence of him in her home. The way he looked at her. The way he took care of her.

"You left me again." She said taking the cup and reaching up to kiss his lips.

"I woke with the alarm. I couldn't go back to sleep. It was either getting up or bothering you for sex. So, I had to distract myself. Plus, you needed the rest for tonight. I want you at your best."

"I love you Kiah." She kissed him again. He kissed her back. "I slept through the alarm again. Gosh Kiah you wore me out."

"As you did me. Do you think you are innocent in all this?"

"Who me?" She asked laughing. Little tingles went off in her chest as she looked over at him from the rim of her cup from sipping a couple sips of the heavenly scent.

"Thank you for always taking care of me. By the way I have an early appointment at the hairdressers.' One came up and I took it. I must be there for nine."

"After that any plans?"

"What were you thinking?"

"I was hoping we could head to **Corrie's** and pick out a ring. We could have the Aunties pick out a couple. Any particular style you fancy?"

"Not really. I never thought of marriage. Especially after David."

"Why the fuck do females do this shit? Let assholes determine the rest of their lives. Damn, he truly did a number on you didn't he sweetheart?"

"He couldn't if I didn't allow him to Kiah. But not anymore thank God. I am awake to experience God's goodness."

"Which is why I am going to spoil you sooo rotten Nia. You deserve this. I mean I wish I could sing like that asshole. I would do Tina Turner Simply the

Best for you. Two seconds later he started to sing. "**You're simply the best. Better than all the rest**..."

Nia sank to her bed and wrapped her feet up under her and rocked back and forth to the loveliest rendition ever.

He reigned kisses on her face through breaths that made her giggle like a schoolgirl. As she wondered again how the fuck did I she get so damn lucky?

When he was ending, she got up and wrapped herself around him like a python.

"I'm not done yet woman." He kissed her. "Big finish. You are simply the best Nia-Belle Corrington."

"What did you call me?"

"Nia-Belle Corrington because that is who you are to me." He said easily. "Now let that asshole try to top that. He thinks he is the only one who can pull some shit. Tell me I didn't melt your heart with that?"

"You were dynamite! Yeaaaaah!" She clapped like a kid presented with a new bike for Christmas. "This is why I totally love you. You make me happy Hezekiah Carter Corrington. Totally!" She threw her arms around his neck and kissed him deliciously. "Are you sure about what you're doing Nia? I mean I don't want too..."

"Shush...C'mon baby. I am hornier than a toad."

"Your wish is my command mi-lady." He teased and deposited her back on the bed.

Nia dressed in mid-thigh length orange baggy shorts, white tank and orange sweater. She selected her chunky **Bonswa** jewellery set of necklace earrings and stackable bangles and rings.

They had commissioned her to do an accessory line this past Heritage Day using the island madras that Seba used for his **Havana** line. The outcome was a masterpiece.

She chose criss-cross kitten heel sling backs instead of the slip-ons. That she placed in her bag for later.

Kiah was dressed in khaki three-quarter length flat front trousers and rust coloured tank and hooded insignia jumper. His feet were encased in espadrilles. His hair was neatly held back.

"You are truly a gorgeous man Kiah Corrington." She tossed at him when she came out of her dressing room. "Have you ever modelled?"

"Yes Nia. I have." He said matter-of-factly.

"See you are so nonchalant about shit Kiah. I bet it was for Ralph."

"I modelled for a lot of brands but only by choice. I've even done some Asian designers as well."

"Bet you made couple covers as well."

"Yes Nia. I made **People's Magazine Sexiest Man a few times** and **Rolling Stones**... I thought Seba gave you all the juicy bits."

"Seriously Kiah. How are you not daunted or jaded?"

261

"I have a balance, Nia. I have money which gives me choice. I am not keen to be in the spotlight. Sorry I am just a simple human being who cares to damn much like you do. Plus, I can only drive one car, wear one pair of shoes. My highlight so far is finding you. So, I am just going to enjoy my time with you until it ends on this earth."

She rushed to him and wrapped her arms around him tightly.

"You're not putting me on are you Kiah?" She asked still in disbelief.

She squeezed him closely.

"I thank God for you Kiah. You make me so damn happy."

When they got into town and parked. He reached for her hand. She was starting to get use to the boys and the reporters following them and taking their pictures. She no doubt believed they would once again be featured on the news.

Some friends had even **What's App** to ask, "how come you never messaged to say you got a MAN!"

Some sent her pictures from what came off their island's news feeds. She had stopped checking and discussing. She did not have that much time in the day for frivolity. Good thing she never craved that kind of life. So, the sooner she stopped feeding into the cess pit she felt the better off she would be.

The guys made sure it was ok for them to enter. Nia had called ahead as well to make all was well. Beverley assured her it was. However, when they walked in Nia knew instantly it was a mistake.

The place was packed with females in all shapes sizes and colour. Loud and itching for melee.

Beverley greeted them.

"You're Majesty! Rarse Nia! They still chasing you-all around and shit? Come in come in." She ushered them over to the waiting area.

Giselle the high-coloured sexy Trini with her pouty lips was working reception. She eyed Kiah up like he was a plate of Sylvie's succulent fried chicken.

"Eyes in you damn head Giselle. This is Miss Nia's blessing. Not yours you horny bitch." Beverley tossed and winked over at the girl. "By de way how you do Kiah? So nice to meet you." She extended her well-manicured hands to him.

"A pleasure to meet you, Beverley." He took her hand in his and shook it gently.

Beverley looked like she was near swooning. Along with all the ladies in the room. They seemed to want to bend over for him.

She loved how he took it all in stride.

Big-Bottom Melda stomped in from the nail section. All the other females followed. She had a magazine in her hand.

"This is you right? Damn Miss Nia. This is him! This is him!" She banged the cover of **GQ** Magazine. She pointed at Kiah animatedly. Shit! We have a real honest-to-goodness celebrity!

Kiah you gonna sign this for us, right?"
"This too! Wait you damn turn Iona! Wait you damn turn. Kiah you gonna sign dem right?"
"Ladies! Ladies! I'm sorry Kiah." Beverley mouthed. "Because I didn't think grown-ass woman would behave like this. Plus, I hope you all know that all these magazines you are holding, is mine. Mines you all hear me. They all mine." She banged her chest artfully. "They belong to me, myself and I! Mine all you hear! Mines." She dramatically stated, "So even if he signs them, they stay right yah! You want one. You ghats to pay me. Right Kiah?" Beverley tossed winking up at him.
"Why you ghats to be such a drama-queen Miss Bev?" Long mouth Janelle asked, kissing her teeth.
"I just stating de facts honey. You don't like. There's de door."
"Kiah, can we get pictures then?" Whoring Betty; she does not like to be stifled or penned in. She sleeps with whomever or whatever she liked. So, she garnered the name. Which she says was like water to a duck's back. She carried long rainbow-coloured dreads. She was also in your face and can defend a point to a fault. She stepped right in front of Nia.
"Ladies! Ladies please. You..." He pointed to her and pulled Nia up close to him. "I will take a photo with you. But please be polite to her." He pointed to Nia. Be nice to her and you get what you want."
"Within reason sweetie." Nia tossed giving Betty the look.
"I'm sorry Miss Nia! We good. We good." She flattered in her New Zealand accent. "I am sorry. Just that its my first time up close with a celebrity in a long time. Please. I am sorry." She cooed like a naughty child.
"Damn Nia. I warned them. They promised to behave. Now look at them. Acting like American people hounding celebrity. "
They all had a good laugh.

An hour later Beverley asked. "You ready to get you hair done?" She draped her arm about her shoulder. "But first off tell me about his hair. Dang! Kiah sweetie, can I get a closer look?"
"Treat her queenly Miss Beverley, and we can have a chat even."
"Damn Kiah! You sure is a fine man."
"Her man Miss Beverley. Her man."
All the females tutted and cackled loudly, as they crowded about him to get their photos.
A girly man wondered in and sashayed over. Seems as though everyone wanted to get their chance at a photo-op.
"Hello Kiah! Nice to finally meet the great man of mystery. Pleasure." He extended a well-manicured hand with red talons.
"Pleasure?" Kiah offered. Looking towards Nia to let him know what sex was greeting him.
"Can I get one of those too?"
Kiah agreed. But he was yanked closer for the picture.
"Jess'E' Ca! Do Ghad bless you! Please to leave Miss Nia's man be. This is not your blessings, he is hers. Get me?"

263

"A feel you Miss Nia!" He offered, flicking at his long braid. "By- the- way Mr Floyd wants a brand new cellular. He believe his men had something to do with it."

"What! Tell him I have Warren on speed dial. All it takes is just one phone call to get the ball rolling."

Jess'E'ca cackled like a laying hen. "I just passing along de message." He offered with his fine and dripping in fake haute couture regalia. No doubt bought from Fake Frankie's Emporium.

"We sure know who get shot in de ass first!" Beverley tossed. "Dang! Why you all got to be so fierce. I just came in to check out de merch and get a mani-pedi."

"Well get your foine ass inside and let them start." Beverley ordered. "Cause we all aiming to be out on time so we could catch the Extravaganza tonight."

"By de way Kiah. You are sporting some damn neat dreads. Miss Nia, you had better keep he ass on lockdown. Cause I know lots of fastie folks who don't give a toss about what happening between you two."

"But I do." Kiah offered easily.

"Word smooth-operator."

"Pretty-girl bye!" Beverley interjected. "Fly fly away."

"But you know I speak truth Miss Bev."

"Zzzip! Ssshew!" Beverley swatted him away with a Jill Scott flourish. Everyone laughed out loud as he sashayed off towards the Spa-Hut.

"Keep he pretty ass on a tight leash Miss Nia." He spat, pausing abruptly. p Don't say I didn't warn yah." She spat back at her.

"Thank you Miss Jess E Ca. I will certainly take your words under advisement."

"You had betta." She cackled. "Cause you know awe no like foo see each other flourish."

"Bite you tongue! Speak foo yourself."

"Stop pretending Miss Bev. You know I speak truth. Cause we islanders don't like to know she doing well while we catching hell."

"Oh, shut it! Go get you damn claws sorted."

Jess E Ca disappeared behind the swing doors after kissing her teeth.

"Damn confused fool. Just don't listen to it."

"But she tells the truth Bev."

"Darling just remember all the good you do throughout this island. God forbid! No weapons formed against you and yours shall stand."

"Amen." Nia finished. Thank God Kiah wasn't in ear shot of the aspersions.

"By the way Kiah," Beverley called back. "You do know you gonna be busting up Facebook, right?" She had taken an instant shine to the man. He was a far cry to that asshole David. Who thought all women should be beholden to his skinny black ass. Nough times she wanted to haul off and slap the black sense he sure did not get from the Creator back into his greedy behind. He sure treated the beautiful kind and freakin creative woman like shit. She always thought she deserved better. The universe had answered her prayers. So no! No weapons formed! She would fight anyone who dare try to steal what God had freely given. The woman had done enough penance; with David who had dragged her through her through hell and back many times.

Some thought she deserved it for the way she treated him: as though his shit don't stink. Thank God she had finally opened her eyes to his philandering-bullshit.

Beverley wanted to praise-worship each time she saw the way her Kiah treated her.

When Nia was finally under the dryer, Beverley wandered over during a lull in the shop activity and celebration. She wanted a touch and chat with Kiah.

He gave his permission to touch his hair. She was in awe and felt weird to touch. The dang things were masterful. She said as much.

"Damn Kiah! They neat as hell! Who did your hair and shit?"

"I will gladly give you the hook up Beverley."

"Damn! Butter could melt in your friggin mouth. But for real though. You lock an dem really neat. How long it tek to do?"

"Almost a day with two assistants."

"Damn! That is dedication."

"I was trying to find myself, as well as support a friend who dared me too. They've grown on me."

"Well, I think on all of us. They are truly sweet. Please share the secret."

He wrote the number on her note pad, with a promise to make first contact for her. Beverley was over the moon when she went back to check on Nia.

"Girl call me when you need a break." She whispered in her ear when she lifted the dryer.

"A break? A break from what?"

"Mr Handsome of course. Girrrl I would fuck him for you when you get tired." She whispered again. "Damn that white dude is even hotter in person than on them fucking covers. I bet he got you in pain and shit all de time?" She chuckled and fanned herself dramatically.

"Beverley behave. Behave yourself oh!"

"When someone lek he around? A bet that lout feels like shit now."

""Don't care."

"That's my girl. Blessed and highly favoured. But seriously call me."

"For what? What would you do? What could you do?"

"Tie his ass up! I would tie that buffed-fucker up in my house and rape his FOINE-ass every second of the day even if I am chaffed to high-heaven! He looks like he could bruise a bitch something proper. Miss Nia, don't he have a clone?"

"Stop it, Beverley!" She was aching with laughter. "So, what you gonna do with Thomas if you get Kiah's clone?"

"Keep the fucker in my spare room and shit! You know like one of them toys we bought from sex class. He makes me so horny looking at his FOINE-ass."

265

"I know right." Nia laughed.
"I'm so happy for you girl. It is bout time you get something special."
"Thank you, Miss Bev."
"By the way is V and Ga'elle doing your hair and make-up tonight?"
"Yes, they are." Nia said easily.

V was the up-and-coming make-up artist on the island. Her makeup could rival some of the American artists. She had attended Cosmetology school in the US and learnt how to hone her craft.
She had even created her own make-up line; **V'unique** and it is doing quite well.
Nia wore her stuff and has given up on the other oversees brands. Her make up brand name carries a range of foundation colours that cater to a variety of skin tones. Not to forget her stunning highlighters. Her products are created naturally100 percent vegan and cruelty-free: no animal testing.
Nia loves her vibrant liquid lipsticks that are quite bold.
"So, I will pin your hair up when I am done. Then they can style it the way they want too later."
"Thank you for doing this, Beverley."
"You are a great client. Plus, I am getting half price on my costume. We gonna be some hot birds in paradise, aren't we?"
"If I can get back to work. You know since that shit happened; I haven't been to the office. I am hoping to drop by today. So, the sooner you sort me."
"I got you Miss Nia."

Florrie the manicurist and pedicurist hooked Nia up after her hair was being hot-oiled. Giving Beverley and her cronies a chance at Kiah.
She looked over at him in the mirror as he held court, chatting laughing and taking photos.
Beverley pulled out the VIP treatment: champagne or cold drinks, fried chicken and patties.
Ella's goat water and rolls were expressed delivered. Kiah had hers sent in. It was still steamy, and the rolls were succulent and warm. He also paid for the sessions and all the trimmings the ladies were enjoying outside.

By the time they were ready to leave, more people strolled in. Islanders could make anything into a party. It was like swimming through a mob to get back to the car. She never knew her people had it in them.
Thank God she had brought her head wrap and her dark glasses.
"I think you were born to do this Nia." Kiah offered when she came up looking like an African Queen.
"You are too. Think I didn't see how all those females were throwing themselves at you. You were just lapping it up. You had them eating out of the palm of your hands."

266

"I just gave them what they wanted. I made them feel important. You yourself reminded me that everyone just needed to be seen."

"I bet you paid for all that in there and all their pampering needs."

"Compliments of you. I bet it was something you would have done. Did you enjoy your goat water?"

"You betcha! I had two bowls. Now all I want to do is lay back and go to sleep."

Her mobile went off. It was Seba.

"Girlfriend! **Facebook** done blowed-up with all them pics everyone posting of your man, wid them at Bev! Some say he paid foo all of them to get the works! Even for the rest of the females coming in until the store closes! They are all gonna get the works!"

Someone else was calling… "Seba I have Madame Cruz on the line. Shit! What could go wrong now?" She clicked over the call.

"Madame?"

"Nia? We have a huge favour. Lucien would like you to sing the songs **At Last** and **Evergreen**. Seems as though Manuela cannot sing this evening. She has a fierce bout of tonsillitis. Lucien is going out of his mind driving me out of my mind. Please can you do us the huge favour?"

"Yes Madame. I will. I just need a run through."

"That's why we are calling. Can you make it to the academy in the next half hour?"

Nia looked at her watch. It meant that Corrie's would have to be quick. She would not be able to head to the office.

"Madame. Can I get forty-five minutes and I will see you then?"

The woman agreed. She relayed the message to Kiah.

"You're singing Barbara Streisand's Evergreen? Do you know that's my mom's favourite song? Gosh Nia, she will love you forever."

"Shit! Talk about pressure."

"Not to worry. You will blow her away. I have every faith in you. Don't forget **At Last** is our theme song." She recalled the first time she sung it for him. "Stop it!" She pushed at him playfully. "You are so sentimental."

"When it comes to us. But seriously if I could sing, I would be singing from the roof tops. You can do this. Stop stressing. You are going to be dynamite tonight. So, are we popping in at the Aunties or waiting until later?"

"Let's do it now. Unfortunately, I will not be able to head to the office today. Thank God I used my time wisely and finished those dresses. Seba will drop your suit and the ones for the guys off at home. He is blown away that you would do this."

"I told you I will support you any way I can Nia."

"Thank you, Kiah." She kissed him sweetly. "Let's call the aunties and tell them we would have to be quick. OMG!!! I am really beginning to freak out. Not just a little but a shit-load!"

They entered **Corrington's** via the freight lift. Upstairs after a round of hugs and kisses the aunties bought out the motherload; the jewels kept in the vault for **VIP** customers.

The stuff in the showcase was one thing. But sitting and staring at what was displayed before her on their bed of black velvet boggled her mind. She began to feel a bit overwhelmed. Bile crept around in her stomach. It churned. Maybe it was a mixture of nerves and goat water and juice. She was up and bolting for the lady's room.

Inside she hurled the contents of her stomach.

When she came up from around the lid of the toilet Kiah was there.

"Nia?" He reached for her. She stopped him. She gave her attention to the toilet bowl again.

"Nia are you ok?"

"Oh God Kiah." Another round overtook her. But there was nothing.

She waited. After a couple more minutes she allowed him to help her up from the floor.

"Nia are you ok?"

"I think so. Perhaps my nerves got the better of me after all."

She untangled herself and went to rinse her mouth. There was a knock. Her auntie came in. Her face was filled with the anxiety she felt. Their eyes met.

"I feel better now auntie. Guess just a case of nerves is all." She hugged the woman.

"Ok Nia-Belle I am glad that you are. However, I hope you have not undertaken more than you can chew?"

"We are wasting time as is. I am ok now."

"Not before ingesting some ginger tea. Now come with me."

"Yes auntie." She said, casting Kiah a pleading look.

He shirked his shoulder and followed behind them.

As soon as Nia sat down and took one look at the ensemble of real diamonds verses the **VVS1** stones; that only the super-rich on the island would be bold enough to have a peek at her stomach churned as the things blinked up at her mischievously.

Swiftly her hands jumped to her to her mouth. She looked over at him anxiously and in total confusion.

It was as if someone was playing a trick on her. When she looked at him, she was calm. When she looked at the magnificent loot on the table her stomach churned.

"I...I...Kiah I can't do this!" She jumped up.

"What do you mean Nia?" Auntie B asked. All eyes pelted her with confusion.

"What are you on about? What do you mean you can't do this? What are you saying? You haven't even looked at any of them."

"Auntie B... Please let's just give her a moment."

When he looked back, he saw her running. She looked caged suddenly. "Nia! Nia!" he called. She ran for the bathroom again.

"Sweetheart! Sweetheart what the hell is going on?" He asked a sort of panic crawling around in his voice. "I don't get this. You were on board with it. This was your idea. Do I need to remind you?"

"I know. I know Kiah. I don't know what is happening. Here with you I am fine. I go out there and take one look at those frivolous things on the table and I want to hurl."

"So, it's not me? You aren't having second thoughts?"

"No! Hell no!"

"Then what? I am so confused right now. Do you want us to forget about getting a ring then? What Nia? Because I don't get it!"

The aunties knocked on the door. "Is everything ok in there you two?" They walked in. "Nia, are you having second thoughts?"

"No auntie B! I want to marry Kiah. But I think. I think." She became tongue-tied and started ringing her hands nervously.

"What sweetheart?" Her auntie asked as she wrapped her up in her arms.

"Auntie the size of those things. They are freaking me out."

"We will get you smaller ones if that is your choice."

"We are doing this because it was your idea, Nia!"

He felt like he was grasping at straws in the wind. She was truly strange. He had never heard of anyone having an affinity to diamonds big or small. It made laughter dance about in his chest and he had no choice but to release it as it scampered up his throat.

"I know. I know. But those things out there are scaring the bejesus out of me."

"Seriously?"

"Yes Kiah. Those things aren't me. I would settle for a little one. Aunties you know I don't go for things of that sort."

"Which is why we decided on those on that tray Nia. Beautiful yet understated."

"I'm sorry." Nia said again her eyes pleading with him.

"So, are you going to do this or what?"

"I want to. I want to do it."

"Well, the interview is tomorrow, and you promised that woman a scoop. So, we need to pick something."

"Wait! I have an idea. Sweetheart, give me your scarf."

"Why?"

"Time is running out. She needs to fulfil her appointment over at the academy. We will deal with things after. But for now, she must do this. So, give me your scarf."

"Okay Katho." She unwrapped the scarf from around her neck and handed it to her partner. She watched as she wrapped the thing over the girl's eyes. They led her out.

Kiah followed thinking what the fuck!!!!

They took her back to the table as though she were facing a firing squad. "Touch one and don't think. Just touch."

269

"Kiah!" she called as she reached out to him.

"I'm here." He walked towards her. "Don't think about it. Just reach down and touch one."

"Help me. Help me Kiah."

"Ok." He took her hand, and just as she was about to touch something he moved his hand. She touched an emerald cut 3.5 carat stone."

"That's my girl." Auntie Katho said. She motioned for B to cover the others. "My Nia-Belle you have always been a unique individual. When children were running around in the sunshine you always had your head buried in a book. That's Rosa-Belle's doing. When teenagers were going about holding hands and planning their weddings you were always hard at work." She hugged the blindfolded girl to her and gestured to Kiah.

"Ask her again." She whispered as she unwrapped the scarf from about the girl's eyes.

"Nia-Belle Castle nee Francois…" He dropped to one knee. "Will you marry me?" He slipped the ring on her finger.

Nia looked at the thing nestling there. She looked to him. She looked to his auntie, her auntie, then back to him, then to the thing. Then she got down on her knees.

"Yes! Yes Kiah! I will marry you!" She threw her hands around his neck. "I love you so very much. Thank you for my ring."

"So, you like it?"

"I do."

"We are not at that part just yet sweetheart." Her auntie laughed. Laughter rang out like a mischievous imp throughout the room. When they rose, both females had tears that left a streak down their faces.

"Nia, you have always been our daughter since your mama exited this plain. We have always seen and nurtured the best in you. Sometimes you've made it oh so damn difficult. But we have never given up on you." Her auntie gushed. Hugging her tightly.

"I have always envisioned this." Auntie B said tearfully. "He is our best Nia. So, I now give him to you. God lent him to us to keep safe for you. Just think he could have been anywhere else this year, but he chose to come home. You two have now found each other without any meddling from us. Someone reminded me that while we plan God laughs. So, he must have had a toe-curling one when you two finally met."

"Hurry B. She must be at the academy."

"Shush sweetie. You had your moment. Let me have mine. As I was saying, she is our family's best too my dear boy. Just like I found your family's best Nia. All we ask is that you two love and treasure each other like we your aunties have done all these years. So now it is up to you two. And so long as there is breath in our bodies, we will always be there to support you. So please be good to each other. "

"We promise." They mouthed to the woman, quickly looking at each other. They were on the same page.

"That is all we ask sweeties. Now sweetheart, I am done."

"Thank God. I was beginning to think we are now married." Kiah teased. Kissing her cheeks.

"Bite your tongue! I have bigger plans for that day." Auntie Katho tossed.

"Now run along you two, and we will see you both later."

They left after the transaction and packaging of the ring was sorted. Then they hugged and kissed each other with a promise to see everyone at the theatre later.

Back to the car. They were quiet, even though he reached for her hand and held it tightly in his. She sipped on the ginger tea in the mug her auntie had given her. It settled her stomach.

"I am sorry Kiah. I got scared." She said softly.

"Are we good now?" He asked as he glanced over at her.

"We are. I just thought those things cost a lot."

"Nia, I have money. I told you not to worry."

"But you just bought me so many extravagant pieces the other day."

"Nia, I like buying you things. You deserve it."

"But Kiah those things cost like mortgages for a few people. Food and clothes even."

"Only you Nia. But I do understand. I promise we will do something about all your causes." He laughed. "But seriously I have never known a female to act like you did when you saw those rings. Who runs away and hacks up the content of their stomach at the sight of diamonds? Not once but twice."

"Me Kiah. I don't really care for them."

"Nia it's an engagement ring! Your ring! You had my heart feeling so crushed in my chest for a while. I thought you had changed your mind about me. Us."

"Never Kiah. I love you."

"I truly had my doubt. I am not going to lie."

"I'm sorry." She snuggled up to him. "Forgive me?"

"You know I do. But seriously, do you really like the ring?"

"Yes Kiah. I like the ring. We chose it."

"You did. With a bloody blindfold! You are the most unique woman I have come across in a long, long time." "Sorry I am not eager to spend your money."

He chuckled. Kissing the bundle, she had on her head. "Why don't you let me see it on your hand again just to make sure I am not dreaming Nia? What do you say?"

"Okay." She whispered a moment away from sleep, fighting a big yawn. She held out her hand to him. She heard the rustling of the paper, then she felt her hand in his. She loved it.

Couple seconds and he slipped the ring back on her finger. She held out her hand and looked at the thing nestling there sleepily.

He brought her hand to his lips and kissed the spot where it laid. He had to admit it suited her.

She was fast asleep when they pulled up outside the building. He hated to wake her. But if he did not, she would be terribly late for the rehearsal. He eased her over.

"No more Kiah. I am sleepy." She murmured.

Her words made him laugh. Nice to know in sleep he was still on her mind. But she had a task at hand that she needed to attend to.

"Nia you must wake up."

"I'm tired." She snuggled into him, kissing his neck.

"I know but you have to wake up." He shook her gently.

"Just do it Kiah. I am tired."

The guys were laughing. He caught them in the mirror.

"Not funny. I need to wake her, or she will be late for her rehearsal."

He brought her up off him and shook her gently.

"Nia, wake up. Wake up baby."

She slapped his hand away. "Do it without me. I am tired Kiah."

"Nia, stop this or so help me. Nia, wake up. Nia...Wake up!" Kiah called with more urgency.

"What? I'm tired Kiah."

"You need to get to rehearsals." He spat with a raised voice. As her cell Interrupted. It brought her up sharply. She reached for it clumsily.

"Hello...Madame... Madame... Yes Madame. There was lots of traffic... I am parked outside the building. I am on my way in...Yes Madame I will be there in five."

Extravaganza Night: Once again they pulled up outside the statuesque building lighted in majestic array with all the Christmas trees blinking a golden warm welcome. They had used them to line the red-carpeted pathway.

Two 12-foot silver glittering trees flanked the entrance way. They were brilliantly lit and even had beautifully wrapped boxes underneath.

The atmosphere reminded him of a New York or California Gala.

Walking the Oscars or even the Grammy's red carpet.

It was an electric atmosphere prickling with sights and sounds.

All types of cars and trucks, limousines and even buses and mini vans were pulling up. Bikes and scooters were kissing up alongside them also.

Coming through the town was just as magical.

Seemed like the Christmas decorations were starting to go up, even on the houses and buildings, and even the trees. Everything sparkled and commanded your attention.

He felt like singing, **it's beginning to look like Christmas**. Everything was twinkly and magical.

Even the fountain was lighted in an arrangement of colours. As was the humongous tree standing guard beside it.

Nia had forgotten all about the customary Christmas tree lighting in the town square. In hiding out she hadn't come down with the choir on Wednesday night to perform.

She had said as much to him.
"I forgot that the tree was being lit on Wednesday evening Kiah. So many things are passing me by."
"Hopefully after tomorrow you can get back to your life Nia. I apologise once again. In the meantime, just concentrate on what you must do tonight. How are you feeling by the way?"
"I am ok. Practice wasn't the greatest, but I pray for saving grace to get me through tonight."
"You think you weren't great? Even Barbara couldn't have done it better. Believe me when I say this because I have seen her perform that song on numerous occasions. I am an untrained ear, so perhaps that is why I couldn't spot a flaw."
"See, that is why I love you Kiah Corrington. You even allowed me to sleep for a bit. I was so tired. I don't know what has come over me."
"Me Nia." He kissed her cheek.

Just before they could enter the building, they had to wade through the media gauntlet ending with Indiria...
Many people shouted out to them. They waved and called back their greetings.
It appeared the theatre was '**the place**' to be tonight.
Young and old, rich and not so rich, local and foreigners...
Seems as though everyone was out here tonight.

Nia's heart rattled in her chest. She prayed again for the strength and the courage to pull things off. Especially knowing that Kiah's parents would be sitting front and centre in the audience.
The regional and even the international reporters and locals tried to get Kiah to speak. He simply posed with her for photographs and gently eased her along the line.
Thank God they had set out early.

She spotted his parents and the aunties. They waved over at them. They were wearing pieces from her **Back to Elegance** line.
These designs were exclusive: that way no one would have a twin at any upcoming event.
The ladies were simply-simply beautiful; auntie B wore a silvery bling black ball gown with off the shoulder huge puff sleeves. Auntie Katho was dressed in a silvery pink A line ruffled floor length gown with fitted bodice and half shoulder. A huge over-emphasized tied bow draped her elegantly to enhance the finish.
Nia recalled sending pictures of the designs to the aunties. They were so ecstatic, and responded immediately, requesting the two dresses, and paid full price for them. They never demanded family discounts or any special favours.
Ooh!!! She still got so excited when she recalled the aunties saying they would play mass this year.

273

She said it to Kiah, and he said, "Sign me up, and all the men too. We will work on the parents."

Kiah's mom wore the magenta off the shoulder ball gown held with a diamante knotted bow at the centre of her breast. The only accessory needed was earrings and wrist cuff. She had pulled it off royally. Especially with the stylish chignon and the diamante hair comb she wore that kept it together.

Kiah had purchased a suit for his dad from Seba's line. They were a mesmerising photo-op as they looked down at them.

Indiria and her team was out and in full force. She would always cover the outside just like on Oscar night. She would interview the haves and even some of the have-nots.

A pleasure for those sitting at home to still be a part of the grandiose and enjoy the glamour.

She too was wearing one of her gowns: a figure-hugging Milky Way number with low cut halter. The woman was gorgeous. Her dreads were pulled back and loose flowing in ringlets to the side.

Nia had to always grudgingly admit that she was made to showcase her designs. She always complimented her. Not to forget Kiah himself. He cut a most dashing figure.

He wore **Imperial;** a tux from Seba's **Holiday Exclusive** line; black shiny three piece appliqued slim fit single-breasted tuxedo and waist coat hugging a crisp white shirt and black tie. He complimented it with shiny black shoes. His hair was loose flowing and held back with a black satin headband.

All Nia could do when he stepped to her, was place a hand to her chest. He had stopped her heart again for a split second.

She had chosen a white form-fitting ankle length dress with a plunging V neckline and asymmetric sleeves. It complemented her gorgeous figure. Even Kiah seemed thrown for a loop when she stepped out of her dressing room.

He told her she was stunning. She knew she was. She felt it when she slipped into the dress. But pity she would have to change a few more times for the evening. It was just for the red-carpet entrance.

Indiria was interviewing Marcus and Yvonne and soon it would be their turn. While they spoke to the press the couple waited at the top with the aunties.

Just as they stepped to the chopping block Seba, and his boys crept up. "Look at you!" He said and twirled Kiah. "Damn you are FOINE! You boys look good too. Thank you for the support, man. I am never going to forget this." He put his hands to his mouth and feigned a cry. "Thanks man. You honour me. You honour us."

"Anytime Sebastin. You do magnificent work." Kiah complimented him.

"Are you saying that you are wearing a **Sebastin Original** Kiah?"

"Hells yes he is! Hezekiah Corrington who has graced many covers such as **GQ, Newsweek, People, Time, Esquire**. Yes people! Yes, Hezekiah Corrington is wearing a **Sebastin Original**. He is wearing one of mine. He is wearing the showstopper. It is called **Imperial** because this tuxedo represents **Royalty**. From the material down to the stitching. Tell me Miss Indiria doesn't he look like a God?"

"Sebastin!" Indiria scolded and gave him a dirty look. She gestured with her head for him to get out of the shot. "Kiah what made you choose a **Sebastin Original** over some of the well-known brands you are accustomed to wearing?"

"Simple really. I visited **Belle** and I was introduced to this ta lented designer and saw some of his work and was blown away."

"Aaaah." Seba beamed. Nia was certain if you placed him on the roof of the building, he would light the way over.

"We must admit Kiah, to say you look dashing would only be an understatement. However, we say well done Mr Sebastin. You have outdone yourself yet again."

"Shucks!" Thank you, Miss Indiria." Seba gushed.

"Now Miss Nia...Are you nervous about performing tonight?"

"Yes, I am Indiria. So nervous. But that doesn't mean that I will not give it my all. You know me."

"We sure do. You are so incredibly talented. So, we know you will be at your best."

"Speaking of best. My God Miss Nia. The ladies at the top of the steps are all wearing your designs. What do you think?"

"They are stunning Indiria. I just want to say a massive thank you to my team and this amazing big brother." She looked to Seba: who was dressed in the equivalent to Kiah's tux in royal blue.

"He has always been my rock, my tower of strength. He supports me in every way. Thank you, Sebastin-Ricardo Quadri Wallace, for all you have done and continue to do. I love you from here to eternity and back. You are a superstar. Thank you also to team Belle. You make me shine always."

"We love you too sweetie. You make it so easy. Ditto my sister. Can I kiss her?" He asked looking to Kiah. "Fuck it! Oops!" He didn't wait for an answer. He thanked God for keeping him true-blue to her and vice versa. Many would always say to him branch off and fly free. But something always told him to stay the course.

That change was coming. He kissed her again.

"You two have always been inseparable." Indiria chimed in. "You teach us the meaning of true teamwork. Gosh, you both have always managed to bring me to the door of tears whenever we speak. We hope that we can all keep learning from you two."

"Thank you Indiria. Thank you for always supporting us as well."

She blew them a kiss. "Now are we still on for tomorrow?" She had written the cheque and handed it over last evening. She prayed it was good stuff as usual. Because in her opinion Nia sat at the right hand of the muse for fashionistas. She was a bloody genius.

"You betcha!" Nia said squeezing Kiah's hand in hers. She felt him squeeze hers back.

"Thank you again for stopping by. I will see you soon. Miss Nia break-a-leg. Especially seeing that Kiah and his parents will be sitting in the audience."

"No pressure Indiria. Play nicely." Nia tossed as they walked away and went to join their little posse that was waiting.

They walked up to join the others amidst all the chatter and clatter of the cameras. No doubt they will be featured in the monthly glossy magazine called **'Interpretation'**. As well as the **Weekly**: the insert that lies in the middle of the weekly paper, that the extremely ambitious woman had started. No doubt she was vying to become the total heir-apparent to her fathers' media company.

Plus, it was something the islanders look forward to, even before they came out.

A round of hugs and kisses as well as thanks accompanied. His mom held her longer.

"You look amazing sweetheart." The woman gushed as he hugged her tightly. They had spoken briefly. Kiah was speaking to her earlier and had handed her the phone.

The woman squealed in delight. It was over her dress. Thank God she was never idle. The dresses she designed must always have a prototype: just in case something went seriously wrong. One never knew. She thought of her mobile team: they were magical. They travelled all over the island just to make her work shine.

"Nia darling let me say again how very talented you are." Elena did a peacock shimmer. "When I saw this dress. Oh, my word! I feel so beautiful. We all look so beautiful. You are an amazing talent." She said and reached out and hugged the girl again. She genuinely liked her. She prayed yet again that things truly worked between her and their son. Just think the magical things they could accomplish as a team. She had said as much to her husband.

"I sent a couple pics to some friends of mine! Just you wait and see Missy. Son don't you ever let go of this one. Do you hear me?" She teased him. But she was totally serious.

"I never will mom. I told you I love her." He mouthed and drew her in closer. She turned her face upward; he kissed her fleetingly.

A chorus of oohs and aaahs went up around them.

"Miss Elena..."

"Mom. Call me mom sweetie."

"Mom..." She squeezed out. As a picture of her mama popped up. She touched her thumbs and knuckles together: Just like she and her mom would, to form a heart shape.

Then she continued, "Let me introduce this lovely lady. She is a wonderful designer as well." Nia offered gesturing over to Yvonne. "This is our beacon. My north star."

"Sweetheart." Yvonne smiled. She blew her a quick kiss. "This is all about you. It is your time. Please enjoy it."

"Son, I think in all this they have forgotten the true superstars." His dad primped. "This is some great craftmanship. I need to speak with the designer. I think the forefathers would have loved his work."

"He is right there, dad." He said and pointed Seba out. "This is Nia's partner Sebastin."

"Nice to meet you Maestro-Sebastin." He extended his hand. "As I said to my son. This is some fine craftmanship. It makes me miss the rag trade. But I know some people who know some people. You get what I mean?"

"Yes Mr Corrington." Seba tossed grinning from ear to ear. It was his dream; for someone other than local and regional to recognise his work. His heart hammered away wildly in his chest.

"Call me Denton."

"Yes sir...I mean Denton."

"Great work." He pumped Seba's hand. Then he turned to Kiah. "It's not all about these beauties. We look like we belong on the cover of **Rolling Stones**." He struck up a pose with his son and gestured to Seba.

The photographers did not miss the op. They clicked away freely.

Nia knew Indiria would be proud.

"Dad, you look spiffy. You sure cleaned up well."

"I can give you a run for a cover or two don't you think?"

"You sure can." He said giving him another bear hug. "Mum, you look like a goddess. You both do too." He gestured over to the aunties.

"Too late Hezekiah." Auntie B teased. "But we understand. You look like a million bucks and so do you Nia. Are you ready for tonight?"

"I am."

"We heard you are tackling Barbara." Yvonne said to her.

"Barbara who?" Kiah's mum asked looking at Nia.

"Nia will be singing your favourite song mom."

"You mean she is singing Barbara Streisand?"

"**Evergreen** to be exact."

"Nia will be singing Barbara's Evergreen?" The woman asked aghast.

"You betcha! You just wait until you hear her sing mom!" Kiah gushed.

"Oh, be still my beating heart! Nia! I hoped my son told you that I adore that song?"

"Yes ma'am. I mean Elena. He did. I pray I do it justice for you tonight." Nia offered humbly.

"I am sure you will sweetheart. God gave you talent five times over. You know this." Her auntie offered. Kissing her cheek. She felt so much pride for the girl who had blossomed so refreshingly into a woman. She could not be prouder if she had given birth to her.

"Thank you, auntie. I love you."

"I love you more."

277

"Everyone I don't want to appear rude. But I really must..." Nia interjected.

"Yes! Yes! We will see you soon."

"Nia-Belle..." Her auntie said. "Forget about everything else. Just do this for your mama. You know she is with you. Honour her."

She gave the woman a strong cuddle. Katholeen had no doubt that her sister would be there with her every step of the way. It was their connection, and she was certain she was defying the keepers of wherever she was to rally around her child tonight.

"Yes ma'am." Nia squeaked before she wandered off with Kiah beside her.

When they entered the backstage area, saying it was manic was a total understatement. Everyone seemed to be running here there and everywhere.

Some were shouting, stretching, humming, and even barking out commands, and begging and dashing back and forth.

V and her partner were already involved in make-up. They quickly gestured her over. For once he was not the centre of attention.

He quickly got the message, and they kissed. Then said their goodbyes.

The costumes were brilliant if she must say so herself. Lucien and his team had been a pain to deal with as usual, but Nia was happy that it all got sorted.

The cast was 60 strong. A synopsis of the electric evening's performance; It was an adaptation from the book **Iridescence** written by the leading playwright Dame Sarah Weekes.

She had delved into the birth, life, love, fears, agony and freedom of an Afro-Caribbean female. From birth...being a child... girl... and woman living in the Caribbean. Her name was Irie.

Nia had read the book a couple times and could relate to where the laureates head was at.

She like many females had lived out loud most of what Irie had experienced at some point in their life.

Nia had also performed a prose from the book of poetry the woman had written.

Dame Sarah had given them a glimpse of who Irie was. So, she was quite familiar with the strengths and weakness of the character.

Some of the highlighted costumes; were deep red silk and toile to represent the Suckna/Sukiyahs; creatures who sucked the life essence from others. They were the modern-day vampires. Remnant cloths were used for their cloaks. Just like they were used for the ballerinas to show poverty and the Afro-Caribbean heritage from the past.

The Jabless; male version of the Sukiyahs, and the Jumbies and Moko-jumbie costumes were made using high-vis-skeletal outlines on black from head to toe.

Nia liked that he had incorporated stilt walkers it was mentioned by her because she thought they represented a sort of deity. She had made them plumes for their heads. She had used iridescent white satin and lace as well as toile and feathers to get the angel and birds' wings fashioned unto wire.

They had small to large angels and birds; she thought she would up-cycle for her troupe.

She had explained to V and partner that she wanted some of the costumes to come alive using their makeup skills; so, some of the dancers had birdlike features to their faces.

They had also painted, stencilled and sequined until she never wanted to see another for as long as she lived. But unfortunately, she had to replenish. Hence the trip away from the island. So, to say she was truly satisfied was an understatement. Because from what she saw on set at dress rehearsal last night, she had every faith that things would be more than grand.

They were incorporating all genres of music and dance from Hip hop to folk dancing, which she and her team had thought to use some of the island madras to highlight.

Nia prayed silently again and breathed deeply. Like she usually did before every single performance.

Pastor Seaton came in to say a quick prayer. She wished them all the best. Then all too quickly Nia found herself waiting on the podium to be quickly spirited up.

She spotted David on his. He mouthed something over to her. Thank God he had stayed in his part with the men and did not come to say anything to her.

He gave her that goofy puppy-dog face that used to make her forgive him anything. She smiled and lifted the flowing iridescent gown in gossamer white over with its elegant puff sleeves. She had also done a satiny white tightfitting pair of trousers to wear underneath.

She repeated her mama's mantra. Then they were being eased unto the stage as the orchestra started.

The Prayer... Her eyes sorted Kiah's and remained there. He was sitting front row with the entire family along with the Premier and his family, the governor and his family.

She was being seen. It felt like she had finally finally met her authentic self. She allowed her lovely voice to join with the angel's choir.

The dancer's rendition and everything came together beautifully.

When the last note climaxed, and the dancers stuck their poses the entire auditorium after a full second erupted into absolute pandemonium.

A glorious and thunderous applause ascended to the ceiling and no doubt shook the realms of heaven to its very core.

David himself was totally incredible. His voice seemed to have matured like fine wine. She smiled. He was terrific with his first love. One could tell that he spoilt her rotten.

Just before she slipped back to the dressing room. He reached for her hand.

"Don't spoil it, David. Let's just do what we are here to do. No drama please." She hugged him quickly.

Then she released him and pushed the door open and disappeared inside.

Impossible Dream… Nia switched the gown for a royal blue and white long sleeve off the shoulder applique and embroidered long sleeve over coat that buttoned from breast to waist.

David was singing with her again. He had chosen a navy-blue suit that complimented her outfit.

Funny he was wearing a Sebastin Original; no doubt borrowed from flashy Kranston; he loved purchasing Seba's suits. He and his cousin have always been the same size. He looked gorgeous. A Teddy Pendergrass lookalike. He could blow even better than the man in her opinion.

She recalled one of the Glee Club concerts where they had done the Stephanie Mills and Teddy Pendergrass number called **Feel the Fire**. They had brought the house down. No doubt he was remembering this. He gave her that silly knowing grin again. Her heart winked. She couldn't help it.

At Last… She sang to Kiah and only him. Her eyes never left his. The audience was still applauding when the curtain closed. Even when she left the stage, she could still hear them as she picked her fiery red and white off-the-shoulder ball gown up off the floor and ran to him as soon as he came around the corner.

"Goddam Nia! You were on fire! How the hell have you not made it up there with Whitney and the likes? You were dynamite!"

"Thank you, Kiah!" She said excitedly. She felt dizzy as he twirled her about. "What did your parents think?"

"Did you not see dad out of his chair? They are waiting out there." He pointed to the door.

"Just for a little bit then."

He took her hands and pulled her along. Just as she saw David coming around the corner.

"Kiah? Kiss me." She whispered.

The next half of the program started. She had had enough time to finish her lukewarm tea. Georgie looked fantastic. She had gifted the girl with a knockout outfit: figure hugging spaghetti strap black diaphanous dress with an enormous split from ankle to thigh. She chose the shimmery black a line halter dress that morphed like small waves crashing to the shore whenever she moved.

280

They were sisters and singing the theme song **Dear God** from the mega Broadway hit **The Colour Purple** for Audra; she was dancing Irie's belief in God, in herself, her mother: how hard she worked to raise her without a man; she never knew him. Her belief in the world and its people. Her illusions of love that caused her to go back into herself and dig deep to find her strength.

Audra interpreted the moves with such grace and fluidity. The girl's body was like a pretzel so pliable and compliant.

My God! It was like watching a master create with spun sugar. The webs she created with her hands and feet were so intricate. It should make a person with limbs who doesn't move when they hear music feel downright ashamed.

They performed like it was only yesterday in Glee Club. Well come to think of it when tensions were high at the office, and they needed a breather they would start to sing.

Sometimes Georgie would spoil it and say, "if only David were here."

"Well, he is not. So, sing."

That was what they were doing now. They were killing it! It was a magical friendship. Nia truly enjoyed performing with the girl. They brought out the best in each other.

Nia wore an emerald shimmery floor length duster with majestic bat wing sleeves over a white body-hugging sweetheart necklace dress with painted bougainvillaea appliques and sequins.

Her heart pounded in her chest when the orchestra started.

She looked to Pascal…When he gave the signal, she prayed.

"Please dear God let me kill this."

She dug deep and called on all her ancestors and begged her mama for help with **Evergreen**…

Kiah's mum was on her feet and clapping like a madwoman. They managed to get her seated, but she was up again. They held her still. But couldn't and would not be contained; she was up and clapping enthusiastically.

Finale: Irie has learnt a valuable lesson; that no matter what has happened throughout her life, if she was breathing, she had hope.

So as Dame Sarah Weekes' words echoed throughout the auditorium. A pin could be heard as it fell to the floor.

"We people of African descent are quite resilient. If many of our forefather's survived slavery; by being hosed, tortured, shot, hanged, lynched, dragged, beaten, burnt, thrown overboard from overcrowded ships, made to sleep and eat where we shit, and starved, and was taught that the colour of our skin meant we were a second-class people. That we weren't ever going to amount to anything…. Yet we survived the trees that were printed on our backs, the swamps with crocs and gators, snarling dogs, being spat on, called Niggers, the killing and raping of our babies

281

and our minds. To this very day they are still trying to tell us we are nothing. Kept ropes and chains about our necks and our fists. They even cut off ears and cut out tongues, and chopped feet so we couldn't run, scream, or beg our Father in heaven for the strength we needed. So, we as afro people had to dig deep to find this hidden strength. We had to find our home; a place where we can look deep within ourselves and say we have every right to BE. Just like you... and you...and You."

Nia recited it all. The words were powerful for any multi-coloured person who believed they were worth something. That their voice will not be silenced, and that they deserved bigger and better. God gave life and no one else should have the right to take it. Because we with life were chosen, so we had every right to be.

She wore the island madras in a huge billowing ball gown. The bodice was a striking green: to depict the green of the rolling hills of the island. She had chosen to wrap her head in a vibrant yellow head cloth: to depict the sun.

She filled the top with white: sea-island cotton; a symbol to remind their people of how our forefathers worked the fields in the burning sun picking it until their fingers were blistered and swollen, bloody and oozing.

Nia waited anxiously for the first note of the violins. Then Mr Pascal gave the signal...

She started to sing Stephanie Mills **Home**...

Tears streamed down her cheeks at the end of the rendition. Especially when the dancers crawled under her skirt; it was made to expand so they could all be covered; symbolising protection for Irie and her descendants.

Nia thought of her island and how much she loved it and will do for its people.

The crowd was going wild!!! She was certain even God himself must have stood to raise his hand in appreciation. He must have pumped his fist and shouted YES!!!!

For she had no doubt that he was pleased with what the theatre had brought to life. Everyone had done their absolute best. Even Dame Sarah Weekes was jumping and shouting at the top of her lungs.

The clapping, whistling, shouting, and the applause was totally infectious. It must have taken a good five minutes to get people calm again.

Pascal came in and congratulated them for the fantastic job. Nia thanked everyone and told them she could not have done it without them.

Curtain call was tremendous. Everyone was off their feet and clapping. The night was a definite success.

Now all she wanted to do was go home and curl up for a couple of hours with her man.

Georgie helped her to pack her things. While a handful of the choir members asked who the woman was that was shouting so much for her.

282

She told them it was Kiah's mother. They said she sure was in the family after that song. Little did they know? But she said nothing.
She quickly packed.

When she opened the door, they were all there. Kiah had an armful of red roses. When the guys took her bags, he handed them to her. She buried her face to the soft perfect petals.
"Did I tell you how magical you were? Nia you were spell bounding!"
"Sweetheart you were fantastic!" Elena screeched and reigned kisses on her forehead and cheeks.
"What a voice! Nia sweetheart you were so fantastic!"
"Sweetheart your mama would be SOOO proud!" Her auntie gushed and kissed her.
"Sweetheart each time you sang you made me weep." Auntie B said.
"You were fantastic! You all were. Everyone was truly so wonderful! Sarah was so pleased. Did you see how excited she got? Not to forget Elena!"
"Gosh child! How come you don't have more international fame?" His dad asked. "That guy as well. The entire choir was amazing! I didn't sleep not once!"
"Well done! Great show!"
"Thank you everyone."
"You are one talented female let me tell you. Heard the costumes were designed by you as well. My goodness is there nothing you can't do?" His mom asked.
"Not really if I put my mind to it."
"I asked her that when I first met her." Kiah gushed.
"I think her mama took her back to God a number of times to be blessed." Her auntie said.
"You should be proud Katholeen. She is a dream."
"I know she is Denton. I thank God." Her auntie said.
"Pascal! Pascal."
They looked up to see Dame Sarah bounding down the corridor. Her shoulder length dreads bobbing.
"Miss Nia! You were **DY-naa-mite!**" She gushed. She wore a shimmery black knee length spaghetti strap tasselled dress. She looked like she could do female body building competitions. She too was another great looking island female.
"Thank you, Miss Weekes." Nia offered graciously. Thinking she was the seal of approval really. Lucien had taken on Goliath and thank God; he had defeated him.
Judging by all the accolades he had received and had bestowed upon them personally.
"You deserve every penny." He said to her when he wrapped her up in his arms.
The woman squeezed her in a bear hug. "Your interpretation with the costumes was phenomenal. I loved the Mocko-Jumbie/stiltwalkers. Lucien said you told him to throw those in. I thoroughly enjoyed the entire

presentation. Not to forget all the superb interpretations tonight. Everyone was magnificent. I need to say this to Pascal. By the way it's good to see you again Bellot. Katholeen you look fabulous. And you Elena. I know I don't have to ask again if you enjoyed the show."

"It was superb!"

"Nice to meet you again Kiah. We hope to see more of you on the island. Heard this lady has sparked your interest?"

"She hasn't simply sparked it." Kiah tossed cockily.

"Touché! Clever man. I wish you all the best. Well, I must find Pascal. Good to see you all again." She bent to give Auntie K a kiss. She lingered to long, as though she had whispered a secret.

A look of trepidation passed over Auntie B. She looked the cagey woman up and down wearily. Especially when she saw she held auntie a moment too long.

Come to think of it, Nia had remembered some rumours that she was Auntie Katho's first love before Auntie B had popped into the picture.

"Bye Sarah." Auntie Katho said to the woman. Watching as she disappeared through the door.

Nia didn't miss the elbow that went into her side either from Auntie B.

"Great looking female." Kiah's dad said. She looks like she could bench press hippos."

They all laughed.

"I am feeling like I have gone pass my bedtime. I am so tired. Can we go home please?" Nia asked softly.

They walked out and into the beautiful hall decorated with wreathes in all shapes and sizes, as well as blinking lights.

Miss D and Miss Ruthie were there chatting with a group.

Almost everyone was out from **Safe Haven** and **Iya's Place**. Nia had bought them all tickets.

She introduced Kiah and his parents to everyone.

They congratulated her and told her she was fantastic. They gave her hugs and kisses and shook Kiah's hand far too enthusiastically. Especially Joyce and Patricia; they were living at the house full time.

Joyce's mum had died: suicide from years of depression.

Patricia was sexually abused at a very young age until pre-teen.

They honoured some with more photo-ops. Even the under-water twins ran over for theirs and to say congratulations.

Seba came over with Munni Gupta and his family.

The Guptas' owned many supermarket chains all over the Caribbean.

Surabhi his wife was very demure in features and manners, but she was magical when she took the stage to dance Bharatanatyam. She took your breath away every time.

The girls were Shankar and Kamla. One had to deduce that the females in that family were gorgeous looking.

284

They congratulated her and was gaga over Kiah; whom they recognised immediately. Seeing they were business majors and had even started their own beauty and fashion vlog. It was doing quite well. They handed him their card. They were very articulate and did not want to converse in another language.

Seba hugged her and told her quite sedately how terrific she was. Nia thought his ass was under **lock and key**; he wasn't his flashy self.

It brought a smile to her lips.

"We did well, didn't we?" Seba asked. Hugging her again. "You were fantastic too."

Gupta told the girls "Nia and Sebastin along with their team are responsible for the brilliant costumes."

"Wow! We are super impressed." They harangued. "Can we visit your store soon?" They asked like over excited teens.

"We would like that very much." Nia said, gesturing to Seba.

His friends wandered over and after introductions were made again and congratulations given. Gupta and his family said their goodbyes and went over to talk with others.

Seba's friends asked if they were heading downtown for late night **Lime and Jump-up**.

Nia said she would pass because she was truly whipped. She fought back a yawn.

"What is late-night-lime and jump-up?" Denton asked.

"Not for you dad." Kiah said laughing. It made them all laugh.

"What are you trying to say son? That I am old?"

"You are dear. Let's not dispute that. Let's go home. You can do the lime there." Elena told him.

"Seriously Sebastin what is a lime?"

"Sir it is sort of hanging out and drinking, chatting, laughing and dancing..."

"To hip hop?"

"No sir. To calypso and reggae music."

"We could do that!"

"Not tonight dad. Maybe another night."

"I'm gonna hold you to that."

"I think Denton just discovered his birth paper." Auntie Katho tossed.

"He ain't the only one." Auntie B tossed crossly. Sucking her teeth and walking away.

"I think that the Dame has put a bee in Bellot's bonnet." Denton tossed. "Come along dear."

"Ok ok. Guess no liming for me tonight. My son thinks I am too old."

"You can always lime with me dear." Elena said kissing his cheek.

"Ok young folks. I just got an offer I can't refuse." He squeezed his wife's ass as they walked away.

"Good night my boy. Stay safe you two. You young ones also."

"I think your dad is definitely getting some tonight." Seba tossed as he and his friend's fist bumped him and each other.

285

"You boys get your mind out of the gutter." Auntie Katho tossed as she gave them hugs and kisses before turning away.

"I think she is in the doghouse." The guys said in Korean.

"We sure know who ain't getting nothing tonight." Seba laughed. "By the way you were fantastic sis. You burned the house down."

"She sure did. Now I think sleeping beauty is ready to expire." He felt her place her head against his chest.

"She deserves it though. Any-who I will not be home tonight. I am heading into town. You know I can't resist live music. See you two soon. Thanks again for the plug Kiah... By the way don't you give those boys any time off?"

"I can drive Nia home. You guys can go relax... We will be fine." He knew what they were thinking. He also had not missed how David had tried to play with her on stage. Yet again. But he was not going to take part in his shenanigans. It was her night and she had worked hard for it. It paid off royally in what she had created all around.

For sure they had a connection. He couldn't deny it. They would always do. They were electric on stage. He had to grudgingly admit it. But that was up there. On solid ground they had even footing, and he had more to offer. Time would tell. Because it seemed he had finally grasped the message. He had not come buzzing around. But he reasoned he wasn't going to rest easy until David was far away.

Kiah took the key and ushered them off with Seba and his crew.

Nia knew where William was heading. He was panting after Georgie and anyone with eyes could see. He offered to drive her home.

"I don't need to tell you that she is very important to me, do I?" Nia said to him seriously.

"I understand Miss Nia. I promise I will be good to her."

"You had better be." Was all she said before she climbed into the car and waited.

"Don't worry about Georgie Nia. She will be safe with him." Kiah offered when he climbed in beside her.

"Okay. Please just let's go home. I can't tell the last time I felt this tired." She yawned as she placed her head momentarily against his shoulder. When he started the vehicle, her head lopped to the other side, and she was out cold.

Kiah tried waking her when they arrived home, but she would not have any of it. So, he simply just reached in and lifted her out.

She placed her arms around his neck and was out again.

He muddled through and got her inside and placed her on the bed and started to undress her.

She stirred. "Kiah I'm tired." she mumbled and turned the other way.

"I know you are sweetheart." He said unzipping her trousers. He pulled it off her finally and tossed it. He then pulled the covers up over her and proceeded in taking his clothes off.

He grabbed a shower and headed out to get a glass of water.

Her phone was going off again.

It was him. He grabbed it.

"Look don't you get it? She is no longer interested. Just let it go man." He hung up the phone and switched it off.

He wanted to throw the thing so far across the room. But he stopped himself. He reached for the bottle in the cupboard, but he quickly replaced it. He had given his word. He settled for a glass of water then went in and curled up beside her.

She murmured and reached for his hand and snuggled up tightly.

Chapter Eleven

Nia turned she wanted to wee. She unwrapped herself and eased out of the bed. He was sound asleep. He didn't stir.

When she stumbled off to the bathroom, she heard thuds and pit pats on her veranda outside. She reckoned it must be raining.

She realised she was still wearing her bodysuit and her top from the night before. She fought to get out of the tight-ass thing almost wetting herself. In the end she simply pulled the crotch aside and sat down thankfully. Thinking this is the price you pay for trying to suck things in.

Task accomplished she wiped herself and flushed the toilet, then undressed.

She then cleansed and washed her face because she had printed a rainbow of sorts on her hands from the old makeup. She took one look in the mirror, "Uurgh!" She murmured at the first glance because her face was still in full regalia.

Shit! She must have messed up her pillow. Because she never slept in makeup. She must have been so exhausted. But how? This was not like her. She was known to be a night owl, but lately things had changed.

She showered... Then she toned and added some moisturizer to her face. She then applied lotion to her skin and dressed in drawstring shorts and a tank and headed back to the bedroom.

He met her on the way. He bent and gave her kiss. "I need to go." He murmured. He headed for the bathroom. Her smell stayed with him. Even as he brushed his teeth she was still on his mind.

When he returned, she was putting new pillowcases on her pillow.

"I tried to wake you." He offered.

"I'm sorry." She said giving her lips when he came over. "What happened?" He pointed to her pillow.

"It was a mess. My makeup was all over it."

"I'm sorry. I tried Nia."

"I was tired, I guess. I can't believe I didn't even know when we got home."

The alarm started. She switched it off. "This is the day that the Lord has made. Let us rejoice and be glad." She opened her arms to him. "I thank God for you Kiah Corrington."

"As I give thanks for you Nia." He squeezed her tightly and kissed the top of her head where her braids were still piled high.

"You were magnificent last night. I think you found a friend in my mom. Did you see how she reacted?"

"Kiah I nearly shit my pants! And your dad. He didn't even fall asleep."

"I think he's had a truly great time."

"Did you?" She asked looking up to him. He kissed her lips.

"Yes, Nia I did. I know you said you couldn't live anywhere else.

288

But my God your voice! It is so amazing! Don't you want to be like Whitney or even Barbara?"

"I like being me Kiah. I like picking and choosing what I do. I like having fun doing it. I have my fans here. I don't like people being in my face constantly. I say I want to be a great designer like so and so. But truth is I am already a great designer. I have my following. I have the respect of many here and around the Caribbean and yes around the world Kiah. Maybe I am small in my thinking. Or maybe it is fear. But all I know is that I have all I need right here. I love my life here to be honest. I like that I don't have to do things I don't believe in, being censored, or put in a box or be compared to others."

"Wow Nia! In that mouthful I think I get what you are saying."

"That there can be only one me and it's up to me to treasure and protect me Kiah. I like that I can walk anywhere in this island, and no one calls me horrible names or treat me less than. You see that song, **Home?** Kiah every time I sing it, it makes me realize that I already have all I need to live my true authentic self. So, no I don't want to be like Whitney because despite all the talent. She died alone."

"My God Nia. Please don't ever change."

"I have no intention to. Well let me correct myself and say never again. Not even for you Kiah."

"Nia, I respect that. I respect you. I just think your voice is so incredible. You could pack auditoriums, stadiums..."

"Like I can do here. Let's get a better transport system in place and I will bring them here."

"You are never leaving this island then?"

"Not for exceedingly long periods Kiah. I told you that from the get-go. I can only do little increments off my island. I love being near the aunties, my friends, my family, and my projects."

"Ok Nia. I hear you. But if you change your mind."

"Thank you, Kiah." She tiptoed and kissed him. "Thank you for your support. But I love my life here. I am not defined by who I wear or know. I like that I can go out and pick mangoes or coconut from my own trees. That when I walk or drive on the streets most everyone knows who I am and are always eager to say hi and ask how I am doing, and really want to know. I love my life here Kiah."

"Ok ok. I was only saying your talent is so amazing. Maybe I should build an arena and bring some artists in so you can showcase that voice of yours. Do you guys have a music festival on island? Perhaps we could get something like that going."

"Good idea Kiah. I will take that. I have performed at Reggae Sumfest and even Curacao Jazz Festival. I would like some Gospel and Soul and R&B... bring some artists like Cee and Bee, Jennifer Hudson, Babyface... Do that Kiah and I am there!"

"Let me speak to a couple contacts. Marcus included."

"But we have to sort that damn travelling to the island shit first."

"Yes ma'am."

They were sitting having coffee at the table and munching on butter and guava jam on thick raisin toast. While the rain beat down mercilessly outside. Kiah had placed the roses in a vase atop the island.

"Thank you for my flowers." Nia said pointing at them. She had smelt them when she walked in earlier. They are heavenly.

"You deserved them."

"Don't forget we have Miss Indiria today."

"I didn't. Anything you need me to do? The boys?"

"Speaking of boys...Where is that blasted phone? I don't know why I even have one." She looked around for the thing.

"I turned it off. He just kept calling."

"Who?"

"Seriously Nia? David. I told him to cease and desist. Then I switched it off. It's over there." He pointed to the sofa.

"Shit! I thought he would get the message. Especially after last night. He is one stubborn... Any who, I am in a good mood. I could tick off the **Extravaganza**. Next on the agenda is the Masquerade & Auction. You are still on board, aren't you?"

"Of course, I am."

"You are the best boyfriend ever."

"Fiancée you mean?" He challenged.

"That too." She tossed. Kissing his lips lovingly. Any ideas since it is raining so much out there?"

"Of course, especially since you allowed me to sleep with my dick in my hands last night."

"I'm sorry Kiah."

"Show me how sorry Nia."

The rain had trickled to a murmur now. It was nice to touch his body and have him caress hers to the powerful essence of the rain. She loved hearing it as it fell.

Sometimes when she was at home and it was raining, she would wander out and sit and just listen or looked at it as it performed and blessed her land.

"Let's go outside." She said to him and reached for his hand. She took a couple duvets and blanks on the way out.

"What do you have in mind?"

"I love the rain and I love you. So, let's see what we can get up to."

Outside they got lost in the exploration of ed each other's naked body on the floor of her bedroom's private veranda. She kissed him languidly. The ambience was so delectable that it didn't take them long before they gave up their essence to each other over and again.

They fell asleep and was later awakened by the sound of waves breaking on the shore. They stayed for a bit longer kissing each other lazily.

"I am so hungry for you Nia."

"Just like I am for you Kiah." She opened her legs and wrapped them around his waist when he climbed atop her. Hungrily he took each nipple in his mouth and sucked delectably. Not much coaxing was necessary, especially as a gently breeze caressed them gloriously.
"Kiah is it a sin to feel this delirious? I can fuck you all day long."
"You are a dirty girl! Listen to you. But honestly, I love fucking you too. It's as if your body was designed only for me."
He adored it with his tongue, teeth and hands. He loved the noises that emanated from deep within her.
"I have always wanted to do this. I love the rain. I love that I can do this with you. You make me so horny Kiah Corrington." She opened her legs so he could enter her wielding his dick like a matador's blade.
She groaned sickeningly.
"Fuck Nia! Ooooh... you feel so good baby." He pulled her up to join him. She moved like a sleepy top over his dick.
God, he recalled she said she did classes that encouraged her to move. But what she was doing to him was downright blasphemous.
He growled like a damn mountain bear. He grabbed her ass cheeks in his hand for sanity. Just to make certain he would cling to a reality that was morphing on him.
She devoured his lips. When she released him, he punished her nipples ravenously. She cried out in ecstasy.
Couple minutes later he was on his back, and she was fucking him genuinely.
Just before he thought he would die he felt her hot on him. He gave himself permission to howl as he joined her a second later.
"I fucking adore you woman." He said exhaustingly keeping her there as his dick deflated and slipped away from her.
"You blow my mind every time Nia. He rested his head next to her heart.
"I seriously think I can do this all-day Kiah. Does it mean that I am a nympho?" She liked that she could talk to him. He never made her feel as though she was silly, or that he didn't care to hear what she wanted to say even if he disagreed.
"As long as you fuck me Nia, we are good."

Kiah's mobile started to chatter as they gave the house a last go over: washing dishes and drying and putting them away, fluffing pillows on the sofa, placing some of her roses strategically around the living room.
They tidied up the bedroom and put new linen on the bed and took the others to the laundry room.
Rosario was coming in the morning. She had already sorted Kiah's things and placed them neatly in her closet. She had called on Monday and Nia explained she had met someone.
"Mamita has found a man?"
"I think so Rosario."
"Is he a good man?"
"He is. He makes me happy."

"Good girl mamita. I will meet him soon?"
"Yes Rosario. Very soon." Nia promised.

Kiah answered. It was Marcus. "I'll put her on speaker." He said and gestured her over. She sat next to him on the sofa and brought her feet up under her.
"Hi Marcus!" Nia said. As she looked at the room with a critical eye. She shushed the thought that Indiria may be negative. But who cares? She had built her house at a young age. She would own it outright in a couple years. She hadn't done anything immoral to achieve it either. Not many had accomplished the things she had. She was very proud of herself and didn't need anyone anymore to tell her she was worth it.
"Miss Nia I am working on a project: **Women of influence in the Caribbean**. My mum, my wife, Sarah Weekes, the aunties, Indiria... Can I ask if you would do me the immense honour?"
"You want to photograph me?" Nia asked aghast. Thinking 'the famous photographer Marcus Winter wants to photograph me?
She looked to Kiah her eyes bulging.
"Why not you Nia? Look at what you have accomplished. My God you were phenomenal last night. My wife has not stopped gushing about you."
"Really?"
"Yes, really Nia. It would be an honour. To many times women from the Caribbean islands get left out in the grand scheme of things. They do so much and are not rewarded for all their hard work. Well things are going to change. Let me do this and I swear the entire world will learn who you all are and the immense difference you make to this world."
"Funny you say this. I just had that talk with her only this morning. She made me promise to sort transportation to the island and build her an arena. She wants to host a music festival here on the island. She doesn't want to live in California."
"She is like my wife mate. She can only tolerate the UK in tiny increments." He said laughing loudly.
"Ouch! But it is true honey."
"Hello Nia. What do you say? I do it, you do it yes?"
"I think it's a brilliant idea. Yes, I will. To be included in a book with the likes of Madam Premier and Dame Sarah Weekes and you Yvonne! OMG! That is the ultimate coming out! I will do it!" She shouted hugging Kiah to herself.
"Well done you." He kissed her. "Thank you, Marcus, for honouring her. Perhaps you can drum up some interest from some leading artists over in the UK."
"What genre Nia?"
"I was thinking R&B, Gospel..."
"Have you heard of the London Community Gospel Choir?"
"Who hasn't? You would have to be living under a rock. I loved when they worked with Luther Vandross. **The Impossible Dream** is my song."

292

"I know Basil Meade personally. I will give him a call."
"That's perfect Marcus. Guess we can get the ball rolling for next year sometime. But first the conundrum about transportation. But in the meantime, we have an interview with Indiria for 2:00 pm.
Let's sort that and we can hammer out these things a bit more."
"You betcha! Thanks again Nia."
"Phenomenal job last night by the way. The performance was brilliant."
"Thank you. I am honoured. Thank you both for thinking of me."
"By the way are you two still on for the birthday barbeque next weekend?"
"You betcha! Great chatting with you. Let's do this again."
"Have a good trip over." They said to the couple. "See you soon."

Nia wore a sky-blue off the shoulder asymmetric jumpsuit with a cinched waistline and flared trouser legs. Her feet were encased in silver sling backs.
She wore the diamond necklace set that Kiah gifted her.
Her makeup was simple but very flattering she had learned from V about proper application, even highlighting.
Kiah suggested putting some bake goods in the oven. They had some raisin and cinnamon cookie dough, which they placed on a greased tray in the oven.

The house smelt and looked divine. The boys were home, so they lent a hand.
She gave William the 'look'. He grinned. He promised he was very good to her.
She smiled because she already knew. Georgie had called. She told her that she was totally in love, or was it lust?
Nia thought the girl a contradiction.
She said they chatted for most of the evening. She told him she would like to take it slow for a while. But then again when he was kissing and touching her it felt sooo good. She gushed and squealed loudly.
"Boss I felt sooo horny. You know it has been a while since I had my garden watered. I was on the verge of changing my mind. But Willie stopped me."
"Good on him."
"Boss he said he wanted to treat me right, and that last night was not the right time. I am in love."
"Good for you sweetie. I pray God bless you as he blessed me." It was the gospel truth. The woman deserved all good things. She reminded her of that.
Nia scanned him as he sat next to Kiah. **Hurt her and I will bury you**, she telepathically echoed to him.
He smiled back as though he had read her mind.

The rain had all but disappeared now. A couple of the guys were checking the perimeter; front and back. They would all head up to the manse when the interview was over. They were having dinner there.

Indiria and her people arrived right on time. They were busy setting up. She went over a few ground rules with the woman; she told her the apartments downstairs were off limits and why.
She agreed readily.
She was a decent individual when she wanted to be. Nia thought magnanimously. She also had a scheme cooking up in her head.
They would be live, so she aimed to milk it for what it was worth.
She was decent but not stupid. No one had ever accused her of that.

Indira gestured them over so they could be positioned correctly for the shoot. Kiah had chosen a navy-blue suit and matching tie. He looked very dashing. She said it to him when he came to wait for her at her dressing room door.
She had oiled his hair while he sat between her legs with some of his products; they were subtle in terms of smell but worked very well. His hair looked so gorgeous.
She promised herself she would sketch the image.
She had accumulated a few more and wanted to present him with them for his birthday. She had been sneakily working on them. Because what do you get a man who had everything for his birthday?
Indiria had also promised her a couple photos from last night and a couple of the stills from today. She would get them framed for him and hang a couple.

It was decided upon that Kiah would be interviewed first. So, the countdown started...
"Good afternoon, everyone. Let us say a very warm welcome to our listeners as well as our viewers. My name is Indiria Osbourne, and this is ECBC, and we are live **In the Hot Seat.** Today we are pleased and so very delighted to have in our presence visiting on our lovely island of Emerald City Mr Hezekiah Carter Corrington 111. He is a philanthropist, a brilliant businessman, model, television personality, and the dashing bachelor who sits on the throne of Carter Incorporated as the CEO. He is also the great-great-grand-son of Carter Hezekiah Corrington; the great haberdasher who came over from Europe hundreds of light years ago. You get where I am heading with this aren't you?"
"Yes Indiria." Kiah laughed. "It's your way of saying that they were old but great at their professions."
"That to Kiah. But seriously your money is up there with God right now, isn't it?"
"Not very nice to ask a fella about his money on the first date my dear."
"Touché Kiah." She teased. "But seriously though."

"We are comfortable Indiria. Thank God I don't have to worry too much about the everyday stuff that life throws at so many."

"Amen! Anyway, let's say welcome once again to our tiny but Talawah beautiful island. Many call it **God's Garden of Eden right here on earth**. Do you agree?"

"Totally agree Indiria. But first please call me Kiah...God's Garden of Eden right here on this earth." He said it slowly as though ruminating. "I like that. It totally sums up the brilliance of the island. Its lush, green and beautiful hills and valleys. The flora and fauna they are so breath-taking. Not to forget all the lovely people I have met, and the foods and drinks I have sampled and enjoyed."

"Tell us about some of the foods and drink you have tried Kiah."

"I have tried your goat water. Ella's preferably."

"What do you think?"

"It's delectable." He looked over at Nia as he said the last word. "I also enjoyed sorrel and ginger beer."

"Nice drinks especially when trying to stay cool on the island. Tell us some of the people you have met so far."

"Wow! I have met someone called Miss D who oversees the **Meals on Wheels** program, and an amazing woman. I still need to meet up for Ital with her. I have also met Sebastin Wallace. As you know I wore one of his suits last night to the Extravaganza. I met Madame Cruz and her daughter Audra. Terrific team. I also met the dancer who played the preteen Irie. She is an upcoming Phenom.

"You mean Pearline?"

"Yes Pearline. She is so talented. The evening was filled with so many wonderful artistry and music from the skilled dancers to the singers and the amazing ECGC choir and their director Pascal. Gosh we don't have time to mention everyone. But so far, I have been truly blessed."

"I was told that you speak a couple different languages?"

"Si...Oui...Ja...Tak...Evet...Si...Sim...Po...Ne...Shi..."

"Wow! I recognised French, Spanish, and Italian. I lost track of the others. Wow Kiah."

"Nice to be able to speak to others fluently when I need to. So, 15 and counting. Plus, English can be rather bland at times."

"Show off!" Nia whispered. Indiria smiled. She thought it but she didn't say it.

"Okay Kiah here comes the murky water bits. I am afraid we must tackle them though."

"I understand Indiria. Go ahead."

"Kiah everyone including all the visiting news journalists are waiting for you to open up about what went down over on Heart Island."

"I understand. I will be as honest as I can be seeing that an investigation is still happening on the island."

"So can you please tell us what happened over there?"

"I bought the island a couple months ago and thought it was a done deal. Then I received a phone call demanding more money. Well, I was not comfortable with it. So, I went over to see if we could come to an amicably solution. However, one brother decided he would play hardball."

"Seriously?"

"Yes. I tried to handle things from this end. However, like I said we couldn't seem to agree. So, I went over to the island in good faith. Somewhere along the line we couldn't agree. An argument ensued and one brother was shot and killed. I deeply regretted that turn of events. Such a mess. Believe me I tried to avoid it. But I wasn't about to go back on an offer that was already accepted."

"We totally understand. Now tell us who shot whom? There are some whisperings that perhaps one of your men shot first. That there was a scuffle, and he was shot..."

"True that one of my men was shot. But the shot was not fired by anyone from my team. Remember we weren't the only ones with guns on the island."

"So, what are you saying Kiah?"

"Not what you want me to Indiria. All I would say is that my men and I are innocent in all this. Anything else you would have to take up with the others who were on the island."

"So, you are saying that ECPD or ECDF are the ones we should be speaking with?"

"Seriously Indiria I thank the police and defend force of Emerald City for saving the lives of not only me. But my men also. I am just sorry someone had to die. Because all life to me is considered precious."

"So, what can you tell us as to further development with the island?"

"Absolutely nothing Indiria. I no longer own the island nor have any dealings with anything that happens there in the future."

"Does that mean that you sold the island?"

"Yes, Indiria I did."

"Can you tell us to whom?"

"No Indiria. Any involvement I had with that island is now over. I just want to get on with my life."

"Thank you so much Kiah. Speaking of getting on with life. In our next segment we would like to introduce our beautiful guest Miss Nia-Belle Castle Francois. Please stay tuned everyone." She said courteously and gave the signal to cut.

Kiah's mobile went off. It was Greta. So did William's.

"It's Ama." He gestured.

Kiah suggested conferencing. He went to the kitchen. He brought Nia with him. She waved to the beautiful females.

"Why are you working on a Sunday?" Nia asked. She felt comfortable because he had introduced her a couple times.

Ama reminded her of Judi Dench and Greta reminded her of Ivanna Trump: her body double. She sounded like her as well.

She congratulated Kiah in his response to Indiria: who she said had great television presence.

"Your home is beautiful Nia." Ama said. She was looking at the live streaming and so was Greta.

"You look healthy and happier." She said to Kiah.

"That's because I am in love ladies. Isn't she beautiful?"

"Stop fishing Kiah." Greta warned. "I said that to you when you sent the photo."

"You sent a picture of me?" Nia asked in astonishment.

"I had to. So, they didn't think I was making it up."

"Which picture?"

"The one the guys took of us before you left for work on Monday."

"Great one." She gave them a thumb's up.

Indiria signalled to her. She was next on the chopping block. Then they would be interviewing together on the next segment.

She said goodbye to the others.

He did not tell them what they were planning. She knew they would no doubt call again.

Nia sat on the sofa nervously after a quick touch up to her face.

"We say welcome back to our listeners and viewers. Again, my name is Indiria Osbourne, and we are broadcasting live from ECBC, and this is **In the Hot Seat**. We will now be speaking with Miss Nia-Belle Castle Francois. She is a wonderful lady and woman, a designer of fashion and costumes. She owns her own fashion house here on the island called **Belle**. She is also an entrepreneur/ humanitarian/ambassador/ and the list continues. Nia, may we ask which hat best describes you?"

"All of the above. It can change at any time of the day. But the one that best describes me is humanitarian/ ambassador. I fight tirelessly for the things I believe in, especially when it comes to supporting woman and children and the elderly."

"Hence the many organisations that you support here on the island such as **Meals on Wheels, Gift Giving, Golden Years, Safe Haven, Live and Learn, Pass it On, and Iya's Place.** Did I call them all?"

"Yes, you did Indiria. They are all near and dear to my heart which is why I work indefatigably to support them all."

"Can you tell us about a couple Miss Nia?"

"Of course, Indiria. **Meals on Wheels** is a program that makes certain **breakfast, mid-day snack, lunch, mid afternoon snack, dinner and supper** gets delivered to the elderly and shut-ins throughout the day. It also means that when you spot those two big blue buses on the street that you should allow them to pass without hassle. Because they are trying to get to the people that require this food the most. Thank you so very much Miss D. I love you. I love the team. Hi Marcelle. Hi Robert and Elvira. Not to forget her husband, Stanley. Thank you so very much Ashton and Orson our drivers. Thank you so much for all your hard work daily."

"I guess they all now know how truly grateful you are Miss Nia." She laughed over at the beautiful woman. She knew how hard she worked. "Without them Indiria. Let's just say I don't ever want to find out." "Tell us some more about your other charities Miss Nia." "Well, there is **Safe Haven** and **Iya's Place**. They are truly dear to me. Well, they all are. But I find myself working harder just to be certain that all women and our children all have a fighting chance. So that is why we are doubling up in terms of offering a safe place to the women, children, and young people." "Explain." "The young ones need their own space. So that is what we are working on. A private space to nurture their health and wellbeing. But seriously if there is a female or a child out there who under any circumstance feel at all threatened by a spouse or is hurt by anyone in their household. I urge you... I mean I cannot stress this enough listener, viewers... If you are in a situation and you feel at all threatened, please call 546-1947 any time. Day or night. There is always someone on the other end to come to your rescue. Just pick up the phone. Please, please please." She encouraged. "Great work Miss Nia. I have heard from many people that these programmes have helped; they are the backbone into contributing greatly to this island. Many say as well if your programs weren't available, they didn't know what would have become of them." "I am honoured. But there is still lots of hard work to be done." "Speaking of hard work. The **Extravaganza** last evening. OMG! What a phenomenal performance from you at the Emerald City Arts &Theatre Centre. May I say how amazing you were?" "Thank you Indiria. The evening was electric. I say thank you to everyone who performed and gave it their all. Thank you. Thank you everyone." "Nia you not only sang. You did the costumes. Even Dame Sarah Weekes commented that they were brilliant. It superseded what she had in mind when she wrote that piece." "It's an immense honour. She stopped by at the end of the show to say congratulations." "It truly was a superb show. We had such great feedback from the online audience as well. We have had quite a few phone calls enquiring after you. I bet you didn't know." "No, I didn't. Indiria wow! The power of the media." "Well don't be surprised if you are contacted by many. I have a few here as we speak. I think I may have a job as your agent." "Thank you Indiria." Nia laughed as she took the white sheet of paper. "Each one teaches one Miss Nia." "Exactly! So that is why I fight each day to make certain that each of us is seen. No matter if it's even in the smallest of measure. If it is even to say thank you to the person who opens your door or pick up the garbage. Down to the person who brings you your coffee. A simple thank you I have learnt goes a very long way."

"On that note we say thank you Miss Nia. Everyone be sure to stay tuned with us. We will be back to interview Mr. Kiah and Miss Nia together after this break."

Nia was so thankful to be up and stretching her legs. She went to grab a drink and offered to the others; Indiria and the crew.
Kiah and his men placed a tray of cookies atop the island and a couple disposable glasses with an assortment of drinks out as well.
Nia settled for a cup of hibiscus and ginger tea. Thanks to Safari Towne and Tafari who made up all the incredible blends of teas and sold them throughout the island.

She needed to use the toilet, but the aunties and his parents were on the phone. They called to congratulate them on the interview so far.
The next segment when she thought about it made her terribly nervous. She couldn't help it. She took off like a bolt of lightning.
She was sitting on the toilet her feet having a mind of their own when Kiah walked in. She opened her mouth, but words failed her.
He looked at her but offered nothing. He just stood there looking at her. Then finally he said, "Nia, you don't have to do this. We don't have to do it if you aren't ready."
"Do what?"
"Don't pretend with me. If you are getting cold feet..."
"Not about being with you Kiah. It's just that after we do it everyone will know. Then all those uncomfortable things are going to pop up. Like has he asked you to sign a pre-nup? Our background, our colour... Kiah I am sort of scared about that. Not about you and I."
"Well, that makes me feel better. But can we not stress over what others think? We don't have to worry about that just yet. One day at a time. So, stop overthinking."
"I can't help me. That is my mind in overdrive. Speaking of pre-nup. Do you want me to sign one?"
"Only if you want to." He offered easily. But as far as he was concerned. She could have it. But he knew in the real world they would have to face it. But call him crazy in love. He would let it rest for now. But he couldn't resist. "Do you want me to sign one?"
"Don't be an ass Kiah! You just must split with Seba and my little sister. They get the house for sure. Seba gets the business. It is all in my will except the bit about you. That is if anything happens to me."
"Don't you think we have to say I do first?" He whispered laughing. "But seriously we don't have to do it if you're not ready."
"I gave my word Kiah. I am not backing down." She tiptoed up to kiss him. Before she went to wash her hands and applied some lotion.
She had to get her hand ready for that thing called a ring and all the questions that will no doubt come later. She had better pull up her big girl drawers and get on with it. She repeated **2 Timothy 1:7 "God hath not given us the spirit of fear. But of power and of love and of a sound mind."**

He repeated it with her. They said it a couple times until she felt calm. She then reached for his hand. "Let's go slay some dragons my love. Got your sword?" She asked.

"You betcha! You crazy woman. Do you know how much I love you?"

"This much." She said opening her arms.

He swooped down and lifted her clean off her feet.

"Welcome back listeners and viewers. I have just heard we have tipped the scale for the very first time in the volume of hits we have accumulated. I am Indiria Osbourne, and this is ECBC, and we are live once again **In the Hot Seat.** We are back with our very own Miss Nia and Mr Hezekiah Corrington, Kiah for those who have met him."

That was when they walked in; him carrying her over his shoulders and sitting with her atop his lap. He held her there with her hands in his and gave Indiria time to recover.

Everyone could tell Indiria was taken aback; she was speechless for a few seconds. It was epic! The woman was never at a loss for words.

She recovered quickly. "You two sure are happy?"

"Yes, we are." He kissed her lightly on the lips.

"Nia is there something you would like to share?"

"I have a favour."

"Yes?"

"In the last segment I told you about **Iya's Place**… Now this next segment will be something. But before we get into it. I want you to promise me that whatever you make going forward from this interview you will donate thirty percent to my charity **Belle Foundation.**"

"I don't understand."

"What will happen next is going to put you at the top of your game Miss Indiria."

"I don't understand."

"Oh, but you will in a few minutes. But you must give me your word concerning my charity."

"You've got me…us. Quite intrigued."

"So, can I count on you? Think very carefully Indiria. Thirty percent for my charity for the exclusive rights to the next piece of footage?" Nia teased. For she knew she had the big Kahuna on the hook, and it was time to reel it in. She could see the woman's brain pulsating.

"I'll bite." Indiria offered as her brain ran the gamut of scenarios; could she be pregnant? Hell no! They only just met. Could the man be gay? Could be a possibility. He was too damn good looking. She had combed through heaps of photos, and she couldn't find a bad shot. The camera bloody adored him. She had stopped at a newsworthy piece; he had a child. But he never spoke of the child in any interview. Coming in she had to sign that she would not venture there unless he opened the door. Was he ready to talk about her? Time was ticking away. She thought she could hear the clock loudly. She could not allow too much empty white noise.

"You will bite?"

"Yes Miss Nia! Yes! I will bite."

"So, you are agreeing to my deal Mis Indiria?" Nia teased.

"Yes, Miss Nia I agree." She offered and watched as the man placed her on the couch across from him and turned to her.

"Indiria we all heard your agreement." Nia mouthed, feeling like her heart would scamper from her mouth now. "Kiah?"

"She sure did sweetheart."

"Ok are we ready?"

"Does this mean that you are ready to tell the world that you two are an item?"

"Indiria, we have been an item from the first moment we laid eyes on each other. Some call it love-at-first sight. But I never believed in any of it. That is until I met this phenomenal woman. Maya Angelou wrote this poem that my mum loves a great deal. Sorry mum let me borrow a few lines. But I will add-lib. **She walks into the room. Just as cool as she please. The fellows stand or fall down on their knees...**"

Kiah got up and sank down on one knee. **"Phenomenal woman... It's in the reach of your arms and the span of your hips. The stride of your steps and the curl of your lips. It's the fire in your eyes, and the flash of your teeth, the swing in your waist and the joy in your feet. It's in the arch of your back and the sum of your smile. The rise of your breast and the grace of your style. It's in the click of your heels and the bend of your hair, the palm of your hand and the need of your care. Because you are my woman. Phenomenally. Phenomenal woman that's you... Phenomenal woman I love you... Phenomenal Woman will you marry me?"**

"Yes..." Nia said softly. Because she was crying. Even Indiria was crying.

"Marry me Nia-Belle." He said lost in her tearful eyes.

"I will marry you Hezekiah Corrington! I will marry you Kiah! I will marry you." Kiah slipped the ring on her finger and kissed it like he had done the night before.

She got down on her knees and tossed her arms around his neck.

"I love you so much you crazy man. You bring me joy." She kissed his lips, and he repaid in kind.

"This is amazing! Did he? I mean was this? Did he just propose? OMG! She said yes! She said yes! Listeners...Viewers...This is ECBC, and we are live streaming. Hezekiah Carter Corrington the III has just asked our Miss Nia-Belle Castle Francois to marry him! She just accepted his proposal everyone! She just told him she would marry him! Congratulations! Congratulations you two!" She gushed and gesticulated hurriedly to Hubert; her camera guy to get a close-up of the ring.

All the mobiles in the room seemed to be speaking to each other.

Kiah picked up for his mom and dad.

"Hello dad..."

"Kiah is it ok if we stream this?"

"Yes, you can." He said to the babbling crying woman. Again, Indiria hysterically gestured to her guy; he zoomed in on the couple as they held each other. Facebook and What's App were blowing up.

"We wanted to say congratulations son. I am so proud. Well done."

"That was beautiful baby! You had mom in tears! Congratulations you two! That was the sweetest proposal ever!" His mom cried happily.

"Congratulations Hezekiah! Congratulation's sweetheart!" The aunties crowed. "How do you feel sweetheart?" Auntie Katho asked.

"I feel on top of the world auntie."

"So, you should sweetie. You deserved for this great thing to have happened to you. Congratulation's sweetheart."

"We shall see you two later. Hezekiah that was a beautiful proposal." His auntie said to him. "You make us all so very proud."

"Suave son. That was brilliant."

"Dad, we must go. Ama and Greta are standing by."

"Good luck son. You did something without her permission. She is going to roast you."

"Thanks a lot dad. I love you."

"Congratulations again you two. We will see you soon." His mom said. Blowing them kisses along with the aunties. His dad waved.

"Well, there you have it everyone! I still can't believe what has just happened! My God Kiah you just proposed to this woman...!"

"Not just this woman Indiria. To me she is one of your princesses plucked straight from your Garden of Eden right here on earth." He kissed her again.

"Kiah do you know how difficult you are making it for guys all over the world to rise to this calibre?"

"It is about time we all recognise when we find treasures Indiria. I know I have found mine."

"OMG! Oh, my goodness all! What a prince! Miss Nia how happy are you on a scale of one to a hundred?"

"I am way past that!" Nia mumbled tearfully. She hadn't expected what he had just done. She tossed her arms around him and kissed him openly. "Kiah you've brought me so much joy." She said when they came up for air.

Indiria gestured for the camera guy to keep recording.

Marcus and Yvonne called to congratulate them as well. Nia looked at her mobile and picked it up with a trembling hand. She was still reeling. It was Seba. She answered and listened as he squealed loudly.

"Seba stop! Seba calm down! You are going to burst something. Plus, Indiria is here so you must be PG if I put you on speaker. Seba...Seba did you hear me?"

"Ok! Ok! I am calm. Where is Kiah?"

"He is here. Everyone can hear you."

"I don't care Nia! Kiah you were amazing! You blew my mind! Congratulations!"

"You are hyperventilating Seba!"

"I know! But fu...I mean I am so happy Nia! I feel like I need oxygen! Congratulations! You freakin rock man!"

"Thank you, Sebastin."

"You will never ever do wrong in my book Kiah Corrington as long as you keep her as happy as you have right now."

"I am aiming to do just that Sebastin."

"I love you two so friggin much." He squealed again and again.

"Seba, we must go. Indiria wants us back on the coach. Can we talk later?"

"You betcha!"

"Talk soon. We are heading to the manse. So, we will catch up later."

They decided they would handle the rest of the calls later. In the meantime, they needed to finish the interview with Indiria. Then they could catch their breaths.

"Shall we start rolling again you two?" Indiria asked as bright as a beacon now. They could literally see her salivating.

"Yes, you can." Nia said looking to Kiah.

"This is ECBC, and I am Indiria Osbourne, and we welcome you back to **In the Hot Seat.** Nia...Kiah we would all like to say congratulations once again. There are so many people calling in to say congratulations. But we have one caller in particular Miss Nia who wants you to answer this question... He wants to know how you can possibly say yes to a marriage proposal after only knowing someone 10 days and him practically all your life?"

"To that person all I will say is why cry over spilt milk? Furthermore, this man right here has given me more joy in 10 days than I have ever had all these years spent with him." Nia said straight into the camera.

"Indiria let me also address that caller..." He too looked straight into the camera. "If he is being honest with himself, he should reason that he had his time from what I gathered over and over to show this beautiful woman how amazing she is, and he wasted it. So your loss is my gain."

"Well said." Indiria said. Thinking it was all so true. Lesson that should be learnt by so many. Don't expect to act a fool and no one will notice.

"Kiah let me say that proposal...I am still shaking. It was sooo amazing! I can tell you right now that not many men can recall let alone recite Miss Maya the way you just did."

"Thank you Indiria. But all the credit goes to my mom for this. In every way. I guess what I am saying is **Phenomenal Woman** is her all-time favourite. To say she loves it is such an understatement. I recall learning that poem at the age of 8 for my mom for Mother's Day. This poem is an anthem, a movement of sorts for modern women. It is liberating. Their liberation."

"Explain Mr Corrington." Indiria teased.

"Well, I think women are starting to embrace and treasure themselves. Their own uniqueness? Standing up for themselves and saying we can do regardless of what you think. Even though some are still stuck; trying to

303

change themselves to fit into whatever box men as well as media say they should."

"I agree."

"So many others are saying hell no I will not. Look at this woman beside me… my mom, our aunties. Even you Indiria and so many others. You are all finally saying take me for who I am or get to stepping. Because this is who I am. You can either love me or leave me."

"Again, Kiah I say amen."

"Seriously Indiria. Strong females are emerging and now we as men must start to learn how to accept you and embrace you as you blossom."

"Wow!"

"Another thing to your listener. I am telling him that Nia was created by God just for me. I know this. I believe this. So, once we met it was instant kismet."

"Wow Kiah! And you say you are no poet? Nia what do you say?"

"Indiria I totally agree…" She turned to kiss him. "One day at a time. All I know is that this man makes me happy, and he keeps me smiling. He brings me so much joy from the time I open my eyes until I fall asleep next to him wrapped in his arms."

"Let's keep our show PG please Miss Nia." Indiria said as she fanned herself dramatically.

"I speak the truth Indiria. Kiah accepts me for me. He doesn't try to change me. So that is why I love him. He is my gift from God."

"Wow! Wow! Wow!"

"Wow indeed Indiria. Every chance I get I give God praise because he sent me a great man. So, I will treasure him as he treasures me."

"How does it feel to hear this Kiah?"

"Amazeballs!" He gushed. "She is my gift and I enjoy unwrapping her each and every day."

"Geez viewers and listeners! This is truly amazeballs! Can I ask a huge favour?"

"Go ahead."

"Can we do this again in a couple of months? I am sure our audience would like to know how this amazing love story blossoms.

"Of course, Indiria."

"Thank you so much. In the meantime, can we have a tour of your lovely home? And perhaps you can sing us something on that lovely piano?"

"You sure can Indiria, and I will."

"Ooh one last question. Any albums or CDs in the works? What of that Jazz mix you were working on, when we spoke a while back?"

"Still working on it. Not enough hours in the day. But in a couple months' time let's chat again."

"We sure will Miss Nia. We sure will."

The still camera guy did his thing while the video camera guy and Indiria took the tour with them.

Nia sang **I Dreamed a Dream from Les Misérables**…

She felt it fitting. Especially seeing how many times she had sat there and sang it when David had come to haunt her. She was going to put him away and leave him there. She was going to embrace her life. God has been tremendously kind to her.

When she got to the end of the song Kiah flicked a tear. As did all the others in the room.

"Audience I did say to you this woman has a voice that has been kissed by God himself, didn't I? I also didn't promise a tear-free Sunday afternoon either."

"Tears can be represented in many ways Indiria." Kiah offered as he wrapped his woman up in his arms. Somehow, he had a feeling that things were sorted between her and David. She no longer seemed haunted.

"These are cleansing tears Indiria. Sometimes to wipe the slate clean all we need is a good boo-woo. So those were good tears." Nia said, wiping gently at her eye. So as not to ruin her makeup anymore.

Last photo-ops and it was over. They finally packed up and left.
Nia quickly reached for Kiah's hand and ran towards the bedroom.

She was only dressed in his ring now. She loved it. He loved how it felt on his body as she touched him.

"Are you ok with it now Nia?" He asked her again.

"No not okay. I love it!" She said and held it up in admiration.

"Do you really?" He asked. Thinking he would have bought her something that they could spot from the moon. But she didn't want that.

She assured him once again the ring she wore was just sufficient.

"We need to call Greta. She has probably blown up the phone by now." Kiah said.

"I know. But it's just that I don't want to do any of that just yet. I just want to stay here with you. Wrapped in your arms and have you make steamy love to me repeatedly. Call me a damn coward. But I don't want this to be rattled by the outside world just yet. Just please hold me and let us just forget about everyone else for a little while longer.

They were sitting in the car and heading out and up to the **manse.**
The numerous reporters tried to stop the car as they pulled out of the gate. A few even tried scaling her wall. Even the police patrol had to chase another boat off that tried to sneak in.

Seems as though they had not quieted anything. They had simply stirred up the hornets' nests.

She had received so many messages; that she disregarded after Miss Ruthie. She said Pearline was over the moon that Kiah had called her name personally.

Pascal was screaming like a female. David of course wanted to have his say. She deleted all his messages. Then she blocked his ass. She wanted no more.

They called Greta and Ama. They were groggy at the start, but wide awake now.
They wanted to know if either of them had thought it through or had any reservations.
"Where the hell are you going to live Kiah?" Ama asked. Rubbing sleep from her eyes. "We sent you to the Caribbean to see your aunt. Now you are engaged! Wow I still can't wrap my mind...Steve can't even wrap his mind around it! But he says you look happier..."
"Congratulations Kiah! She is a beauty. Incredibly talented too."
"Hi Steve." Nia said. Waving to the man. He was sitting up in bed with his wife.
"Nice to finally meet you. All I have been hearing this past week is Nia this, Nia that."
"Nice to meet you too. I hope it was all good. If not, I hope you will be kind."
"It has been all good Nia. I hope he has been treating you well. Well, he treats my wife like a star, so I have no doubt he is treating you like a supernova."
"Oh, stop flirting!" She tossed over at him and kissed his cheek.
They all continued chatting until they got to the house.
Greta said she was contacted by a couple major headliners who wanted an interview. She said she would contact them later.

His parents met them on the drive. They chatted warmly with the oversees crew. They seemed like a well-blended family.
When they got inside, the aunties joined in by saying a quick hello.
After another round of hello and chit-chat they clicked off.

Dinner started after auntie K said grace. Nia's favourite: prawn pasta bake was on offer. She knew her auntie had made it specifically for her. No one does it quite the way she does. Nia would always say this.
It was the only dish her mama liked and could cook well. She taught auntie K how to prepare it.
"It is just in case." Her mama would always say. Little did she know how significant those words would become in their lives.
There was toss salad, roasted chicken, potato salad, macaroni and cheese; his mom baked. Southern style she said. She had even sprinkled paprika over it just like most islanders did theirs.
She also made corn pie. Nia liked it. They had steaks as well.
They ate in the comfy dining room area that was partitioned to accommodate them. It gave a lovely view of the rose garden.
Most still grew quite lovely even around this time of the year.
As a girl she liked to see them strolling, or out cutting stems for the tables inside.
The dining table posed elegantly with the two lovely vases of white and pink roses sitting in the middle.

Silcott; hugged her and whispered congratulations in her ear. He asked her if she was happy. She told him she was. He winked over at Kiah and gave him a thumb's up.

Terrence and William joined them at the table. They were family. Elena and Denton seemed to treat them like their sons as well.

"What are we doing this week?" Denton asked Kiah. "You can't stay cooped up indoors all week.

"Can't I dad? I seemed to recall you telling me you and mom did just that one time. That I wasn't here by immaculate conception."

"Boy watch your mouth around the table." His dad tossed. Then he whispered to him, "we didn't watch any television either."

"Denton honey don't scare Nia." Elena tossed winking over at her. "Tell me Nia I hope my son doesn't disappoint?"

"Good God mom! Talk about scaring her!"

"No, he doesn't Miss Elena, I mean mom." Nia added popping a piece of pasta bake in her mouth. Which was true. She loved the hell out of her son. And if truth be told. It was carnal every time she laid her eyes on him.

"But seriously son. Let's do something. I miss you. Guys what do you say?"

"Sounds like a plan dad. We could go scuba diving. Nia has a friend. We can probably meet up."

"From my recollection this island has some greet reefs along the coast. Nia do you scuba dive?"

"Absolutely not! I don't do water like that sir."

"You don't?" He sounded flabbergasted.

"No sir."

"Denton please leave her alone. Each of us has the things we don't like. Plus, I hear Nia will be very busy won't you dear?"

"Yes, our festival village opens this Wednesday afternoon. The choir is singing, and we will be presenting some of our costumes for the kiddies' carnival. By the way will you be joining us to play mass this year? Kiah has already signed himself and the guys up."

"I will be honoured. I mean **we** will be honoured. What will we be presenting?"

"Dressed as, you mean!" Nia said. Laughter escaping. "We will all be birds of paradise that has evolved because of the impact we are imposing on our planet and the island."

"Interesting." Denton said. "I never pictured myself as a bird."

"Too late sweetie. You've already signed us up. So, we are in her hands."

"You always like to preen dad. Just think what a beautiful peacock you will make."

"Yeah, keep being a crow over there on your branch. I will show you how to shimmer." He shimmied like a peacock.

Laughter broke out around the table. Nia had forgotten how she loved the simple dinners.

"Silcott will you be joining us? Let's make it a family affair." Nia teased.

"Count me in." The man said. "But make sure I am an Oriole."

"The national bird right Nia?"

"You're right Kiah." Nia said. "Auntie K you will be presenting, aren't you?
"Yes, I will! I will be presenting a check to a very well deserving recipient
from the Rotary Club."
"Do you know who the lucky recipient will be?"
"You know I don't Nia. Plus, even if I do, I can't tell."
"Spoil-sport!" Nia tossed. "But I hope it goes to a very worthy recipient."
"We hope so too." Auntie B said. Knowing full-well who was chosen and
was so thankfully to Kiah for the huge influx that was infused. Even as they
sat there, many things were in the works.
Kiah truly wanted it all to be ready for her birthday. His parents had
asked what he wanted for his birthday. He had simply told them to
donate to her causes.

Giving thanks; this was done after they ate their mains and just before
dessert was served. They would each take a turn in saying what they were
most thankful for, for the past week.
It was a ritual in the manse household; To never take for granted the
kindness of the Creator. Take everything as an immense honour.
Auntie K started. "I give thanks for my love. She has made me so incredibly
happy these past few years. From the moment we met. Many still to this
day didn't understand why she chose me, and chose to live here on our
little island, giving up so much. But I give thanks that she did, and that she
chose us, and our girl, and so much more, and has never once said she
regretted making those decision." She bent and kissed Auntie B and
reached out for Silcott's hand as well. Then she opened her fist, and said,
"B sweetheart would you do me the honour?"
"Of what K?" She asked. Too busy wiping tears from her eyes. She hadn't
looked at auntie's opened palm where a ring lay nestled calmly.
Auntie K gestured to it. She took one look and sprang up from her seat.
She threw her arms around auntie's neck.
"K darling! Are you sure?"
"As my love has been for you from the moment, I laid eyes on you."
"Then my answer is yes! Yes K! Yes!"
"Those upstarts over there stole my thunder." Auntie K laughed. "My dear
boy I may not be able to recite Maya. That was brilliant by the way. I
totally loved it. Well done. But after last night, I don't ever want you to
doubt how much I treasure you, my darling. Because you mean the
absolute world to me."
"Ooh, sweetie I love you so very much."
"And I you." She kissed her lips. "I love you so very much."

It was Nia's turn after the excitement abated.
"I give thanks for everyone around this table. I know it is not easy at times
loving and caring for me. My mind runs ahead, and my tongue plays
catch-up, and let's not forget my crazy temper. But I thank God for your
love and care. I most especially give thanks for Kiah..."

The tears came. "Thank you, God, for saving his life... Thank you for saving him just for me. For creating him just for me. Thank you, mom Elena and dad Denton, for nurturing him that he can daily teach me, and in turn show me what a great love should feel like and be like. Thank you, God, for my aunties, and for Silcott: who has cared for me, and my brother Seba and our May, no less than he would his own children."

She pictured May's face and again prayed for her safety like she did every day.

"Thank you for sneaking Kiah down to my house even though you knew those two would be so angry."

Everyone laughed and the aunties wagged their fingers at him.

"Thank you for William and Terrence and all the guys who put their lives on the line to make sure we are all okay. I was very resistant at first, but I thank you for daily taking care of me, and all those that I love. Most especially for bringing Kiah back safely to us. Thank you for my ring, and thank you so much for our eclectic life... Ooh, and thank you for his parents accepting me... I thought they would take one look and think what the hell did our son got himself into? But they have accepted me, and I thank you for that."

"Thank God it wasn't that hellion Jordanna!" His dad said. "He was crazy for a while. But thank God he woke up and came to his senses." The man finished.

"Amen." His mom said before they swallowed her up in hugs and kisses.

"C'mon now. No more tears." Auntie B said through hers.

"This is prayer time. Let us give our God all the praise." Auntie K said.

It was Kiah's turn. "I give thanks for my life. More so when I was staring down the barrel of a gun and thought I would never see the faces of everyone around this table...But more so for this beautiful woman. I thank you God that I was given another chance to wake up beside her, close my eyes and sleep beside her... Nia knows what I am speaking about. I thank you for the arms that she extends each time to hold me and caress me... I am sorry mum and dad... aunties... But when I am in her arms, I feel safe and strong." Kiah said flicking at a tear that had escaped.

"Preach it!" Auntie K said. "Speak your truth!"

"Oh baby!" His mom said going over and kissing the top of his head.

"I thank God for you mom that you have never given up on pops. Thank you pops for loving the hell out of this beautiful woman. She has taught me how to love this woman. Aunties thank you for keeping her wrapped for me so I can unwrap her myself. Loving each nuance of her uniqueness. You are one hell of a woman Nia. I thank God for the strength and the ability to show you just how much I treasure you. I pray for his protection most to show you daily just how much I love you."

"Kiah!" Her tongue ran off with her because she felt the intensity of his words. Her hands came up to cup her mouth. She had forgotten how wonderful it felt to be loved in its infinitesimal measure. Kiah fell to his knees before her.

"Are you ok sweetheart?"

"Yes." She whimpered. "Thank you for loving me so incredibly."

"I thank God for you, my Nia."

"I treasure you Hezekiah Corrington. You bring me so much joy."

"Mom...Dad...This is how she greets me every morning. Since I've met her again."

"What do you mean by **again** son?" His parents asked. Even the aunties looked with confusion to him.

"She was the girl I saved all these years ago on the island."

"What! You mean? No! You mean?" They pointed to her.

"Yes mom. She is the girl that has haunted my dreams ever since."

"Oh my God!" They all chorused. A pin could have been heard hitting the floor after Kiah said what he did.

"You mean Nia was... is that girl?" Elena asked. As she recalled the hideous sounds her child made whenever he drifted off to sleep. She had even allowed him to sleep with the light on in his room. She would sit in a chair just to be there to offer him comfort when he woke thrashing and screaming. A couple times he had wrapped his hands around her neck. He had kicked her in the gut. Leaving bruises to compensate.

Even his dad didn't come away unscathed.

They had sent him to therapy; it worked for a while, then it started again. She was slightly relieved when he started sleeping away from home. But until she heard the key in the door her rest was never easy.

Her thoughts were consumed with prayers for her son. She placed him in God's hands every moment she got. It had become as easy as breathing. Most times she woke with a start and thought today would be the day for sure when she would receive the call to say they had arrested her beloved. Her hand came to rest on her heart, and she touched his face.

"I'm okay now mom. I can sleep."

"Oh my God son! You can sleep through the night and not?"

"Yes mom. I can."

"Thank God. Thank God. Thank God." They all chorused.

Bea and K had also forgotten about the incident. Something always came up that was more important to talk about.

That was a major life changing event that had been wrapped up and somehow put neatly away.

Elena decided she would give thanks next. "I thank you God that my son can sleep...Oh God! I give you thanks that my son is finally at peace when he rests. I thank you for his great love. I thank you for the great son that he is. I thank you for keeping him safe. For watching over him while he was in danger. I thank you that we have our baby. I also thank you for my great love..." She reached for her husband and kissed him. For she too had fallen head over heels with him the moment she had laid eyes on him in her studio that day. She has loved him through it all ever since.

"I give thanks for our new daughter. For the peace she has bought to our son..." She kissed the girl's cheek and placed her hand in her son's.

"Continue to bless their union and allow them to always bring out the best in each other. I thank you for all the wonderful things they will accomplish together with your help." She kissed their hands together. "I thank you for Bellot who has always been there for me and my family. I thank you for providing her with such a great love and for their beautiful life. Thank you for allowing us once again to be a part of it."
"Thank you, God... Amen." Chorused about the room.

Denton spoke. "I thank you for my family and for the many things they have taught me. The biggest ones are tolerance, forgiveness and integrity. Since meeting this gorgeous woman, she has brought me absolute joy. We have had bumpy patches, but I thank you God she stayed the course. She gave me my son in whom I have been really pleased. As you have blessed him, he has blessed us, and so many others. I thank you for sparing his life this week. Man! God you are one awesome so and so!" He raised a fist in gratitude.

William went next. "I thank you for all the wonderful people we have met these past few days here on this beautiful island. Meeting you, Miss Nia; you are an incredible woman. I have been praying about meeting one like you and being just as good to her as my boss is to you."
He blinked over at her. "By seeing how you love this guy. Man! I haven't seen him this pumped in an awfully long time. So, I thank you for being such a massive presence in his life. Our lives." He raised his glass to her.

"Same here." Terrence said next. "Boss is happy. I like that. I thank God that we can continue to support him in all the ways he needs us to."

It was Silcott's turn. "I thank you God for a different kind of love." He offered as he looked from one auntie to the other. He squeezed their hands under the table
To the outside world, many still think loving in the way they do was strange, an abomination. They would cast aspersions. Hell, they already did. But after years of cultivating; meditation and prayers, as well as manoeuvring through everyone's expectations and even their own... He had grown to love them with a fierceness.
So, he continued, "I give thanks for all the females here. They sure are a complicated bunch. Yet , yet so soft, and still so strong. So, for great love I give thanks. These two came along when I needed them most. I have never regretted a single moment. I have met all kinds. But I am eternally grateful for meeting these two who has allowed me to be a part of their daily lives. As well as their families. I thank you God for all Mister Kiah has done for everyone here in this house. He is an inspiration."
He raised his glass to them...Then to Kiah and Nia; he winked over at her. He thought of May and wondered how the girl was doing. They were daughters to him because of the two females in his life. Not to forget Sebastin, that crazy ball of twine. He smiled easily.

311

"We give God thanks for you too Silcott. For you continuing to love us so purely." The aunties said and blew him kisses.
"I think we had better get ready for dessert, or we will all be sitting here crying for the rest of the night." Elena interrupted.
"Let's adjourn to the drawing room." Auntie B said and rang the bell.

Just before they walked into the room the lights came on. Then the aunties and his mum and dad started to sing...
"Happy Birthday..."
Martha and Margaret; two of the household stood next to a table with an assortment of desserts and a cake with burning candles.
When the song was nearly over his mom led them over to the table...
"Make a wish Hezekiah and you as well Nia."
Kiah pulled her along and they made their wishes and blew out the candles while the others took pictures.
They chatted and laughed and reminisced about past birthdays.
It seemed as though Kiah was always overindulging his parents, but he never allowed them to reciprocate.
"He is always away in Bali, Hawaii...Someplace all on his own seeking." Denton said hugging him happily.
"I don't need to seek anymore. I found what I was looking for." He reached over and kissed her.
"So, what will you be doing tomorrow on your birthday?"
"You don't really want to know mom."
"Of course, I do. Tomorrow is your birthday son."
"Spending every moment with this beautiful woman."
"You get it now Elena? A chip off the old block, right? Remember how we spent my 50th birthday on Martha's Vineyard, and no one saw us for days?"
"Denton!" His mom feigned alarm.
"He's an adult. If he wants to spend his day with his best girl so be it. Silcott will take us into town, and we will explore for a bit. Leave him be. Let him enjoy his birthday." He winked over to his son.
"Then how about you dance with your mom then Kiah. For old time's sake?" Elena rose and waited for auntie B to put some music on.
Nia watched as Kiah danced with his mom. They danced a combo of a waltz and a fox trot... Apparently it was their warmup dance back in the day. She had created it.
She was so giggly and carefree with her son who indulged her. When they were finished, she collapsed on her husband, and joined everyone in the clapping.
"Twinkle-toes go dance with your girl." His dad said. Kissing him. "You still got it baby. I have a treat for you later." Denton whispered to Elena and slapped her bottom.
"C'mon dad!" Kiah teased. Holding out his hand to the man who ignored him.

312

"You just make sure you fleckle yours, and I tickle mines." He dropped a big smooch on him and one on his wife.
"Come dance with me baby." Elena said pulling him up. "No complicated stuff, ok? I want to conserve my energy." "Dad, I think you had too much wine." Kiah teased. "I am always drunk on your mom's love boy." He twirled her easily. "You should know how that feels. Now go dance." His dad said to him. Giving him a wink.

They continued dancing and enjoying the rest of the evening and feasting on cake: red velvet with buttercream icing. There were also mini tartes; guava and coconut, pineapple and mamciport as well as mango. Kiah's favourite: sorrel was available. They had picked up a good amount from Miss D. She sent a couple extra bottles for them. over some. There was fruit punch along with wine and spirits.
Nia wanted to finish a couple more of the sketches at home, so she told the family she had something very important she needed to sort out. She was feeling tired too. The family said they understood. So, after accepting a hamper of goodies and amongst a flurry of hugs and kisses and congratulations, they set off.

They were home in record time. Seemed like the reporters had gone for shelter. It was raining again. The temperature had changed as well. Thankfully she had dressed earlier in a milky pink Palazzo jumpsuit that stopped at the top of her breasts. She had also brought along a rose printed **Tis the Season** scarf and tied it into a chic bolero jacket.
The jumpsuit had a matching lined knee length jacket. It was a **Mulcaire Original** that she had treated herself to when she visited Star Island earlier in the year for a Black history event called **Drumming for the Ancestors**. She was always mesmerised with hearing the beating of drums. So, when she heard the event was added she was on a flight over.
She had wandered into the woman's shop again, because she loved visiting it when she travelled over there.
It was elegantly decorated and designed just as beautiful as **Belle**.
The aunties had commented on the outfit, because they carried some pieces from the **Mulcaire** line.
Elena once again gave her gushing compliments on her impeccable eye for details.

At home Nia told Kiah she had a couple things she wanted to sort out in her work room. He asked if she needed any help. She told him she did not. She gave him a quick kiss.
"Go chill out with the boys for a change. I will demand your attention in a couple hours. Just give me this time please."
"Are you sure we are, ok?" He asked coming into the room.
"Come to think of it. We have never…"
"I know. I know" she said and kissed him with as much urgency as she felt from him. But she had to get his gifts sorted.

313

"Kiah give me some time. Shew! Go see the boys."

Couple hours later when she came out of the room. He was nowhere to be found. Not in the kitchen or even in the living room.
"Kiah? Kiah?" She called but got nothing for her efforts. She felt a tad disappointed. She had wrapped some of the sketches in a piece of white material and tied it with a blue ribbon.

She walked into the bedroom. He was fast asleep atop the bed face down wearing only his pyjama bottoms. His birthday was in twenty minutes.
Quickly she grabbed a shower and salivated as she slathered herself in tuber rose lotion then dressed in the sexiest lingerie, she had: a Brazilian cut lacy thong bodysuit in bubble gum pink with elasticised side slings and waist.
She left her braids hanging loose and applied pink lip gloss. She didn't need any of the other stuff. She had one minute to spare by the time she switched the lights off and ran back to the bedroom.
She held one of the roses at the grove of her breast. Knowing she was gagging for it. But it was all about him.
Nia began to sing after she propped her foot atop the edge of the bed.
"Happy birthday to you...Happy birthday to you..." She used the petals of the rose to gently caress his back.
"Happy birthday my love Kiah..." She continued to use the petals.
He turned... he rose up languidly and rubbed sleep from his eyes.
"Nia...?"
"Yes Handsome..." She purred as she caressed his chest with the rose.
"Happy birthday my sexy Kiah. Happy Birthday to you."
She finished perfecting a gymnast's final pose with extended arms.
He shook himself together. "You...you look...Fuck Nia!" He buried his face in her mid-section.
"Happy Birthday sweetheart." She whispered using the rose to caress his bare back. He trembled against her.
"Do you like?" she asked stepping out of his grasp. By the way how come you are sleeping? Where are the boys?"
"They retired. I was tired sweetheart, and my head was pounding."
"Does it still hurt?" She asked as she knelt before him and took his face in her hands.
"Aaah...No not anymore. Nia. You look...You smell..." He buried his lips in the crook of her neck. "Damn! I can eat you all up."
"I am yours Kiah...Happy Birthday baby."
"You are delicious." He helped her to her feet and laid her down on the bed. He trailed hot kisses all over her body. From her feet all the way to her lips. He suckled them hungrily.
"I love you so damn much, woman." He said as his fingers snaked into her and she opened invitingly to him as she moaned delightfully.

He was driving her insane from the way his eyes smouldered, to the fingers lodged deep within her.

"I want you Kiah." Nia moaned. As she eased him out of his pyjamas.

"I want you too baby." He mumbled hiking her legs high as he eased over her and slipped deep within her.

"Fuck! Fuck! Nia, you feel so good." He moaned.

"Do you like it?"

"Fuck yes! I love it!

"How much Kiah?"

"Soo fucking much Nia." He drove deeper. She moaned, locking her legs around his waist tightly.

"Then fuck me Kiah!"

"Yes baby!" He rammed deeper...deeper...

After a while he slipped out of her and flipped her. She was on all fours now. He opened her wide and licked her wet pussy and her asshole.

She squealed.

He rammed into her. He pumped wildly. He wanted to devour her heated body. He licked his thumb then massaged her asshole.

She was on fire. She screamed wildly when he inserted his thumb.

He slapped her ass a few times. She bucked. He yanked her back.

"Let me fuck you, Nia!" He begged as sweat dripped like a faulty tap.

She shrieked.

He continued the insanity. He felt like he was about to unload, so he slipped out of her front and gingerly inched into her back.

She screamed.

"Fuck! Kiah! Ooh God!" she moaned.

He picked up the pace and matched her movement. He dug deeper and deeper...deeper...

"You are so fucking tight! So, goddam delicious!" He squealed. Reaching under and sorting out her clit; massaging it sweetly applying a bit of pressure.

She howled loudly for the feeling was utterly maddening.

He knew she loved it. She had told him as much the first time he had done it. He continued the pressure using his forefinger and thumb, a couple seconds later she swelled as he inserted a couple fingers into her heated furnace.

"Kiah!" She sang his name prayerfully as they rocked like ships in a tumultuous sea.

Minutes later he felt her gushing all over him. He followed quickly behind.

They laid spent in each other's arms. "I didn't hurt you did I Nia?"

"No Kiah." She caressed his face. "You would tell me if I did, right?"

"Yes Kiah. I am a big girl."

"I just never want to do anything to hurt you. I got carried away."

He ran his hand along her flat smooth stomach. She was still wearing her bodysuit.

"I love this by the way. You looked so delicious. I got ravenous. Thank you for my present."
"That's not all." She said kissing his lips.
"I still need to unwrap this one fully Nia." He gently tugged at her lingerie.
"You do. But first I need you to open something else."
"What? These?" He asked finally getting her boobs unclasp from the sexy lace padding. He suckled each one teasingly.
Couple minutes and they betrayed her and were standing to attention again.
"Nia, I love the way your body responds to me."
"I love what you do to my body Kiah. I have never felt as horny about anyone as I do about you."
She draped her leg over him. She kissed him with as much urgency as he did her. She dug into his butt cheeks as he climbed atop her and kissed her sensuously and deeply.
"Where are your condoms?" He asked after an eternity of kissing and caressing. He didn't want to fuck her uncovered. She pointed to her night drawer.
He reached in and came out with one from a box.
"You are so beautiful Kiah." She said watching as he dressed his dick. He re-joined her and slowly helped her out of the bodysuit and tossed it.
For that, she jumped on him and pushed him back on the bed and devoured his lips in her mouth. They kissed each other all over until their bodies became feverish with want.
When he entered her again, she was more than ready.
"I want to be on top Kiah." She begged as he suckled at her strained peaks.
"Only if you sing me the happy birthday song again, and slower this time." He whispered, his hands coming up to grab her ass cheeks.
"Sing Nia." He urged.
"Okay baby." She teased. "Happy...birthday...to you..."
She rode him slowly.
"Happy...birthday...to you... Happy... happy...happy birthday...to my man Kiah... Happy...birthday to...Oh God Kiah!"
"Sing Nia! Sing!" He pleaded loudly. His fingers clawing at her slippery ass.
"Happy...birthday...too..." She quickened the pace. "I can't hold it any longer Kiah!"
She rode him like a leading jockey all the way to the finish line.
They exploded together clutching desperately to each other.

After a long while, they laid chase to the bathroom, where they had a quick shower lathering up each other.
She sang him happy birthday again as he covered her in foam adoringly.
They dried and lotion, then dressed in bathrobes and sat on the bed.
She handed him the cloth wrapped parcel.
"What's this Nia?"
"Open it and see for yourself Kiah."

He pulled the bow, then set it aside and unfolded the A4 papers.
His eyes filled with tears.
"Nia, you did this didn't you?"
"Yes Kiah. I did."
"This is us on the ferry... this is me kissing you for the first time... me waking up next to you... Me overlooking Isle's Bay Bluff...Wow! Wow! Fuck Nia! I can't let anyone see this one!"
"Why? This is how I feel when you make love to me." She had sketched a picture of the two of them fucking. He was buck-naked and deep within her. They were lying on her floor atop her blanket.
"We will have to keep this in our boudoir." He kissed her. "But I love it. I love them all. They are brilliant. When did you? How did you?" He asked pointing at the sketches.
"Every chance I snuck away from you, and at the office. I finished the last two when I got home tonight."
There was one of her grooming his hair while he sat between her legs. She had done it naked as well. She did one of him laying back on the sofa only wearing his pyjama bottoms. His hand was atop his forehead.
The last one was of him, her and his daughter; she was sitting in the middle of them. He had only shown her a picture of the girl on Saturday morning when they were having breakfast.
"You have such a photogenic, not to forget vivid imagination Nia."
"Thank you, Kiah."
He dropped the papers and pushed her roughly down on the bed. He started to kiss her hungrily. She tasted the saltiness of his tears.
"Have I told you lately how much I fucking adore you Nia-Belle? My God! How did I get so fucking lucky? I am going to spend the rest of my life adoring the fuck out of you. Thank you for making my birthday so special. I love them. I love you. Everything about you." He kissed her lips.
"Let us refuel. Then I am going to fuck the hell out of you until the first ray of light scampers across the sky."

They laughed loudly as they ran towards the kitchen. They enjoyed more cake, and drank tea; for her, and strong black coffee for him.
She told him she felt like taking a walk.
"At this time Nia?" He looked to the clock. It was almost 3:00 am.
"Why not Kiah. Is there a specific time that people should walk?"
"Well come to think of it. I guess not. Where should we walk?"
"Outside my property we are gated so no one can get to us. Plus, you know Kung- Fu and I am very adept at screaming."
"Lots of other things too." He said winking over at her.
"Tease." She said kissing his lips. "Plus, I also have my trench."
"What use is your trench?"
"It is very special to me."
"Why?"
"Because Silcott gives me things to put in it."
Nia..." He looked at her strangely. "What are you on about?"

317

"Just c'mon Kiah."

"Don't we need to change out of these robes for a walk?"

"Says who? Now come on." She pulled him over to the door and pressed the button on the side by the light switch.

The white panel slipped back, and she pulled a couple trenches out from the nook. Black for him; a bit too snug but it was okay.

She chose a navy blue for herself and slipped a small black bag into the pocket. Not that she needed it. But one never knows.

Silcott's words jumped to mind. "You never know what craziness would step off that ferry to spoil our unspoilt island for Festival. Bearing grudges usually breathes nastiness in de heart of mankind."

Nia smiled, as she recalled reminding the man. "Don't forget we were voted in the top three of the **Most Safe** Islands in the Caribbean."

"That's exactly what I'm talking about. Not many like that."

"Silcott..." Nia whined.

"You need it now these crazy reporters are here." He said when he called to ask if she needed a refill.

"What is that?"

"I take it when I go for walks."

"Why?"

"You never know Kiah. I took it when I walked with you in the tunnel... and when we went to the bluff..."

"Nia!" He laughed totally flabbergasted.

"Come on Kiah." She opened the door and stepped out.

The rain had disappeared again. But it left the night air fresh and crisp; moist and tinged with earthy and heady smells.

"Isn't this just heaven on earth Kiah?" She hooked her hand in the crook of his. "Let's walk sweetheart."

They went to the end of the gate and around the expansive circular drive. That lighted up automatically as they strolled. She took him over to her mom's memorial.

"Hello mama. It's Kiah's birthday today. So, we are just out and enjoying this time together. I know you already know how much I love him."

"I love her too. So very much." Kiah interjected. "She makes me so happy. I thank you for her."

"Mama! Look! He gave me a ring!" She held out her hand. "Please bless it and bless our union. Oh, I forgot! Auntie asked auntie B to marry her last night and she said yes! So, we are both engaged mama!"

"Please ask for an extra blessing for us all." Kiah added.

"Mama as you can see, he brings me so much joy...Yes, he does. Now I know what you meant when you said I would find the one who brings me that absolute joy. He is amazing."

She brought her hands girlishly to cover her mouth. "I am finally satisfied mama. He fills me up."

"I do?" He asked pulling her to him and wrapping her up in his arms.

"Yes Kiah! Yes mama, and I am no longer made to feel ashamed of the things I want sexually. I can explore my sexuality with him and not feel inferior." She kissed him.

He kissed her long and hard. "Nia let's go inside…" He whispered to her. Let me fill you up." He continued.

"See mama." She said, giggling up at him as she kissed his lips.

"See you soon mama." She was hungry for him again.

"Nia, I want you again."

"I know. I can feel it Kiah." She snaked her hand inside the robe and massaged him gently. "You want me Kiah? Then you must catch me first!" Before he knew what was happening, she took off running.

"You little minx!" He called out running after her. He caught her just before she got to the door. He pressed her up against it and clamped his mouth over hers. He kissed her breathlessly.

"Your hands are like magic Nia." He said, "Touch me there again." He commanded breathlessly.

She did.

"Yes Nia! Fuck! Do you feel what you do to me?"

"I am making you grow Kiah. Grow for me baby."

"Yes baby! Keep doing that…He was losing the fight to hang on. Especially when she took his dick and massaged her heated crevice.

"God Nia! I want to fuck you! Yes baby…Let me fuck you Nia!" He spat the words out hotly, as he tried to push his way into her.

"No, you don't! Not yet Kiah." She rubbed him vigorously between her heated furnace, getting even more excited as she listened to him beg and strained to disobey.

"Please Nia…Please…Please…" He begged. He felt like he was going insane.

She eased up on her toes and extended her leg slowly upwards.

"Then fuck me Kiah." She purred. Taking a ballerina stance with her agility. It drove him over the edge.

He dove into her before she could finish. He was like a starving madman finally given permission to eat food. He devoured her maniacally.

When he exploded inside her she was certain her body would snap in half. She held unto him weakly. He bore her up.

"You drive me insane Nia." He panted. They collapsed against the door. "You are magical."

"Just like you Kiah."

After another couple minutes they hobbled inside, and grabbed water from the fridge, took long gulps, switched off the lights and shuffled to the bedroom.

Nia tossed her trench and robe and flopped unto the bed. He followed suit and came to join her.

"Sweetheart your man must be getting old. I am truly shattered." He moaned as he reached for the covers and brought it up to cover them.

"I have to agree Kiah." She teased.

319

"You little minx!" He said and pulled her body over to his. She squealed with delight. He could feel Johnson trying to rear its head. But he knew they would not get far. Because the greedy bastard was truly a tad sore. Plus, he was totally wiped out.

"Truth be told I am too Kiah." She stifled a yawn. "Can I grab an IOU?" She felt him kiss her neck as they spooned. He brought his leg up and draped her.

"Thank you for a wonderful birthday, Nia. Best by far." He offered, fighting a yawn.

"You're welcome baby." She said pressing into him.

Chapter Twelve

When she turned in bed. It was stark daylight outside. The sun was streaming through the windows. It almost hurt her eyes.
"Good morning sleepy-head." He said and kissed her neck.
She rubbed sleep from her eyes.
He kissed her again.
"Can I collect my birthday IOU now?"
"Can I have a wash first?"
"Can I join you?"
"Come on then." She tossed.
They sprang from the bed and raced towards the bathroom. She flopped down on the toilet first. He walked by and went to put the shower on. He came back and waited.
He was a glorious and remarkable sight. Her insides started to ping as little electric currents shot off.
"Happy birthday you glorious man!" She said and gestured for him to come over. When he did, she kissed his protruding dick.
"I love you." She whispered and stroked its head with her tongue.
Then she lovingly licked it as though it were an ice lolly.
He exhaled... "Fuck!" He forced himself to be still.
She bathed him deliciously with her tongue. He was so ready to unload but he didn't want to do it her mouth. After another few unbearable moments, he reached down and lifted her. He carried her towards the dressing room where he placed her atop the edge of the cold bathroom counter.
She groaned.
He hiked her legs up. "You have teased me long enough." He groaned as he pushed gently into her. She shifted; he gained deeper access as she balanced on the sink.
"Extend your legs like you did earlier Nia." He begged. It was mind blowing. She astounded him. The agility of her body was phenomenal.
She obeyed. He eased her forward and close to the edge.
He felt his body convulsed as he lurched and plunged deeper within her. He cradled her in his arms, he was almost atop her. As he delved into her as though she were a bestseller's novel. He could not get enough. He did not finish until the last word; he closed the covers as they came together maddeningly.
"Fuck Nia! You are so delicious!" He barked as he lifted her and carried her to the shower.

Before they got dressed. Nia massaged his body with her rose oil and couldn't resist the urge to kiss, lick, nip and lick his body adoringly.
She sang the first verse of **Unforgettable**...

She loved how he moaned and whimpered under the expertise of her hands. She was encouraged, so she reached for her abandoned silk scarf and used it to caress his body.

"Come with me baby." She teased. As she led him over to her makeup chair and pushed him gently unto it. She tied his hands expertly. Then she used her entire body to light a burning trail.

He exorcised the right to her name in every tone.

Her body heated like a Bunsen burner. It became the balm to his heaving chest. She rubbed him slowly, softly and ooh so rhythmically.

He whimpered. Johnson was putty once again to her tutelage.

She loved the way he blossomed and grew.

"Nia please." He pleaded as he strained in the chair she had pushed up against the counter. She rummaged in the drawer and pulled out a tube of lubricant.

"Are you ready for me baby?" She asked softly, sweetly against his ear. She kissed his quivering lips, and gently anointed his circumcised bulging dick lovingly. She was starved. She sat astride him on tiptoes.

He groaned sickeningly, especially when she moved seductively up and down his shaft as though it was a fireman's pole.

He yelped. It was magical what was happening to his body.

The slight chaffing that was annoying her body was long forgotten after she anointed him. She was ticklish from head to toe. She grabbed his sweaty form fiercely. She felt lightheaded and free.

"This is what you do to me Kiah. This is what you do." She prophesied. As she clamped him to the chair.

"Fuck me! He squealed. "Nia! Oh God! Fuck me! Please baby!"

"You want me to fuck you Kiah?"

"Yes Nia! Please...please baby!"

"Okay Kiah!" She teased "I will fuck you."

She took his dick and teased her entrance as he strained.

To support herself she used the counter as leverage and eased up on her tiptoes. Then slowly ever so slowly she eased down unto his shaft.

He groaned sickeningly. She coaxed her breast into his mouth.

"Sssssh baby." She teased as she moved slowly atop him. She loved how he felt as he bulged and strained.

He bit her breast feverishly. It intensified her movement. She rode him hard and fast.

He shrieked... She screamed...

"Ooooh God! Nia! Nia!" He cried maddeningly.

The intermingling was so intense in its explosion it caused them both to weep.

"Where did you learn to do that Nia?" Kiah asked with incredulity. As they laid splayed against each other. Thank God the chair was a friend. It bore them up.

She had totally blown his mind. Especially when one thought they had done everything else already.

Most all the crazy shit he had done. They had left him unsatisfied. But she seemed to always manage to take his body, his mind, his very soul to the heights of heaven.

At times he wished he could stay tucked deep within her. Now he knew what Prince Charles meant by that tampon-comment.

"You had Madame Ito. Well just think that I had her twin sister here on the island."

Kiah laughed. "I must thank her Nia. You blew my mind. I thought I was going to die."

"You do that to me too Kiah. I mean it." It was the naked truth. Thank God, she had found him, or she thought she would have withered and died.

She thought of the many females out there who were starving silently having not found that partner to nurture that sexual ache within them.

"You bring me joy Kiah." She said and cupped his face in her hands. "But right now, I am starving. I am suddenly ravenous for food."

"Come on let's go grab some."

Out in the kitchen the coffee was on timer. They each grabbed a steaming cup. Bless the boys she thought. They had even done a bowl of fruits with a note at the top. Nia read it aloud.

Happy Birthday Boss.
We've gone away like you asked us to do. We are taking the boat out for a while. Seba gave Rosario the day off as well. So, you two can have the house all to yourselves.
The Gang.

"So, we are alone?" Kiah asked. He came up behind her. He wrapped his arms around her. He kissed the crook of her neck. His hand wandered down the front of her baggy khaki shorts.

"According to this note." She held it up for him. "But I am hungry."

"Sustenance first then..." He released her.

"Anything I want?"

"It's your day Kiah."

"By the way I feel like a swim. Let's head down to the beach."

"Your wish is my command today." Nia said as she poured herself another cup of coffee. She ate her fruit and so did he. Then she made him toast with butter and sorrel jam.

He poured orange juice for himself. They took them out to the veranda and sat eating heartily.

"I love this, Nia. It is so peaceful out here."

"I love it too Kiah, and I love being here with you. Are you enjoying your birthday?"

"So damn much. I am thinking of... God Nia. I want you again. I am being greedy."

"You have my permission Kiah." She gave him her lips. "Do you know how much I have prayed for a day just like this? So now I am aiming to enjoy it."

323

"Do you not ever say what you are thinking?" He laughed.
"Do you Kiah?"
"Absolute truth when it comes to you."
"Ditto Kiah." She munched her toast and crossed her legs. "I would love to see us this way when we are old and grey. Even though I am trying to picture you old."
Kiah laughed out loud. He dropped the toast and pulled her atop his lap. "Picture this Nia. Even if I am old and grey, I will still find a way to fuck you. Make no mistake." He buried his face in her ample bosom.
"Eh Eh! Old people don't have no have sex! Do they Kiah?" She asked laughing her head off.
"We will! Even if I must balance on my cane woman! I will be paying attention to your glorious body. I wish we could swap so you can feel how delectable your body is to me Nia."
"Bless you Kiah. But I guess in some ways I do because I love when you touch me, kiss me, make love to me…and when we fuck too. It's like billions of electrical surges hit my body all at the same time. I can light up a tiny island, I am sure."
"Gosh Nia! You do drive me insane! He buried his face deeper. He kissed the place above her heart.
"Distract me a bit. Better yet, let's go grab a swim down on the beach."

They took a couple towels and beach blankets, the hamper with the cakes and tarts, bread cheese, fruits, ice bucket and drinks.
"Let's not forget this." She reached in for the leftover tray of prawn pasta bake. She popped it inside the basket.
"Looks like we are having a picnic."
"You betcha! We will grab an umbrella on the way out.

After setting up in the alcove. Kiah pulled her along. The water was very inviting, no wild swells breaking, only welcoming babies lapping to the shore.
There was also no prying eyes; reporters. One boat skipped by but way out not to intrude. She believed it was the police patrol or the guys, because their boat wasn't there.
"Shit! In everything I forgot my swimsuit!"
"Do you really need one?" he asked slipping out of his shorts and tank.
"Suppose…You know?" She gestured out to sea. "C'mon Kiah."
"Trust me, Nia. God will not let them. Plus, we are wasting time. And you will not need one soon anyway. You are wearing a panty and a bra, yes?"
"Yes."
"Swim in them. Or you don't swim in anything. Remember it's my birthday Nia."
"Kiah!"
"You promised to obey whatever I ask."
"Shit! I really walked into that didn't I?"

324

"Plus, I saw what you were wearing so…?"

"Okay birthday boy." She shimmied out of her shorts and striptease her top. Thank God she had piled her hair up in a bun earlier. It held. She struck a pose.

"Satisfied?" She asked. He laughed loudly. God he was gorgeous. He wore black speedos.

"Keep stoking the flames, Nia!"

"Talk talk Kiah." She sashayed pass him seductively. She loved playing tease.

"You really are going to get it!" He chased after her.

She ran the length of the bay before he caught her.

"I really am off my game woman." He caught her with his hands about her waist.

They collapsed at the shore as a little wave lapped at their feet. She squealed.

"Come swim with me Nia." He said breathlessly.

They swam about for a while after she plucked up the courage to just throw it all to the wind and get on with it. She could swim so why continue to lay about in fear's arms especially when he was right beside her.

He reminded her of this when he reached out and pulled her into his arms and kissed her sweetly, gently.

She started to have so much fun.

After their swim. They laid about; wrapped in each other's arms. He could feel Johnson stomping like a cross horse. He ignored him.

Nia didn't miss the welcome. She smiled.

"Come on Kiah!" She tossed and jumped to her feet. They headed to the alcove hand in hand. There he pulled her to him and kissed her sweetly. He wanted her so very much. He lifted her in his arms.

"I want to make love to you Nia." He ground out feeling so hungry for her.

"I want you too Kiah." She said grabbing his face in her hands and burying her lips on his. "I want you so badly. I tried to be good…"

"You don't have to be Nia." He offered, wanting to bury himself deep within her. He knew she would be warm and oh so inviting.

He laid her on the blanket. He buried his tongue deep and sometimes allowed it to wander about in her mouth.

"You are driving me insane Nia." She was salty and heady.

"You do the same to me. I am on fire. I want you so much. My heart is beating so wildly in my chest Kiah." She took his hand and brought it to the spot.

"Feel mine sweetheart." He brought her hand to his heart. "I am feeling like this is my first time. I know I sound like a fucking novice. But I want to rip into you with such ferocity Nia."

"C'mon then Kiah." She said sweetly. Yanking on his shorts. Like he was yanking on her panty. They only got halfway.

"Nia I can't..." He slipped into her. He loved when she moaned in such a carnal and passionate way. He unclipped the bra. "You are so gorgeous woman!" He buried his mouth over her salty mounds. He suckled them fanatically. It was as if he couldn't get enough.

He felt almost clumsy as he fondled her like a maniac. Everywhere he touched just seemed to burn his hand. Even his body felt feverish.

"Nia I am on fire!" He pulled her up to him as perspiration seemed to pierce his body.

"Help me! Help me, Nia! Help me!"

Nia tried anchoring her body to his. It was too slippery.

She braced her hands on the blanket and arched her back.

"Baby I can't wait!" He eased in deeper, and finally got a grip on her ass. He held her firmly there like a plug and shot off like a rocket into her. He roared like the alpha wolf. He lapped and sucked at her breast as her body quickly quivered and she flowed like a river unto him.

They laid on the blanket in each other's arms. Her head resting on his beating chest. The breeze was thankfully caressing their naked bodies. She used her leg to rub deliciously against his. He kissed her sweetly. She felt satisfied and suddenly she slipped off to sleep...

Kiah spent the time on his elbow simply looking at her beautiful face and stature.

He loved that there were no enhancements; she was wearing no makeup. Her breasts; were just as subtly and pert. Her stomach: was firm not totally flat but he liked her with all her curves and edges.

He pictured her carrying his child. Tears stung the back of his eyes. He caressed the spot lovingly. She shifted.

"Kiah...?" she moaned. Her hand sought him. She snuggled her face into the crook of his neck.

"I love you so very much Nia." He whispered.

She mumbled his name again then threw her well-toned leg up and over him. He couldn't resist the urge. He ran his hands along the curve of her, all the way down to her leg. He could have sworn his body vibrated again.

He must have fallen asleep. He was having the most delicious dream... Someone was kissing him as he laid spread-eagled. She was at his waist and trailing hot wet kisses down his body, she lingered at the space between his legs...

He moaned delightedly. Johnson was dancing in abandoned delight. She was adoring his body in the most intimate of ways. She kissed, caressed, stroked and licked him gently.

He reached out, and pleaded, "please don't wake me."

Then in his mind he saw the head slowly wandered back and the mouth covered Johnson. It suckled him delicately. He breathed the only name he loved and had come to call next to his God.

"Nia!"

"Yes baby." She murmured and lifted her head.

It started when she woke and saw him asleep beside her on his back. Her breath had caught in her throat at the sight of him. She couldn't resist and reached out and touched and caressed him.

He stirred but didn't awake. She longed for him as she stared long and hard. She imagined many lifetimes; their wedding; everyone she loved was there and was happy and was wishing them wished them well.

She saw herself pregnant and sitting on the veranda as they caressed her bulging tummy and he kissed it lovingly, as he sang and told the baby stories while she ate happily.

She saw them cradling their son and putting him in his basinet. It made her weep. She reached out to caress his face. Before long she was touching him intimately. She wanted him again. He stirred but he did not wake.

"Nia...Nia..." He purred sweetly as she continued the beat on his manhood. She loved the taste of him, how he swelled to absolute perfection in her mouth.

He sang her name. His hand sorted her. He had to see. He forced his eyes open. She crawled up slowly to view...

"Nia?"

"Yes baby." She purred softly. Johnson greeted her opening.

He begun to behave impertinent. She spoilt him by easing him into her. He waited for just a little to be fed while she moved suggestively and very succinctly. She clamped him sweetly using her Kegel muscles. It brought him up in a seated position.

"Do that again Nia!"

"So, you are awake now?"

"Please!" He begged. She happily obliged.

He groaned sickeningly. He clamped unto her breast. He ate one hungrily. Grabbing at the other. She loved it. Her fingernails went to his back.

"Nia!" He bellowed. He buried his in her ass cheeks and swallowed the other nipple into his mouth.

She clamped Johnson again. He got mad. He sliced into her for a couple minutes. Kiah was going insane as Johnson was being reprimanded.

He flipped her for a perfect view as the fight continued.

He slapped her ass as he pumped into her; Johnson sought revenge as he plunged deep.

"Kiah! Kiah! Kiah!" She called out carnally.

His hand continued the torture ever so often as Johnson dug deeper. She regaled his name loudly. It spurred him on. He wasn't ready to end the game. He forced himself to slow down. Then he eased out.

"Please..." She pleaded her head thrashing from side to side.

"Not yet Nia. Not yet baby."

"Please Kiah!" She turned. "Please..." She begged tears sliding from her eyes.

"Okay baby." He helped her unto the blanket. "Okay"

327

He slipped back into her easily and started slowly. She wrapped her arms and legs tightly around him. He swore her body was like magic. He swallowed her lips. She matched him stroke for stroke.
Their bodies were dancing in unison. Making loud noises. She loved it. She released him and splayed her arms and legs. He ground deep, deep, and deeper.
He sang her name on his lips. He begged for strength. He did not want it to end as he rode her ferociously now. He hiked her legs up and pressed into her. He was in a trance and so was she it seemed, as she purred prayerfully just above a whisper. Then she locked her arms into the crook of his and anchored him. It spurred him on. He gushed like a geyser inside her and felt her heavily explode all over him.

He laid on top of her totally spent. She bore him up. "I love you so much Kiah." She whispered in his ear. Her fingers making tiny imprints in his back. "Sex with you is always so mind-blowing. You set my soul on fire."
"You complete me, Nia." He spoke his truth. "It's as if I cannot get enough of you woman. Nia, I totally adore you."
"And I you Kiah." She said and kissed the top of his head as his breathing caressed the peak of her breast. "It's as if my body was made for you and only you."
"I swear I feel the same way, Nia." He managed to ease on his elbows. "At times I get so greedy. I am so sorry baby. I just wanted to devour you whole. I tried to savour each moment, but I just get ravenous."
"I love you." Nia said kissing his lips. She felt like her heart would burst right through her chest each time she looked at him, touch him, and have him touch her. He lit her body from the inside when he entered her. She kissed him again.

He managed the strength to roll off her. They lay looking up into the semi darkness. As the beginning of the evening started to creep in.
"Come swim with me Nia." He sat up. "Nothing will happen. I will take care of you." He extended a hand. He pulled her up. "Come on Nia." She was up. They ran to the water's edge. They splashed each other for a bit. Then they ventured in. The water was like a balm especially when it covered their chest.
"It's so beautiful here." He said pulling her to him. They stayed that way for a very long time. She even chanced extending her legs and splashing. She was so gorgeous. He thanked God for the umpteenth time today.
"Kiah I am hungry." She uttered. "Let's go get something to eat."
"Ok sweetheart. I'm hungry too."

They left the cool water and walked back to their hideout. They prepared plates and ate what they had in the hamper. Every piece of it before they said their first word. Then they packed up and put the empty stuff back into the hamper. They snuggled up and laid back in each other's arms and pulled the blanket up to cover their waist, as they stared off into the horizon.

It was a great day they concluded. She couldn't remember the last time she had done something like that.
"We haven't looked at our mobiles today, Kiah. Do you realise this?"
"I know. I didn't want to. I just wanted to be with you."
"What if something happened?"
"Like what Nia? Don't you think they would have found us by now?"
"Just let's finish the day together. I want to sit with you until late into the evening."
"Anything else Kiah?" She asked sweetly looking up at him.
"You little minx! I will do that again. Trust me."
"I had a dream earlier." She wanted to share it with him. She hated waking.
"Want to tell me what it was about?"
"I dreamt of us. I dreamt we got married, we had a baby. A boy..."
"Nia, I pray God grant us this someday. I came to a comfortable place earlier in my life, but since meeting you and falling in love with you I pray for possibilities."
Truth be told that was his wish when he blew out the candles on the cake. He would be satisfied if he blessed them with one. He would be eternally grateful. He kissed her forehead.
"Me too Kiah. I have allowed fear to hold me back for far too long in my personal life. Not anymore."
Her wish on those candles was to live truthfully, to push fear away and embrace her authentic self. Help her to face whatever the universe throws at her. Knowing; believing that whatever it is he would not ever give her any more than she could bear.
She reached for his hand and pulled them tightly around her.
"Let's keep believing in possibilities Kiah. Yours and mine. Let's not block our blessings."
"I hear you sweetheart."
"Today was a good day Kiah."
"Best birthday ever Nia!"
"Did you get anything you wanted?"
"Everything and then some. I wanted a day of no interruption with my best girl, and I got it. I got some beautiful sketches that I will treasure until my last breath. I love that you incorporated Jourgette into our lives. That meant the world to me Nia. It just proves to me what a special person you are."
"Thank you, Kiah. By the way I am planning to go back to the office tomorrow. I am not going to allow those people to stop me any longer. We have nothing to hide. The sooner we talk to them then I figure they will get tired and leave us alone."
"I understand Nia. But unfortunately, that is not how it works with the press. But like you say we can't hide out forever. I did promise mom and dad to

do something with them. We could probably meet up for lunch if that's ok?"

"Sounds like a plan." Nia said and reached for her glass and swallowed the rest of her passionfruit juice.

"Are you ready for us to head up? I feel like I need a nice warm shower."

"Can I join you?"

"Of course, you can! You know I love being with you."

Creatures scurried about in the bushes as they picked their way up to the house.

They switched the lights on and sorted the hamper as they listened to their messages.

Georgie called and left her a girlie one: she gushed about her day with William. They had lunch, and he treated her so incredibly special.

He even bought her flowers, and a stuffed animal for London. She had such an amazing time.

"I think I have fallen madly in love with him."

Kiah received calls from so many people. But he decided to call Jourgette after he listened to her lovely voice singing him happy birthday.

Her mum picked up. She switched to video.

"Happy Birthday Kiah. How are you?"

"I am good. How are you two doing?"

"We are good too. But your daughter is chomping at the bit."

"Then put her on."

"Hello daddy!" The child called out after a couple seconds. "How are you?"

"I am fine sweetheart. How are you?"

"I'm doing fine. But I miss you daddy."

"I miss you too pumpkin." He said tearing up a bit.

"Where are you again?"

"I am in the Caribbean. I am visiting Emerald City remember?"

"Like in the Wizard of OZ?"

"Just like that sweetheart."

"How is Nia?"

"She is fine. Want to say hello?" He motioned her closer.

"Hello Jourgette. How are you?" Nia asked loving the child's little cherub face.

"I am fine. Did you have a party for daddy?"

"Not today. But we are having one on Saturday."

"Can I come?"

"Of course, you can. I am sure daddy can arrange something."

"Mommy can I go to daddy's party?"

"We...we..." Jasmine stammered. She did not plan to.

"I will speak to Ama. You can take the Lear into Antigua. I will organise something from there over. Sorry Jasmine. It wasn't planned."

"Well at least they can get you tied down to something. It is a big one this year."

"I know. Mom and dad are here on the island. Just let Ama know which day you want to fly in. It's a barbecue at my auntie's."

"So, are we going to see daddy?"

"Guess so sweetheart. Perhaps we will spend Christmas with him. Is that ok Kiah?

"Thank you, Jasmine!" He felt his eyes well up again.

"Kiah you are her dad."

"Thank you. Mom and dad will be so excited."

"I can see you are too. By the way congratulations on your engagement."

"Thanks Jasmine."

"You know who is not happy? She is fit to be tied."

"Who is fit to tie momma?"

"Let's not worry about that. Why don't you go pick out a pretty dress for daddy's party? We will spend Christmas with him as well."

"Yippee! Yippee!" The child squealed. "I will be with daddy after all. Thank you, thank you so much mama!"

"Jourgette! Jourgette! Pick one with lots of bows. You know daddy loves your bows."

"A pink one daddy?"

"Yes baby. A pink one with bows. I love you. See you soon?"

"Yes daddy! I love you too. See you soon! Bye Nia!"

"Bye sweetheart." Nia said as she watched the child run off.

"Kiah. She is not happy. I am just saying, ok?"

"Got you Jasmine. I will see you soon. Don't worry about Jordanna. She will be over it soon."

"I don't think so. Just watch your back please. You know how ridiculous she can get when she feels backed into a corner?"

"Ok Jasmine. See you guys soon."

When Kiah hung up Nia looked questioningly at him. "Do we need to worry Kiah?"

"Don't worry about Jordanna Nia. Plus, it is still my birthday I don't want to spoil what little time is left talking about her."

He reached for her and pulled her to him. "You still owe me a shower."

He did not mention to Nia that she had been calling and leaving him stupid messages. The last was borderline crazy. Threatening even.

They washed each other; more like used their tongue like animals. He made her scream for the onslaught she delivered to Johnson in the shower. He reciprocated in turn. She was whimpering by the time he allowed her to put her leg back on the floor.

They applied lotion to each other's body and ended up fucking hard and fast collapsing on the dressing room floor. By the time they crawled into bed they were totally spent. Neither knew when the other fell asleep.

331

Chapter Thirteen

The next time they opened their eyes it was nearly light outside. A quick kiss and cuddle, then a trip to the bathroom; toileting and brushing their teeth.

They were back and chose to sit on the floor for meditation and prayer. They then headed outside for stretches and a couple laps around the grounds. By the time they got back to the house and had a cup of coffee and started breakfast. They were ready to face the world.

The guys wandered in. Seemed like they too had been out for their daily exercise. They were wearing short jogging bottoms and tank when they came in via the dining room door. They said good morning and asked Kiah if he'd had a great birthday.

He thanked them for being discreet yesterday and giving them time together.

Turned out Terrence, Onrey and Russell went fishing. They claimed they got lucky; they caught a couple snappers and tilapias, lobsters and crabs in their free diving. They said they bagged them and placed them in the freezer.

"Hope you sorted them before you put them away?"

"Yes Ma'am. I mean Miss Nia." Terrence offered.

"By sorting I mean cleaned, gutted and sliced. I am not doing any of that stuff."

"Yes Miss Nia. We sorted all of that."

"Well, I do hope so or you guys are going to be in big trouble" She said her hands akimbo on her hips.

They all laughed. Kiah copied her. "Big trouble." He comically tossed.

"I mean it. I am not operating on fish. The only thing I cut is style and fashion."

"We hear you." They laughed out loud. "But yes, we did all of that. We parcelled them in bags as well. We are fishermen Miss Nia."

"Wow! Colour me impressed. By the way I am suddenly in the mood for some good fish broth. Let me call Rosario and ask her to stay off at the market and get us some green bananas, some peppers, celery and okra. Then I can whip some up when we get home later."

"That sounds good Miss Nia."

"William how is our Georgie?"

"She is well Miss Nia. I stopped by to see her."

"I know. She called." Nia said and winked to him. "I also would like to head to the office today... I have been away for far too long. Don't give me that look either. There comes a time when I must face this head on. I am not turning back. Plus, I did nothing wrong. We did nothing wrong."

"We've got your backs with whatever you decide."

"We will be heading out soon. The aunties will be getting ready to leave home in a couple of hours." Dimitri said finishing his coffee.
"Mom and dad should be meeting us in town today. I was hoping we could grab lunch and a chat. Perhaps at the mariner."
"Sounds like a plan. We will check in when it's decided. We will see you later."
They finished and said their goodbyes and were off.

Nia and Kiah took another cup of coffee and headed out to the veranda. They called the manse. Everyone wanted to know how his birthday was.
"It was out of this world." He gushed. Winking over at her.
"What did you two do?"
"What didn't we do?"
"That's my boy!" His dad enthused. They had a good laugh.
Nia reminded him to tell them about Jourgette and Jasmine. He did.
"They are flying in for the barbecue on Saturday. I am awaiting word on what day they would come. "
"Sounds great." The aunties said. Everyone was delighted.
They concluded it was no trouble having the extra guests at the manse. The more the merrier. They were looking forward to finally meeting the two in person. Meeting at the mariner was the plan.

Nia dressed in a navy-blue suit and white silk top. She chose black kitten heels. They complimented the outfit. She braided and bun the braids and created a beautiful chignon.
Kiah clipped her diamond necklace in place, and she slipped her ring and bracelet on her finger and hands. One more dab of powder to her face and lip gloss to her lips and she was ready.
"You look gorgeous Nia." Kiah said. "Are you ready to slay dragons?"
"With you by my side. You betcha! You look gorgeous as well." She said and kissed his lips.
He was wearing grey flat front trouser and white buttoned top. He had the jacket for later. His feet were encased in white loafers. He wrapped her up in his arms.
"You bring me joy Kiah."
"You bring me joy too Nia."

When they left the house a couple reporters were waiting by the gate. They snapped photos of them. Kiah held her proudly and they walked closer to give them a better shot.
After their meditation they reasoned to just get on with their lives because they had done nothing wrong. And why should they continue to be prisoners? So, they telephoned Indiria and informed her they would give a short press conference outside **Belle** at 11:00 am when Nia was free.
Well, she was not about the silly. Because people were hounding the shop. From locals to visitors along with these many reporters.

Seba told them business was grand, and things kept flying off the shelves. So, she figured they should head in and see for themselves.

Greta called to relay some information. Nia learnt she was also Jordonna's agent. She said that media giants such as **Sky, CNN, NBC, and CBS**... wanted interviews.
They were planning to pay a shitload of money. He told her he would deal with that later. She also told him the titbits about Jordanna; she kept calling and had even threatened.,
"The psycho is in Miami finishing a photo shoot. She would then be heading to the Caribbean; Barbuda to shoot a commercial. She had thrashed her hotel room and had to pay a fine to prevent her going straight to jail."
Kiah promised he would keep an ear as well as an eye out. He mentioned it to the fellas. He also reminded them he did not want to discuss anything to do with her in the presence of Nia.

Nia was super happy to see her shop again. She got a bit teary when they pulled up outside it.
"I can see you are happy to be back." He opened his arms to her after unclipping his seat belt.
"So happy Kiah." She closed her sketch pad and crawled into his arms. "I am sorry that it seemed like I was ignoring you."
"Not at all. It gave me some time to take care of some work." He gestured to his computer. He stuffed it in the sleeve pocket of the seat. It was flat and sleek.
"Thank you, Kiah. I truly missed this." She kissed his lips. She saw a couple workers. "Do you mind if I get out now. I just want to say hello, then go open my shop for a change."
"You go ahead Nia. You go do your thing." He urged; thankful he could have some time with the guys.

Nia stepped out when William opened the door to her. She spotted Georgie and called out to her.
The woman turned and ran towards them. They embraced, as did all the other females who spotted her and came over. Even the security team for the shop. Amelda, Marilyn and Lucille. They all came over to greet and congratulate.
Nia felt a tear slid from her eyes. "I've missed you guys." She offered. Hugging them tight.
"We missed you too boss."
"Then let's get in and get some work done."
"Are you sure boss? Because those reporters have been relentless."
"Which is why we decided to face it head on. I am tired of being a prisoner in my home and on my island. This is my land not theres."
"Amen boss."

Seba broke the silence with his loud music as usual. He screamed from his lowered window.

"BIATCH! BIATCH!"

He stopped his truck in the middle of the private space and jumped out.

"Girl it is so good to have you back!" He picked her up and twirled her.

"You are a sight for sore eyes."

"I missed you guys too. So very much."

"Like we did you."

"Seba, can I open? It just feels like I have been gone for forever."

"You go right ahead. You do you." He placed her on her feet, gave her the keys, and gestured; lead the way.

"Thank you Seba." She did not miss the group who was clicking away like crazy with their cameras in the far corner.

"Glad those fools are listening. We had to tell them to stand over there and stop blocking the customers from coming in." Amelda said.

Nia thanked them all, then led the way to the door.

"You can go see him." She whispered over to Georgie. She didn't wait to be asked twice. She took off running.

Nia inserted the key, and the shutter went up. She marvelled in the sound. Her heart pitter-pattered in her chest.

"Are we ready to start the day team?"

"Yes, we are boss-lady!" They chorused.

The doors slid back, and she watched them walk in.

They all stood looking up at the ceiling. Nia raised her hands to the heavens. Her beat loudly in her chest. She could hear it. Because time hadn't stood still. The shop was already decorated. Taken straight out of the 2016 Christmas sketches. She did it each year.

This year the decorations and theme were silver and white. She had designed a few birds; she wanted nesting or perched in flight. She had discussed it during staff meeting before she left on holiday. Now they had brought it all to life. Seba added huge orb balls in silver white and red with reams of green garland.

"You like boss lady?" Seba asked. Draping his hand across her shoulders. "

"Oh gharm! Oh gharm! I love it!" Nia shouted. Then she started singing **it's beginning to look a lot like Christmas.** Georgie joined in.

When they finished, she asked. "Seba when did you find the time?"

"I did it on Sunday with Graham and the boys. Finishing touches were done last night when everyone left."

"Remind me to put something more in his envelope."

"You say that every year sis. You do it without being reminded."

"Thank you for being here when I could not." She threw her arms around him.

"Should I be jealous?" Kiah joked.

She released Seba and turned to hm. "Never."

"Thank God." He laughed. "It is beautiful and festive in here Nia."
"Seba and the team did it."
"This is all her idea. She designs how she wants things done every year."
"That she does. She told us her vision and firmed it up before she left on holiday. We simply just followed through." Georgie said to him. "She has such a brilliant mind."
"That she does." Kiah said. He held up her bags. She took them.
"I will let you get on with your day. I have occupied enough of your time. I will be back for the press. In the meantime, Onrey and Russell will be here. Don't let her out of your sight, got it?"
He had already briefed them on the contingency plan concerning Jordanna. He knew how reckless she could be. He would have stayed, but he didn't want to distract or take time away from her getting back to business.
He also wanted to check in with the workers on that special project. It must be sorted by the time her birthday came around. It was great that money could do so much. Get ticklish things expedited speedily.
So, he kissed her one last time.
"Oohs and aahs." Echoed about the room.
Nia did not care. This was her man, and she was not ever going to kick her blessings in the teeth. So, her hands tightened about his neck.
"I love you Kiah Corrington. You bring me so much joy."
"I love you too Miss Nia." His eyes never left hers.
His hands encircled her waist tightly. "You bring me joy too. Now off to work you go. I will see you in a couple of hours."
He didn't miss the clicking of the lenses in the back. Because she had followed him to the door and kissed him one last time.

When they left. She closed it. Staff could come through the smaller doors using their code. They weren't ready to be opened yet.
Staff meeting was brief; Nia apologised for being truant and told them she would make it up to them. They congratulated her; concerning her engagement and came over to exam the ring closer.
After a joyous inspection from all. She informed them of the press conference she and Kiah would be holding outside at 11:00 am.
She told them it was just to set the record straight and hopefully bring about some peace.
"That doesn't seem likely Miss Nia. The more they get is the more they will want." Amelda interjected. "One even offered me $20.00 US for some info."
"What did she want to know?"
"She asked me when next you would be in the office... But that was after I took her money. I told her maybe never."
They all laughed heartily.
"So, you are twenty US heavier." Seba stated.
"You betcha!" Amelda laughed. "I ain't no fool. Lesley needs a pair of Jordon's for Christmas."

They all laughed. "Well mama Rose didn't raise a idiot eh! But hear yah! They offered me about $500.00 for intimates." Seba offered.

"Five hundred!" Nia asked her hands coming to her mouth.

"I told them that was chomp change."

"What?"

"Seba stop it!" she laughed.

"Seriously sis."

"Seriously?"

"He said he would go to $1500.00 if I could place a camera strategically..."

"Sebastin!"

"What!" He spluttered jumping from his thinker's pose.

"Seriously though let's not waste time with dem and foolishness..."

Mischief scampered briefly across her mind's eye; she pushed it quickly away. She believed Seba would never betray her in such a vile way. She prayed her faith and trust would not ever be misplaced or compromised.

"You would never betray me, right?"

"Seriously! Sis, you didn't go there! Tell me you didn't!" He guffawed.

"Money usually cause many of us to do unforgettable things..."

"Tell me you know me, right?"

"Seba, I do. But I wouldn't be human if I didn't..."

"Sweetie we are fist in glove. Never forget that. You are my ride or die. Believe that."

"I know." She reached for him. She held him tightly. "Please don't ever change."

"Plus, Nia you know that man of yours would bury my high-yellow-ass in a second. Don't you deny it! You know he would. So, this had better be a lesson to learn. You do anything to hurt her, and that drop-dead-syrupy-fella would make life for you all very difficult."

"On that note. Let me say that Kiah and I are having a barbecue on Saturday evening. You are all invited. With only people from your immediate household. Please do not show up with more cousins and siblings than you have. Yes, Amel you heard me. I know you have only four so please do not come with ten."

"Oh gosh boss! Amelda laughed. "Is de food and licka. You know when dat free we all dey."

"Well, just remember not all ten."

"I hear you boss." She snickered. They all joined her.

"That's settled then. So, remember discretion is the key here. You know how word can spread. This is a warning to you all. " She laughed.

"Eh Eh!" Some chorused. Looking at each other and pointing fingers.

"It starts at 5:00 and will go until around 10:00 or 10:30 pm. It will give us all enough time to head home and prepare for church the next day. And let me say please... please be on your best behaviour. Because it would be held at the **manse**."

Huge applause and jubilation went up about the shop floor. She told them all they had to do was simply show up; this according to the aunties. She also reminded them about Secret Santa. Also, that they needed to firm up a venue for where they would like their Christmas Party this year. Or tell what they would like to do?

"Team please let me know by the end of the week so we can do something together. Remember teamwork makes the dream work."

She looked at her watch. They had ten more minutes before the shop opened.

She decided to end things. "Have a great day everyone and let us always give all praise and thanks for another blessed day."

Seba opened after everyone looked about and made sure everything was totally ready for the customers when they started to pour in.

Nia walked the steps to her office. The guys followed. She paused long enough to say, "how about you go spend time in security fellas?"

"No ma'am. I mean Miss Nia. The boss says..."

"I know what the boss said Onrey. But seriously what fun is there in following me around all day? Come on go make yourselves useful. Then again... Come with me so we can make some space for you in my office."

She showed them a desk in the far corner, and they helped to shift things around. They already had their computers. She smiled. Thinking they could watch porn for all she cared. Just so long as they aren't her shadow.

Couple minutes later she had a thought. She placed her sketch pencil down. They were busy on their computer.

"I think your boss will need a spot when he visits, so help me move some of these."

They helped her move the sketches and folded them and affix bands to them and put them in the corner next to the others.

"Your store is beautiful. The things you design are equally as beautiful. I would like to purchase acouple pieces to take when we leave for home."

"Just tell me what you like, and I will sort it."

"Thank you, Ma'am. I mean Miss Nia. The boss is very lucky."

"I am as well Onrey. I give thanks for him. For you guys as well. You have been taking such loving care of us. You are brilliant."

"Shucks Miss. It's what we do."

Seba wandered in after a couple minutes. "Hey... I see you two are already sorted. But don't forget to come across to my store. I have a lot I know you guys would like."

"Thank you, Sebastin. We will have a look later. Boss does not want us to leave her. Especially having those reporters wandering around out there."

"Gotcha!" Seba said. "Come when you can. By the way Lady, I am so glad to have you back. Are you going to make the opening of Festival? Plus, we must decide which of the kiddies section you want to display? I know your birthday is on Wednesday I can handle it if you want me to."

338

"Thank you Seba. But I will be working. I want to work. It seems like I have been away for far too long. As for the opening of Festival I want to be there. I think we should highlight the Oriole and the Heliconia flower in red and yellow?"

"Fantastic. We can highlight the bird and the flower and leave the hybrids for Costume Day... Then again, we can give them a taster. How about London? She can highlight the hybrid kiddies."

"I think that can work. A taste of what is to come."

"That is it! Your boss signed you all up for costumes. We will need to measure you both. I take it you have never played mass before?"

"No, we have not. But I look forward to it. Sounds like fun."

"How is Gupta and the girls?"

"They put down a shitload of money the other day. They should be back in a couple of days. They were crazy about the store. They were vlogging. I promised I would check out their site. But I was too damn tired."

"What are their names again?"

"Shankar and Kamla. I think their vlogging site is something called ANKARA."

"Got it. Here is the feed about the store." Onrey said turning the laptop so they could see.

Nia and Seba watched the girls hamming it up for the camera. Seba was equally as hammy as he plugged the shop she thought. The pieces they had purchased were the ones they Vlogged.

They were getting lots and lots of hits. More as they were viewing. Many gave them and the store lots of thumbs up. It made Nia quite happy. Then she remembered what Yvonne said to her about social media. She walked away from the screen and over to her desk and reached for the phone. She dialled Mandy and Tara. They told her they were already in the costume room. She told them she was heading up.

Nia walked in and saw that most of the costumes were already done, and the females were in the process of finishing the Hybrids. There were twenty-one.

The **Oriole; mama and baby, Cattle Egret, Heron, Cobo, Hummingbird, Hawk, Pigeon, Dove, Crow, Thrush, Blackbird, Swallow, Sparrow, Flamingo, Cuckoo, Seagull, Brown Trembler, and Parrot.**

These were birds found throughout the eastern Caribbean that were in fear of losing their natural habitats if we are not careful. They would be the fantasy of what the species could evolve into. She made mention to the team that she thought it would be brilliant if Mother Nature and Father Time came to play Mass this year as well, and that her vision would lean towards the exotic: an albino eagle and a peacock.

"OMG! Ladies they are beautiful!" Nia said as she caressed the humongous beings; that would open and allow the host entry. Headpieces and makeup would complete the appearance.

Initially she envisioned Seba as Father Time alongside her as Mother Nature. Now since Kiah had entered her life...She pictured him beside her. "You have changed your mind, haven't you?" Seba asked coming up behind her as she caressed the being.

"You don't mind do you Seba?"

"Of course! Absolutely not sweetheart. Have you ever reigned on my parade? You stood with me through it all. I will stand by you now with whatever decision you make."

He pulled her to him. He kissed the top of her head. She was his sister. Not even death could change that. Plus, she deserved her moment to shine in love. She has always allowed them all to. So why not give her this now?

"So, you really don't mind Seba?"

"Girl please. This is your time. However, I do love the fact that your peacock will shimmy in the gay pride colours. Nia, I love your mind, your spirit, the way you think about others to the point of forgetting about you. I thank you. I love you so much boss for how you take care of us and our people around the island. I've got your back. We've got this."

"Seba. Don't make me cry. Remember I have a press conference soon."

"Happy tears my love." He chirped. Wiping at his eyes. "Happy tears."

"Seba?"

"Mmmmh"

"Every girl should have a best friend like you. You know I love you from here to eternity and back, right? No matter how many times we fuss and fight. I thank you for always being my cricket."

"As you are to me. You keep my gay ass happy. Thank you for always being present when my mama was absent. You and your family presented me with the most wonderful gift of acceptance. I love you all for that Nia. Your aunties are amazeballs! They are my icons."

"Ooh! Ooh! I forgot to tell you! She asked auntie B to marry her on Sunday evening!"

"Fuck! I mean yes!!! Shit! How is Silcott taking it?"

"He seemed ok. You don't think they have not discussed this? They talk Seba. I believe they have gone over this. It would not surprise me if he walked them both down the aisle. They have had this special kind of love. This bond that is so rare. That is how he explained it to us when we asked him to remember?"

"He said it was a love that transcended what society edicts." Seba reminisced. That It's his agape faith that has allowed him to love so unconditionally. But seriously I don't care what they have Nia. I will be front and centre when the day comes to shout long and loud. It is hard to love as a transgender, gay or hetero. I say more power to them to love as a trio."

"They need to pen a book." Nia said to him.

"Amen." He said and snuggled up to her.

"Do I need to be jealous? I asked this earlier." They turned to see Kiah standing there his arms laden with a bunch of heliconia's.

"Kiah! You're back!" She shouted and took off running.

340

He handed the bouquet to the guys. Then opened his arms to welcome her. She was truly a sight for sore eyes. Even though he had only seen her a couple hours ago.

She jumped into them. She kissed his lips hungrily. He wrapped his arms tightly about her waist. He had missed her something fierce.

"Kiah! You're back!" Seba copied sashaying over. He stopped short.

"Don't you Kiah me you two-timer." He teased.

"Huh? I am so hurt." Seba feigned. "I was only keeping her warm for you."

"Good answer my friend. Come here." He threw an arm around Seba.

"Aaaah. Kiah you are too sweet." He cooed and kissed the man's cheek.

"Thank you for your support to her my friend."

"You mean brother, don't you?"

"I stand corrected brother."

"Guys what do you think?"

"Nah!" They said after taking a good look. The room erupted in peals of laughter.

"Are you ready?" Kiah asked Nia. Because he could see that the piranhas had already circled outside.

"Can I sort a brave face first?"

"You are absolutely beautiful just the way you are."

"That is why I love you so much Kiah Corrington. You are so blooming good for my ego." She said and slapped his rear.

"Those pieces are gorgeous. Which one will I be?"

"I will tell you later." She said and kissed his cheek. She thanked the women before they said their goodbyes.

After Nia refreshed her makeup and Kiah slipped into his jacket. He reached for her hand, and they walked down the steps amongst clapping and hooting from her staff and many of the shoppers.

They walked out into the sunshine amidst numerous flashings and clicking and under the awning.

They were flanked by his security team. Seemed as though they were quite versed in protocol.

Even Onrey and Dimitri had re-joined the others.

Nia's heart was beating wildly in her chest as she looked to Kiah; he smiled down at her and squeezed her hand.

His heart was banging away in his chest like a bongo drum. He was back in the spotlight, and he hated every second of it.

Indiria and her people and so many others were gathered like vultures.

Nia spotted crews from CNN, SKY, ABS, FOX, NBC, and CBN...

She gave up counting for fear of snatching her hand and running like a hell hound. Instead, she just closed her eyes and simply asked for help from above.

She mouthed, "**Hello Eternal Loving Presence** the acronym for **help**. Please watch over us and guide the words we speak. Help us to face the things thrown at us with an open and honest heart. Help us to stand in our integrity and speak our truth."

"I like that, Nia." He wrapped his hand tightly around her waist and led her out.

The moment erupted; with loud chatter shouting, arms raised and cameras clicking...

"Good morning, everyone..." He said using his press voice. "I just want to say thank you on behalf of this beautiful woman, myself and family and her team. For the kindness and understanding that you have shown so far. I know it got a bit dicey at first. But I thank you for being kind. Now with that said. We will give you 10 minutes. So, I hope you have had time to think about what you need to ask. Make it count. I will not answer offensive questions. Nor will I tolerate disrespect. So here goes... Good morning ABS?"

"Good morning, Hezekiah. Good morning, Nia. My name is Alfredo... and we at **ABS Antigua Broadcasting Station** would like to congratulate you on your engagement... We would like to know what you can tell us concerning the incident and the death that occurred over on Heart Island."

"Absolutely nothing Alfredo. Other than what I have already said before. The police are still working over there and as soon as they are finished, we would all know. But for now, I can offer nothing while they are still investigating. That is all I know...**ZIZ**?"

"Good morning, Mr Corrington. Good morning, Miss Nia. My name is Fenty I am an associate of **ZIZ Broadcasting Corporation**, and we would like to congratulate you both on your engagement...May we have another look at that gorgeous ring?"

Kiah held up her hand and she showed off the ammo nestling on her finger.

"Is that a 3.5 carat diamond?"

"Yes, it is."

"Miss Nia did you choose?"

"Yes and no. I think it was a collaborative effort."

"Wow! By the way Hezekiah...Kiah. How are you enjoying your stay on the island so far? And why Nia?"

"I am totally enjoying this island. Not to forget its people. They have been the absolute best. There is so much to do, and I am aiming to enjoy it all. Especially the Festival season this year. As to your second question. Why the hell not Nia? She is one hell of a woman, an incredible act to follow. I think I said before that she is phenomenal. She is my gift from God. Fenty, would you say no to the big guy? Well, I didn't."

Laughter erupted.

"Indiria?"

"Congratulations to you two once again. Thank you for collapsing our online network in one afternoon."

Another peel of laughter rang out.

"Miss Nia my question is to you… Since that awesome proposal. May I ask how has it been? And what would the future be like for you living here and Kiah on the other side of the world?"

"Absolutely amazing Indiria!" she turned to look at him. "I still feel as though I am in a dream loop. But please people don't wake me… But to follow on from what Kiah said before. I think that he too is my gift from God, and I plan to enjoy him one day at a time. I don't know about tomorrow so I will enjoy today. I will do my absolute best to make this special thing we have between us work. Plus, frequent flier miles… I know they will add up. But sometimes it is working out the details that makes it more fun. A friend reminded me that you do not always have to live your life in a box. Make tracks around it and you never know what you can create."

"Amazeballs!" Kiah said and smiled over at her. He could not resist kissing her either.

"SKB?"

"This is to you both. What have you learnt so far by being in this relationship? Of course, a lot of people will try to not state the obvious. But we can clearly see. So Nia how will you deal with it? And you Kiah?"

"Good question…What is your name?"

"Ezra."

"Well Ezra. To recap what Nia has already said we will nurture this great relationship one day at a time. Because when I look at her, I just see the amazing woman that I was given the immense pleasure to get to know a little bit every day. She has taught me so much in the short time I have known her. About caring for others and her island, as well as its's customs and people…"

"I am speaking about the obvious Kiah. Can I call you that?"

"I understand Ezra." He ignored her dig with his name. She seemed as though she had an axe to grind. "But like I've said before. Nia and I are two people who love each other. We are not as different as you think we are…"

"What are you saying Kiah? That you are black?"

Laughter erupted yet again.

Ezra smirked. She was not about this sugar and cream shit. He was not getting off the hook so easily.

"Ezra what does skin colour have to do with the way we feel about each other? I love her. She loves me. We are likeminded in the way we view this world…"

"All well and good for you Kiah, but what about your relationship with the well-known supermodel Jordanna? Isn't she more your speed than our small island Miss Nia?"

"Kiah loves me. He is here with me. He proposed to me. Why are you bringing up the past?"

"It will always be there Miss Nia. Don't kid yourself. A ring does not make a relationship, nor does it cement anything in stone. He lives there with her and you live here. Let's not get it twisted and think those rose-coloured glasses you are wearing…"

"Ezra! Nia and I know what we are getting into. We do not need you or anyone else to dictate how we should live our lives. This…" Kiah gestured between them. "Is between Nia and I and God. We cannot help who we fall in love with. We just need to be tolerant and treat each other with respect. An important thing we should all learn don't you think?"

"I was just stating the obvious. What you two will no doubt be facing in the future. How about a pre-nup? And where will you two live?"

"One day at a time Ezra. One day at a time."

"Nice save Kiah! Congratulations once again. The future is left to be seen."

"No doubt Ezra… CNN your question."

"Congratulations on your engagement Kiah. You prefer to be called that? I have a couple questions. You stated you no longer had any affiliations with Heart Island. But can you tell us anything as to what is happening there right now?"

"No, I can't."

"Not even a smidge? I mean someone died in the incident."

"Unfortunate…Mike. I hated that it came to that…"

"Can you tell us who shot him?"

"No, I cannot because I honestly do not know… Things happened so swiftly. There was an altercation and from it a squabble ensued and there were gunshots…"

"C'mon Kiah! Be straight with us. For god's sake someone died."

"I know Mike. But you will know when I know."

"Are you saying that your people didn't have guns as well? They are your elite team after all. So, give us something."

"Mike…" He wanted to reach out and squeeze the life out of him. But he was not going to play the game. "You will know something when we know. I have said that before."

"I see that you are still deflecting…Anyway let's shift the subject…Can you tell us why you proposed so quickly? Did you two know each other before?"

"Well yes and no. But none of that really matters. All I will say is that we listened, and we paid attention when God spoke. That is why I proposed."

"That is why I said yes."

"**CBN**?"

"Is it over between you and Jordanna?"

"Yes, it is." He was getting fed-up. "**CBC** and **Fox**. Then that's it."

"**CBC** here Kiah. We would like to say congratulations again on your engagement. Have you set a date Nia?"

"Not yet."

"Will you be living here or in the US after your marriage?"

"Can we chat again when we decide? Last question. **FOX**?"

"You speak of God a lot. Do you believe in him? And can you tell us what your parents think of the suddenness of your decision?"

344

"They absolutely love this. And yes, I believe in God. Look at what he has given me. All I will say is when God says jump, I jump. That's it."
"Your faith is that strong?"
"Yes, it is. Nia has proven that. Now on that note. We thank you all for coming. We wish you a wonderful holiday when it comes. Please tell me you will not be out chasing us and leaving your families? Go home. Enjoy what God has given." He waved them off and wrapped his hand about her waist and led her away.
"Kiah! Nia!"
"Thank you everyone. Thank you again."
"Nia! Nia are you pregnant? Nia when is the wedding? Nia?"
"Thank you again." Kiah offered and led her back inside.
Some tried to follow. The guys kept them at bay.

Inside the shop they stopped. "How are you holding up Nia?"
"I'm fine Kiah. I guess there is blood in the water."
"We are better than them. Let's just get on with our lives. It's up to them if they still want to follow us. By the way are you ready for lunch?"
"Lead the way Kiah."
"The car is parked in the back. We can leave that way if you want."
"Let's go out the way we came in. We have nothing to be ashamed of. The only people we need to please are ourselves and our family. So let me get my bag."
"You rock!"
"You are solid."
"By the way I ordered lunch for everyone. **Sylvie's** will deliver at 12.30 pm."

The reporters followed them again to the mariner. But thank God they only got as far as the gate.
The aunties and his parents were just exiting their car when they pulled up. They waved them over.
They exchanged hellos and hugs. They spoke a little about the press conference until Victor the club manager came out to greet and lead them to their very own private dining room; overlooking the serene crystal-clear water, where boats were bobbing about, as huge herons and gulls dived in and out to grab their lunch.
The warm afternoon sun shone down on the palm trees as they swayed gentle in the breeze.
This was all enjoyed from the private veranda that housed loungers and colourful pillows and potted palms to enjoy if they decided to walk through the sliding doors.

The buffet was already set up and smelt heavenly. Nia could feel her insides getting quarrelsome. They each went off to grab drinks and starters; spring rolls, samosas, patties, fruit salad, butter and rolls, cheese and biscuits, salami, ham...
"I don't think this is going away any time soon son."

"I am trying dad. Nia and I just decided to get on with our lives."
"That's all you can do." Auntie K said.
"We aren't going to put our lives on pause because of silliness."
"Amen. We are here to enjoy the holidays. Please let us do so."
"I like your reasoning. So that is what I intend to do. I am not hiding out anymore."
"That's my girl." Auntie K said. Giving her a shoulder squeeze.
"You look lovely by the way."
"So do you Auntie." Nia said loving the fit of the salmon-coloured pant suit she wore topped off with beige tank. She complemented it with a printed scarf knotted in a bow. Her hair flowed freely. She liked when she wore it like that. She reminded her of her mama today. She lingered a bit longer in the woman's arms.

Kiah wandered outside with his dad and the guys, as well as Silcott. Giving the women a chance to sit and chat.
"You did well with the press today, Nia. I always hate those things."
"I know what you mean. It feels like you are under a microscope."
"That Ezra and Mike. They were so ferocious." His mom said. "I would have throttled them if I was standing there."
"They were doing their job. People want answers. But honestly, I just wish it would go away." Nia said.
"Me too. But to bring up Jordanna? Nia my son was never at his best with her. And this is not because I know your family. Kiah is not about bells and whislles. He would much rather spend his time working and retiring to some faraway place where no one knows him. But Jordanna yearns for attention, and she would do whatever it takes to get it. I for one am glad that my son has finally gotten her out of his system."
"Amen." Auntie B added. "Hezekiah is thriving since you two have come together. Even you dear. I would like to say that you are glowing. You two are great for each other."
"I raise my glass to that. Just think Nia-Belle all these years and you avoided him like the plague. One look and you two are thicker than thieves."
"I can't even wrap my mind around it at times. I always say thank you God for bringing him home to me. Sometimes I scarce can understand just what a blessing he is in my life. I have been so foolish to think I would never find a great love."
"You have Nia-Belle."
"Just be good to each other. He can be a workaholic at times."
"Just like her." Auntie K tossed. Pointing to her. "She has been working since she discovered what legs and arms are."
They all laughed, and paused when the guys came back in for more food.
"Are we planning things for the soiree on Saturday?" Kiah teased.
He walked over to the buffet. Nia joined him.
"Please no soiree. I mean it." She begged. Pinching a chip from his plate.

346

"Get your own." He kissed her lips.

"But I like yours."

"You'll get it later." He tossed and walked over to get salad and steak. He tossed her a wink.

"Aaaah." His mom gushed. Looking over at them sweetly. "Kiah you are positively beaming."

"I know mom." He tossed back and winked over at her as he disappeared outside again.

The others wandered in. His dad paused long enough to kiss his wife and enquire if they were okay. He seemed even more relaxed now as he wandered off to get more food.

Once again Nia looked to the three and tried to reason who Kiah got his good looks from. She surmised that he did from both: a total combination. She loved the little family that had emerged. She felt truly blessed that with him she had inherited more family and they were looking out for her.

"Just think how much we have grown this past few days B. We went from five to how many now?"

"Not complaining. But our family has certainly grown for Christmas. Gone are the days when we thought we would have no one in our house when we got old."

"You two will never get old. I have it on guarantee."

"From your lips to God's ears Nia-Belle. My prayers were always for you to meet that other half that will compliment you in every way. The way that Bellot has been to me and Silcott to us, and Denton to Elena. We have seen how much you have blossomed since Kiah came into your life."

"It is not all one-sided Katho. Nia my son has also blossomed. He worships you. He called us the first time he laid eyes on you. Do you know what he said? He said mom I've met the woman of my dreams. She is prenominal! I am going to marry her. My son has never spoken like this before. Every day he tells us how much he loves you, Nia. We thank you for loving him too."

"I do love him a great deal. He is my miracle for Christmas. I say to God that I am now standing out of the line so he could bless someone else in the way he has blessed me."

"Surely Goodness and Mercy will follow us for the rest of our lives."

She pointed to the three females. "Thank you so very much for all you have done." She walked over and gave each one a hug. "And for all you will keep doing to guide us on our journey."

They gave the girl a cuddle.

"You will be another year wiser Nia. I pray our Creator's blessing on you and your union with Kiah. He is a good one."

"I know he is." Her eyes found his as he came through the door.

"Nia?" He called to her a look of worry plastered on his face.

"I'm ok Kiah."

"She is ok son. We are just having girly time."

"So, I have nothing to worry about?"

"No son. She is fine."

"Nia?"

"I love you so very much Kiah Corrington." She said and wrapped her arms around him. "You bring me joy."

The men came in to get their lunch. They all sat at the table and had fun chatting and laughing as they ate.

"So how are the plans coming along? Is there anything you need us to do Ma'am?"

"Just bring yourselves boys."

"What is the head count now?" Kiah asked?

"With all of Nia's supporters and a few people from **Corrington's**. We are at a hundred."

"So why don't we do a beach thing then Bellot?" Denton tossed. "You are already having it catered. So why not let them have it down on that lovely part of the beach? Gosh just the other day I was saying to Elena that I could see us living here. Taking the boat out. Going fishing and snorkelling…"

"Denton! Can you really?" Bellot chorused. Her face beaming like a lit-up Christmas tree.

"You are my only sister. I love California. But you are here. I have missed you Bellot. I think I am getting more nostalgic in my old age. But now that they are going to be married, and I don't see Nia giving up all that she does here. My son is going to be here more. Elena has proven she is a mermaid. She has found her cove. What do you think son?"

"What do you think mom?"

"I like the idea. We can trial it for a couple months at least. Plus, I can get to know Nia even more, and help her with planning the wedding. Bellot and Katho I can help you as well."

"Yippee!!" Auntie B squealed.

"Someone is sure excited. "Auntie Katho said. "You are always saying you wished he would come. Well, your cup doth runneth over."

"Oh, Denny I am so happy." She squealed again. As she rushed over and hugged him tightly.

Kia's mobile pinged. He looked. "It's Ama."

Everyone said a quick hi and hello. Then Kiah excused himself especially when she gestured that she wanted to talk about Nia. She told him about the updates on plans for Jasmine and Jourgette and asked what he would like sent for Nia's birthday.

"What do you think of us taking advantage of the spa today, Nia?"

"A birthday treat from us dear." Elena said coming over to her. As she looked at Kiah out on the veranda.

"Let me call the office."

"No need. We spoke with Sebastin. Now come along." Auntie B said. Pulling her along. "We will join them later for dessert."

"Why don't you take a boat out with the guys?" Auntie Katho said to Denton. As Ellie and Caroline came in to take them out to the private spa suite.

Nia had forgotten the team at Spa Mariner were sent straight from heaven. By the time they re-joined the men her body felt light and free from Jimmo's expert hands, and her face like a baby's butt after Caroline was finished.
Nia would sometimes treat herself, or the aunties would treat her like they did today. She loved it.
They all felt like they were on cloud nine and serenaded by the heavenly harpists. She smiled delightfully to herself because of the surprise she had instore for him.

When they entered the room again, everyone immediately started singing the happy birthday song.
Georgie was there and so was Seba. Nia took them and the transformation of the room in. She was totally surprised. They had filled it with many pastel-coloured roses and decked out the tables with succulent desserts.
There was a beautiful white cake with sprinkles and candles.
"Make a wish sweetheart." Her auntie said to her. Leading her over to the table.
"Is this coconut cake with toasted coconut frosting auntie?" She asked.
It was her favourite that her mama would always make for all her birthdays.
"You betcha my girl. The Rodriguez' sends their love."
"Oh auntie…" She said as tears stung the back of her eyes.
She reached down and stuck her finger in and licked it. She did this every time with her mama, who never scolded her.
"Still the same Nia-Belle." Her auntie K said. "Make your wish."
Nia gestured for Kiah to join her. When he did, she said, "Wish with me."
"Ready?" He asked. They blew the candles out together while the others took lots of pictures.
"Do you like your surprise?" Seba asked coming over to give her a hug.
"You knew about this Seba?"
"I know everything sis. And I will help with everything to keep a smile on that gorgeous face. But it is all him." He pointed to Kiah.
"You did this?"
"With the help of everyone here. We all wanted to remind you how very special you are to each of us."
"Thank you so much everyone."

They continued to enjoy the rest of the afternoon; food and drinks and lots of dessert. They danced, chatted and laughed and enjoyed each other's company.

349

Kiah suggested a walk down to the end of the pier. Thank goodness she always carried a spare something in her bag. She took a pair of flats from it and quickly slipped them on.

They enjoyed the setting of the beautiful yellow and reddish hues the sun dazzled with as it sunk on the horizon.

"Did you enjoy the afternoon, Nia?"

"Yes, Kiah I did. Thank you for reminding me that I am special."

"I will never stop reminding you of that." He kissed her sweetly.

They did not realise they were being photographed...

"They've resisted this for so long. Now look at them. One can't tell where the other begins or the other ends." Bellot said. Tears pricking her eyes.

"She has found another bestie Sebastin." Silcott teased. Giving Seba a bear hug.

"I know."

"Ooh Mister Seb. I'll be your bestie." Georgie teased.

"To play second fiddle to him? I bet I know who is taking you home tonight."

"Ooh shoosh."

"Are they?" Silcott asked gesturing to the two.

"Uh huh. By the way I heard the ladies are engaged. How do you feel?"

"Nothing's changed my boy. Plus, you know how we feel about each other. They have waited long enough for this. Things changed with the law this year. So, they wanted to move with it."

"Damn pops how have you evolved into such a human being?"

"Agape son. Agape love. It transcends everything."

When they were ready to leave. Seba said he would take some of the food and drop to **Safe Haven** and **Iya's Place**, as well as to his friends, where he had been staying.

Nia commented on it.

"Just want to give you some time with him. You need it. "Happy birthday Chicca. Sure, is different when you didn't have a man. Hold up! It's fiancée." He whispered incredulously. "See I told you our God works in mysterious ways. Have fun sweetie. You so deserve to. And stop worrying about me." He kissed her one last time.

Georgie also took some food for her neighbours, as well as cakes for London. They decided William would drop her off.

Everyone took something for their trip home. She had received a lovely pre-birthday celebration that she would never forget. Nia said thanks to everyone again before she climbed into the car.

When she opened her door the smell of flowers immediately accosted her nostrils. When she switched the lights on, she spotted vases of the same pastel-coloured roses everywhere, from either side of her hallway and even in the living room. Even the kitchen was filled, along with the dining room...

"Oh Gharm!" Her hands flew to her mouth. "Kiah you didn't! OMG! There's so many of them. It's like I am in my very own rose haven."
"You like it?"
"I love it Kiah!"
"I love you, Nia. So very much. I just wanted to give you as much joy as you have given to me."
"Kiah it is beautiful. They smell gorgeous." She buried her nose in the petals. "How did you do all this?"
"Rosaria. Sebastin gave me her number. She was so pleased to oblige." Of course, he did not tell her he had left the woman an envelope with $2000.00 as an early Christmas present.
She deserved it after the way she took care of them all. She did all their laundry and dropped things to the cleaners, as well as the cleaning and cooking. He recalled Nia saying she had lots of family. So, he thought why not put a smile on all their faces. She had done a fantastic job out here. He had told her he wanted some in their bedroom as well.
He said nothing as she took in all that was before her.

The fellas bought the things in from the car and sorted them. She said she was going to change. He allowed her to go in….
She screamed loud and long.
"Guess she found them." He said to the guys as he followed her squeals.
When he entered, he saw that Rosaria had strategically sprinkled red rose petals along the floor leading into the bedroom. She also placed vases of red roses on the side tables and arranged a huge heart shape on the bed with the words **I love you Nia** inside it.
He had bought out the flower shop again. But come to think of it… Rosario needed a new job. For she surely had gotten the gist of romance down pat. He made a mental note to give her a call to say a massive **'thank you'**.
He thought he should send her some more money. She had even put some roses on display on her dressing room table and sprinkled some petals on the floor. Even in the bathroom on the counter and sprinkled some petals on the floor as well. He had to admit the sight was breathtakingly beautiful.

The fellas decided they would go downstairs to chill because the two deserved the time, and they didn't want to get in the way. Even the reporters seemed to have finally been satisfied. They weren't there when they left the mariner, and they weren't camped outside the house for a change.

Nia kissed Kiah hungrily; with all the passion stored up in her body as he eased her out of the confinement of her clothing. She was delirious with want for him and overwhelmed by what he had done for her today. When they came up for a little pocket of air, she helped him out of his clothes as quickly as she could.

"I want you so badly Kiah."

"I know Nia. I want you too. But I need a quick shower."

"I am coming to."

They took off towards the shower stall, where their bare feet crunched on the petals scattered there. The scent was intoxicating.

They washed each other performing the most heated make out session imagined, using all the accoutrements to hand; water, soap, suds and petals. Not to forget each other's hands, as they fondled hungrily.

"I want you so damn much Kiah." She breathed hotly and buried her mouth over his. She then clamped her body against his and felt just how much he wanted her.

"Fuck me Kiah." He folded his arms about her and lifted her high.

He walked a few steps and pressed her up against the shower stall.

She was so ready for him by the time he dove in.

"I have wanted you all day long Nia."

"Me too Kiah." Nia ground out. As she arched her back so he could probe deeper. She grabbed a hold of the fixture so he could gain deeper impact. She moaned in delirium.

He pumped into her savagely. Her body always gas-lighted him.

She groaned with delight. It spurred him on. He pumped into her with as much fervour and vigour as a runner on his victory stretch.

He saw the finish line. He felt it to. But he was frenzied.

She squealed delightedly and screamed his name.

He gave her everything he had. He was shooting to the stars like a launched rocket. He exploded deep within her. She followed mere seconds later.

He used her scents to anoint her body attentively. Then he lifted her and took her quivering body to the bed and splayed her in the middle of the petals. He used his tongue and hands, and asked his breath, teeth and fingers to join the presentation. By the time he had mercy on her, her body had already begun to dance melodiously. She screamed in fits of salacious ecstasy, as she thrashed about like a mad woman.

She exploded. Shaken to the very core.

Nia switched the music on low as they ate fish broth in the kitchen. Rosario had cooked and left it in a big pot on the stove. She heated some for them. He said his friend Ninja had made him fish tea when he stayed with him. He had eaten fish stew, broth, tea and soup and enjoyed it all. The smell was to die for.

"This stuff is a good aphrodisiac many islanders claim." Nia offered.

"I know Night Ninja believed in it. He tossed some mussels and cockles or even chunks of conch in as well."

"Did it work?"

"I do just fine Nia. Any complaints?"

"Nah!" Nia laughed gleefully. "You always make my body sing delightfully."

352

"Oh, shucks woman! I like it when you talk dirty."

"Drink your soup Kiah. There is more work yet to be done."

"Yes mam!" He hissed. She dropped a pinch of the scotch bonnet pepper on the top of his. "I forgot how superhot this stuff can be." He said, fanning his tongue.

"Kiss me Kiah." She covered his mouth with hers because she had popped an ice cube in. She used her tongue and the ice cube to encircle his tongue. It was a delicious sensation.

"You are such a weak heart Kiah Corrington." She said when they came up for air. "That smidge was child's play. Suppose I had dropped a bit of bud/bird pepper in it to?"

"Cheap trick, right?" He laughed. "I got a delicious reward for my acting. God, you taste so good."

"Keep talking like that and I will make you pay."

"Damn Nia. I can't wait."

After they finished eating and sorted the kitchen, storing food and washing up. They took their ice-cold glasses of water with them down to the living room.

They attempted watching a Steven Segal movie. But after a while she was too distracted by the sight of all the flowers strewn around, and the invisible smell that kept crawling up her nostrils causing her heart to scamper about in her chest for the umpteenth time that she asked, "Are you ready for bed?"

"Only if you are."

"Let me put the glasses away." She offered and extricated herself from the confines of his arms.

"Let me head to the toilet."

"Okay I'll sort things out here. See you in a jiffy."

When she walked into the bedroom after turning out the lights, she found him naked and smiling delectably on the bed amongst the pillows in the crucifix pose. The red throw pillow propped up on his private. A black box nestling atop it.

"Kiah what are you doing?"

"If you have to ask sweetheart it means I am not doing it right." He laughed. Gesturing come-hither over to her.

Nia placed the glasses of water she had refilled on the side table.

She went to him. Her heart was beating wildly in her chest.

"Kiah you are spoiling me." She said crawling up unto the bed.

She paused at the pillow. Then she reached out, the pillow swayed from side to side. She brought her hands to her mouth to stifle the scream.

"Take it baby." Kiah teased.

Nia reached out again; the pillow moved. She did it again...This time like a chameleon's tongue. She swiped the box and clutched it to her.

"You're a devil Kiah Corrington!"

"Your devil Nia-Belle." He said and winked over at her, watching as she opened the box. A confused look crossed her face.

"There's nothing in it."

"Really?" He asked. Making the pillow move again. "Maybe you aren't looking hard enough." He said mischievously over to her.

"Kiah. Where is it?" She asked innocently. Looking at the pillow as it moved again. "Is it under there?" She pointed.

"Look and see." He shirked.

Nia bent. She used her mouth to pull the pillow aside. The sight that greeted her had her vagina jumping deep within hysterically.

For lying dramatically around his thick-standing–to-attention dick was a shiny platinum diamond tennis bracelet.

"For me?" She purred. Pointing again.

"All for you... Take it." He teased as he watched her reach out.

Then she seemed to change her mind. His eyebrow raised. She then bent to the gift and used her mouth to kiss his shaft slowly...

"Dear God...Nia...You are truly a little minx."

"You love it... Or else you wouldn't have tempted me like that."

She took the bracelet and crawled over him, sliding expertly over Johnson.

Kiah felt him jump excitedly.

She opened her leg wide enough for Johnson to slide up and down teasingly.

"Help me Kiah." She said and extended the bracelet. He eased up and took it, as Johnson stole the distracting moment and slipped in.

She moaned delectably.

It took him a little while before he could open the clasp and slip it back in place when he got it on her wrist.

Nia's opening danced deliciously with his shaft inside her. He unbelted her robe and devoured one mound, then the next. He suckled each one gloriously.

She tingled all over. She rode his dick slowly.

"Gosh Nia you feel so fucking good baby." He clamped his hand on her ass cheeks under the robe. She grooved like a spinning top. She moaned and groaned hungrily as he drilled her deeply inside.

He continued the melody until it seemed he would lose his mind. He tilted her so she fell backwards on the bed. He gained better leverage. He drove into her.

"Nia... I don't want to cum yet..."

"Then slow down baby! Slow down." She admonished as she snaked her hands up and under the pillows. She needed something to anchor herself. The music he was playing inside her was causing her body to spasm.

Her fingers collided with something cold. Her heart quickened. She snatched it out and held it up.

It was a two-strand choker to match her bracelet. It fell from her quivering fingers to her elbow. The thing was even more beautiful.

"Kiah! Kiah!"

"You like?" He purred as he squirmed deep within her.

"I love! Oh God! Oh God!"

"Say you love it, Nia!"

"I love it! I love you more!" She whimpered as tears stung her eyes.

"Show me Nia!"

She paused long enough to ease out of her robe and slip the necklace about her neck.

Then she proceeded in riding him to what seemed like a slow death waltz.

"You are so fucking gorgeous!" He managed to grind out as he took her writhing body above him in.

"Let me look at you." He paused the task at hand and pushed her gently back on the bed.

"Kiah you shouldn't have."

"Yes, I should. It's your birthday. Let me spoil you. Please...?"

"Okay."

He bent and kissed her breast, using the necklace to massage the other gently.

"You are so fucking beautiful Nia." He kissed her hungrily trailing a heated path down her stomach all the way to her toes. He worshipped and adored her body with his tongue. When he came back up to the spot between her legs, he licked her ferociously.

"Fuck! You are so fucking beautiful! I love that!" He growled.

"You finally noticed?" She asked opening her legs wide. She had treated herself to a Brazilian wax.

"Amazeballs! You are fucking gorgeous woman!" He spat pressing her legs down and creeping closer to her entrance.

Nia allowed the heady moans to fly free as her body arched in anticipation.

"I am going to fuck the hell out of you Nia." He spat and rammed like a madman into her spreading her agile legs wider.

She screamed in rapturous lamentations.

They laid spent; their bodies crisscrossed. He felt Johnson extricate himself from inside her. But he couldn't move. He could feel her hands running up and down the length of his body. It felt nice.

She brought her leg up around him.

"I swear to God your body makes mine act in delirium Nia. It's like I can't get enough of you."

"Same for me too."

"Happy birthday sweetheart."

"Thank you, Kiah. Thank you for another lovely day. It was so much fun. I wish every female had a Kiah. I think there would be more peace in the world."

He laughed and willed his body to obey as he turned. He made it onto his back. She snuck up and snuggled better into his arms.

"I love you sweetheart." He whispered. He could feel the sand man creeping by.

"I love you too Kiah. You bring me joy."

"That is all I want to bring you Nia-Belle. I wish you a lifetime of love. You deserve this. I want us to be just like this when we are old and grey."

"Me too Kiah."

"Did you make a great wish today?"

"Yes, I did. I am not going to tell you what I wished for though. But I will tell you when it comes through."

"I hope it does. You are too good to this world not to have your wish granted."

"Something tells me it will Kiah." She kissed him sweetly. "Thank you for a great start to my birthday. I love you Kiah Corrington."

"I love you more Nia-Belle. Now close your eyes and get some sleep. When you wake. I will show you again just how much you mean to me." He wrapped her up tightly in his arms.

Jordanna threw a fit yet again. She saw the shoot manager looking like he wanted to punch something. Like she wanted too as well.

"Ouch!" She yelped when the fat bitch sorting her hair yanked on her prized tresses. "That fucking hurts." She spat up at the woman.

"Sorry." She squealed making friends with the corner it seemed. Jordanna ignored her. She furiously thought of Kiah and what he had done with that bitch. It consumed her. Another second and the bitch yanked again.

"Fucking cunt!" Jordanna spat. Propelling from her chair. She didn't recognise the imp that had laid siege to her body because the next second she raised her hand...

She saw it happening, but ferocity had taken hold of her body.

The slap sent the woman clean across the room.

"That fucking hurts bitch!" She screamed. "Do that again and I will beat the shit outta you!" She screeched in her face. She didn't even feel an ounce of sympathy for her when she saw her recoiled into the corner clutching her hand.

All that consumed her thoughts was that bastard! How dare he dump her for that black bitch? He only just met her! Now he is fucking engaged!!!

What the fuck was wrong with the picture?

Granted she couldn't stand his workaholic and boring ass sometimes. He hated the spotlight and always wanted to hide away like he was some fucking cave dweller. It was such a fucking shame. Seeing he was such a gorgeous looking man. Smart as fuck.

Which is why he had made so much money. He had the Midas touch for a brain. She had thought be patient to the point of trying to live like a fucking nun. All because she couldn't find a better fuck.

She loved the way he turned her insides to mush. He had a dick that knew how to beat a woman's pussy into submission. He would always make her squirt like a spraying hose. Everyone knew when he was fucking her. She screamed like a banshee.

She could not forget the look his mom had given her when she stayed over with him one Thanksgiving. She did not apologise, and he never took her back. She had tried many others, but most had come up short.
No wonder she took all the shit.
Now this was what she got for being patient?
Suddenly, he was on camera acting like a cunt. What the fuck!!! What does that braided black overweight bitch have over her? Her breast was way too fucking big, as well as her hips and ass!!!

She had thrashed her hotel room when she caught the live feed. They had thrown her out.
She too was trending on the news. Every fucking where she went, the media was in her face. She pushed a few. A couple tried to accost her, and she had beaten the crap out of them.
He had taught her to fight. They used to work out together.
She pictured them as they would. Then they would always end up fucking like rabid animals. She enjoyed voyeurism as much as she loved her body and equally loved when they fucked so the entire world could see.
He drove her body totally insane with want.

She couldn't stop herself, she swiped everything off the counter. It hurt so fucking much. It was like the life was being sucked from her lungs using a tiny straw every time the picture popped up of him being an asshole by proposing to that ugly black bitch!!!
She screamed like a wounded animal.
One of her few best friends/ personal trainer/assistant/ fuck-friend/ confessor/ anything slashed Chardonnay tried to grab her.
She pushed his too-fine-ass up against the wall and wrapped her hands around his throat.
"Don't fucking touch me! Don't fucking touch me!" She screamed hotly in his face. She had fucked him a couple times. Most especially when Kiah would act like a boring asshole. He was good and gave as great as she got. But he was not Kiah.
None of them were Kiah!!!
She pictured the lucky bitch's face. She wanted to punch it into oblivion and pull all those braids from her scalp plait by plait. Show her just how much it hurt to have a dream pursued snatched so easily from your grasp.
"Bitch calm down! Calm the fuck down!" He spat at her when she relaxed her hold a bit.
He sucked in a few gulps of air. He spluttered. "You have been spiralling ever since you saw that fucking interview…"
She spun around to face him looking like a hungry hyena.
"Baby! Baby! You must calm the fuck down!"
"Shut the fuck up! He was mine! Mine do you hear? He was mine Chardonnay. I played the game the way he wanted it. He said he was not ready for a fucking commitment…"
She relaxed her hold on his neck again.

357

He pushed her hand away. But it was more like she allowed him too. The bitch was fucking Xena.

"I thought you said, he said..."

"Shut up! Shut the fuck up Chard! Not helping."

"Look I hate to be the bearer of unwelcomed news. But you two have not been a thing in so long."

"But he is mine. He has always been mine Chard."

"I know sweetie. I know." He placated and reached for her again. If only she would give him the time of day. He was by no means a bloody pauper. His family had a good amount of money.

They were champagne merchants in Europe. But their money had nothing to do with him. He had made his money by being an A list stylists/slash whatever the fuck the rich and famous kids of celebs wanted the world to perceive them as.

If they wanted to fuck, he fucked them, for a price. He was a modern-day gigolo of sorts. But he didn't give a fuck. He didn't believe in labels. He drew the line at animals though. But the one person that has been constant for him was her. He had fallen head over heels in lust with her the first time he saw her; she was walking the runway for London fashion week about seven years ago.

Their eyes had met, and he had not wanted anyone as much since. Even when she fucked about with Corrington, and he broke her heart over and over he would always be there with open arms.

He had told her every time it would be the last. Yet here he was.

He had come running when she called. He could hear the rawness in her voice, along with all the things she was not saying.

"Let me get you something sweetheart...A drink...some blow...?"

"No!" She shrieked. That was one of the reasons why Kiah said no to her. She had tried to get him to try the stuff. He flatly refused.

She had sniffed a pinch; too regularly. He threw her out.

Once she had even slipped him a mickey. They fought as hard as they fucked. Breaking lots of things in his home. He refused to see her after he found out what she had done. He assured her he would not participate in her dangerous spirals.

He in a matter-of-fact tone told her to go get help. He accused her of being an addict. She broke up with him.

She had spent the time with Chardonnay.

When she returned, he would have nothing sexual to do with her. He still treated her as though they were together, but he never fucked her again. That is until she drugged his ass again and flipped the script; she fucked him all night.

He was very resistant at first, but she knew what buttons to push and before long he was putty in her hands. That is until she stupidly cut him loose. He threatened to call the cops. She silenced him; she showed him the USB stick that had all the videos.

358

She knew he did not like the press. She held it over him for a couple months, saying she had copies. That is until she was robbed one night, and her phone was stolen, and her safe ransacked.

She had no doubt it was his men. He had frozen her out again. He would do things for her in the press but as soon as the cameras stopped, so did he. She was no longer allowed to come to his house or his office.

He did not spend time alone with her anymore. She couldn't stand it. It almost drove her over the edge.

She had finally listened. She went to get help. Which meant she had to be open and talk about all the fucking shit that happened to her while she was growing up... Later for that shit.

Right now, she couldn't take Kiah walking away. Treating her as though she were shit, messing up the bottom of his shoes. He owed her.

Even that two-timing bitch Jasmine was all hunky-dory with him. She was laying in the lap of luxury with that kid that he spoilt rotten, and she was not even his.

She had called to say he had sent tickets for them to travel on Thursday. That she was taking the **Lear** down because the two lovebirds were having a party.

The set manager flew over. "You are so fucking fired Jordanna!" He squawked. Interrupting her train of thought.

"Good! I didn't want the fucking job anyway. I was only doing Kuran a fucking favour!"

"Jord! Jord! You can't do this." Chardonnay admonished. But to no avail.

"You fucking watch me! Watch me Chard!"

"Sweetheart where are you going?"

"I am catching a flight to this fucking Emerald City, and I am going to kill that motherfucker!" She screamed. "And that bitch too! I am gonna rip their fucking hearts out. How dare they treat me like this? Who the fuck does she think she is? That is my mother-fucking life! My life you hear me bitch?" Jordanna shrieked feeling as though madness had taken a hold of her and was wrestling with what little sanity she had left.

Glossary of dialect words

Friggin- damn

Nham- eat

Parpus- porpoise

Tek-   take

Mek-   make

Eh-   yes?

De-   they

Ma-   me

Brudda-   brother

Bum-   beg

Ova dey- over there

Tassin- tossing

Lek-   like

Buss-up- hurt yourself

Farsin-   nosey

Gee- give

Le awe go-   let us go

Oh Gharm- Oh my! Oh gosh!

Lek- like

Ghat-   got

Eh eh- oh dear

Ain't fraid- not afraid

Wha-   what

Bruk- break, broke

Outta- out

A Ghad! - it's God

Wid- with

Tark- talk

Dutti- dirty

Honky- derogatory term for Caucasian

Em- them

Drunkin- drunk

Nuf or pret up- uppity

Ain't- not

Dardie oh!- oh gosh

Ain't- not

Gonna- going

Grun wuk- ground, hard work

Foo- for

Melee- news

Bout- about

Oh dear

Gyel, ghal- girl

Wha ya- what is this

Nough- enough

Rarse- ass

Renking- smelly, stink

Tark- talk

Woulda- would have

Tings- things

The journey for Nia and Kiah does not end here. Ride the wave all the way to the end. Find out what amazing things can happen when you believe and step out on Faith.

Part 2 of Emerald City will be with you soon.

Printed in Great Britain
by Amazon

11003895R00210